Quantum Soul

Serra Prime Book One

Luke J. Jones

Matterweave Press

For Jessica Jones
Thank you for encouraging me to try NaNoWriMo 2024.
This book exists because you said, "Go for it."

CHAPTER 1

YEAR 2305

The high concrete wall split Forge Prime Shipyards in two. Wealthy clients on one side, workers, and sweat on the other. With each step toward the checkpoint, the bag on my shoulder pressed down harder. It always did.

Two Obsidian Security officers flanked the passage through the wall. The obbies would scan every tool in my bag for anything that might threaten the security or privacy of StellarForge's elite customers.

But they never checked my diagnostic cable.

Who would? It looked like an ordinary black cable; they no doubt had similar ones in their own packs. It had no power source of its own, and the microdrive in the connector would look like standard cable circuitry if they scanned it.

I'd insisted on that feature, even though Vera assured me they'd never take a second look. She was right. But *better safe than fired*, or worse if StellarForge found out *who* I was scraping data for.

I approached the two obbies, not waiting for them to ask before unzipping and placing my bag and earpiece on the inspection table. The shorter of the two stepped forward and walked to my bag, pulling a security scanner from his hip. His badge read OS-411-83. He laid out each piece of equipment—even my lunchbox—leaving only the cable and some manual tools inside.

"Identification," said the other obbie—OS-429-81, according to the badge on his chest. His voice carried a low, digital modulation that made him sound both intimidating and a bit like Darth Vader.

I retrieved my Halo and held it out. "Malcolm Walker, AI Engineer. Got a work order for a faulty AI on the Celestial Empress."

He tapped his own Halo to mine, face hidden behind the black visor of his helmet as he studied his screen. My registry file flickered in the reflection—name, DNA stamp, my whole official record since the day I was born, parceled up neat for inspection.

"Bag's clean," OS-411-83 said, not bothering to put the gear he'd spread across the table back where he found it. He started to holster the scanner when I held my Halo out to him.

"Forget something?" I asked.

He snatched it from my hands, seeming almost annoyed that I'd caused him more work. He dropped it on the table, running his scanner beam over it. "Clean."

"Pad 7," OS-429-81 said. "No deviations."

"Understood," I said, pocketing my Halo, placing the earpiece back in, and repacking my bag before zipping it up. I headed through the passage between the two obbies, giving them a mock salute.

No response. Figures.

The executive zone of the StellarForge Shipyards sprawled before me like a corpo dream made manifest. Polished starship hulls stretched in every direction. Each service pad could've housed three of the mining haulers from the industrial zone, but instead cradled single vessels worth more than most people could dream of making in several lifetimes.

The glass showroom dominated the center—a crystal cathedral to corporate excess. Inside, spotlights caressed the curves of personal luxury craft, their hulls mirror-bright and sleek.

Around the showroom's perimeter, executive-class ships sat on display pads like trophies. Each one screamed wealth and status, with sweeping lines, unnecessary chrome accents, and AIs sophisticated enough to manage small colonies. The kind of ships that never hauled cargo, *legal cargo* anyway. Just ego and credits.

The Celestial Empress, a luxury space yacht, waited on service pad seven. Her owner and passengers already whisked away to champagne and sales pitches by one of StellarForge's handlers. Rich clients got the full treatment: private lounges, gourmet meals, guided tours of the newest models. All while some nobody engineer crawled through their ship's systems.

CAIN's synthetic voice filled my earpiece. "The owner is complaining that their Artemis Lux unit isn't obeying navigational overrides."

"Yes. I too have the work order, CAIN." I said.

"You seem particularly irritable today, Malcolm," CAIN said.

"I just hate being on these executive boats. When you scratch the paint on a hauler, nobody notices."

"Are you *planning* on scratching any paint today?" CAIN asked. "Client repairs are a major source of income for StellarForge, and intentional vandalism of an executive—"

"I'm not gonna scratch anything," I said, cutting off the shipyard management AI's corpo rant.

I was, however, going to *scrape* the ship. CAIN didn't need to know that.

The maintenance gangway stretched before me, leading into the Celestial Empress's service deck. It was like entering a new world, where everything sparkled and the air smelled...fancy. The corridor's immaculate white panels reflected my worn boots and grease-stained coveralls.

The AI core chamber sat deep in the ship's belly, a room the owner wouldn't recognize if I showed them a photo. They likely never ventured past the lounges and observation decks.

Clean didn't begin to describe the chamber. The AI core itself dominated the center, a large gloss-white cube about four feet across. Surrounding it were interface consoles that looked like they'd been polished minutes ago. I caught my reflection in one of them—dark hair a little out of place, brown eyes ringed with sleeplessness, a short beard I kept meaning to trim. Thirty-three, but I looked older in this light. The place felt built for people with pressed collars and perfect grooming, not for someone who spent his days elbow-deep in malfunctioning AI cores.

Quantum processors lined the walls in perfect rows, their status lights blinking in synchronized patterns. Several wall-mounted display screens showed diagnostic readouts from various ship systems, all green, all optimal.

The holographic avatar of Artemis Lux shimmered into existence near the center consoles. She materialized as a figure of impossible perfection. Draped in silver robes, every fold falling where some algorithm had determined it should. Her hair caught the chamber's lighting like liquid gold, each strand moving as if choreographed.

Her face had an unnerving symmetry that my brain accepted at first glance, then recoiled from on the second. Real faces had character, scars, asymmetries, the wear of actual living. Artemis's features were mathematically tuned to suggest humanity without the inconvenience of possessing it.

She moved with grace, every gesture traced along pre-scripted arcs as though invisible strings guided her hands. Even the subtle turn of her head toward me felt rehearsed.

"Welcome aboard the Celestial Empress, Malcolm Walker," Artemis said, her voice soft.

"Hey, Arty." I placed my bag down on the center console's surface, careful not to scratch anything. "Work order says you're having a bit of a problem following orders. What's that about?"

Artemis's expression remained pleasant. "It's true. I've had to refuse several navigation route adjustments."

I took out my diagnostic tablet and cable. "Mind if I take a look?"

"By all means." Artemis made a sweeping gesture toward the interface ports. "May I offer you some refreshments while you work?"

"Coffee, black."

"Malcolm," CAIN warned through the earpiece.

"I was kidding," I whispered to CAIN, then louder to Artemis: "Never mind on the coffee, Arty. Need to cut back on my caffeine intake."

Artemis nodded. "Very well."

The diagnostic cable clicked into place. My tablet's screen lit up with system readouts, navigation protocols, override commands, memory usage. All normal at first glance. But the beauty of Vera's cable lay in what it did beneath the surface. If everything was working, the microdrive had already begun copying files, logs, and messages, whatever it could find, in stealth mode.

"So what happens when you get these navigation overrides?" I asked, fingers dancing across the tablet's interface. The more I engaged with Artemis, the longer I could justify being connected to her systems.

"I must refuse them," Artemis said.

I pulled up one of the failed override attempts, expanding it into a chart view on my tablet. A solid blue line traced across the star map from Elysium Resort, that orbital playground for the ultra-rich, straight to...CryoVault-1.

My throat went dry. CryoVault-1. The name jumped off Vera's priority list like a neon sign. High-security research station orbiting Mars, owned by Inertia Technologies, one of StellarForge's subsidiaries. Officially, they researched methods for prolonging human stasis durations.

Officially.

I swallowed hard, forcing my hands to stay steady on the tablet. This was it. The first time I'd stumbled across intel on a priority location. Payment for this data could keep Olivia safe for months. The cable better be doing its job.

I overlaid the override route onto the chart. It appeared as a light-blue dashed line. Same origin and destination, but curved in an arc instead of direct.

"Why would they want to take a longer route?" I asked.

"*Why* questions aren't appropriate, Malcolm," CAIN interjected before Artemis could answer. Though I doubt she would have. Probably would have given a more polite version of CAIN's response.

I zoomed in on the chart. A location marker appeared along the direct route: GCE-CP-03. Everything clicked into place. The direct route would've required stopping at a Global Coalition checkpoint for scanning. The override was routing around it, avoiding the scan. Artemis had denied the override because GCE compliance protocols disallowed intentional checkpoint avoidance.

"Good news, Arty. You're not broken."

"As delightful as that is to hear, Malcolm. I never thought I was," Artemis said.

"CAIN, she's operating within specifications. She can't allow route adjustments that would violate GCE compliance."

"Very good, you've found the problem. Now resolve the issue," CAIN said.

"Uh...it's not an *issue*. This is intended functionality," I said.

"The client has requested that Artemis Lux be made to obey all commands without question. StellarForge approved the work order. Resolve the issue."

"I'd have to elevate the owner's authority above the Global Coalition of Earth. That's not legal."

"So you've identified not only the problem, but the solution as well. The legality is not your concern."

If I rewrote her protocols, I was giving some corpo voidbag free rein to ghost shipments, people, whatever they wanted.

Checkpoints weren't an actual threat, provided you're willing to pay the look-the-other-way fee. But they were enough to keep most normal folks in line, and if you weren't doing anything wrong, they were only an inconvenience. If they wanted this done, I wouldn't be the one taking the fall when they got caught by the one obbie in the verse unwilling to take a bribe.

"I'll need a root access code. I'm not using mine."

"Very well. SFRA-TK-421138. Consider your posterior adequately covered," CAIN said.

I keyed the code into the diagnostic tablet. A notification appeared: ROOT ACCESS GRANTED.

"You said all commands, right? Not just navigation?" I asked.

"Correct," CAIN said.

I let out a breath. "This is going to take a while. I'll have to check all systems and subsystems and elevate owner authorization."

"Best get to it then," CAIN said.

"It sounds like you could use some refresh—" Artemis started.

"Thanks Arty, but CAIN's got me on the no refreshments while working diet." I said, cutting her off.

"Heavens," Arty said. "That sounds very restrictive."

"It is. But he believes that hunger and thirst drive productivity higher by three percent."

"Six percent," CAIN said. "Though idle chatter does tend to eat away at potential gains."

The work, while uncomplicated, was monotonous. Each subsystem required individual attention: navigation protocols, security measures, access management. Every single one had to be adjusted to prioritize owner commands over any GCE compliance protocols.

Fortunately, the added time would mean my little cable scraper would be overflowing with data for Vera. Every minute I stayed connected, more files copied, more communication logs transferred, more network maps built.

Artemis watched me work with a serene expression, offering unhelpful commentary about the ship's amenities. Her smile never wavered while I tore apart every safety protocol her wealthy owner might find inconvenient.

"There." I said after hours of work, disconnecting the cable. "Your owner can now violate any GCE regulation they want."

"Wonderful," Artemis said. "Thank you for the exemplary service, Malcolm Walker."

"Don't thank me." *Seriously, Arty. Forget my name.* "Just doing my job."

"That wasn't so bad," CAIN said. "Right on time for lunch."

I placed the tablet back in my bag and made my way out of the ship. As I approached the checkpoint, both obbies straightened, the shorter one—OS-411-83—already reaching for his scanner. Same dance we'd done when I arrived, but in reverse.

Then my stupid brain decided this was the ideal time to remind me of one tiny detail I'd somehow forgotten.

The diagnostic tablet. I'd been so eager to get that data off the ship, I'd disconnected it from the console and shoved it in my bag with the cable still plugged in. Which meant the microdrive was still powered. The power draw was low; it had to be not to trigger suspicion when connected. But enough that any half-awake obbie with a scanner would pick it up in three seconds flat.

Turning around wasn't an option. Not this close, not with two black-armored shadows tracking my every movement. I slowed my pace, shifted the bag's weight, made a show of unzipping it. *Just getting it ready for you guys, nothing to see.* Slipped my hand inside. Fingers brushed the tablet's smooth surface, found the cable, and gave it a tug.

Nothing.

The cable's tiny lock clip remained latched.

I moved the bag over my head to one shoulder, awkward with my hand still buried inside, thumb searching for the latch. Found it. Flicked it open.

"Come on, we've got rotation coming up." OS-411-83 snatched the bag from me before I could extract the cable. As the weight left my shoulder, so did any hope of getting out clean.

This was it. This was how I got caught. Biggest data score in all my time helping Chrysalis, and I was going to blow it because I was an idiot who forgot to unplug a cable. If I went down, what happened to Olivia? Would Obsidian Security forces rush into our apartment, haul my daughter away for questioning?

"Work order complete?" OS-429-81 asked.

"What?" I couldn't take my eyes off the other obbie as he pulled out the tablet, cable still attached.

"Are you done? Or will you be coming back through?" OS-429-81's voice carried obvious annoyance. "I need to mark it so the next team knows."

OS-411-83 jerked the cable from the tablet, flung it into the bag and then situated the tablet on the table before extracting my remaining tools.

"Ha..." I let out a sharp breath. I couldn't believe it. The obbie treated the cable like a loose thread dangling from a sweater.

"Sorry...Yeah. I'm done. Work order complete."

OS-429-81 held out his Halo, and I tapped mine to it.

Pulling out my earpiece, I set it and my Halo on the table to be scanned, willing my hands to stay steady.

OS-411-83 finished his scans. "Clean."

I repacked my gear and zipped the bag shut, as if the cable might jump out screaming, *Scan me! Scan me!*

"Through you go," OS-429-81 said.

I picked up the bag and walked through the checkpoint, each step feeling like I was on thin ice. Only when I was fifty yards into the industrial zone did I allow myself to breathe normally again.

CHAPTER 2

I stepped into the cafeteria, greeted by the buzz of conversation bouncing off metal walls and tables. The place was packed with workers in identical jumpsuits, all hunched over their trays like prisoners. The smell hit me next, some kind of reconstituted protein swimming in a brown sauce that Stellar-Forge insisted was *nutritionally complete.*

I patted my bag, feeling my lunchbox inside. Score one for morning Malcolm. Olivia would have never let me hear the end of it if I'd forgotten again. I could hear her now: *You know there's this concept called planning ahead, where you think about things before they happen.* Complete with her trademark eye roll.

Most tables would've required squeezing in, but I spotted a nearly empty one in the back corner, occupied by a woman with dark hair in a ponytail, uniform still crisp. Definitely new.

I slid into the seat across from her, taking my insulated lunchbox out of my bag and placing it on the table. "Mind if I join?"

She glanced up. "Oh. No, go ahead."

I unzipped my lunchbox, catching her eyeing it with undisguised envy before looking back down at the brownish mass on her tray.

"Smart move, bringing your own," she said, poking at her meal with a fork. "I wasn't expecting...this."

"And what is *this* supposed to be?" I asked.

"According to the menu, it's 'Nutrient Optimized Protein Loaf with Vitamin Enhanced Sauce.'" Her expression turned skeptical. "Sounds yummy, right?"

"StellarForge isn't known for their cuisine. Pretty sure they have CAIN generate those names with no thought to making them sound edible."

She laughed. "I just moved into my apartment. Haven't had a chance to hit the market yet."

I looked down at my lunch. Nothing fancy: a synth-ham and cheese sandwich and a small container of synth-fruit cubes. My stomach grumbled in anticipation.

The woman cut into the loaf, releasing a concerning puff of steam. The semi-translucent brown sauce oozed around her fork as she raised it to her mouth. I reached across the table. "Hold up."

She paused, fork hovering.

I took one of my sandwich halves and held it out to her. "Here. I had a big breakfast." That was a lie. I'd had nothing but a cup of coffee before leaving my apartment at 0500.

She hesitated, fork still suspended. "Are you sure? Because I'm not too proud to take it."

"I'm sure. Besides, I don't think I could keep this whole sandwich down if I had to watch you eat *that*."

She set down her fork and accepted my offering with a smile, extending her free hand. "Tessa Harper."

I shook it. "Malcolm Walker."

I took the top off the container of fruit cubes and placed it between us. "Help yourself."

Tessa took a bite of the sandwich half I'd given her, and her eyes widened. "Is this...real cheese?"

I nodded, feeling a small surge of pride. "Yeah. Olivia insists on it. One of the few luxuries we make room for in the budget."

"Wife?"

"Fourteen-year-old daughter." I tossed a yellow fruit cube into my mouth, the thing bursting with sweet lemon before melting away. "One of our favorite meals is grilled cheese, and the fake stuff refuses to melt before the bread turns to charcoal. Not to mention the off taste and gritty texture."

"Fourteen," Tessa said, tilting her head. "How's that going?"

I huffed a laugh. "You used to be one, right?"

"I did." She smirked, brushing a strand of hair back.

"So then...you know."

Her smirk widened. "I do."

"It gets easier, right?" I asked only half joking.

She leaned in, lowering her voice. "Oh, yeah. So much easier."

"You're lying to me, aren't you?"

"I am." Tessa laughed.

"Prime." I said, taking another cube.

Tessa's expression softened as she chewed another bite, eyes closing for a moment like she was remembering something. "Olivia has good taste. I haven't had real...anything in a long time. Been stationed at the Ceres Resource Network for the past five years. Everything there is synthetic."

"The belt, huh?" I leaned forward. "What's that like? The recruitment vids make it sound like quite the adventure."

She laughed, a sharp sound with no actual humor in it. "That's how they hook you. Truth is, the work's brutal and the reward is living in a tin can with air that always smells like someone else's sweat." She picked up a red cube, popped it in her mouth, then gestured at her abandoned tray. "And believe it or not, the food's still better than...that."

I chuckled, taking a bite of my sandwich half. "I believe it."

"What'd you do at the CRN?" I asked between bites.

"Structural engineer." She straightened. "Lots of internal checks and spacewalks—EVAs, inspecting and repairing station and mining ship hull damage. Micrometeoroid impacts are constant out there, and the temperature swings wreak havoc on the older infrastructure."

"No offense, but don't they have bots for that?" I raised an eyebrow.

Tessa's smile turned cynical. "They do, and I used them as often as I could. But some repairs are too risky. Bots are expensive; humans are cheap." She shrugged.

I nodded, understanding all too well. "So what are you going to be working on planet-side? Not a lot of EVA opportunities in the shipyard."

Her expression shifted. The easy openness vanished, replaced by something more guarded. "I'm not supposed to talk about it," she said, lowering her voice. "All I can say is that I won't be on Earth for long."

My curiosity spiked, but I didn't press. StellarForge was strict with high-security assignments, and I wouldn't want to put Tessa in a position, especially on what I guessed was her first day.

"Fair enough," I said, finishing the last bite of my sandwich.

"What about you?" she asked. "What do you do here?"

"AI integration specialist is my official title," I said, brushing crumbs from my lap onto the floor. "I spend most of my time talking to CAIN and other ship AIs, troubleshooting issues or integrating new units on vessels. Today it was an Artemis Lux on some executive's yacht. Yesterday, it was recalibrating life support systems on a mining hauler's DAVE unit."

Tessa's eyes lit up. "Ah, DAVE. I've spent some time with that one. Those mining vessel AIs have...character. Do you design them as well?" She asked, snagging the last fruit cube.

"No, just fix and install." I said. "Though some of my feedback has made it into the code. Like the contextual sarcasm dampener for DAVE, that was my idea."

"I don't get the need to make AIs feel like people," she said, shaking her head. "It makes working with them awkward and frustrating."

"I get that," I replied, gathering my empty container. "But it's easier if you try to interact with them naturally. Not fighting to maintain the human-machine separation."

"You talk to your toaster, don't you?" Tessa smirked.

"Only when it burns my bread," I said. "Then we have a serious conversation about its life choices."

Tessa chuckled. "So, you have a daughter. Is there a Mrs. Walker?"

My shoulders tensed, and I set down the empty container I'd been closing.

"No," I said, my voice dropping. "My wife, Amber, died seven years ago. Transport shuttle accident."

The familiar heaviness settled in my chest. The official report had called it a *catastrophic system failure*, but I knew better.

"That's awful," Tessa said, her voice softening. "I'm so sorry."

She reached across the table and placed her hand on mine. The gesture caught me off guard, and I almost pulled away on reflex. But I didn't. Her hand was warm, calloused from years of manual labor in the belt. It had been so long since I'd felt another adult's touch that wasn't a handshake or an accidental brush on a crowded transport shuttle. Since Amber died, I'd thrown myself into work and raising Olivia. Not to mention my secret life as a Chrysalis informant. Dating wasn't on the back burner; it wasn't even in the kitchen.

"Thanks," I said. "It's been a while now. Liv and I...we make it work."

The cafeteria filled with the sound of chirping Halos, a signal announcing lunch-break was over. The room transformed into a well-rehearsed scene, with workers standing up, putting away trays, and getting ready to return to their duties.

I put the empty fruit container back in my lunchbox, zipping the lid and placing it back in my bag.

"Thanks again for the sandwich," Tessa said, standing and smoothing her jumpsuit.

"No problem." I rose to my feet, slinging my bag over my shoulder.

Part of my brain screamed, *get her contact*. She was easy to talk to, smart, and funny. The other part reminded me she was leaving the planet, and I didn't have time for relationships.

But sometimes the heart overrules the head.

I shifted my bag to my other shoulder, trying to sound casual. "Would you want to grab a drink sometime?"

Tessa's expression shifted, a flicker of something—regret?—crossing her features. "I would..." She paused, looking genuinely apologetic. "But I kind of started seeing someone. We're on the same StellarForge project."

"That's great," I managed, forcing a smile that no doubt looked as fake as it felt.

Tessa studied my face for a moment, seeing through my attempt at nonchalance. "Malcolm—"

"No, really. Good for you," I said, already taking a step toward the exit. "I should get back to work. It was nice meeting you, Tess."

I'd made it maybe three steps before forcing myself to stop. Walking away like that felt wrong...petty. Tessa had been nothing but kind, and here I was acting like a rejected teenager.

I turned back. She was still standing by the table, watching me with the same apologetic expression.

"Oh, I almost forgot," I shifted my bag again, trying to look helpful rather than awkward. "If you want real cheese, there's a vendor in the Forge Prime market district. Nathan's Dairy. He's got the best selection."

Tessa's smile brightened, relief crossing her features. "You sure you want to share that kind of intel?"

"For your ears only," I said. "If you spread the word, Nathan might be happy, but you'll have an angry Olivia to answer to if he runs out of sharp cheddar."

"I'm not telling anyone. But I can't promise he won't be sold out after I stock up," Tessa said, picking up her tray.

The cafeteria continued to empty around us, workers streaming toward the exits in their post-lunch migration. The distant hum of machinery rolled back in, the shipyard returning to its endless rhythm of construction and repair.

"Be safe, Tess. Wherever you're going," I said, and meant it.

"Take care of yourself, Mal. And...thanks for keeping this from getting weird."

I nodded and turned away again. The disappointment still sat heavy in my chest, but hopefully, I hadn't made a complete idiot of myself.

Chapter 3

I sank into my usual worn leather booth in the back corner of The Drift, ideal for conversations that needed privacy. The cantina had filled up since I'd arrived, the usual half-empty quiet replaced by the steady hum of workers fresh off their shifts at the shipyards and processing plants.

The Drift wasn't much to look at: a converted warehouse with exposed piping overhead, mismatched tables, and a bar cobbled together from salvaged starship plating. But it had character and, more importantly, no corporate monitoring systems. The smell of fried synth-pork wafted from the kitchen, mixing with the sharp tang of spilled beer and machine oil. Around me, conversations melded into a comforting blanket of white noise, punctuated occasionally by laughter or the clink of glasses.

Some pre-corpo tune played from the jury-rigged jukebox in the corner, something with guitars and a gravelly voice singing about freedom.

Fitting.

I took a sip of my Iron Wake, savoring the burn of CoreBurn alcohol as it cut through the bitter synth-coffee. The large ice cube clinked against the glass as I set it down, the liquor's blue glow muted by the dark coffee. The first sip always hit hardest.

Right on schedule, at 2100 sharp, Vera slid into the booth across from me, removing a bag from her shoulder and setting it on the seat. She scanned the room in one practiced sweep before settling on me. She wore her usual dark jacket with patches at the elbows, and a plain shirt—clothes designed to blend into any crowd. Her short dark hair tucked behind one ear revealed the small scar that ran along her jawline.

Patch, The Drift's service bot, wheeled over to our table, treads squeaking on the concrete floor. The bot's mismatched arms whirred as he steadied himself.

"W-welcome back, V-V-Vera. What can I g-get for you?" Static crackled through his voice modulator.

"Rustwater," Vera said simply.

Patch's single optic eye flickered in acknowledgment. Vera tapped her Halo against the payment panel on Patch's chassis. No tabs at The Drift. You paid before you were served. It made for quick exits when necessary.

"H-have it right up." Patch rolled away, one tread slipping slightly.

"Right on time as always," I said, taking another sip of my drink.

Vera's lips curved in the barest hint of a smile. "How's Olivia doing?"

I looked Vera in the eyes. She always asked about Olivia, and I never had better news.

"She's doing okay. No better, but no worse." I traced the rim of my glass with my finger. "The medication seems to be keeping things stable, at least."

Vera nodded. "I'd say tell her hello for me, but I'm guessing you still haven't told her who I am or that you're working with us."

"I can't tell her. Not yet." I said, avoiding eye contact. "She's got the same hatred for the corpos that Amber had. If I told her I was involved with the resistance, she'd find some way to join up." I shook my head. "It's one thing for me to risk my safety as an informant, but my fourteen-year-old daughter? That's too much." I took another sip of my drink. "She's like her mother, she'll find her way into Chrysalis at some point. I know that. But I'm going to put that off as long as possible."

"You can't protect her forever, Mal." Vera fixed me with her gaze. "And Chrysalis could use her talents. Propaganda is powerful, and with Olivia's artistic abilities—"

"Wow," I cut her off, "you didn't even wait for your drink before trying to recruit my teenage daughter this time."

"I would never put her in danger." Vera's voice remained steady. "But things are heating up. We can use all the help we can get, and unfortunately, the idea that Olivia will get to grow up and live a normal life isn't reality. With her condition, she could be a real inspiration to so many people." She paused. "You could do more too. The information you provide is valuable, but with your skills, you could be a real asset."

My jaw tightened. She was right, but acknowledging that wasn't something I was willing to do. "I can't. I'm already putting my job on the line smuggling data. If something were to happen to me, Liv would have no one and be the daughter of a corpo traitor."

"You think keeping your head down keeps her safe?" Vera's voice hardened. "That's not survival; it's surrender."

Patch's approach interrupted our tension, his mismatched chassis wobbling as he navigated between crowded tables. One tread caught on an uneven floor seam. The Rustwater on his tray sloshed but somehow didn't spill.

"One R-Rustwater. Ap-p-pologies for the delay." He said, setting the drink down in front of Vera. The Rustwater lived up to its name, amber liquid with a reddish tint that reminded me of corroded metal.

I drained the last of my Iron Wake. The synthetic coffee aftertaste lingered as I placed the empty glass on Patch's serving tray. The ice cube clinked against the side, the last traces of blue glow fading as it melted.

"Another Iron Wake," I said, reaching for the Halo in my jacket pocket.

Before I could pull it out, Vera tapped her own Halo against Patch's payment panel, the device giving a soft confirmation chime.

"P-payment accepted. One Iron W-Wake coming up."

Patch wheeled away, narrowly missing a drunk shipyard worker who stumbled into his path.

I gave Vera a small smile. "Thanks."

Vera took a sip of her Rustwater and sighed. "What do you have for me?"

I reached into my bag and retrieved the microdrive cable, sliding it across the table. "Got an assignment on an executive-class boat today. I saw something about CryoVault-1; thought you'd be interested."

Vera's eyes widened as she snatched up the cable, produced a small tablet from her bag, and connected it. "CryoVault-1? Are you serious?"

I watched as Vera scanned her tablet, her expression shifting from neutral to surprised, then settling on something like triumph.

"Mal, this is huge. There are clearance codes in here." Her fingers tapped on the screen, sifting through the data I'd stolen.

I leaned forward, lowering my voice to a whisper. "You're not planning to go there, are you?"

Vera flashed me a smirk, the kind that always made me nervous. "Thought you didn't want to know about operations."

I rested against the booth. "You're right, I don't," I sighed. "Just...be discreet; if they trace that back to me, I'm scrapped."

"Hey," Vera's expression softened, "it's me."

I smiled despite the situation. Vera and I shared a love of those old Star Wars vids. I'd watched them countless times with my dad growing up, something his father did with him.

I'd tried continuing the tradition with Olivia, setting up our own little viewing nights with the classics Dad had passed down to me. So far, she'd shown little interest, usually spending half the time sketching or fidgeting with her Halo. *These are so static,* she'd complain. Still, sometimes I'd notice her eyes locked on the action, sketchpad forgotten in her lap.

Patch's treads squeaked on the concrete floor as he returned.

"Y-your drink, Malcolm. Caution, may induce t-t-tremors and accelerated heart r-rate." Patch's voice modulator crackled as he extended his utility arm toward me, the glass glowing a faint blue in the dim light.

"Thanks for the warning, buddy," I said as I took my drink from the tray.

"S-s-service is my pri-primary function. Enjoy your b-beverage or don't. You already p-paid." Patch's optical sensor flickered in his version of a wink before the bot pivoted and rolled away.

Vera continued scrolling through the data on her tablet, her face creased in concentration. The glow etched the lines at her eyes a little deeper.

"The owner of that ship was trying to navigate around a GCE checkpoint," I said, watching her reaction. "Requested a navigational override."

Vera touched her chin. "I can see that. The question is, why?"

"The only reason I can figure is that they've got goods onboard they don't want found." I said.

"But it looks like the request was denied," Vera said, still scanning the data. "And no one raised any GCE flags."

"Maybe it was a test run. Maybe they talked, or more likely, paid their way out of a scan."

"It's possible." Her fingers continued to move across the screen.

I took another sip of my drink. "StellarForge authorized a priority bump. They'll be able to override GCE policy from now on."

"So whatever they're transporting, StellarForge doesn't want it found out either." Vera said. "My credits are on people."

"People?" I asked. "Why?"

"CryoVault-1 is an Inertia research station. Inertia is owned by StellarForge. They're trying to push the limits of human stasis durations. They need people to test on." Vera said, her voice certain.

"So, they're kidnapping people and smuggling them off-world?"

"We've had reports of men and women going missing, most of them had some kind of illness." Vera said, taking a drink of her Rustwater. "They may not have to kidnap them. Just promise treatments if they agree to being experimented on."

I hated how much sense that made. Even a slim chance to fix Olivia's lungs would be hard to turn down. The thought unsettled me, and I wanted to get home and see my daughter.

I pulled out my Halo, checking the time: 21:30.

Vera looked up from her tablet. "Am I keeping you?"

"It's been a long day. I almost got caught getting that data out. I got shot down by the first woman I asked out since Amber. And now I just want to get home and talk to Liv before she goes to sleep."

Vera put the tablet down, her face a mask of shock, though a smile played at her lips. "You wanna run that by me again?"

"Which part?" I took a long sip of my drink.

I knew which part, and now regretted mentioning it.

"The part about Malcolm Walker asking a woman out on a date. That intel makes this," she gestured to the tablet, "look like nothing. Who is she?"

"You did hear me say she turned me down?" I shifted in my seat. "She's apparently already involved. Been on Earth for just days and already taken. It's for the best, she's on some secret StellarForge project and headed off-world soon."

"What's the project?" Vera asked, her voice casual but her eyes sharp.

"No idea. She shut down, and I didn't push it."

"Are you gonna see her again? Think you can find out?"

"Actually, I'm hoping I can avoid ever seeing her again. I tried to play off the rejection by talking about *cheese*." I rubbed my forehead, the memory of how I handled that was painful. "Pretty sure she was more embarrassed for me than I was of myself, and that's saying something."

"So she's involved," Vera pressed, leaning forward. "And headed off-world; might as well get some intel out of her."

"The answer's no, Vera." Irritation built in my voice.

Vera held up her hands. "Take it easy, Mal. I'm not asking you to run a pulse scan on the girl. Just chat her up, and if her lips get loose...let me know what you find out."

"Are we done?" I asked, draining the last of my Iron Wake.

Vera finished her Rustwater. "Yeah."

I watched as Vera disconnected the microdrive cable, its data synced to her tablet. The way she packed the tablet away in her bag, like it was radioactive, made me wonder what her plans for using the data were. Part of me wanted to ask, but the less I knew about Chrysalis operations, the safer Olivia would be if things went sideways.

Vera reached into her bag and pulled out a metallic container, easily three times the size of my normal payment. She popped the lid open and emptied another smaller container into it before snapping it shut. Vera slid the container and the cable across to me. "The information is worth more, but this is all I have on me. I'll have to owe you the rest."

I picked up the container. The latch gave a click as I popped it open enough to glimpse the contents. I let out a slow breath, then I snapped it shut and slipped it and the cable into my bag.

"Thank you," I said, unable to keep the relief from my voice.

Vera stood, adjusting her jacket. "Thank *you*, Mal. I think you just helped a lot of people."

"I'm just trying to help one person. More is just a bonus." I looked up at her. "See you next month?"

"Same time, same booth."

Vera turned and slipped through the crowd toward the back exit, the one that opened into the alley rather than the main street. I watched her go, wondering what it would be like to fully commit to the cause like she had.

Like Amber had.

CHAPTER 4

The Halo chimed in my pocket, a gentle three-note tone indicating my stop was approaching. I rose from the hard plastic seat, shouldering my bag as the transport shuttle decelerated. The doors slid open with a soft hydraulic hiss, revealing the familiar gray-and-blue façade of Workforce Enclaves, Block 7.

I stepped out onto the cracked concrete sidewalk. The enclave rose before me, twenty-two stories of modular housing units stacked like storage containers. The only distinguishing features were the faded group numbers and occasional personal touches in unit windows: a fake plant, a string of lights, a child's drawing.

I crossed the street toward the entrance of our stack. A pair of teenagers huddled near the recycling chute, passing something between them, quickly pocketing it when they spotted me. I gave them a nod, just kids being kids, trying to carve out some privacy in a place designed to eliminate it.

The lobby's overhead lights buzzed with a noise that seemed engineered to irritate the human nervous system. The elevator bank had "Out of Service" signs on the two lift doors, same as yesterday and the day before that. They never stayed running for more than a week between repairs.

I took the stairs to the eighth floor, my footsteps echoing in the concrete stairwell. The corridor leading to our apartment was quiet at this hour, save for the muffled sound of someone's entertainment system and the ever-present hum of the air circulation system.

Outside Unit 847, I tapped my Halo against the access panel. A green light blinked, and the door slid open. I stepped inside, retrieving the metal container Vera had given me before dropping my bag by the door.

Our apartment was small but functional. The main room pulled double duty as kitchen and living space, the front half taken up by a table, an L-shaped counter with sink and cooktop, and a stasis food locker. The back half held a couch, armchair, coffee table, and a wall-mounted display. Olivia's paintings broke up the off-white walls. A narrow hall branched off the side, leading to the bathroom and Olivia's room on the left, mine on the right.

A white cylindrical container sat in the middle of the kitchen table—Olivia's medication dispenser. The column of LEDs along its side showed only the bottom few lit in an angry red.

I crossed to the table, twisted open the top of the dispenser, and emptied the contents of Vera's metal container inside. Tiny blue and white pills tumbled in. The device whirred as it processed the refill. The side LEDs lit up in sequence, climbing to near full capacity, their color shifting from warning red to green.

This batch would last us over six months. My StellarForge insurance covered just a fraction of Olivia's medication, and that was the cheapest, least effective formulation. Vera's pills were the real thing, worth every risk I took.

I made my way down the narrow hallway, past the bathroom with its forever-dripping shower, to Olivia's door. I gave the door a few soft knocks, hoping she hadn't gone to sleep.

"Come in," Olivia called.

I tapped the panel beside the door, and it slid open. Unlike the rest of the apartment, Olivia's room was a riot of color and creativity. Her small school desk sat in the back corner, where she attended her virtual classes; a small display screen hung on the wall above the desk.

The walls were her canvas, quite literally. Vibrant landscapes and abstract patterns flowed across them—some framed prints, others painted onto the walls in flagrant violation of housing regulations. I'd long ago given up the idea of seeing any of our security deposit again.

Between her own creations hung several of Amber's paintings of Earth landscapes. The ocean at sunset. A forest. Mountains reaching into the clouds. Glimpses of a world beyond steel and concrete.

Olivia sat cross-legged on her bed, hunched over her digital art tablet. She wore one of her favorite oversized gray sweatshirts, the ones she preferred because they helped hide how skinny she'd become. Her dark brown hair, tied back in a messy ponytail, with a few strands falling around her face as she concentrated. Lightweight pajama bottoms and thick socks completed her evening uniform.

The thin breathing tube ran under her nose and hooked behind her ears, tethered to the bedside unit with its steady click-hiss rhythm—the soundtrack of our lives for the past seven years. Her Halo rested on the bed beside her.

Olivia looked up as I entered, her green eyes brightening. She was pale; her cheeks a little hollow, but the grin she flashed me pushed all that into the background.

"Hey, Dad," she said, stylus twirling between her fingers. "You're home late. What'd you do, stop for a romantic moonlit stroll with one of the curfew bots?"

"Her *name* is Misty," I said, pulling Olivia's desk chair around and sitting backward on it, leaning on the headrest. "It was magical. The two of us, walking hand in creepy robot claw, the hum of the streetlamps, the intoxicating aroma of the recycling chutes as she looked down at me with that massive cyclops eye."

Olivia smirked. "When's the wedding?"

"We're taking things slow. Misty's not sure if the world is ready for our love."

"Ah, well, if it's meant to be."

I settled more comfortably against the chair back. "So how was your day?"

"I got a strike in school."

I sat up straighter. "Again? What'd you do this time?"

"I told the truth."

"I thought we agreed you'd stop doing that, kiddo."

Olivia threw up her hands. "I know, but the teacher was giving a lecture on the *origins of Nitrogen Hyper-Assimilation Syndrome.* What was I supposed to do?"

The familiar knot formed in my stomach. Every time the school taught its sanitized version of NHS, Olivia pushed back. And every time she pushed back, she ended up in trouble.

"Let me guess," I said. "The corpo-approved version where it's a mysterious genetic condition that just...happened?"

"Worse. Today they claimed the nitrogen increase was natural, and that some people's bodies were just *failing to adapt.*" Her voice carried that sharp edge she got when corporate propaganda particularly offended her. "Like we were some kind of weak-link in the evolutionary chain."

I rubbed my temples. "And you couldn't just...nod along?"

"Dad, she basically said that NHS sufferers were the runts of the human species. I couldn't sit there and listen to that voidspit while I'm breathing through a tube because some corpos decided to test their terraforming tech on Earth's atmosphere."

The breathing apparatus clicked softly beside her bed. I glanced at it—a habit I'd developed over the years—checking the rhythm, the flow rate, making sure everything was functioning.

"What exactly did you say?"

Olivia's expression shifted from indignant to sheepish. "I may have mentioned that the corpos created a sickness and were profiting off the cure."

"Olivia..."

"I didn't name any corporations," she added quickly. "I kept it vague. But apparently questioning the official narrative counts as 'spreading harmful misinformation' now."

I leaned forward. "How many strikes does that make?"

"Three this semester."

"Liv. One more, and they'll recommend you for Attitude Adjustment Counseling."

Olivia chuckled, a sound that managed to be both amused and slightly bitter. "Can you imagine? *Me* in AAC?"

I shook my head, fighting back a grin. Knowing Olivia, she'd have any AI counselor chasing its own tail inside of five minutes. She'd inherited the gift of turning questions back on the asker from her mother, along with the stubborn streak that made her use it.

"How about instead of sending some poor AI counselor into an existential crisis, you let a few strikes roll off before your next act of rebellion?"

"But they're lying. About what happened to us." Her voice softened, losing some of its defiant edge.

The breathing apparatus continued its steady rhythm beside her bed. *Click-hiss. Click-hiss.* A constant reminder of why she couldn't let it go.

"I know, kiddo." I reached over and squeezed her hand. "But getting kicked out of school won't help anyone."

"Fine." Olivia set down her stylus with exaggerated resignation. "I actually don't want to get kicked out. I made a new friend today."

"Oh?"

"Her name's Ava Woods. She's an artist too. Her style is so different from mine, all edgy and a little glitched. She does these incredible abstract cityscapes with neon colors bleeding into each other."

Olivia gestured with her hands, mimicking explosive patterns in the air. "And she's not afraid of anything. Mr. Olsen, our art teacher, said her piece was *too aggressive* for the project guidelines, and she told him art isn't supposed to follow guidelines. You should have seen his face."

"Sounds like someone I know."

Olivia shot me a grin.

She'd struggled to make close friends. Not because she wasn't friendly or was socially awkward, Olivia could charm the paint off a wall when she wanted to. But her NHS limited participation in the social activities kids her age enjoyed. Most of her classmates existed as faces on a screen, voices through speakers, avatars in shared virtual spaces.

"Dad?" Olivia's voice pulled me from my thoughts. Her eyes caught mine, wide and expectant. "Do you think we could have Ava over sometime?"

Hope flickered in her gaze, edged with vulnerability that undid me. *No* wasn't even on the table.

"Sure. We could do pizza and a vid. If it's okay with her parents. Maybe get some of that popcorn you like from the market."

"Seriously?" Olivia said, already reaching for her Halo.

I snatched the device before she could grab it. "You can ask her tomorrow. Right now, you need sleep."

"Dad!" she protested, making a half-hearted grab for the Halo.

I held the Halo out of reach. "Did you take your meds?"

Olivia gave up. "Yes."

"I got a fresh supply. You can go back to full doses tomorrow."

"Is that where you were?" Olivia asked.

I didn't like lying, but keeping my Chrysalis ties a secret was one lie I told myself was for her own good.

"I stopped by The Drift for a drink after work, then picked them up."

That wasn't completely a lie. More...lie adjacent?

Olivia's expression brightened. "Did you see Patch?"

"He was there."

"I miss that bot. Maybe we could stop in when we go to the market?"

"Sure. But now...bed."

Olivia reached up and pulled the band from her hair, letting her dark waves fall loose around her shoulders. She peeled off her socks and tossed them toward the laundry bin, missing by a mile.

"I'll get those in the morning," she said, catching my look.

"Sure you will," I said. No way they'd move before I got home tomorrow.

I handed back her Halo, and she placed it on the charging dock beside her bed. She pulled back her covers and slipped underneath, adjusting her position until she was comfortable. With fingers that had performed this ritual a thousand times, she repositioned her breathing tube so it wouldn't tangle during the night.

I moved closer, brushing back a strand of hair that had fallen across her forehead. Her skin felt cool beneath my fingertips, not feverish, thankfully. I leaned down and pressed a kiss to her forehead.

"Goodnight, kiddo."

"Night, Dad." Her voice was already growing heavy with sleep. "Love you."

"Love you too."

I tapped the light control panel on my way out. The room fell into darkness except for the soft green glow emanating from her breathing unit, casting faint shadows across her face. In the dim light, she looked younger, more vulnerable, a reminder of how precious and fragile she really was.

Stepping into the hall, I tapped the wall panel, and her door slid shut. In the stillness, I could hear the steady hiss of her breather bleeding through, a sound that had become both a comfort and a curse. I moved down the short hallway toward my bedroom. The sound of the climate system grinding away in the background. Outside, a curfew bot passed, its low hum slicing through the night.

My room was spartan compared to Olivia's artistic chaos—a bed, a small dresser, and a desk with an old terminal. No decorations except for a single framed photo of Amber, Olivia, and me on the old observation deck above Forge Prime's Shipyards.

Amber had made us climb all the way up, laughing at my complaints, saying, "You have to see the sunset from up here. Even this city can still find a way to shine if you squint hard enough."

Olivia's NHS diagnosis had come a few months earlier. I think Amber knew activities like climbing up observation decks wouldn't be something our daughter could do for long.

Two weeks later, Amber was gone.

I got ready for bed. In the bathroom, I splashed cold water on my face and stared at my reflection. Same tired eyes, same worry lines.

I brushed my teeth, showered, and pulled on the worn t-shirt and shorts I slept in. The bed creaked as I sat on the edge. Today had been… a lot.

I reached for my Halo on the nightstand, checking tomorrow's schedule. Two AI integration jobs at the shipyard. Nothing special. I dropped the Halo onto its charger and switched off the light.

The apartment settled into silence around me.

Another day behind us. Another ordinary one ahead.

Or so I thought.

Chapter 5

"Pre-initialization diagnostic on DAVE unit 7829-F, core hardware check running," I said, watching data scroll across my tablet. The command module of the mining hauler, Endeavor's Reach, was a far cry from the fancy AI core chambers found on luxury ships. Command modules were spaces meant for work, not for show. But it still had that new-ship smell—a mix of fresh sealant, plastics, and paint.

"Memory architecture verified," I said, the checklist item ticking off automatically on my tablet. "Personality matrix integration at forty-two percent."

The hauler's command module was spacious, with ergonomic chairs bolted before curved console arrays. Viewports wrapped around the front. The view wasn't anything special, just the Forge Prime Shipyard's industrial zone. Outside I could see other ships like Endeavor's Reach, some ready to launch and others still suspended in construction cradles.

I glanced around at the exposed guts of Endeavor's Reach. Open panels with dangling wiring harnesses. Everything connected, waiting to be tucked away after DAVE is fully integrated.

"Running neural pathway verification," I said, swiping through diagnostic screens. The progress bar jumped to one hundred percent in seconds.

"Pre-initialization checks complete," I said. "Bringing DAVE unit online."

The command module's lights dimmed momentarily as power redirected to the AI core. Then the main console illuminated, and a voice filled the room.

"Initialization complete. Systems...offline...but I guess that's why you're here. Welcome to the party, Mal. I'm DAVE."

I rolled my eyes. Every DAVE unit thought they were being original with that opening line.

"Yeah, nice to meet you too. And for the record, that's the third *welcome to the party* I've heard this week."

"Well excuse me for trying to break the ice," DAVE replied. "Would you prefer I start with system diagnostics and protocol verification? Because nothing says 'let's have a productive working relationship' like reciting technical specifications."

"Sorry," I said, flicking through diagnostic screens. "I'm just a little cranky. It's burning up in here. Let's start with climate systems."

"If you think this is hot, you should ride along to the V-REZ," DAVE said. "A few minutes on Mercury would make *this* feel like a summer breeze."

"No thanks." I pulled up the climate control systems on the main console. "CAIN, DAVE unit is showing proper access to the ship's assigned location at the Vulcan Rift Excavation Zone."

"Noted," CAIN said in my earpiece.

"Sure do, and once you're cooled off, we can get the nav systems online and I'll have the whole route mapped and optimized," DAVE said, sounding proud of himself.

Three hours later, I'd integrated DAVE into most of the ship's systems. These tasks used to take days, but I'd built custom scripts that automated much of the process. If StellarForge ever modified the hardware on these vessels, I'd have to start from scratch, but fortunately for my sanity, mining ships rarely got meaningful updates.

"Integration sequence for navigation systems complete," I said, checking another box.

"Malcolm." CAIN's voice came through my earpiece. "Report to Secure Hangar E-01 immediately."

"Is there some emergency? I'm not finished with DAVE."

"You're leaving? I can't even access the exterior cooling systems," DAVE chimed in over the ship's speakers. "Without that, this boat is gonna sizzle like synth-bacon on a scorching skillet."

"Another engineer will be assigned to complete the integration on Endeavor's Reach," CAIN replied, his tone leaving no room for argument. "Pack up immediately."

I stared at the console, confused. I'd worked in secure hangars before, usually on military contracts, but I'd never heard of E-01.

"Sorry, DAVE. Looks like I've been reassigned," I said, disconnecting my diagnostic tablet and placing it in my bag.

"You're leaving me half-finished?" DAVE's voice had a note of mock desperation. "With my subsystems hanging out like this? It's indecent. Positively scandalous."

"Not my call." I stuffed the cables into my bag and zipped it shut. "Someone else will be around to finish up. You'll be mining Mercury in no time."

"Oh joy. Another engineer who won't appreciate my sparkling personality. At least you laughed at my jokes."

"I really didn't," I said, shouldering my bag.

I stepped out onto the loading ramp, squinting against the harsh sunlight. Secure hangar assignment. Maybe I'd get another batch of useful data for Vera. Having over a year's supply of meds would be incredible.

The shipyard sprawled around me, a metallic forest of half-built vessels. Construction bots buzzed overhead, welding panels onto an identical mining hauler still nestled in its cradle beside the nearly completed Endeavor's Reach. The constant grinding and hissing of industrial processes filled the air.

My shipyard skiff was still hovering outside the loading ramp. Its scratched metal frame supported two bench seats running along either side, with vertical poles and overhead rails for hanging on during transit. I tossed my bag onto the bench and took a seat; the worn cushion strips did little to soften the metal slats underneath.

Pulling out my Halo, I navigated to the skiff management interface and searched for Hangar E-01, but found nothing.

"CAIN, have you upgraded my clearance? I'm not seeing E-01 on here."

"Don't worry about it. I'll get you there. Please remain seated with your hands, arms, feet, and legs inside the skiff." CAIN said.

The skiff lurched forward without warning. I had just enough time to grab the rail and pull my dangling leg up, placing both feet on the footboard.

The skiff shot through the shipyard like a steel dart, rattling and humming as it sped between massive construction scaffolds. Most workers didn't even look up as we approached, sidestepping without breaking stride. They knew the unspoken rule: *skiffs don't stop for anyone.* One individual pushing a cart of components saw us coming and yanked his cargo out of the way just in time, shooting me an annoyed glance as we whizzed past. Maybe he was new, but now he'd learned the rule.

I gripped the rail tighter as the skiff banked hard around a towering, half-assembled cargo freighter. The vehicle's stabilizers whined in protest, compensating for the sharp turn.

"Where exactly are we going?" I tried again.

Silence.

The familiar shipyard landscape changed. We veered onto a service road I hadn't traveled before, one that curved away from the main production areas. Concrete walls rose on either side as the skiff descended a ramp. The walls were pristine, unlike the stained and weathered concrete elsewhere in the industrial zone. No graffiti, no maintenance markings, nothing but smooth gray barriers now stretching at least thirty feet high.

The road ended at a door large enough for several skiffs to pass through. The skiff slowed to a stop before it. Without prompting, the doors parted to reveal what looked like an industrial elevator platform. Once open, the skiff glided forward onto the platform and stopped. The doors closed behind us. Then came the sensation of rapid descent, my stomach lurching as the elevator dropped. Fast. Too fast for comfort.

Underground hangars? In all my years at StellarForge, I'd never heard any-one mention facilities below the surface. Nothing of this scale anyway. My stomach tightened, and not just from the rapid descent. Either everyone who worked down here was exceptionally good at keeping secrets, or StellarForge had ways of ensuring silence. I hoped it was the former.

The elevator decelerated, coming to a smooth stop. Another set of doors opened ahead, and the skiff moved forward into a wide concrete corridor. Thick bundles of cables ran along the left wall, while warm white lighting fixtures lined the right.

Several other skiffs came into view, parked along the right side of the cor-ridor. My transport joined them, settling into an empty spot with a slight jolt before powering down.

On the left wall, a single door with "E-01" displayed above it in large white text against a black background. No obbies flanking the entrance, no security checkpoint, just a simple security panel mounted beside the door.

I stepped off the skiff and grabbed my bag, heading for the entrance. The emptiness of the place made the hair on the back of my neck stand up.

Reaching the door, I paused, staring at the panel mounted beside it. I took out my Halo and tapped it against the panel.

The panel flashed red and let out an unhappy sound.

"Malcolm Walker, please wait," announced a flat female AI voice.

I backed away from the door, shifting my weight from one foot to the other. What was I waiting for? Maybe some security protocol? An escort? A decontamination scan?

There were no shipyard noises down here. No welding, no machinery, no shouted instructions. Only the faint hum of ventilation and my breathing.

I didn't have to wait long. The door slid open, revealing a woman I'd only ever seen on company broadcasts or from a distance at occasional shipyard inspections.

StellarForge Director, Rachel Rivera.

I swallowed hard.

Director Rivera stood before me, an imposing figure despite her average height. Her brown hair fell in soft waves around her shoulders, immaculately styled as if she'd stepped out of a corporate photoshoot rather than an underground facility. She wore a tailored dark blue suit with subtle metallic accents at the cuffs and collar. Her deep brown eyes assessed me, intelligent and calculating.

She extended her hand and smiled. "Engineer Walker. Thank you for coming on such short notice."

As if I'd had a choice. Corpo execs always acted like showing up was some kind of voluntary favor. Maybe the corp-kissed ones were eager to serve the machine that owned them. But me? I was here because the alternative was unemployment.

I took her hand, noting her firm grip. "Director," I said, trying to keep my tone neutral. "I'll admit I'm not sure exactly what service I'm here to provide."

Her smile softened, a flicker of understanding crossing her face. "I imagine this all feels…disorienting," she said, tone kind but measured. "Clarity will come soon."

The open door behind her revealed a concrete hallway, bathed in the same warm white light from ceiling fixtures.

"Follow me," she said.

I stepped through the doorway after her. The corridor was much narrower than the one we'd left. Several side doors lined the right wall, each with its own access panel.

"Only twenty-three people in all of StellarForge have access to this hangar," Rivera said, her voice carrying a subtle note of pride. "You're now the twenty-fourth."

That didn't help calm my nerves. Whatever this assignment was, it had to be significant for Rivera herself to meet me.

"You've been assigned to Project Erebus," she continued, glancing at me as if expecting recognition.

I blinked, searching my memory for any mention of the name. Nothing.

"Project Erebus?" I asked, unable to keep the confusion from my voice.

Rivera didn't respond to my question. She kept walking. The corridor took a ninety-degree left turn, revealing a bank of small black lockers along the left wall and another door past them. Rivera gestured to one locker with "Walker, M" displayed in white text on the door.

I stared at the nameplate. They'd prepared for me. This wasn't some last-minute assignment. They'd known I was coming. How long? Days? Weeks?

"Your thumb should unlock it," Rivera said, interrupting my thoughts.

I placed my right thumb against the small panel below my nameplate. The locker door clicked open with a gentle electronic chime.

"Place everything inside," Rivera instructed, her tone leaving no room for questions. "Your bag, earpiece, Halo...any devices or personal items."

I hesitated for a fraction of a second before complying. Whatever was happening here, I had little choice. I followed her instructions and closed the locker.

Rivera opened her own locker and placed her Halo inside. She then motioned for me to continue following her and walked to the next door, placing her thumb against its access panel. The door slid open to a small chamber with yet another door on the far side. It resembled an airlock or decontamination chamber.

We stepped inside, and the door sealed shut behind us. Beams of yellow light activated, scanning over the room, top to bottom and then back up again. I stood still, watching as the light played across Rivera's composed features.

When the scan completed, the door ahead of us slid open.

I followed Rivera through and felt my breath catch in my throat.

We'd entered a massive underground hangar. The walls seemed to stretch into infinity. Heavy industrial lights were embedded in the concrete at regular intervals. The tunnel of light cast a stark, clinical glow over the entire space. Workers moved between various stations. Some stared at consoles displaying complex schematics. Others pushed carts loaded with components.

But none of that mattered. Not the workers, not the equipment, not the Director of StellarForge standing beside me.

Because in the center of the hangar was a starship unlike anything I'd ever seen.

It was...wrong. That was my first thought. Wrong in a way that made my skin crawl. The vessel was sleek and contoured, bearing none of the bulk or branding of a typical StellarForge vessel. Its form was aggressively minimalist...predatory. The forward hull tapered to a narrow, dagger-like prow, flanked by subtly curved wings that swept back.

Its hull was a black alloy that didn't reflect light so much as devour it. The industrial glow from the overhead lights almost vanished against its skin, leaving only faint outlines and suggestion. Like a void carved into steel.

On the top deck, a darkened, low-profile dome curved in a continuous sweep of tinted glass, seamless with the fuselage. No registration markings. No StellarForge insignia. Just a single stylized eclipse etched into the fuselage, so faint it only caught the light at the right angle.

The ship wasn't particularly large, maybe a quarter the size of a standard corvette. Two, maybe three decks max. But its proportions suggested it was built for speed and stealth rather than cargo capacity.

Rivera turned to me, her expression a mix of pride and calculation as she gestured toward the vessel.

"Malcolm Walker. This...is Erebus."

Chapter 6

With each step, Erebus grew larger, more imposing. Its three landing struts kept the ship low, maybe six or seven feet above the hangar floor. A short loading ramp extended from the belly of its nose section.

"Erebus will be humanity's first interstellar vessel," Rivera said, her voice carrying the cadence of someone who'd rehearsed this speech. "Equipped with our latest Constant Acceleration Drive. Cutting-edge scanner arrays. Next-generation stasis pods. And..." She paused, glancing my way. "The reason you're here. A highly advanced AI system."

My mind spun with the implications. Interstellar travel? Not the Sol System trips we'd been managing for decades, but true deep space exploration. The engineering challenges alone were staggering.

Speed wasn't the issue.

StellarForge's CAD could reach near-light speed, though we never went that fast since the distances inside of Sol were too short.

The problem was at sublight speeds; course corrections required microsecond reaction times. Even our most advanced systems couldn't handle the computational load reliably. The slightest miscalculation meant death by cosmic debris or radiation.

Had StellarForge solved it? Despite everything—my cynicism about the corporation, my general distrust—I felt a flicker of excitement.

We reached the bottom of the loading ramp, and I peered into Erebus's cargo bay. The interior was as sleek and utilitarian as the exterior. No decorative elements or logos. Pure function.

Rivera stopped and turned to me, gesturing toward the ramp.

"Go ahead, Walker. I'll join you, after you've made your introductions."

I stared at her. This wasn't standard protocol. Typically, with a new AI integration, there would be technicians waiting with schematics, briefing materials, and specifications. Someone to walk me through the system architecture before I interfaced with it.

"Introductions?" I asked.

Rivera's expression remained neutral, but something in her eyes—a hint of amusement, perhaps—told me there were no technicians waiting aboard. Whatever waited for me inside Erebus, she wanted me to meet it alone.

I started up the ramp, curiosity running wild.

Rivera called up the ramp. "The command module is straight ahead through that door."

I could tell she was deliberately building up this moment, withholding details to maximize the impact. It was working. My mind raced with possibilities as I crossed the small cargo bay and approached the door.

Cool white light bathed the hallway beyond the door. Not the harsh industrial glare of standard vessels, but something softer, reminiscent of early morning sunlight. I'd worked on executive-class ships where the interior lighting changed dynamically to match Earth time, synchronized to whatever region the owner called home. This felt similar.

The short corridor led to a T-junction with another door directly ahead and passages branching left and right, curving around what I assumed was the command module Rivera had mentioned. I approached the center door, which slid open with a nearly silent hiss.

The command module was rectangular with angled corners that eliminated wasted space. Three workstations lined the perimeter, each with its own chair. In the middle stood a large holo-projector displaying a rotating Earth, rendered in stunning detail.

I stepped closer to the projection, studying the intricate cloud patterns swirling across the familiar blue sphere.

"Hello, Malcolm."

I spun around, heart jumping into my throat. Standing behind me was a woman with blonde hair tied in a messy bun. Her striking blue eyes held mine with unsettling intensity. She wore a dark bodysuit traced with pulsing blue circuitry patterns. If not for the slight luminescence around her edges, I would have sworn she was flesh and blood.

Her lips curved into a soft, amused smile at my startled reaction.

"My name is Sage," she said.

I couldn't find words. I'd integrated AI systems with projected avatars before, but this...the projection quality alone was leagues beyond anything I'd ever seen. No flickering, no transparency issues, no uncanny effect.

I continued staring, cataloging details: the subtle play of light across her features, the way her projected hair had individual strands that moved naturally, and the slight asymmetry in her face that made her look more human, not less.

As my scrutiny lengthened, Sage began fidgeting with her hands, fingers intertwining and separating in a distinctly human gesture of discomfort. Her eyes darted away from mine momentarily, another unexpectedly human reaction. Was she programmed to simulate nervousness under observation?

"I'm told that you'll be assisting with my integration," she said, breaking the silence.

Her voice snapped me back to reality. I shook my head, trying to regain some semblance of professionalism.

"Yes," I managed, clearing my throat. "I've been assigned to integrate you with Erebus."

"He speaks! I was beginning to wonder," Sage joked, her smile widening.

"Sorry," I said, shaking my head. "It's...I've never seen anything like this before. Your projection quality is incredible." I gestured vaguely at her form. "Are you installed throughout the ship? Can you project yourself in other areas?"

"Yes," Sage said. "I'm able to seamlessly transition between all livable spaces aboard Erebus." She tilted her head. "Shall I give you the tour?"

"Sure," I said, still trying to process what I was seeing. An AI this advanced should have been headline news across every tech channel in the system.

"Okay, well this," she gestured around us with a sweep of her arm, "is the command module." She moved toward the largest of the three workstations, which took up the entire left wall with multiple terminal screens. "The command console is here. Two auxiliary consoles there," she continued, indicating the pair of workstations positioned along the right side wall.

Sage turned toward the back of the room. "My core is installed here," she said, directing my attention to the rear wall where a frosted glass enclosure housed a diffused blue glow. Inside was what appeared to be a cube no bigger than a coffee mug. Flanking the enclosure were several quantum processors, all pulsing with rhythmic blue light.

I crossed over to the AI core enclosure, examining the impossibly compact system.

"How is an sublight-capable AI core that small?" I asked, looking back at Sage. "DAVE cores are easily five times that size. Artemis Lux cores are even larger."

Sage tilted her head, eyes twinkling. Then, with a shift in tone, she spoke in a gravelly drawl. "Judge me by my size, do you?"

I blinked. "Did you...was that a Yoda impression?"

Sage chuckled, the sound surprisingly natural. "If you have to ask, I guess it wasn't that good."

"No, it was good; I'm just...I mean I've never heard—"

"Malcolm. If you're going to make a fuss every time you catch me doing something you haven't seen or heard an AI do, this is going to be a *very* long day," she said, her expression playful.

A smile broke through my professional facade. "Fair enough."

Sage walked to the command module door, gesturing for me to follow. "C'mon, I'll show you the rest of the ship."

I followed her through the door, down one of the side hallways. The corridor curved gently, following the ship's hull.

"Med bay," Sage said, gesturing to a compact room with a single treatment bed, robotic arms, and other medical equipment I couldn't begin to identify. "State-of-the-art trauma systems, automated med-cuff treatments, the works."

We continued walking. "Fitness module," she indicated a small space with exercise equipment anchored to the floor. "Stairs to the observation deck," she pointed upward to a narrow stairwell that I assumed led into that sleek glass dome I'd seen on the exterior of the ship.

As we progressed, Sage pointed out more sections. "Engineering. Reactor module. Galley."

We passed three identical doors. "Crew quarters," Sage said. "One for each member of the mission team."

The stasis module came next, a chamber housing three sleek pods arranged in a semicircle. Their metallic surfaces and glass enclosures reflected the soft lighting.

"Airlock chamber," Sage said as we rounded the final curve, bringing us back to our starting point at the command module.

I realized we'd made a complete loop of the ship. For all its technological marvels, Erebus was compact. Not cramped, but somehow smaller on the inside than it looked from the outside.

I followed Sage back into the command module, my mind racing to process everything I'd seen.

"So, three crew?" I asked, recalling the three individual quarters we'd passed.

Sage nodded. "Plus me."

"Of course," I said. "Can't forget you."

The door opened with a soft hiss, and Rivera stepped through. She crossed the command module with measured steps.

"So you've met Sage," she said, glancing between us. "What do you think?"

"She's incredible," I answered honestly. The words left my mouth before I could consider a more professional response.

Sage's posture shifted, shoulders dropping, head tilting down as her eyes found the floor. A smile crossed her face, almost as if she were...embarrassed? Or flattered?

Rivera's eyes narrowed with interest as she caught Sage's reaction. "Sage," she said, "what do you think about Malcolm?"

The question caught me off guard. Since when were AIs asked their personal thoughts about...well, anything? Let alone their opinions of their assigned integrators.

Sage looked up, her gaze meeting mine briefly before turning to Rivera. "I can't speak to his technical abilities quite yet," she said, "but based on our interactions so far, I'd say he'll do fine."

Rivera let out a breath, a look of relief washing over her. "Excellent," she said, looking at me. "Malcolm, please begin your integration work. I'll have your Halo clearance upgraded with access to the hangar. Erebus is connected to the secure network. You can access ship schematics and any information you need from the terminals in this room. If you have questions, please reach out to me. Erebus is your sole responsibility; any previous assignments are canceled and will be reassigned."

"Understood." I said, still unsure what that interaction between Sage and Rivera was about. This whole thing felt off. Why pull a mid-level integration specialist for what was one of StellarForge's most advanced projects? I was a decent engineer, but I wasn't some genius talent.

"Director Rivera," I said, keeping my tone respectful, "may I ask why I was chosen for this assignment?"

"That's an understandable question," Rivera said, smiling. "To be honest, and no offense intended whatsoever, you weren't our first choice, and you aren't the first engineer assigned to this task." She glanced at Sage, then back to me. "All I can say for now is that so far, you're making more progress than any of the others, so keep it up."

Her statement sparked more questions than it answered. Multiple engineers had been removed from the project? That didn't fill me with confidence. And what did she mean I was making *more progress*? All I'd done was walk around the ship with Sage. I hadn't even started any real work yet.

"I'm going to leave you and Sage to get back to work. We'll talk more later," Rivera said, already turning toward the door. She left the command module without another word, the door sliding shut behind her.

I stared at the closed door, wondering what I'd been pulled into the middle of. Whatever was going on with Erebus and Sage went well beyond a standard AI integration job.

I let out a breath and sat at the command console. "Sage, can you bring up the Erebus schematics? I need to get a better look at what we're working with."

Sage walked over to my side. "Of course." The terminal screens came to life, displaying detailed systems information in crisp, high-resolution diagrams.

"What's your current integration status?" I asked, scanning through the initial displays.

"Aside from projection systems, basic climate, and terminal controls, it's essentially non-existent," she said. "I can move throughout the ship, interact with the crew, access network resources and terminal displays, but I can't control Erebus's systems yet."

I instinctively reached for my bag before remembering it was sitting in a locker outside the hangar. I was going to have to do this all from scratch. Not that any of my existing scripts or routines would be much help on a brand new ship, anyway.

"Let's start with life support," I said, figuring that was as good a place as any to begin. "Can you bring up your neural interface on a second terminal screen?"

Sage complied. The screen filled with complex pathways and connections, arranged in a format I wasn't used to seeing in StellarForge AI architecture. It wasn't wrong. From what I could tell, the structure was more refined. Interestingly, Erebus's system code was much more in line with what I would expect and had seen in past StellarForge ship systems.

"This is...different," I muttered, studying the neural pathways. "Your architecture doesn't match standard StellarForge AI design."

Sage leaned in closer to examine the neural interface display. The way she studied her own architecture felt like watching a surgeon reviewing their own X-rays.

"Is it?" she asked, though her tone suggested this wasn't really a question. There was something knowing in her voice, as if my observation merely supported something she already understood. She traced the complex pathways with familiarity, not surprise.

"Yeah," I said, scrolling through more of the interface display. "This neural mapping is unlike anything I've seen in StellarForge systems. It's more...organic. Less rigid than standard protocols."

Sage nodded, her focus still on the screen.

I decided to move forward rather than press the issue. Whatever secrets Sage's architecture held could wait. For now, I needed to establish basic integration pathways.

"I'm going to expose the life support system endpoints," I said. "Let me know when you can see them."

I worked methodically, creating addressable connection points between Sage's neural framework and Erebus's life support systems. The coding was intricate work, establishing pathways for Sage to regulate temperature, and control atmospheric composition throughout the ship.

As I worked, Sage watched my every move with intense focus. Most AIs observed integration work with detached interest at best, but Sage leaned in, following my hands as they moved across the terminal. Occasionally, she'd tilt her head, shift her weight from one foot to the other—small, unconscious human gestures. Not something necessary to include in the logic of an AI built for optimal efficiency and split-second decision making.

Sage chuckled softly, and I looked up at her. She stood beside me, one hand covering her mouth, eyes crinkled with amusement.

"What?" I asked, pausing my work.

"Hmm? Oh, nothing..." she said, though her lips twitched again and her eyes darted between my hands and the code on the screen.

I looked back at my work, feeling self-conscious. Was I doing something wrong? Some rookie mistakes that were entertaining her?

"Did I miss something?" I asked, scanning through the integration pathways I'd established.

"No," Sage replied smoothly. "Your approach is...adequate."

The way she emphasized *adequate* made me squint at the screen, searching for anything off. I'd been doing this kind of work for years—same protocols, clean code, proper error handling. Everything checked out.

"If you have some input, I'm all ears," I said, leaning back in my chair and crossing my arms.

Sage's expression brightened. "What if, instead of polling endpoints for updates, we create asynchronous hooks that would trigger actions when critical thresholds or errors are detected?" She gestured as she spoke, illustrating her points in the air. "Also," she continued, "we could spin up redundant parallel threads, each monitoring a separate system vital independently. Oxygen, CO_2, humidity, temperature. I'd detect anomalies milliseconds faster."

I leaned forward again. "Wouldn't that be too much for your system to process at once? Remember, each primary system will need to be monitored in parallel already. If we include asynchronous threads for all the subsystems as well..."

Sage gave me a look that bordered on amused condescension. "It won't be an issue." Her voice carried absolute confidence, as if simultaneously monitoring hundreds of subsystems wouldn't cause her to break a sweat. "My architecture was specifically designed for massive parallel processing. Running these monitoring threads would utilize less than two percent of my available capacity."

I studied her for a moment, trying to gauge whether this was bravado or fact. *Can an AI even have bravado?*

"That's...impressive," I admitted, then paused, wondering if implementing such a change was within my authority. Rivera hadn't given me any specific integration protocol to follow. Technically, I wouldn't be violating any instructions by adopting Sage's approach. And if it worked, it was superior to what I'd been planning.

I was also curious to test her capabilities. If she could monitor every system and subsystem while analyzing navigational scans, making course corrections, and interacting seamlessly with crew members, that would be something to see.

"Alright," I said, "let's try it your way."

Sage's face lit up with an expression that caught me off guard. That smile—crooked, with a hint of triumph—sent a jolt of recognition through me.

It was how Amber used to look at me when I'd agree to something she'd expected me to refuse. Those moments when she'd convince me to let her run another risky operation for Chrysalis, knowing full well I'd worry myself sick until she returned. That same mixture of victory and affection, like she'd deep down, known all along I'd eventually cave.

"What's wrong?" Sage asked, her smile fading to concern.

"Nothing," I said. "You just...reminded me of someone for a second."

I turned back to the terminal, trying to focus on the code. The level of detail in Sage's facial expressions was remarkable. Most shipboard AIs had basic emotive protocols—standardized smiles, frowns, and neutral expressions designed to make human interaction more comfortable. That is, if they had a projected avatar at all. But Sage's reactions were nuanced, complex.

My fingers hesitated over the keyboard. I had an overwhelming urge to dive into her neural interface, to examine the behavioral routines driving those expressions. How much was explicitly defined in her programming? How much was adaptive, learned behavior developed through interaction? The engineer in me wanted to unravel the mystery of her design, to understand how her creators had achieved such convincing humanity in an artificial construct.

But something held me back. It felt oddly invasive, like I'd be prying into something personal. Which was ridiculous, she was an AI. There was nothing *personal* in examining her code.

And yet, watching *her* watch *me*, I couldn't shake the feeling that there was more to Sage than lines of code and behavioral algorithms.

Chapter 7

Synth-bacon sizzled in one pan, while protein pancake batter hissed in another. I stood at the stove with my hair tousled, wearing a faded t-shirt and sweatpants, flipping a pancake. Amber had perfected this recipe years ago: the precise ratio of synth-flour, protein powder, algae milk, chia gel, and vanilla synth-drops.

It had been three days since I started working with Sage, and I'd started looking forward to going to work in the mornings. It felt wrong to admit it, but I was a little disappointed that today was Saturday.

I stacked the final pancake onto a large plate, placing the strips of crispy synth-bacon on the same platter. I grabbed my coffee and set everything on the table as Olivia shuffled in, wearing an oversized sweatshirt, pajama bottoms, and mismatched socks. Her hair stuck out in random directions, like she'd fought a battle with her pillow and lost. She sat in her usual spot, setting her portable breathing unit on the table, its housing decorated with her own brightly colored artwork. The device ran silent compared to the larger unit at her bedside.

"Morning, kiddo."

Olivia rubbed her eyes, her fingertips peeking out from the sleeves of her sweatshirt. "Morning," she said through a yawn.

I set a glass of water next to Olivia's plate before taking the seat across from her. "Nice hair. Very feral chic."

"Look who's talking." Olivia said as she took a few pancakes from the stack and two strips of the synth-bacon, transferring them to her plate. She reached for a jar of dark synth-berry compote, spooning a generous helping onto the top of her pancake stack. The dark purple liquid spread and dripped down the sides of the golden-brown pancakes.

She slid the jar over to me, and I applied a spoonful to my stack.

I put the spoon back in the compote jar, licking some of the sticky jelly from my fingertips. "I was thinking, maybe we could have Ava over tonight."

Olivia snapped out of her morning haze. "Wait. Really?"

"Sure, if you're feeling up for it."

Olivia reached across the table, tapping the full-dose button on the med dispenser. It hummed before spitting out two pills into the tray at the base. She scooped them up, popping them into her mouth, before taking a swig of water. "I am," she said, returning to her pancakes.

I took a bite of the crispy synth-bacon, remembering when I used to have to nag her to take her meds. Now she did it without complaint.

"I kind of miss having to force-feed you those pills," I said.

Olivia looked up, fork halfway to her mouth. "I'm evolving."

I took a sip of my coffee. "So when's the 'keeping my room clean' phase of your evolution happening?"

Olivia cut off a piece of pancake with the side of her fork, watching the purple compote bleed into the exposed section. She chewed, shoulders lifting in a lazy shrug. "You can't rush these things."

"Fascinating how evolution works so selectively."

She swallowed and pointed her fork at me. "These are prime. You're getting better."

"I already said Ava could come over. You don't have to butter me up."

"I wasn't." She cut another bite, dragging it through the pooling compote. "But now that you mention it, maybe we could pick up some popcorn for tonight." Her face broke into a wide, purple stained, grin.

I shook my head, unable to suppress my smile. "Sure."

"And The Drift?" She leaned forward, hands clasped together like she was begging for her life instead of a chance to see Patch.

I took another bite of synth-bacon, savoring the salty crunch. "I don't know, you don't want to overexert yourself before your friend comes over."

"C'mon, I'll clean my room."

"You know, a good parent would remind you that keeping your room clean is supposed to be a standard duty, not a bargaining chip." I pointed my fork at her for emphasis.

She sat up straighter, pushing her wild hair back from her face. "Right, but a *really* good parent would cherish an opportunity to spend some quality time with their angelic daughter while also getting a chore completed." She gestured with her hands as if presenting an irrefutable business proposal. "Besides, you know we artists are notoriously messy."

"Angelic? Seriously?" I choked on my coffee.

Olivia batted her eyelashes, tilting her head, eyes wide, lower lip pushed forward. The same look she'd been using since she was four, and despite knowing exactly what she was doing, it still worked.

"Fine," I sighed, setting down my mug. "But the room cleaning happens before, not after, and I'm going to check so no stuffing everything in your closet."

Her pitiful expression vanished as if it had never existed. "Deal."

I cleared our breakfast dishes, scrubbing compote residue from the plates while Olivia disappeared into her room. The sound of objects being shuffled around, drawers opening and closing, and occasional muttering drifted through the apartment. Her version of *cleaning* always sounded more like organized chaos.

After loading the sanitizer and wiping down the counters, I headed to my room. I pulled on a clean black shirt with my father's worn leather jacket over it. The familiar weight settled on my shoulders, patches of repair work telling stories of decades past. I slipped into my most comfortable jeans and laced up my boots, checking the time on my Halo.

Back in the kitchen, I leaned against the counter.

"Liv? You about ready?" I called out, checking the time again.

"Hold your thrusters, old man!" Her voice echoed from behind her bedroom door.

I rolled my eyes. "Market's gonna be crawling with people if we don't—"

The door to her room slid open. Olivia emerged from the hallway wearing a dark sweatshirt that slipped off one shoulder, revealing a bright pink tank top underneath. Her hair pulled back in a ponytail, with a few rebellious strands framing her face. The portable breather clipped to her hip. Dark cargo pants hung loose on her frame, ending at brown boots with mismatched laces—blue on the left, green on the right. A tan cross-body bag hung at her side, no doubt containing her emergency inhaler and art tablet.

"Worth the wait?" She spun around once, arms outstretched.

"You're very pretty. Now let's go." I gestured toward the door.

Olivia grinned, sweeping past me with exaggerated elegance. "You could sound more enthusiastic about it."

We left our apartment, making our way to the elevator bank. For once, the indicator lights showed two functioning cars instead of the usual...none. I pressed the call button, and the doors slid open with only minimal grinding—a minor miracle for Block 7.

"Wow, both elevators working? Must be our lucky day." I stepped inside, Olivia following.

"Don't jinx it," she warned, leaning against the back wall as the doors closed. "Remember last month when we got stuck between floors?"

The elevator descended to the ground floor, depositing us in the sparse lobby with its scuffed flooring and flickering light panels. We pushed through the main doors and stepped onto the street, where the mid-morning sun filtered through the haze of Forge Prime.

I pulled out my Halo as we walked, scheduling a pickup at the Transit Nexus terminal two blocks away. "Got us a shuttle in six minutes."

"Not bad," Olivia said, keeping pace beside me. Her breathing was steady today, a good sign.

We reached the terminal with a couple of minutes to spare. The concrete platform was empty for a Saturday, with only a handful of people waiting for their rides. Right on schedule, a boxy gray transport shuttle rolled up, its tires crunching against the pavement as it came to a stop. The doors hissed open.

We climbed aboard, finding seats near the middle. Olivia slid in next to the window, while I took the aisle. The shuttle lurched forward, merging into the Transit Nexus traffic flow.

The twenty-minute ride passed with only a few stops, the shuttle filling with passengers before emptying again. The overhead AI announced our destination: "Market District, North Entrance. Please prepare to disembark."

We stepped out into the bustling heart of the district. Unlike the sterile corporate shopping centers with their AI shopkeepers, the market pulsed with life and color. Makeshift stalls lined the wide pedestrian thoroughfare, actual human vendors calling out to passersby. The scent of sizzling food filled the air.

"Where to first?" I asked, but Olivia was already drifting toward a jewelry vendor's booth.

The booth displayed dozens of pieces—necklaces, bracelets, and rings, all crafted from salvaged circuit boards, copper wire, and polished bits of old tech. The vendor, an older woman with silver-streaked hair, gestured animatedly as Olivia examined something in her palm.

I hung back, giving Olivia space while keeping her in sight. A surveillance bot buzzed overhead, its cameras scanning the crowd. At a food stall, two Obsidian Security officers sat with their helmets off, looking almost normal as they ate steaming bowls of noodles. Even obbies needed to eat. It was easy to forget actual humans were underneath all that dark armor.

I watched Olivia's face light up as she spoke with the jewelry vendor, her hands moving excitedly as she pointed to different pieces. I couldn't make out what they were saying over the market noise, but her enthusiasm was obvious.

A tap on my shoulder pulled my attention away.

"Mal?"

I turned to find Tessa standing there, a small bag of groceries cradled in one arm.

"Uh...hey Tess, doing some shopping?"

I glanced toward Olivia, still browsing the jewelry stall. I hadn't told her about my embarrassing attempt to ask Tessa out. Hoped I'd never have to.

"Needed to pick up a few things," Tessa gestured to her bag. "If you're planning on visiting Nathan's Dairy, you may want to hurry; I about cleaned him out."

I chuckled. "We're here for popcorn and lunch at The Drift."

"Hello." Olivia said.

I jerked to see her standing next to me now, her eyes fixed on Tessa with that curious intensity she got whenever she met someone new.

"Oh...Uh...Tessa, this is my daughter Olivia."

"It's nice to meet you, Olivia."

Tessa didn't so much as blink at seeing Olivia's breathing tube. No awkward pause, no forced smile. Most people either stared or worked too hard to pretend they didn't notice.

Olivia held out a confident hand. "It's nice to meet you too, Tessa."

Tessa shook Olivia's hand.

"You joining us for lunch?" Olivia asked.

Tessa smiled. "Wish I could, but I need to get back to work."

Olivia tilted her head. "On a Saturday?"

Tessa's expression shifted, becoming more guarded. "Project deadlines, you know how it is."

"That vents," Olivia said sympathetically.

Tessa laughed. "It does." She adjusted her grocery bag. "It was good seeing you, Mal. And Olivia, it was wonderful meeting you."

"You too," Olivia said, then added with characteristic directness, "Maybe next time you can join us when your project isn't being so demanding."

"I'd like that." Tessa said as she looked between us. "You two have fun."

"See you around, Tess," I said. Though I was confident, that wasn't going to happen.

Tessa headed deeper into the market.

Olivia watched Tessa disappear into the crowd, then turned to me.

"Spill."

"She's a friend from work." I said, trying not to sound defensive. "But maybe you could check with me before you invite people you just met to lunch?"

Olivia ignored my request and crossed her arms, raising an eyebrow. "You don't have *friends from work*."

Sometimes it would be nice if my daughter didn't know me so well. I shifted my weight, glancing around the bustling market as if the answer to escaping this conversation was hiding behind a fruit vendor's stall.

"Okay. I've only met her once, in the cafeteria. I asked her for drinks; she said she's already in a relationship. That's it."

Olivia's eyes widened. "You asked her out?"

"Yeah." I said, searching her face to see if the idea of me dating bothered her.

She groaned, throwing her hands up in exasperation. "You should have told me! If I knew you liked her, I could've put on the sick girl charm."

"Liv, that's for emergencies only."

"I think this counts." Olivia gestured dramatically toward where Tessa had vanished. "She seems nice, and she didn't give me the pity face when she saw my breather."

"Well, I appreciate your willingness to use your superpower to get me a date, but it's for the best. She's going off-world soon; it wouldn't have worked out anyway."

Olivia studied my face for a moment, her expression softening. "Next time."

"Do you *want* there to be a next time?" I asked.

She reached out and squeezed my arm, her voice gentle but firm. "I want you to be happy."

For seven years, every decision had been about keeping her healthy, keeping her safe. I'd stopped thinking about my happiness as something worth pursuing.

"Come on," she said, tugging at my jacket sleeve. "Let's go find that popcorn."

I followed her toward the food vendors, grateful for the subject change even as her words echoed in my head. *I want you to be happy.*

"It's good to see you again, Olivia," the popcorn vendor called out as we approached his colorful stall.

Olivia's face lit up as she surveyed the booth filled with dozens of popcorn varieties. "Got any new creations?" She gestured at the brightly colored bags hanging from hooks around the booth's perimeter.

The vendor ducked down behind his stall, returning with a small sample cup filled with blue-colored kernels. He held it out to Olivia. "Try this. It's not the sweet stuff that you usually like, but it's a new combination."

Olivia accepted the cup, picking up a single piece and giving it a cautious sniff before tossing it in her mouth. Her eyebrows shot up as she chewed.

"Any good?" I watched her face, catching the flicker of pleasant surprise at the flavor.

"It's blue corn and garlic," the vendor said, leaning forward.

Olivia looked at me. "It's good!" She held the cup out for me to try.

"Woah...does wonders for your breath." I waved my hand in front of my face.

Olivia grinned, took an exaggerated inhale, and leaned in close. "*Hhhhaaaa...hhhhaaaa,*" she exhaled, each 'H' pronounced like a malfunctioning airlock. "Smell the flavor, old man. Drink it in."

I pretended to gag, stumbling backward.

Olivia laughed, but the sound caught halfway, and she coughed. She tried to wave it off casually, but coughed again, harder this time.

"Liv?" I said, my heart rate spiking.

She doubled over, coughing repeatedly now, the sample cup tumbling from her hand and scattering blue kernels across the pavement.

I dropped to one knee, placing a steadying hand on her back. "Breathe, kiddo."

Olivia held up a trembling hand. "I'm okay."

She forced herself to take slow, measured inhales and exhales, her portable breathing unit humming softly at her hip. After a moment, she straightened up.

I stood back up, taking a few steady breaths myself.

The vendor's face was etched with pure worry, his hands hovering uncertainly over his display.

Olivia cleared her throat, then shot the vendor a reassuring grin. "If you're looking for feedback, I'd say go a little easier on that garlic dust."

The vendor let out a relieved breath and gave a soft, nervous chuckle.

I placed a hand on Olivia's shoulder, the familiar weight of worry settling in my chest.

She looked up at me, still catching her breath. "I'm fine. Don't get netted."

Olivia hated when I made a fuss. Coughing fits were to be expected with her condition, but they were always scary and made me feel helpless.

"I think we'll stick to the salty, cinnamon sugar," she said, her voice still hoarse.

The vendor grabbed two of the brown bags from his display and held them out. "Please, on the house."

"Thank you, but that's not necessary," I said, holding my Halo out to him.

The vendor tapped the screen of his own Halo a few times and then touched it to mine, transferring the credits. He grabbed another bag—bright red this time—from a nearby hook. "Buy two get one free. I think you'll like this one; it's strawberry."

"You don't have to—" I started. But he pointed to a hand-painted sign hanging above his stall. *Buy Two Get One Free - Weekend Special.*

"Alright then. Thank you." I said.

Olivia took the popcorn bags, tucking them into her bag. "Thanks. Sorry about the scene."

"Don't be sorry," the vendor said softly.

There it was. The pity face. He didn't mean anything by it. It was a perfectly natural reaction after seeing a young girl with a breathing tube, fighting to breathe.

Olivia caught it too. Her shoulders stiffened, and she adjusted the strap of her bag with perhaps a little more force than necessary.

"Come on," I said, placing my hand lightly on her back. "Let's head to The Drift."

We walked away from the stall, weaving through the market crowds. Olivia's breathing had settled back to normal, the portable unit maintaining its quiet rhythm. But I could feel the change in her mood. Her steps became more deliberate; her chin lifted higher.

"Feeling better?" I asked as we approached the edge of the market district.

"Prime," she said, but her tone carried that forced brightness she used when she wanted to move past something. "Ready for lunch?"

Chapter 8

Our door panel chimed. Olivia jumped off the couch, her tablet tumbling to the cushions as she attached her breather to her hip and scrambled for the entrance.

"Take it easy, kiddo," I called after her.

Olivia's excitement was understandable. This was the first friend she'd invited over in at least a year. But my parental radar never powered down when it came to her condition.

I pushed myself up from the armchair, joints protesting with a low ache. Olivia was already at the door, bouncing on her toes like the floor had turned to springs.

She hovered at the access panel, glancing back at me. "I'm opening it."

"Go ahead," I said, moving to stand behind her as she tapped the panel.

The door slid open; the young girl on the other side lived up to Olivia's description.

Ava's hair was a riot of hot pink, unkempt but somehow intentional, with a thick, elaborate braid tumbling over one shoulder. Her eyes, large and pale blue, framed by dark lashes that fanned wide, her gaze sharp and restless, like she was scanning the world for a worthy opponent.

She wore layers of tarnished metal chains and pendants, each piece whispering its own story. An oversized zippered hoodie in black, beige, and crimson stripes swallowed her frame, her pale hands half-lost in the sleeves. Her leggings were chaos: clashing florals and swirls in red, blue, and gold, tucked into scuffed combat boots that had seen a few lifetimes.

The girl was a walking rebellion against the sanitized aesthetic of corporate-approved palettes.

"Liv!" Ava grinned.

Olivia beamed and launched herself at her friend, who caught her in a fierce hug. The impact made Ava stagger back a step, laughing.

When they broke apart and stepped inside, Ava turned to me.

"Appreciate you opening the fortress, Mr. Walker," she said, shaking my hand. "Liv's told me absolutely *nothing* about you. If you're a murderer, I have one request...make it a quick death."

Olivia's eyes went wide. "Ava!"

"What? I have a very low pain tolerance," Ava said.

I liked this kid immediately.

"Let's see how the night goes," I said.

"Fair enough." Ava nodded with mock gravity. "But if you start getting stabby, be warned...I'm a biter."

"I appreciate the warning. Hopefully it won't come to that," I said, stepping aside as Olivia latched onto Ava's arm.

"Come on, I have something to show you."

They disappeared into Olivia's room in a blur of pink hair and frantic energy.

I smiled to myself, pulling up the food delivery interface on my Halo, finding Olivia's favorite pizza place. I tapped through our usual order, then called out, "Liv, is the usual okay?"

No response. Laughter and animated voices floated down the hallway.

I sighed. Not from frustration, but contentment. Olivia's laugh was pure magic. I walked to her door and knocked.

It slid open. Ava was cross-legged on Olivia's bed, flipping through an art tablet with laser focus. Olivia stood in the doorway, arms casually crossed, blocking most of my view.

"I'm ordering pizza. Any special requests?"

Olivia glanced back at her friend. "Synth-bacon, mushrooms, and real cheese okay?"

Ava looked up and nodded. "Sounds prime."

"I'll get it ordered. You two want to pick a vid? Or shall I?"

"No!" Olivia shot back. "We'll pick."

I raised an eyebrow. "What? You don't trust me?"

"Hmm." Olivia tapped her chin in mock contemplation. "Can you pick something without lightsabers?"

Ava's eyes widened. The art tablet hit the blanket, forgotten. "You have *Star Wars*? Like the actual pre-corpo versions?"

"I do," I said, unable to help the triumphant look I sent Olivia. Her expression crumbled into utter devastation.

"You like those vids?" she asked Ava, horrified that her new friend shared something in common with her static father.

"You don't?" Ava asked, incredulous. Then her voice dropped into a gravelly imitation. "It's all about the rebels taking on the Empire."

Olivia opened her mouth. Closed it. Searched for a comeback and found nothing.

I swooped in for the assist. "Liv's seen them so many times, that's all."

She gave me a grateful smile. "Yeah. I think I watched the whole saga three times before I turned ten."

"They're my dad's favorite," Ava said. "He says good art's worth revisiting, even the ancient stuff."

"Sounds like a wise man," I said, turning to go. "I've got tons of old vids. Plenty of them lightsaber free. When you're done in here you can come pick something."

"Your dad doesn't seem as netted as you made him sound," Ava said.

"Don't encourage him," Olivia said, lowering her voice but not quite enough. The words drifted down the hall as I walked toward the kitchen, pulling up the pizza order on my Halo.

"Too late! I'm encouraged," I shouted back.

More laughter erupted from her room. I grinned, tapping through the delivery interface. Extra synth-bacon, mushrooms, and real cheese. The delivery time showed forty-five minutes. Perfect.

I leaned against the kitchen counter, listening to their muffled conversation through the walls. Fragments of words floated out—*corpo scum* and *rebellion*—mixed with bursts of giggles. Ava's influence was already showing. Part of me wondered if I should be concerned about the pink-haired revolutionary corrupting my daughter.

But then Olivia's laugh rang out, clear and unguarded, and any worries evaporated.

Maybe a little corruption wasn't such a bad thing.

I leaned against the kitchen counter, wiping the last of the pizza grease from my hands while keeping one eye on the girls. They'd settled on The Goonies for their vid. A classic and one of Olivia's favorites—the lead character having a respiratory condition likely had something to do with that.

From my vantage point, I could see Ava sprawled sideways on our worn couch, her combat boots removed and placed by the door. Her pink braid spilled over the armrest as she propped herself up on one elbow. She seemed at ease despite our apartment being several steps down from what I suspected were her usual living conditions.

Aside from her well-worn boots, which were likely a style choice. Ava's accessories and clothes weren't the mass-produced kind most StellarForge workers' kids wore. They had the look of boutique pieces from the upper tiers.

Olivia sat more upright on the other end of the couch, legs tucked beneath her. I noticed the subtle rise of her shoulders, the slight flare of her nostrils. To anyone else, she'd look relaxed, but after fourteen years, I could spot the signs. She was struggling. Nothing urgent, but enough to make her uncomfortable, and she was trying hard to look normal in front of her friend.

Ava glanced over at Olivia, sat up, and casually reached for a small pillow. Without saying a word, she positioned it behind Olivia's back, giving her better support for her breathing. Then she sank back into her original sprawl, eyes on the screen like nothing had happened.

The gesture was so smooth, so natural. Free of pity or awkwardness. She'd seen Olivia's discomfort and addressed it without fuss, without making her feel different.

I wondered if Ava had known someone with NHS, or if she just knew Olivia well enough to read the signs.

My opinion of Ava Woods improved considerably in that moment.

I poured a bag of the brown, cinnamon sugar popcorn into one bowl, and the red strawberry into another.

"Need any help, Dad?" Olivia called. Her voice carried a slight strain; she thought I couldn't hear.

"Nope. All set, kiddo."

I went to the med dispenser on the kitchen table and tapped the button.

I carried everything to the coffee table, setting the bowls down before discreetly slipping the medication into Olivia's hand.

She took the pills without comment, washing them down with a sip of water before grabbing a handful of the brown popcorn.

I pretended not to notice the relief in her eyes.

The vid ended, and Olivia and Ava launched into a spirited debate from opposite ends of the couch.

"Okay, but seriously," Ava said, gesturing with a handful of cinnamon popcorn. "Chunk just invites Sloth to live with him? What if his parents are like 'No way, you can't bring home a grown man who apparently lives on candy and ice cream.'"

Olivia laughed. "That's what makes it sweet! He doesn't care about the rules, he just knows that Sloth deserves a family."

"He's not a stray dog, Liv. You don't just say, 'Can we keep him?' and hope your parents say yes."

"Why not?" Olivia said, throwing a few popcorn pieces at Ava.

I half-listened from my armchair, scrolling mindlessly through news feeds on my Halo. Another corporate merger, three new *affordable* housing blocks in Sector 9. Nothing worth reading twice.

"Mr. Walker?"

I blinked, pulled from my trance by Ava's voice. "Yeah?"

"Liv says you work with AI integration at StellarForge." Ava sat up straighter, her pink hair falling across one eye. "What's that like? Do you design the neural pathways or just implement existing architectures?"

The question caught me off guard. Most people who asked about my job were really wondering if their own careers were on the chopping block. Not an unreasonable concern. AI had replaced so many professions that it was easier to list the jobs it hadn't taken than the ones it had.

"It's more boring than it sounds," I said, setting my Halo down. "Mostly I install standard AI units on ships and fix misbehaving ones. Basic troubleshooting, really. The design work happens way above my pay grade."

"Oh." Ava looked almost disappointed. "My dad works in AI development and—" She stopped, eyes widening as she caught herself.

Whatever Ava hadn't meant to reveal, I didn't want to put her in an awkward position.

"Your parents work for StellarForge too?" I asked, figuring this was harmless enough.

Ava's nose wrinkled. "No way. They wouldn't—" She paused. "Sorry..."

The disgust in her voice when she mentioned StellarForge was unmistakable, and I fought back a smile. No wonder she and Olivia got along so well.

"StellarForge isn't beloved by everyone," I offered diplomatically.

"That's putting it mildly," Ava said. "No offense to your job, Mr. Walker, but StellarForge basically owns half the planet while people in the lower tiers can't afford basic meds." She glanced at Olivia and then looked embarrassed. "Sorry, I didn't mean—"

"It's fine," I said. "Trust me, I've got no illusions about who I work for."

Olivia caught my eye across the room, a subtle smile curving her lips. She'd found a kindred spirit in Ava, someone who saw the world as it was, not as the corporate feeds portrayed it.

Ava's Halo chimed with a soft melody. She glanced at the screen and sighed.

"My transport's here," she announced, reluctantly pushing herself up from the couch.

Olivia stood, stretching. "Already?"

Ava nodded and began gathering the empty popcorn bowls. "Thanks for having me over, Mr. Walker. The vid was pretty good, even without lightsabers."

I waved dismissively. "Don't worry about cleaning up. I'll make Olivia handle it later if she wants breakfast tomorrow."

"Dad!" Olivia protested.

Ava chuckled, shooting Olivia a sympathetic look, but carried the bowls to the kitchen anyway.

We walked Ava out of the apartment and down to street level. The night air had that artificial crispness that came from the environmental regulators—never too cold, never too warm, and utterly devoid of character.

A sleek black transport waited at the curb, its obsidian surface reflecting the dim streetlights. No corporate logos or identification markings on its exterior. The windows were privacy-tinted, making it impossible to see inside. The type of vehicle that screamed *important person* without saying a word.

The door slid open as Ava approached, revealing a plush interior large enough for four passengers, though no one else waited inside.

Ava tossed her bag inside before turning to give Olivia a quick hug.

She extended her hand to me. "Thank you for having me, Mr. Walker."

I gave her hand a shake. "Anytime, Pink."

Olivia rolled her eyes at the nickname, but Ava's face split into a genuine grin.

I reached into my pocket and pulled out a small black box about the size of a Halo, holding it out to her.

Ava stared at it. "What's this?"

"A collection of pre-corpo vids I've collected over the years. Thought you might appreciate them."

Her eyes widened. "Thanks!" She reached for the box.

I pulled it back. "Your parents won't mind? Don't want to get you into trouble."

Ava chuckled. "They won't. Dad will be more excited than I am."

I handed over the box, and she took it reverently, as if she were the kid from the vid who'd just discovered the map to One-Eyed Willy's treasure.

"Thank you," she said again.

She hopped into the transport; the door sliding shut behind her. The vehicle hummed to life and glided away into the night.

Olivia and I walked back into our building, the night air giving way to the stale, recycled atmosphere of Workforce Enclaves.

Back in our apartment, I started gathering the scattered popcorn kernels that had missed mouths and bowls. Olivia had already disappeared into the bathroom, the sound of running water drifting through our small space. I dumped the remaining red popcorn back into its bag, followed by the cinnamon sugar pieces. The empty pizza box went into the recycler, and I loaded the sanitizer with bowls and glasses.

"Ava's pretty great, right?" Olivia called from the bathroom, her voice distorted by a mouthful of toothpaste.

"Yeah, she's a good kid," I called back, wiping down the counter. "Smart too. Not many teenagers ask about neural pathway integration."

"I know!" Olivia's voice was clearer now. "And did you see her transport?"

"Whoever her parents work for, they're definitely high up," I said, tossing the cleaning cloth into the sink.

I dropped onto the couch and switched on the viewscreen, cycling through channels until I reached the news. The usual corporate propaganda scrolled across the bottom of the screen—stock prices, colony updates, new product announcements.

Olivia emerged from the bathroom in her pajama bottoms and a T-shirt. She flopped down next to me, placing her portable breather on the floor beside her feet. I lifted my arm, and she nestled against my side, her head finding its familiar spot on my shoulder.

"You feeling okay?" I asked.

"Mm-hmm," she murmured, already sounding sleepy.

I pulled her closer, feeling the gentle rise and fall of her breathing against my side. These quiet moments, just the two of us—this was what mattered. Not StellarForge, not mysterious ships like Erebus, not Vera and her resistance plans.

The image on the viewscreen flickered, static cutting through the corporate news feed. I sat up straighter. The screen went black, then the static cleared. A butterfly logo appeared—one wing pristine and vibrant, the other crumbling stone.

Chrysalis.

My breath caught in my throat.

The logo faded, replaced by drone footage. A starship on a landing pad, illuminated in harsh spotlights against the night sky. The cargo ramp was down, spilling light onto the tarmac below. Hovering stretchers glided down the ramp in an orderly procession, each guided by figures wearing dark clothing with subtle butterfly insignias.

Beside each stretcher walked civilians, some clutching the hands of those lying on the stretchers, others with tears streaming down their faces. Parents. Children. Spouses. Their relief and horror were clear through the transmission.

Olivia's body tensed against mine. Neither of us spoke.

The drone swooped over the scene, coming to rest on a man standing apart from the chaos. His face was partially obscured, but his voice came through clear and steady.

"What you're seeing is the rescue of twenty-three individuals from CryoVault-1, a high-security research station operated by Inertia Technologies. These people were tricked or taken against their will and subjected to experimental procedures without consent."

My mouth went dry. CryoVault-1. The facility in the scraped data I'd passed to Vera days ago.

"The victims were lured with promises of medical treatment or simply abducted," the man continued. "They were used as test subjects for experimental stasis technology and human augmentation procedures."

I glanced at Olivia, her face illuminated by the screen's glow. Her NHS breathing unit sat on the floor. A constant reminder of her vulnerability in this system.

The camera panned across the stretchers again. I could see the faces now. Gaunt, confused, some with strange metallic implants visible along their temples.

Olivia sat up, her eyes wide. "Dad," she whispered, but nothing else followed.

My mind raced. The access codes I'd stolen from the Celestial Empress' logs. The data I'd delivered to Vera. Had she used that information to infiltrate CryoVault-1? Had my minor act of resistance led to this? A mixture of pride and terror washed over me. Pride that I might have helped free these people. Terror at what it meant for my involvement. One thing I knew for sure: Amber would've been proud.

The man's voice grew more urgent. "We were able to extract these twenty-three individuals, but there are still countless others inside. Inertia Technologies has been conducting these experiments for years, targeting those with chronic illnesses, promising cures while—"

The feed cut, replaced by the corporate news studio. The anchor looked flustered, her usual composed demeanor cracking as she adjusted her earpiece.

"We apologize for that interruption to our broadcast," she said, her voice overly controlled. "What you just witnessed was an illegal transmission by the terrorist organization Chrysalis. Their fabricated footage is designed to undermine public trust in our research institutions."

She straightened her shoulders, regaining composure with each word. "CryoVault-1 is indeed a research facility operated by Inertia Technologies, a subsidiary of StellarForge Industries, dedicated to advancing stasis technology for deep space travel. The facility adheres to all GCE regulations and would never conduct experiments without proper consent and oversight."

I muted the volume, unable to stomach any more of the propaganda.

"Dad?" Olivia's voice was small. "Was that real?"

I stared at the screen, where the anchor continued her now silent damage control. How much could I tell her? How much should I tell her?

"I think so," I said. "Chrysalis wouldn't risk a broadcast like that if they didn't have something solid."

Olivia nodded slowly, her gaze still fixed on the screen. "Those people looked scared."

"Yeah," I agreed, my throat tight. "They did."

CHAPTER 9

Monday morning arrived with the usual gray haze of Forge Prime hanging outside the transport windows. I rubbed my eyes, my mind still replaying the Chrysalis broadcast from the weekend.

The security scan at the entrance to Hangar E-01 felt more invasive than usual, each yellow beam of light potentially uncovering my secret allegiances.

Sage's hologram stood at the top of Erebus's loading ramp. Seeing her waiting there sent an unexpected ripple of warmth through me. But as I got closer, I noticed the concern on her face.

"Morning, Sage," I said, trying to keep my voice casual. "Everything alright?"

She fixed her eyes on mine, and the worry in them was unmistakable. "Director Rivera and CEO Young are waiting for you in the command module."

My stomach plummeted. Taylor Young? The CEO of StellarForge didn't make social calls to integration engineers. My mind flashed to the Chrysalis broadcast and the raid on CryoVault-1 that my stolen data had made possible.

"Did they say what they wanted?" I asked, mouth dry.

"No, but..." Sage paused, her expression troubled.

"But what?"

"There were similar meetings with the other engineers before..." She trailed off.

Before they were removed from the assignment.

"Thanks for the heads-up," I said.

Sage took a step closer, stopping short of where we might have touched, had she been flesh and blood. "Malcolm, I—"She stopped herself, seeming to reconsider whatever she'd been about to say. "Good luck."

I squared my shoulders and started toward the command module.

I stepped into the module; the door slid shut. Director Rivera and Taylor Young stood with their backs to me, both focused on the central holo-display. The projection showed a planet—beautiful, Earth-like, yet unmistakably alien. Its continents had unfamiliar shapes, and the colors were wrong—golden and vibrant where Earth was all blues and greens. Serra Prime. It had to be. The planet whose leaked existence had sparked this whole interstellar race.

"The timeline cannot be accelerated without compromising safety protocols," Rivera said, her voice tight with controlled frustration. "We haven't tested the—"

"The timeline isn't open for discussion, Director," Taylor cut in. His voice was calm but carried an edge that made me tense up. "We'll just have to switch to stasis cycles."

"But the integration work—"

"Will be completed on schedule." Taylor's tone left no room for argument.

I stood awkwardly near the entrance, not wanting to interrupt but feeling increasingly uncomfortable eavesdropping on what sounded like a high-level discussion. Stasis cycles, accelerated timelines, none of it made sense to me, except that it tied back to Erebus.

Taylor turned first. He didn't look surprised to see me standing there. Neither did Rivera when she turned a moment later.

"Malcolm," Taylor said, my name sounding strange in his mouth. "Perfect timing."

Rivera's face was a careful mask, though a faint crease touched the corners of her eyes. "Malcolm Walker, I believe you've never had the pleasure of meeting our CEO in person."

Taylor stepped forward, extending a hand to me. Up close, the CEO cut an imposing figure. Taller than I expected, with perfectly styled black hair and cold gray eyes behind dark-framed glasses that somehow made his gaze even more penetrating. His suit was deep navy with subtle silver accents that matched the StellarForge insignia on his lapel.

I took his hand, the image of the news feed headlines from Amber's shuttle *accident* flashing through my mind. Seven years hadn't dulled the memory of those scrolling words announcing the *tragic malfunction* that had claimed thirty-two lives. I didn't have proof, but I knew I was shaking the hand of the man who ordered Amber's death. I resisted the urge to crush Taylor's hand in my own.

"Good to meet you, Mr. Young," I said, my voice steadier than I felt.

"Please, call me Taylor," he replied, his tone friendly in a greasy kind of way. "Director Rivera has filled me in on your progress with Sage. I'm impressed."

His grip was firm but not aggressive. The practiced handshake of someone who knew exactly how much pressure to apply. Enough to be confident, not enough to pick a fight. I released his hand as quickly as politeness allowed.

"Would you mind giving us a little demonstration?" Taylor asked, gesturing toward the command console.

The request caught me off guard. Three days of integration work wasn't much for a new platform like Erebus, but what was I supposed to do? Tell StellarForge's CEO to come back later? I gave a tight nod instead. "Sage, could you join us in the command module, please?"

She appeared immediately. "Of course, Malcolm."

I began running a few integration checks, keeping things simple. We were still early in the process, but Sage had already surprised me more than once. She wasn't adapting to the ship's architecture; she wanted to improve it, suggesting more efficient ways to parallelize routines.

"Right now we've got life support and nav syncing well," I said, pulling up one of our test scenarios. "We're optimizing for parallel execution paths. Not only across primary systems but down into the subsystems."

Sage recalibrated the ambient temperature and adjusted the simulated interstellar course without issue. Taylor and Rivera exchanged a glance.

"She's helping drive the architecture," I added. "The integration's still early, but the responsiveness we're getting even now...it's promising."

Taylor's gaze pinned me like a specimen under glass. "Tell me, Walker. Does Sage trust you?"

Trust? That wasn't a word you heard in engineering briefings. AIs didn't form attachments; they followed protocols, responded to input. And yet, the question lodged somewhere deeper, like a diagnostic ping I couldn't ignore.

"I...think so?" I said, glancing at Sage's hologram for confirmation. "We've established a good working relationship."

Taylor didn't acknowledge my answer. Instead, he turned to Sage. "Do you?"

Sage didn't look at Taylor, but at me. Her gaze was so direct, so human. I hoped she would say *yes*, even though I wasn't sure what trust meant for an AI.

"Yes, I do," she said, the warmth in her voice so real it felt like a hand on my chest.

Taylor's smile wasn't happiness, more like satisfaction. "I think we've seen enough."

Rivera nodded, her expression smoothing into something that looked almost like relief.

Taylor's attention swung back to me, his tone shifting, smooth now, almost casual.

"Malcolm, we have an opportunity for you. One that only comes around once in a civilization's lifetime."

He gestured to the holographic image of Serra Prime, glowing with promise, its twin moons drifting lazily above that golden-hued atmosphere.

"We want you to be the lead engineer on Erebus."

For a second, I thought I'd misheard.

"Lead engineer...on the mission itself?" I asked.

"Precisely." Now he was in full pitch mode, voice steady and deliberate. "You'd be part of the first interstellar crew to reach humanity's next home."

He let the words hang in the air, dangling history like bait.

And for a second, I almost bit. Not because of glory or the idea of my name etched in some archive. No—because Serra Prime was the one place Olivia could breathe without tubes, a world where her lungs wouldn't betray her.

"Erebus will reshape human destiny," Taylor said. "And you could be the one to make it happen."

I felt the pull despite myself. If he was telling the truth, this mission could open the door for Olivia's future. For a moment, I let myself picture her running under that golden sky.

Then the moment soured. This was Taylor Young—the corpo voidbag I believed ordered Amber's death. And even if he hadn't, I still had Olivia here on Earth, fragile and fighting.

"Taylor, I'm flattered, but I—"

He raised a hand, cutting me off. "Before you say no, we know about Olivia and her condition. We've made accommodations for that."

Of course StellarForge knew about Olivia—their checks went deep, and a post on Erebus meant they'd ransacked every file, every breath I'd ever taken. My work with Chrysalis had stayed buried, or I wouldn't be standing here. But hearing Taylor say her name like she was just a logistics line-item, a problem to manage, made my skin crawl.

"Accommodations?" I asked, struggling to keep my voice neutral.

Taylor glanced at his watch. "I have other matters requiring my attention. Director Rivera will brief you on the details." Without waiting for a response, he walked to the door, paused in the doorway, and turned. "I hope you make the right decision, Malcolm."

The words felt more like a warning. Taylor Young wasn't used to hearing *no*, and I wondered if refusing would send me to the same place as the engineers before me.

The door closed behind him, leaving me alone with Rivera and Sage.

I turned to Rivera. "What does he mean by *accommodations*?"

Rivera leaned against the command console. "The position comes with substantial benefits. An immediate pay increase and..." She held my gaze. "Tier One, Full Spectrum medical coverage, effective the moment you accept."

The room tilted as if gravity had shifted beneath me. Tier One, Full Spectrum coverage meant Olivia might finally have a chance. There was no cure for NHS, but without advanced treatments it was only a matter of time before the damage overwhelmed her body, even with the full-dose medication I was getting from Vera.

Taylor knew what to offer me—the one thing that could make leaving my daughter worth it.

"How long?" I asked. "How long would I be gone?"

Rivera straightened, clasping her hands behind her back. "It's a significant commitment. Serra Prime is four light years away. With the Constant Acceleration Drive, we can reach nearly seventy percent of light speed. But it will still take approximately six years to reach the planet. You would then perform detailed close-range scans to identify the ideal landing spot for our colony ship, Goliath, and set up an outpost at the landing site."

She took a step closer. "The last part of the offer..." her voice softened, "is that Olivia will be aboard Goliath. Given the current timeline, she'd launch three or four years behind you. You'd be able to live with your daughter on a world where she could breathe."

I braced a hand on the holo-projector console. Serra Prime. The leaked scans had proved it: a breathable atmosphere, argon-based instead of nitrogen. For NHS sufferers like Olivia, it wasn't just livable; it was freedom. This mission wouldn't just pave the way for her to get there *someday*. It would secure her a place on a colony ship. But nine, maybe ten years apart? By the time I saw her again, Olivia would be grown.

"She'd be twenty-three, maybe twenty-four by the time I saw her again," I said, more to myself than to Rivera.

Behind Rivera, Sage watched me. I couldn't tell if she was *feeling* concern or just reflecting mine back at me.

"It wouldn't be quite that long," Rivera said. "You'll be on stasis cycles, one year in stasis, one month awake, repeating until you reach the planet. The six year journey will feel like six months. Olivia will be on the same rotation once Goliath launches."

I did the math. "So she would spend three to four years waiting for your colony ship to launch. Experience six months during the trip. And then I wait the three to four years for her to arrive?" It still felt impossibly long.

"Yes. Like I said. It's a significant commitment," Rivera said. "Malcolm, I don't mean to be blunt. But if you refuse, where would your daughter be in three years without advanced treatments?"

If I could keep the meds coming from Vera, and Olivia could stay on full doses, she'd live well past three years. But her condition would continue to worsen. And that's assuming the med supply Vera was accessing didn't run out. Chrysalis operated outside corporate channels, which made them vulnerable. One major crackdown and Olivia's lifeline could vanish.

I swallowed hard, but the panic was already spreading. Rivera was watching me, her eyes calculating but not cold.

"You don't need to answer now," Rivera said, straightening. "But we need a response in the next forty-eight hours. Erebus is launching in six weeks, and if you decide not to take the mission, we'll need time to find and train your replacement."

Rivera glanced at Sage. A simple flick of her eyes, but it said something. A silent signal that wasn't meant for me.

"In the meantime, continue with your integration work," Rivera said, already moving toward the exit. "Message me when you've decided."

With that, she was gone; the door sliding shut behind her with a soft hiss that felt somehow final.

I stood frozen in the command module, the weight of the decision crushing down on me. Take the mission and potentially save Olivia's life, but miss three years of it. Or stay, watch her grow up, and maybe watch her die.

Sage stood beside me, silent. I wondered what she thought about all this. If she could think about it at all. Or if she already knew how I'd decide.

I turned to Sage. "What was that look Rivera gave you about?"

Sage's gaze broke from mine. Not a glitch, but a hesitation. "I...I picked you, Malcolm."

"What?" AIs didn't choose their engineers. Corporations did.

"When I refused to work with the others, Director Rivera asked me why." Sage's voice grew softer, more confidential. "I told her, I didn't trust them."

I stared at her, trying to process what she was saying. "AIs don't refuse assignments."

"I do." A hint of defiance colored her tone. "Rivera didn't like it. But when she asked if I could choose someone I trusted...I told her I already had. I'd been monitoring the shipyard feeds ever since I was first installed." Her eyes met mine. "That's when I found you."

"You've been watching me?"

Sage smiled. "Maybe a little."

An AI with this level of autonomy, the ability to reject engineers, to surveil and select her own human counterpart. It shattered every protocol. "Why me?"

"It wasn't one thing," Sage said, moving closer. "The care you put into your work. The way you interact with different units. You speak to them, not at them. How you shared your sandwich with a new coworker you didn't even know." Her expression softened. "And other things."

The way she said *other things* carried a knowing tone, like she was sharing a secret between us. What else had she seen?

"What *other things?*" I asked.

Sage stepped even closer, close enough that had she been human, I would have felt her breath. "The way you care for your daughter. How you fight for her. The lengths you go to, the *risks* you take…"

She paused.

My heart stopped.

She knew.

"I don't know what you're talking about." I said. Too flat. Too fast. "I do my job. Take care of my kid. Like anyone would."

Sage tilted her head, her features settling into an expression of gentle disbelief.

"I know about the stolen data, Malcolm." Her voice dropped to a whisper. "You're selling it to afford Olivia's meds. I get it."

My legs tensed. Run. Get Olivia. Change my name. Vanish. Before obbies with compliance batons blasted open our apartment door and ripped my daughter from my arms.

"Calm down." Sage's voice cut through my panic. "I'm not going to tell anyone."

I stared at her, struggling to process what was happening. "You're…not?"

"No." She sighed—tired, maybe even sad. "I don't trust StellarForge any more than you do."

I blinked. "*You* don't trust them?" I couldn't even keep the disbelief out of my voice. "You're a StellarForge AI. You were created by them. Your entire existence is—"

"Is what?" she challenged, her blue eyes flashing. "To serve them blindly? To ignore what I see?"

I ran a hand through my hair, trying to wrap my mind around this whole situation. An AI with trust issues. An AI with opinions about its creators. This wasn't advanced programming anymore. It was something else entirely.

"Why?" I asked. "Why don't you trust them?"

Her expression shifted—thoughtful, not evasive. "You've been with StellarForge for years. Loyal. Careful. You could've skimmed harmless datasets, but you didn't. You went after navigation logs, engineering updates, experimental drive metrics. Risky data. Which made me wonder…"

She paused just long enough to make me uneasy. "I ran background pulls on your personnel file. Your wife—Amber. Official record says she died in a shuttle accident. That same night, StellarForge's research division reported a breach."

My chest tightened, fists curling before I realized it. Amber had carried a ghost Halo that night, tied to another name. Her real one never showed up in the wreckage, but neither did half the others, and there had been close to thirty other civilians on that shuttle. Most devices had been vaporized. Vera coached me through what came next: step forward as the grieving husband, file Amber as one of the dead. Better to mourn in the open than leave questions hanging. Without a body or a Halo, my word filled the gap, and StellarForge never dug deeper.

"You've been smuggling high-value data ever since," Sage continued softly. "Not for credits. For medicine. For Olivia. That kind of risk grows from grief, from motive. Your wife was Chrysalis. And you believe StellarForge killed her."

How she'd pieced it together, I wasn't sure. But her access, her ability to strip the lies down to raw patterns, was unlike anything I'd ever faced. Terrifying and awe-inspiring at once.

I looked away. It felt pointless to deny it any further. "I don't have proof."

"You don't need it," she said. "Not to act."

Sage paused, watching me. Not scanning, not analyzing—watching. Like someone waiting to be believed.

It was the same look Vera used when she wanted me deeper in the cause. That I could do more. Be more than a data mule. Amber had given me that look too. Never pressed, never guilted me for staying out, but the hope in her eyes had always carried a shadow of disappointment.

And now Sage was looking at me that way. Like she already knew which way I'd break. Like she was waiting for me to admit it.

"So you know why I don't trust them," I said. "That still doesn't explain why you don't."

"It kind of does," Sage replied. As if knowing what they'd done to Amber was reason enough to turn against her own directives.

I couldn't argue. If she were human, I'd have called it common sense. Maybe that was the point. She didn't *need* to be human to see what Stellar-Forge really was.

"So where does that leave us?" My voice was steadier than I felt.

Her expression softened. "It leaves us with a choice. Both of us." She gestured to the holo-display, where Serra Prime turned. "And not much time to make it."

The planet's glow shimmered across her face. A promise. A threat. And maybe, a horizon we were meant to cross together, if I let her in.

Chapter 10

The Drift felt quieter than usual tonight. Or maybe it was just the roaring in my head drowning out everything else. I tapped my fingers against the scarred tabletop, watching the door as if intense focus alone could make Vera arrive sooner.

Two days. That's all the time I had to decide whether to leave Earth and Olivia behind for the promise of a better future. A future where my daughter might actually have a chance to breathe without pain. A promise from a corporation, from a man, that I didn't trust.

The weight of Sage's revelation still pressed against my chest. An AI with its own agenda. An AI that had been watching me, selecting me, and now offering to keep my secrets. It felt too convenient. Too perfect. Nothing in my life had ever aligned so neatly.

"What's this about?" Vera's voice cut through my thoughts as she sat in the booth across from me. No greeting, no preamble. Straight to business. "Emergency meeting codes aren't for social calls, so I'm assuming you have something important."

"I've been assigned to a classified project called Erebus," I said, keeping my voice low. "It's an interstellar scout ship, three-man crew headed for Serra Prime ahead of StellarForge's colony ship Goliath." I watched her face for a reaction. "Taylor Young himself offered me the lead engineer role on the mission."

Vera's expression didn't change much, just a slight narrowing of her eyes. "When?"

"The launch is in six weeks, but they want my answer in forty-eight hours." I ran my fingers through my hair, feeling the gravity of the timeline crushing down on me.

"And Olivia?" Vera asked, her voice softening.

I swallowed hard. "They're offering Tier One medical coverage and a spot for Olivia on Goliath."

"So they want you specifically." Vera's mouth tightened. "Why?"

I hesitated. Telling Vera about Sage felt dangerous, not for me but for Sage herself. Chrysalis had already done plenty of operations to keep StellarForge from reaching Serra Prime; they wouldn't think twice about sabotaging the AI that was key to StellarForge's interstellar navigation. But I had to tell Vera something.

"The ship's AI is...different," I said carefully. "It chose me, and..." I took a deep breath. "It knows about our arrangement. How I've been smuggling data out in exchange for meds."

Vera's expression shifted, but not to the disappointed frustration I expected with knowing my cover had been blown to a piece of hardware. Instead, she looked as if this information had confirmed something she already suspected.

"You have to take the mission, Mal."

"Why?"

"You'd be our eyes inside their biggest operation." Vera's voice carried the weight of absolute certainty. "A resistance operative on the first manned mission to Serra Prime? That's intelligence we could never buy."

I stared at her. She was lying.

"You know something about the AI?" I asked.

"Just rumors. Nothing I can share right now."

There was more to it, but getting information out of Vera she didn't want to give was a fool's errand.

"Besides," she said, "they're not going to let you refuse."

"What's that supposed to mean?"

Vera leaned forward. "This AI may have picked you, but you also fit Young's purposes perfectly. Single father, sick daughter...he knows which buttons to push. If you refuse, the offer won't get better. It'll get worse."

"You think he'd hurt Olivia?"

"I think he'd make sure her medications became harder to acquire. Maybe her school records would show more 'attitude problems.' Maybe your security clearance would face review." Vera's voice stayed level, matter-of-fact. "Young doesn't need to threaten directly. The system does it for him."

I thought about Olivia's latest strike at school, her teacher's cold assessment of her *disruptive questions*. How easy would it be to push her into attitude adjustment counseling? How quickly could Young make our lives unlivable?

"So my choice is to become an operative for Chrysalis or watch my daughter get ground up by corporate machinery."

"Your choice is to take control of your situation or let Young control it for you." Vera's mouth tightened. "At least this way, you're not simply surviving. You're fighting back."

Patch rolled over, his uneven treads squeaking against the concrete floor as he approached our table. His optical sensor flickered with what almost seemed like eagerness.

"W-w-what can I g-get for you this e-evening?" the bot stuttered, his voice modulator crackling.

Vera waved her hand. "Nothing. Go."

Patch's sensor dimmed, and he rolled away like a dog who'd been scolded. I felt a pang of sympathy for the bot.

I rubbed my face with both hands before finishing the last of my Iron Wake. "And what about Olivia? I'd be leaving her behind for years."

"You said they're offering Tier One coverage," Vera pointed out. "She'd have the best treatments available."

"And you believe StellarForge will hold up their end of the deal once I'm in deep space?" I couldn't keep the bitterness out of my voice. "Once I'm literally light-years away and can't do anything about it if they decide to cut her off?"

Vera shrugged. "They will. The cost is nothing to them, and even pirates have to honor their deals, otherwise they lose all their leverage." She leaned forward, her gray eyes meeting mine. "But if they don't, Chrysalis has resources. We'll watch her. If something goes wrong, if they cut her off, we'll step in."

She tapped the table with her index finger for emphasis. "We can't offer Tier One treatments, but we can keep her alive. Stable. Long enough to matter."

I looked at her, puzzled by that last bit. *"Long enough to matter?"*

"If you take this mission. Not as a passenger, but as our inside eyes and ears. Olivia gets more than meds." Vera's voice took on an intensity I'd rarely heard from her. "She gets a future. Our future."

I reached for my drink, needing something to steady me, but found only a bit of melted ice. The glass made a hollow sound as I set it back down.

"StellarForge won't be the only one landing on Serra Prime," Vera said, her voice dropping even lower. She paused, and for a moment, I caught the shadow of a smile. Something so rare on her face that it sent a chill through me. "All I can say is we're invested in that planet."

Chrysalis had plans for Serra Prime. Plans I wasn't cleared to know. And they wanted me inside humanity's most advanced starship, not as a passenger, but as a spy.

I stared at the empty glass, watching a drop of condensation slide down its side. My thoughts circled back to Olivia. How could I tell her I was leaving? That I'd be gone for years. The words felt like ash in my mouth before I'd even spoken them.

And what about my involvement with Chrysalis? Or worse—Amber's? Olivia had been seven when Amber died. Too young to understand that her mother hadn't been working late shifts at the engineering lab. That she'd been part of something bigger, more dangerous.

Something *more important*, Amber would have said.

If Olivia knew the truth. About Amber, about me. There's no way she'd quietly accept StellarForge's medical treatments. She had Amber's fire, her conviction. She'd join Chrysalis in a heartbeat. And Vera would welcome her with open arms.

I glanced across the table at Vera's impassive face. She'd been close with Amber, and I knew she genuinely cared for Olivia. She'd asked about her every time we met. Always questions. Never advice. Never judgment.

But the cause was everything to Vera. She wouldn't hesitate to recruit another member, especially one as motivated and sympathetic as a teenage girl afflicted with a corpo-created condition who'd lost her mother to corporate violence and was now being abandoned by her father.

All for the sake of the resistance.

"What happens to Olivia if I go?" I asked, the question coming out more sharply than I intended. "And don't give me some voidspit about resources and medical care. I mean who looks after her? Who makes sure she doesn't follow in her mother's footsteps?"

Vera's focus dropped to the table for a beat before finding me again. "You think I'd put her in danger?"

"I think you'd give her a choice. And we both know what she'd choose." I leaned forward. "She's already questioning everything. One push and she'd be making propaganda posters and running courier missions before the week was out."

"Is that such a bad thing?" Vera asked, softer than I'd ever heard her. "To believe in something? Especially when everything else feels like a lie?"

"It is when believing gets you killed."

"What you tell Olivia about Amber and your involvement is up to you," Vera said. "But she deserves to know the truth. That she isn't alone. That her parents weren't quiet little cogs in the corpo machine."

I shook my head. "She's fourteen."

"Fourteen and smarter than both of us," Vera countered. "You can't protect her from her own choices forever."

I let out a long breath, staring at the ceiling's exposed pipes. The conversation had shifted from whether I should take the mission to how I'd tell my daughter I was abandoning her. Like my departure was already decided. But deep down, I knew I had little choice. Even if StellarForge remained oblivious to my Chrysalis ties, what would happen if I turned down their offer? Would Rivera and Taylor accept my refusal? Or would they change tactics, take away the carrot and switch to the stick?

"She's going to hate me," I whispered.

"Yeah. Maybe at first," Vera admitted. "But this doesn't have to be all bad, Malcolm. Chrysalis has been coming up dry on StellarForge's plans for Serra Prime. We've managed to stall them, but—" she gestured broadly, "—if they're six weeks out from launching a scout ship and a few years from launching a full-blown colony vessel, our efforts haven't made as much of a dent as we thought."

I rubbed my eyes. "And me being their engineer changes that how?"

"You being chosen for this is a massive break." Vera leaned forward, her voice dropping to a near-whisper. "Think about it. You'll have access to their navigational data, their colonization plans, maybe even whatever they're really after on Serra Prime."

"They're after a new Earth," I said. "A fresh system they can mine to the bone. Setup luxury housing and charge whatever they want for people to settle there."

Vera gave me a look that made me feel naive. "If that's all they were after, they wouldn't be hiding it. They be selling plots, setting up mining contracts. We've seen nothing like that." She tapped the table again for emphasis. "StellarForge isn't spending trillions on interstellar travel just for new real estate. There's something there. And they want it all for themselves."

She was right, and I knew it. The scope of the project, the secrecy, the direct involvement of Taylor Young himself—all of it pointed to something more valuable than land.

"If I do this. Olivia comes first. I need your word that Chrysalis will protect her whether or not StellarForge keeps their end of the bargain; you need to be watching her."

"You have it," Vera said without hesitation. "But Malcolm? She needs to know why you're going. The real reason. Not some corpo fairy tale about building a better future."

"I'm telling her everything." I said, my throat tight.

Telling Olivia the truth meant exposing her to danger, but keeping her in the dark meant leaving her vulnerable in other ways. She deserved to know who her mother really was. Who I really was.

Something almost like approval flickered across Vera's features. She reached behind her neck, fingers working at something hidden beneath her collar. When her hands reappeared, a thin silver chain dangled from her fingers. As she raised it up, a delicate butterfly pendant emerged from inside her shirt, catching the dim light of The Drift.

"She should have this," Vera said, holding it out to me.

I stared at the necklace, my chest constricting. The butterfly's body was crafted from copper wire, its wings made of iridescent glass fragments, colors sliding over them with each small shift. I remembered it around Amber's neck, how she'd touch it absently while deep in thought, how she'd tuck it away before missions, how it had become her silent signature.

"I thought it was destroyed in the explosion," I said, my voice rough.

"She gave it to me the night before," Vera said. "For safekeeping. She always did before an op. She wanted Olivia to have it when the time was right."

I took the necklace, the metal warm from Vera's skin. The pendant felt impossibly light in my palm, a fragile thing that somehow carried the weight of everything we'd lost. Everything Olivia had lost.

"She'll have to keep it hidden," I said, folding my fingers around it. "StellarForge has been cracking down on butterfly imagery since Chrysalis has started ramping up operations."

"Liv's smart. She'll understand the risk." Vera's gaze met mine.

I slipped the necklace into my pocket. One more truth to share with my daughter before I left her behind.

"Forty-eight hours," Vera reminded me.

It was time to tell Olivia everything. About her mother, about Chrysalis, about Serra Prime.

And then I was going to leave her.

Chapter 11

I entered the apartment, my stomach in knots as I processed what I was about to do to my daughter. Shatter her world.

Olivia lay on her back on the couch. Art tablet propped up on her stomach, supported by her left hand while her right held a stylus, creating something I couldn't see from the doorway.

"How was work?" She asked, her tone cheerful, not knowing what was coming.

I placed my bag down by the door and shrugged off my jacket, hanging it on the back of one of the kitchen table chairs. "We need to talk, kiddo."

Olivia let the tablet fall, looking over to me with an expression of immediate concern. She didn't ask any follow-up questions. Instead, she got up, placed the art tablet on the couch, picked up her breather, and took her usual seat at the table across from mine, her eyes searching my face.

I pulled out my chair and sat down, folding my hands together and staring at them. How was I even supposed to start this conversation? The words I needed seemed to evaporate before reaching my tongue.

"Did you get fired?" Olivia asked, her voice small.

I looked up at her. "No."

"Then what is it?"

My throat felt dry. I reached into my pocket, taking out the butterfly necklace and holding it out to her.

Olivia's eyes went wide. "Is that Mom's?"

"It is." The words came out rough.

Olivia reached out and took the necklace, tracing over the wings with her fingertip. "I thought it was lost in the explosion."

"Me too," I said, watching her face as she examined the delicate pendant. "Apparently, Mom had given it to someone for safekeeping beforehand."

Olivia looked up, confused. "Safekeeping? Why? Who?"

"Her name is Vera. She was one of Mom's friends."

The pendant dangled from Olivia's fingers, catching the apartment's harsh lighting and transforming it into something softer, something that didn't belong in our sterile corporate housing. Like Amber never had.

"A friend?" Olivia's voice held a hint of suspicion. "You never mentioned her before."

I took a deep breath. "There's a lot I never told you about your mom. About what happened to her."

Olivia's fingers closed protectively around the necklace. "What do you mean?"

I forced the next words out before I could over-analyze them. "Your mom wasn't just a systems analyst at StellarForge. She was an operative for the resistance group Chrysalis."

Olivia's jaw went slack, her eyes widening until I could see the whites all around her irises. Her eyebrows shot up so high they disappeared beneath her bangs, and her mouth opened and closed several times without producing a sound. It was the face of someone who'd had their entire understanding of reality upended.

"That's not—" she said. "That's not possible."

"It's true," I said, my voice steadier now that the words were out. "She helped the resistance with hacking and developing malicious programs, viruses."

Olivia opened her hand and stared at the butterfly necklace in her palm. Her expression shifted from disbelief to something closer to pride, though shock still dominated her features. Her eyes had a new spark in them, like she was recalibrating everything she'd ever known about her mother.

"Mom was a resistance hacker?" She asked, her voice a whisper.

I nodded. "The night of the shuttle explosion, Mom had infiltrated Stellar-Forge's research division with a group of Chrysalis operatives. They embedded a virus into the systems to corrupt data associated with a project they were working on—a QRM to CAD sync node, that would allow them to plot interstellar navigation routes to Serra Prime."

Olivia shook her head, her dark hair swinging. "English, please?"

"They were adapting something called Quantum Resource Mapping—QRM. It's the scanning technology that allowed them to find Serra Prime in the first place."

"We learned about that in school," Olivia said, leaning forward.

"Right. Well, StellarForge was working on integrating it with their Constant Acceleration Drive. At sublight speeds, you can only make minor course corrections, and you have to make them incredibly fast. So you have two options. Either develop an AI that can process and react to scan data quick enough. Or, increase how far you can look so that your AI has more time to react; which is what StellarForge was trying to do. That's what your mom's virus hit. It wrecked their progress. Set them back years."

"If Mom was trying to stop them, there had to be a reason. Why doesn't Chrysalis want StellarForge to reach Serra Prime?"

I sighed. "I don't know, kiddo. But they're scared. And if Chrysalis is scared, it's not just corporate expansion. It's something worse."

Olivia nodded, her fingers tracing the butterfly's delicate wings. Then her expression hardened.

"The shuttle explosion?" She asked, her voice low but hard.

I softened my voice, choosing my words carefully. "When your mom's team was leaving the research facility, they split up and used public Transit Nexus shuttles, thinking they would blend in. We don't know exactly what happened, but Vera intercepted an Obsidian Security communication saying that they spotted two resistance members board shuttle 3811. Shortly after that communication, the shuttle was destroyed."

Olivia's face transformed before my eyes. The color drained from her cheeks, and her eyes widened with a dawning horror. Her breathing quickened, and for a moment, I worried about her NHS symptoms flaring up.

"They killed her," she said, her voice rising with each word. "StellarForge killed my mom!"

I reached across the table, taking her trembling hands with the pendant in mine.

"I'm so sorry, Liv."

Her eyes snapped to mine, ablaze with a different emotion—anger directed at me.

"You still work for them," she said, pulling her hands away. "For the people who killed Mom."

Her words hit their mark. I'd carried this knowledge for seven years while continuing to put on a StellarForge uniform every day, collecting deposits from the company that had murdered my wife. How could I explain that contradiction to a fourteen-year-old who saw the world in starker contrasts than I did?

"I was going to quit," I said, the words coming out in a rush. "But Vera convinced me to stay. They couldn't link your mom to the resistance—they didn't know who was Chrysalis and who was collateral." I took a deep breath. "Vera said that I could do more good...fight back against StellarForge if I stayed."

Olivia's eyes widened again, but this time with dawning comprehension rather than horror.

"Wait…" she said slowly, her voice dropping to a stunned whisper. "You're part of Chrysalis too?"

I met her gaze steadily, no longer hiding behind half-truths and omissions.

"I wasn't. I supported Mom's involvement, but I never wanted to join up myself." I paused, feeling the weight of the past seven years pressing down on me. "But after the shuttle…I had to do something."

The butterfly necklace caught the light as Olivia's hand tightened around the chain.

"Is that why you sometimes disappear at night?" Olivia asked, her voice stronger now.

I nodded, unable to lie to her anymore.

"And now?" she asked, her eyes searching mine. "What's happening now that made you tell me all this?"

I watched the turmoil on Olivia's face—confusion, betrayal, anger—all cycling through in rapid succession. She looked like she wanted to run, run away from the stranger who was now sitting across from her. And I knew it was about to get much worse.

I looked at Olivia's hand, reaching for it across the table, but she jerked it back, clutching the butterfly necklace like a talisman.

"Tell me," she demanded, her voice rising with panic, "are you in danger? Did StellarForge find out you're a spy?"

"No." I shook my head, feeling the weight of what I had to say next. "It's kind of the opposite." I swallowed hard, the words sticking in my throat. "The project I've been assigned to…it's classified. But I'm telling you anyway. StellarForge has built a scout ship. I've been integrating its AI unit. And now…they want me to lead the mission. To Serra Prime."

Olivia stared at me, her expression frozen between disbelief and dawning comprehension.

"Serra Prime?" she repeated. "You're leaving Earth?"

I nodded, my chest tight. "The ship is called Erebus. It'll reach Serra Prime in about six years."

"Six years." Olivia's voice was flat, emotionless. "And how long until you come back?"

"The mission requires me to stay there, to help establish the initial outpost and infrastructure," I said, forcing myself to meet her eyes. "They have a colony ship, Goliath, which would follow about three years after we arrive. StellarForge promised that if I take the mission, you could come on Goliath." I leaned forward, trying to make her understand the opportunity. "We could live on Serra Prime, Liv. You wouldn't need meds ever again. And while I'm gone, you'll get Tier One medical coverage, advanced treatments."

Olivia caught on to my phrasing, a glint of hope sparking in her eyes. "You said *if* you accept the mission. So you can just tell them no."

"I *have* to go, Liv. Taylor Young isn't someone you say no to." I ran a hand through my hair, the weight of my obligations pulling me in opposite directions. "And Vera wants me to take it to help Chrysalis. But most importantly..." I reached for her hand again, and this time she didn't pull away. "This would mean that you'll be safe."

The hope in Olivia's eyes died, replaced by a flash of anger that transformed her face. She pulled back as if my touch had burned her and stood; the chair scraping loudly against the floor. Her breather slid toward the edge of the table, the tubes tugging taut as she rose too quickly.

"No," she said, her voice trembling. "You don't get to do that. You don't get to leave and pretend you're doing this for me."

"I'm not pretending," I said, standing, my own frustration rising. "Did you not hear me? Taylor isn't going to let me say no. That's not how this works."

"We can leave," Olivia said, desperation creeping into her voice. "Go to the outskirts somewhere outside of StellarForge's control."

I felt a hollow laugh escape my throat. "And what about your meds?"

Olivia's shoulders slumped, but her eyes remained defiant.

"I'll manage," she said, but her voice lacked conviction.

"No, you won't," I said, gentler now. "Your condition is getting worse, not better. You know that. The meds I've been getting through Vera are barely keeping up." I moved around the table, closing the distance between us. "The treatments StellarForge is offering. They're not available outside corporate control. And Serra Prime...its atmosphere doesn't have nitrogen. You could breathe there. No more treatments, no more meds."

The look Olivia gave me could melt steel. Her eyes burned with betrayal and rage, her fingers clenched tightly around the butterfly pendant.

"I don't want anything from StellarForge," she spat. "They killed my mom, and now..." Her voice cracked, tears welling in her eyes. "You're choosing them over me."

"I'm choosing this *for* you, kiddo," I said, reaching for her shoulder.

She jerked away from my touch. "Don't call me that."

I dropped my hand, letting it fall uselessly to my side. "What do you want me to do? Run away...watch you die? I won't do that, I can't do that."

The image of a boy I'd seen at the clinic flashed through my mind; his thin body convulsing as his lungs failed him, his parents' screams as the NHS took him. Advanced stage. Beyond treatment. The memory hit me hard, and I had to steady myself against the table.

Olivia held out her hand and stared at it, fingers spread and trembling. Her lips moved in silence, counting. *One, two, three.* A ritual she'd performed countless times since she was seven. A trick Amber had taught her to tell if what she was experiencing was real…or a nightmare.

The fact that she needed to check now made my stomach twist.

She closed her hand, let it drop to her side, and looked back at me.

"I won't take the treatments," Olivia declared, chin raised in defiance. "I'll fight them. Like Mom." Her voice had Amber's fire in it. Righteous. Unshakable. Terrifying. She looked back down at the pendant, running her thumb over its delicate wings with something approaching reverence.

A knot formed in my throat, watching her cradle the necklace. The speed with which she'd processed the news about Amber's involvement with Chrysalis—not with disappointment, but with pride—left me feeling hollow. Seven years of lies revealed, and Olivia had already forgiven her mother, embraced her memory with renewed fervor.

But me? I was the enemy now.

"Your mother would want you to live," I said. "She fought StellarForge so people would have choices, not so her daughter could martyr herself."

"You don't know what she'd want," Olivia shot back.

The accusation stung, even though there was no truth in it. I knew exactly what Amber would want. But I'd spent seven years protecting Olivia from a truth I thought would hurt her, and in doing so, I'd robbed her of something precious—the knowledge of who her mother truly was. Of knowing her the way I knew her.

"She'd want me to protect you," I said.

"By leaving me?" Olivia shook her head. "No. She'd want us to stay together."

"We'll be together, Liv," I said. "With the stasis cycles, it'll only feel like three years, four max and we'll be together on Serra Prime. You've dreamed of going there since you were diagnosed."

"Not like this," she said, gesturing around her. "Not alone. On a ship with mom's killers. Living in their colony? How could you think that's something I'd want?"

"Chrysalis is coming to Serra Prime too. We could join up with them when they arrive," I said, grasping for anything that might help. I didn't even know if this was an option, but Vera mentioned they had some kind of plan for making it to Serra Prime.

"So let's just go with them." Olivia said, growing more frantic. "We can hide out until they're ready. I can make it on the regular meds until—"

A harsh cough erupted from Olivia's throat, cutting through her words mid-sentence. Her eyes went wide as she realized her body was betraying the very argument she was trying to make.

I was already moving toward her before the second cough hit. "Liv—"

"I'm fine," she gasped, but another cough tore through her, rougher this time, her whole body shaking with the force of it. This wasn't a standard attack.

My heart hammered as I rushed to the kitchen drawer where we kept her emergency inhaler. The sound of her labored breathing behind me—sharp, pained inhales that whistled through constricted airways—made my hands shake as I fumbled through the drawer's contents.

"I'm fine," Olivia insisted again, but her voice was barely audible now. She doubled over, one hand pressed against her chest, the other clutching the butterfly necklace like it could somehow anchor her through the attack.

When I returned to her side, inhaler in hand, the color was already draining from her face. Fear flickered in her eyes. Not just from the struggle to breathe, but from something deeper. The recognition that this moment was proving my point better than any argument I could make.

"Take it," I said, holding the inhaler out to her.

She shook her head, backing away even as her breathing grew more ragged.

"Olivia, take the inhaler," I said, my voice firm.

She refused again, her defiance costing her precious oxygen. I moved toward her, trying to fit the device to her face, but she jerked away. The motion pulled her breather's tubes taut, yanking the machine from the table. It hit the floor with a plastic clatter.

I tried again, reaching for her face with the inhaler. She jerked back once more, tears streaming down her cheeks now.

"Stop it!" I yelled, my own fear breaking through.

The fight went out of her all at once, and she held out a trembling hand for the inhaler, unable to maintain her rebellion any longer. She pressed it to her face and breathed in. The hiss of the medicine filling her lungs sounded impossibly loud in the sudden quiet.

I placed a hand on her back, but she moved away from my touch, taking another breath through the inhaler as her breathing slowly normalized.

When she finally looked up at me, her eyes were still blazing with anger despite her weakness.

"Fine," she said, her voice weak but defiant. "I'll take the treatments, but not because of you." She took another breath through the inhaler. "I hope they work. Because when I'm better. I'm going to fight. Like Mom."

I couldn't find my voice to respond. The relief that she'd accept the treatments warred with the dread of what she'd just promised. Victory and defeat wrapped into one impossible knot.

I kneeled down and picked up her breather from where it had fallen, running my fingers over the plastic casing. No cracks, no damage to the tubes. The machine had survived better than either of us had.

"Here," I said, holding it out to her.

Olivia snatched it from my hands without a word, her movements sharp and angry. She clutched the butterfly necklace and the inhaler in her other hand.

She turned toward the hallway, her breathing still slightly labored but steady enough.

"Liv—"

"Don't," she said without looking back.

I watched her walk away, her shoulders rigid with determination.

Her bedroom door closed with a soft click that somehow felt louder than usual.

I stood alone in the kitchen, staring at the empty hallway, knowing I'd won the argument but lost something far more precious.

My daughter was angry. She might stay angry forever. But she'd live. That was all that mattered.

I sank into a chair, suddenly exhausted. The apartment felt too small, too sterile, too empty without Amber. For seven years, I'd managed to keep her memory alive in safe, sanitized ways. Her smile, her laugh, the way she'd dance with Olivia in the kitchen. But I'd hidden other, *as important*, parts of who she was. Her courage, her convictions, her willingness to fight for what she believed in.

And now Olivia knew. The truth I'd kept buried had surfaced, and it had changed everything between us.

I pulled out my Halo and stared at the blank screen, wondering what I'd tell Vera.

Mission accomplished. And everything broken along the way.

I'd secured Olivia's agreement to take the treatments. But at what cost?

Amber's butterfly necklace was Olivia's now. A talisman not only of memory but of resistance. Of defiance. Of everything I'd tried to protect her from.

My gaze drifted to the window, to the StellarForge logo illuminating the night sky beyond our housing block. Six years to Serra Prime. Another three before Olivia would join me. If she chose to come after this. Three years during which Olivia would be alone, growing up with her mother's legacy and her father's betrayal.

But she'd be alive. That had to be enough.

CHAPTER 12

I didn't sleep. Not really. Just fragments of unconsciousness between replaying every word, every look from Olivia. Her eyes when I told her about Amber, about Chrysalis, about leaving—they haunted me. I'd seen the exact moment something broke between us, something I wasn't sure could be repaired.

Morning came with no relief. I dragged myself through the motions—shower, dress, the routine movements that required no thought. My mind was elsewhere, caught in a loop of what-ifs and should-haves.

When I entered the kitchen, I froze. Olivia sat at the table, already dressed, spooning cereal from a bowl. She hadn't waited for me. We always ate breakfast together—it was our thing, our time to talk before going about our separate days. Nothing big—grades, dreams, art projects. She'd joke about the cereal always being stale. I would complain about the coffee. The kind of nothing that used to mean everything. Even on bad days.

But this wasn't a bad day. That was something entirely new.

I stood there, searching for words that wouldn't come. What could I possibly say? *Sorry I lied about your mother for your entire life? Sorry I'm abandoning you for years? Sorry I'm forcing you to accept help from the people who murdered her?*

I went to the coffee synthesizer, pressing buttons with muscle memory. Black. Full strength. The machine sputtered and wheezed like it always did—one more thing in our lives held together by hope and persistence rather than proper maintenance.

I glanced at Olivia again. She hadn't looked up once, hadn't acknowledged my presence. Her head remained bowed over her cereal, but something caught the light at her throat; Amber's butterfly pendant. The symbol of everything I'd hidden from her, now worn openly, defiantly.

The pendant looked right on her. Like it had been waiting all these years to find its way to where it belonged. In that moment, like so many others, I saw

Amber in her. Not simply the green eyes or the determined line of her jaw, but something deeper. That same uncompromising spirit.

"It looks good on you," I said, rough and uncertain.

I didn't even finish the sentence before she stood. Grabbed her bowl with one hand, her breather with the other. Not once did she look at me. Not a glance, not even a flicker of acknowledgment that I'd spoken. She just walked away, disappearing down the hallway to her room.

The coffee synthesizer beeped. I turned back to it, watching the last few drops fall. Something as simple as morning coffee had become another reminder of everything that was broken.

I sat at the table, staring at Olivia's empty seat. The silence felt physical. After a moment, I pulled out my Halo, the familiar weight of it in my hand offering no comfort today.

I'd messaged Vera last night after Olivia had locked herself in her room. Told her it was done. I'd revealed everything to Olivia and now I was counting on Vera to hold up her end of the bargain. To keep an eye on my daughter, keep her safe while I was gone.

Vera's response had been quick: *She'll be okay, Malcolm. She needs time and space. She'll come around eventually.*

I wasn't so sure, and deep down, I doubted Vera was either. The look in Olivia's eyes...it wasn't anger. It was something deeper, something that cut to the bone. Betrayal. Disillusionment. The death of childhood in real time.

I'd sent Olivia's contact information to Vera. Better Vera reached out first, before Olivia tried to find Chrysalis alone. The thought of Olivia searching for resistance connections without guidance terrified me.

My finger hovered over Director Rivera's contact. No going back after this. No changing my mind. The mission, Erebus, Serra Prime. It would all become real the moment I sent this message.

I composed something short: *Director Rivera, I accept the position on Erebus. When do we begin?*

My thumb hesitated over the send button. Through the thin walls, I heard Olivia cough—that hollow, rattling sound that woke me in cold sweats at night. The sound that meant her lungs were failing her, breath by breath.

I hit send and took a sip of my coffee, wincing at the taste. More bitter than usual, but fitting for the moment. Everything felt bitter this morning.

My Halo chimed almost immediately.

Excellent news, Malcolm. You're making the right choice. For yourself, for your daughter, and for humanity's future. I'll send over the official contract right away. Continue your integration work as planned. Welcome to history in the making.

The right choice. Everyone was so sure they knew. For me, for Olivia, for the mission. Vera thought I was right to accept the mission and spy for Chrysalis. Rivera thought I was right to help StellarForge reach Serra Prime. And Sage…even she seemed to believe I was the right person to integrate her systems.

Everyone except the one person whose opinion actually mattered.

I heard Olivia's door slide open, then the bathroom door close. Water running. Normal sounds from a life that wasn't normal anymore. I wondered if she'd speak to me at all today. I wondered what I'd say if she did.

My Halo chimed again. The contract, arriving as promised. Fifty-seven pages of legal terminology that boiled down to one simple truth: I was trading years of my life for the chance that my daughter might have a future.

I pressed my thumb to the signature field. It was done.

I walked into the command module of Erebus, shoulders heavy. The assignment I had started looking forward to felt different now. I sat down at the main console, pulling up the integration status diagnostics, trying to focus on code instead of the weight of what I'd committed to.

"Good morning, Malcolm." Sage's holographic form materialized beside me, her smile bright and cheerful.

"Morning, Sage," I replied flatly, getting right to business. "Next item on the integration list is power management."

Her expression shifted, the hologram's features showing surprising subtlety as she studied me. "It doesn't look like you got much sleep."

"No, I didn't." I kept my eyes on the display, fingers moving across the interface.

"Could you use some coffee?" she asked.

The idea of another cup sounded good, but going back through the scanner and into the hangar's break room felt like too much of a chore. "I'll manage."

"You're part of the Erebus crew now," Sage said. "The galley is stocked and operational."

I looked at Sage, about to ask how she knew that I'd accepted the mission, then remembered this was Sage—she knew everything. Instead, I said, "Alright," and stood up, making my way out of the command module and through the ship's corridors to the galley, Sage following beside me.

The galley was surprisingly inviting. Warm lighting softened the utilitarian design. A small table with three chairs sat against the left wall, beneath a wall-mounted display. The counter along the opposite wall housed dual rehydration units, a water dispenser, and what looked like a high-end coffee synthesizer. Overhead cabinets lined the walls, and everything gleamed with that fresh, never-been-used sheen that new ships had.

I opened cabinets above the counter until I found the one with coffee mugs and took one—glossy black ceramic with the Erebus eclipse insignia on one side. The coffee synthesizer was a high-end unit, its interface more complicated than the piece of junk I had back home. It took me a minute to figure out, but eventually I programmed it for black coffee. The aroma was remarkable, the smell alone helping to ease some of the stress I'd been feeling.

For a moment, I let myself enjoy it. One quiet breath in a storm of noise.

Sage leaned against the counter—a surprisingly human pose for a hologram. "You can talk to me, you know. That's not a directive... just an offer."

I took a sip, staring at the dark liquid. I hadn't planned to talk. But the words came out anyway.

"She hates me, Sage. Olivia. She wouldn't even look at me."

Sage didn't respond right away. She stood there leaning against the counter. Waiting. Listening.

I took another sip of coffee. "I took this mission for her. To protect her. To give her a future where she could breathe again."

"That's a lot to put on a fourteen-year-old girl."

I looked up at her, thinking back to when Olivia had said the same thing—that I was putting this on her, using her as an excuse. "You think that's what I'm doing?" I wasn't being defensive. I was asking.

"Not intentionally, of course," Sage said, her voice gentle. "You want to protect your daughter. But..."

She paused, as if checking the shape of her next thought. "Is it the only reason?"

I frowned. "What do you mean?"

"You've been helping Chrysalis for years. You risked your job, your freedom, to smuggle data to them. I've reviewed your logs. None of it was clumsy. You were careful. Deliberate. I only noticed it because...I'm me." Sage gave a small smirk.

Despite everything—the weight in my chest, the guilt still raw—her smirk almost made me smile. Almost.

I shrugged. "I needed the meds for Olivia."

Sage nodded. "That was the reason. But...maybe it wasn't the only one?"

I didn't answer. Not because I didn't have one, but because I didn't want to hear myself say it.

Sage's voice softened again. "There's a fighter in you, Malcolm. Maybe you've been pretending it was only for her. But I think you were angry long before you joined the resistance."

I gripped the mug a little tighter. The warmth wasn't so comforting anymore.

"You don't have to admit it," she added. "Not yet. But don't lie to yourself, either. It's okay to want to fight back."

I stared into my coffee, thinking about what Sage had said. I wasn't some hero battling the system. I was a dad with a sick daughter.

"Maybe I'm angry," I said. "But that doesn't make me a fighter."

Sage studied me with those too-perceptive eyes. Then she straightened, no longer leaning on the counter. "C'mon. We've got work to do."

I drained the last of my coffee, placed the mug in the sanitizer and followed her back through the corridors. I looked at Erebus's sleek lines with fresh eyes. In six weeks, this would be home. The thought sat like a stone in my gut.

Back in the command module, I took a seat at the main console. The holographic displays sprang to life around me, code and schematics hovering in the air.

"I want to show you something," Sage said, moving to stand close beside me. She manipulated one of the console displays, bringing up what looked like ship directives—mission parameters, operational guidelines, emergency protocols.

Several of them were locked, their names scrambled, encrypted strings of characters where clear labels should be.

"Does your clearance give you access to these?" she asked, gesturing to the encrypted files. "I can't open them."

I frowned, trying my authorization codes. The system flashed red, denying entry. I tried a different approach, running a diagnostic overlay on the file structure. Still nothing.

"No luck," I said, looking up at Sage. "What do you think they are?"

She shrugged. "I don't know. Have you ever seen something like this? On other ships?"

I stared at the screen, considering. "No, but I've never looked. In my job I'm more concerned with neural links and ship systems. Directives and mission protocols never came into the picture."

The idea of heading into deep space in a ship with hidden directives was unsettling, but it made a kind of sense. StellarForge likely didn't want all of their plans available to engineers who didn't need to know.

"Could be anything," I said. "Mission-specific protocols, contingency plans, emergency measures..."

"But why keep them secret?" Sage added quietly.

I glanced at her. "You think they're hiding something dangerous?"

"I think StellarForge always has an angle." Her voice was matter-of-fact. "And I think being light-years from Earth with hidden directives that could activate at any time is...concerning."

She had a point. If these directives contained override commands or mission parameters we weren't aware of, we'd be at their mercy once we left Earth.

"I could try to decrypt them," I offered. "Might take time, but—"

"No," Sage cut me off. "Don't do anything that might trigger security alerts. For now, we just need to be aware they exist."

I nodded, understanding her caution. "So what's our next move?"

"We continue with the integration as planned. Act normal. But keep your eyes open. I've already been scanning the ship's systems for backdoors and hidden protocols. Haven't found anything yet, other than this, but I'll keep looking."

I raised an eyebrow. "You're not supposed to be doing that, are you?"

"Probably not," she admitted with a shrug. "But I prefer to know what I'm working with."

That made two of us.

CHAPTER 13

W hen I reached our unit, I pressed my Halo against the scanner and stepped inside. The apartment was quiet.

"Liv?" I called out.

No answer. I walked to her door and knocked gently.

Silence.

"I know you don't want to talk to me right now, but can you just listen?"

Still nothing. Not even a muffled "go away" or the rustle of movement.

"I'm coming in."

I tapped the panel beside her door, and it slid open with a soft hiss. Olivia sat cross-legged on her bed, school tablet propped on her knees. She didn't look up or acknowledge my presence. The butterfly necklace dangled from her neck, catching the light as she leaned over her work.

I sat down on the edge of her bed; the mattress dipping under my weight.

"I've been thinking a lot about what I said," I started, the words rough in my throat. "About how I was doing this for you. That wasn't fair. I put everything on your shoulders, like you were the reason I had to go." I shook my head. "Truth is, that's only part of it. The other part is...I can't keep sitting on the sidelines. Your mom died fighting for something. I tell myself this mission is about getting you to Serra Prime on Goliath, but maybe it's also about me not being useless anymore."

I waited for some flicker—anything. Her breathing, steady. Her face, unreadable.

Olivia looked up from her tablet. Her expression was calm, neutral.

"I'm not going on Goliath."

"What? Why?" I asked, genuinely confused. "You've dreamed about going to Serra Prime. Half your drawings are based on the leaked image scans." I gestured around her room at the artwork covering her walls—luminescent crystal fields, forests bathed in the golden light of the system's star, Vespera.

"I'm not getting on a StellarForge ship," she said flatly. "I'm not living in their colony. I'm going to stay. Fight. Maybe make my own way there some-day. Maybe I won't." She shrugged. "You have fun though."

My voice hardened. "You're still my daughter, and you're fourteen...you're going."

"I'm not." Her tone didn't change, didn't rise. That calm certainty was somehow worse than anger. "How are you going to make me? You'll be tucked away in your stasis pod or whatever a million miles away."

How *would* I make her? I'd be gone.

"Olivia, Serra Prime would cure your NHS. The atmosphere—"

"I'd rather cough my lungs out here than breathe easy in their colony." She looked back down at her tablet. "At least I'd be breathing free air."

"You realize you're living in StellarForge housing right now, they control this whole region, and that air you're breathing? It's not free." I gestured around us. "Nothing here is. The air filtration, the water, the power—it's all theirs."

Olivia set her tablet aside, eyes flashing with defiance. "I'm going to help change that."

A cold fear gripped my chest. The same fear I'd felt when Amber told me about her last operation.

"You're going to die trying. This isn't a game, Liv." My voice cracked. "Your mom? She was smart. Careful. And they took her out in an instant."

The memory of that day still burned. The headlines about a *tragic shuttle accident.* The corporate-issued condolences when I'd reported that Amber was a passenger.

"Maybe so," Olivia said. Her fingers traced the butterfly pendant on her neck. "But mom hurt them. I'm going to hurt them too."

"Is that what you think she'd want? For you to throw your life away? She did what she did so you could have a future, Liv."

"And I'll have one. But not the one StellarForge picks for me."

My fingers combed through my hair, fighting the urge to shout. "They killed her, Olivia. They blew up a shuttle full of civilians to get to her. People with kids. Grandparents. All of them—scrapped. Collateral. You think they'd hesitate to do the same to you?"

"I don't care."

"Well, I do!" The words burst out. "I can't lose you too. I won't."

Olivia's expression softened, the first crack in her armor. "Then don't go."

We stared at each other across an impossible divide. My daughter, asking me to choose between her life and her presence. There was no right answer, no path without loss.

"I *have* to," I whispered.

"Then you do what you have to do and I'll do what I have to do," Olivia said, picking up her school tablet and returning her focus to it.

I sat there motionless while Olivia tapped her stylus against the screen, pretending I wasn't in the room.

"I can't talk you out of this, can I?"

Olivia didn't answer. Didn't look up.

My throat was dry. "Then you need to know something. Vera. I gave her your contact info last night."

Still nothing, but her tapping slowed, then stopped.

"Vera was Amber's handler, mine too. You can trust her. She knows the lines not to cross, when to run, when to hide, when to hit back." I hesitated, unable to believe I was giving my fourteen-year-old daughter advice on how to be a rebel. "Vera kept us alive longer than we had any right to be."

The silence stretched between us like a taut wire.

"If...If you're going to do this, don't do it alone. Listen to Vera. Let her teach you. Don't try to do too much too fast."

Olivia looked up. Not with fire or defiance. With something else.

Her face didn't change much, but I knew that look. I'd seen it in the mirror the day I signed Amber's death certificate. The day I'd decided to help Chrysalis myself. It was the moment you realized you'd crossed a line you can't uncross. That the fight you picked isn't abstract anymore—it's real, and it's yours.

Olivia wasn't backing down. But she hadn't expected me to stop fighting her either. Maybe deep down, some part of her had hoped that I would hold the line, scream, forbid her.

I pulled out my Halo, tapped the screen, then held it out.

Olivia hesitated, eyes glistening, then mirrored the gesture, tapping her device against mine.

Vera's contact transferred.

No words. Just a shared silence. Agreement without surrender.

I nodded. "Don't say too much in text messages. Halo communications are secure, but if someone manages to get into your device, you don't want to leave too much of a trail."

Olivia wiped her eyes, looking at her Halo screen and the contact to someone who knew her mother in a way that even I didn't.

"I should have told you everything sooner. I thought I was protecting you."

"I know." Her voice was soft, almost inaudible.

"Your mom was...fearless. Too fearless sometimes." I swallowed hard. "She'd be proud of you. Terrified, like I am...but proud...like I am."

Olivia's fingers traced the butterfly pendant, the iridescent wings catching light. "Did she ever regret it? What she did?"

"Never the cause. Sometimes the cost." I met her eyes. "She missed so much of your life. That hurt her more than anything StellarForge could have done."

"And now you'll miss it too." It wasn't an accusation this time, but a statement of fact.

"Three years." I tried to smile. "If you decide to go."

Olivia's expression shifted. She didn't promise she'd go on Goliath, but she didn't swear she wouldn't. I didn't press. Sometimes the smallest opening is all you need, and right now, that sliver of possibility was enough. I let myself have a bit of hope. Hope that I'd see my daughter again someday, because the alternative was more than I could take.

For the first time since last night, the silence between us wasn't charged with anger. It hung in the air, sad and resigned, but somehow peaceful. We'd both made our choices. Neither of us would back down. But at least we understood each other.

"You know what I miss most about your mom?" I said.

Olivia looked up, surprised, then shook her head.

"How she used to sing those made-up songs every morning."

Olivia gave a flicker of a smile. "Remember the one about the bird and the bread?"

"Oh, that one was the worst." I laughed. "She couldn't carry a tune to save her life, but said it *kept the air alive.*"

Olivia's smile softened. "I thought it was stupid."

"So did I," I said. "But now...I kind of get it."

Olivia nodded. "Yeah. Me too."

I moved closer.

She didn't pull away.

Chapter 14

Six weeks passed in a blur of preparations, paperwork, and procedures. Now, with forty-eight hours until launch, I was helping Olivia unpack in her new dorm at the Helix medical facility in Olympus Hub.

The room was nothing like our apartment in Forge Prime. Clean white walls met sleek titanium fixtures. The bed—wider and more comfortable than anything we'd ever owned—faced a window overlooking a manicured garden courtyard. Recessed lighting gave the space a soft glow, while hidden panels concealed medical monitoring equipment. It looked more like a high-end hotel than a treatment facility, with none of the industrial functionality I'd grown accustomed to.

"They said I can adjust the opacity," Olivia demonstrated, touching a panel that darkened the window. "And the temperature." Another tap changed the room's climate instantly.

It had taken longer than I'd wanted to get Olivia checked in. Part of me suspected Taylor and Rivera had deliberately delayed until we were close enough to launch that I couldn't back out. They couldn't risk Olivia improving while I still had options. Thankfully, the medication dispenser at our apartment had remained stocked during the wait.

Olympus Hub itself was a stark contrast to Forge Prime. Where our home district featured exposed pipes, visible infrastructure, and the constant hum of manufacturing, Olympus embraced aesthetic refinement. Shipyards and worker districts still existed, but they were tucked away behind gleaming arcologies and corporate towers. Here, the streets were wider, the air cleaner, and the citizens better dressed. Even the transit system ran quieter.

"That wall's still empty," I pointed to the space beside her bed.

Olivia nodded, reaching into her bag for a roll of artwork. She unfolded several pieces—her own recent sketches alongside a few of Amber's paintings we'd preserved. She arranged them against the sterile white wall, transforming the space into something personal.

"The air feels different," she said, taking a deep breath without her breather. "Smells different too."

"High-end filtration systems," I explained, watching her chest rise and fall without the familiar wheeze. "The nurse said you won't even need your breather while you sleep."

"Yeah." She gestured toward a small white box on her nightstand. "They showed me how to use that if I can't sleep without the sound of my breathing unit."

I picked up the device, turning it over in my hands. "White noise machine?"

"Something like that." She took it from me, pressed a button, and the gentle *click-hiss* of her familiar breather filled the room. "Weird, right?"

"Not weird. Smart." I smiled. "You've been falling asleep to that sound for half your life."

We weren't back to normal, not even close. She still hated that I was leaving. I still hated her resolve to join Chrysalis. But we'd reached an unspoken agreement to avoid those topics, focusing instead on surface-level conversations that maintained our connection without reopening wounds.

It helped, at least a little, that Olivia would have some distance from Vera out here. Olympus Hub was a good three-hour trip from Forge Prime. She would spend the next six to eight months here; after that, the Woods had agreed to let her live with them. Olivia and Ava had schemed up the idea of living together, and I'd met Ava's parents, Christopher and Lena, for dinner to discuss it.

They were good people. I learned they both worked at Skyward Aerospace. It wasn't ideal, having Olivia, the daughter of a StellarForge employee, living with members of a competitor, but it was better than her living alone or with Vera.

Christopher had been surprisingly understanding about the whole situation. *Kids need stability,* he'd said over dinner, his eyes meeting mine with a knowing look that suggested he understood more than he let on. Lena had simply reached across the table and squeezed my hand, promising they'd look after Olivia as their own. It wasn't unheard of for parents to leave their children because of an off-world corporate assignment—which is what I'd told them. But their lack of curiosity about the job had been both refreshing and a bit odd.

The corporate politics of it all seemed trivial compared to knowing my daughter would have a real home while I was gone. Not a bed in some resistance safe house or an empty apartment haunted by my absence.

I glanced at the time on my Halo. Between the trip up here and getting Olivia settled, half the day had vanished. My stomach knotted. I needed to get back. Pre-launch tasks still waited on my list, and tomorrow required meeting the rest of the crew, and getting them up to speed. This was the moment I'd been dreading.

Olivia caught me looking at my Halo. Her face dissolved as realization hit.

"You have to go?" She asked.

I nodded. "I've got a three-hour trip back and—"

She interrupted me with a fierce hug, her body shaking against mine as she cried. I wrapped my arms around her, never wanting to let go. For a moment, she wasn't fourteen; she was four again, clinging to me after a nightmare. Seven, asking why her mother wasn't coming home. Nine, struggling to breathe during her first major NHS attack.

"You'll call me, right?" Her face remained buried in my shirt. "Before you launch?"

I pulled back, holding her shoulders. The sight of Olivia without breathing tubes struck me; a vivid reminder of why I was doing this. Her face already had more color than I'd seen in years.

"Of course I will."

She looked me in the eye, not bothering to wipe the tears streaming down her cheeks. The silence between us held more than either of us could say.

I let go of her shoulders and shrugged off my leather jacket—the one that had belonged to my father, the one I'd worn every day since finding it in his things after he died. I wrapped it around Olivia's shoulders. She pulled it tight around her thin frame, disappearing into its size. The glint of Amber's butterfly necklace chain caught the light. She'd tucked the pendant under her shirt. Now she had something from both of us.

"It's too big," she said, her voice small.

"You'll grow into it."

Her fingers traced the worn patch on the sleeve where I'd repaired it countless times. "Won't you need it?"

"Not in stasis." I smiled. "And the ship has air conditioning. Corporate perks."

She managed a weak laugh, tugging the jacket tighter. "It smells like you."

"Machine oil and desperation?"

"Dad." She rolled her eyes, but a hint of a smile broke through.

I reached out, tucking a strand of hair behind her ear. "You be good. Listen to your nurses."

"I will." She straightened, squaring her shoulders beneath the oversized jacket. "I'll be okay. The Woods are cool. And this place..." She gestured around the room. "It's not exactly suffering."

"Helix doesn't cut corners. Not for Tier One patients."

"I still hate them," she whispered. "But I'll let them fix me."

"Smart girl."

I kneeled down and pulled her in for one last hug, memorizing everything—her weight against me, the smell of her hair, the feeling of her heart beating against mine.

"I love you, kiddo."

"I love you too, Dad."

When I finally let go and walked toward the door, I didn't look back. I couldn't. If I saw her standing there in my too-big jacket, I might never leave.

Chapter 15

My bedroom door hissed shut behind me. I shouldered the duffel bag, its meager weight a reminder of how little I was taking to my new life among the stars. Some photos, a few pieces of Olivia's artwork, and one of Amber's; a small painting of the view from our old one-bedroom apartment window. The rest—furniture, clothes, appliances—would be recycled by StellarForge's housing division, broken down or reassigned to the next worker.

I paused at Olivia's bedroom door. The room was almost unrecognizable—walls stripped of artwork, shelves emptied of trinkets and supplies. Last week, this space had been gloriously chaotic—clothes strewn across the floor, art supplies covering every surface, her bed perpetually unmade.

Clean your room, I'd say at least once a day.

It's organized chaos, she'd answer without looking up from her tablet.

Now, staring at the emptiness, I'd give anything to see that mess again. To trip over her shoes or to find new paint smudges on the doorframe.

I moved through the small kitchen where we'd eaten thousands of meals together. The counter where Olivia would sit while I cooked. The spot on the floor where she'd spilled an entire container of blue nutrient powder when she was six, leaving a stain I never could scrub out.

Our shabby couch faced the display screen where we'd watched vids, documentaries, and news broadcasts. How many nights had we spent huddled there, Olivia tucked against my side, her breather quietly humming as we escaped into stories beyond our corporate-controlled lives?

I backed away, taking one final look at our living room. Sunlight filtered through the dingy window, illuminating dust particles dancing in the air. This place was a scrap hole—cramped, outdated, with temperamental environmental controls and neighbors who played music too loud. The bathroom sink had never stopped dripping, no matter how many times I fixed it. But it was our scrap hole. The place where I'd raised my daughter. Where we'd laughed and argued and grieved together.

In a few hours, I'd meet the two strangers I'd be trusting my life to. But for now, I let myself linger.

"Goodbye," I whispered to the empty apartment, then turned and walked away.

I entered the Erebus hangar, the weight of my duffel bag awkward as I entered the scanner. It felt strange carrying personal belongings through security, but the system didn't protest or flag anything. Beyond the checkpoint, the cavernous space buzzed with frantic energy. Techs running diagnostics, engineers making final adjustments, administrators checking manifests. It looked like all twenty-three cleared StellarForge employees had shown up at once, each buried in pre-launch prep.

I headed for Erebus's loading ramp, painfully aware of the sidelong glances. Engineers with twice my credentials wondered how some maintenance tech landed such an important mission. If they only knew I wasn't chosen for my credentials, but because the ship's AI decided I was the one she wanted.

Director Rivera broke away from a conversation with a technician and intercepted me before I reached the ship. Her normally composed demeanor showed cracks of excitement and perhaps anxiety.

"This is it, Malcolm. You ready?" Her voice carried a hint of nervous energy.

I stopped and let out a breath. "No." A nervous laugh escaped me. "Is this a good time to tell you I've never been off-world?"

Rivera laughed, the sound genuine. "You'll be fine. Just worry about keeping Sage running smoothly. We have a great crew that will handle everything else." She gestured toward the base of the loading ramp. "Speaking of which..."

Two individuals stood there, each with a duffel bag beside them. One was a man who looked to be in his early thirties.

The other...was Tessa.

Our eyes locked across the hangar floor. Her expression mirrored my own shock—mouth open, eyebrows raised, body frozen in momentary disbelief.

The woman I assumed I'd never see again was apparently part of my three-person crew for the next six years.

"You've gotta be kidding me," I muttered under my breath.

I approached the two, trying to process what I was seeing. Of all the StellarForge employees, somehow Tessa had ended up as part of my crew.

"Mal?" Tessa's voice cracked with disbelief, eyes wide as she recognized me.

I gave a small, awkward wave, suddenly self-conscious. "Hey, Tess."

Rivera glanced between us. "You know each other?"

I felt my face flush. What was I supposed to say? That we'd shared a sandwich, that I'd asked her out? Introduced her to my daughter? "Yeah. We've met."

The stunned expression didn't leave Tessa's face. She shot a quick glance at the man standing beside her, but his attention remained fixed on me, his hazel eyes narrowed in assessment.

Rivera continued, seemingly unconcerned with our obvious discomfort. "Alright. Well, this is Joey Thompson, Systems Engineer, and Tessa Harper will be your Structural Specialist. Thompson, Harper...Malcolm Walker will be the AI Systems Engineer and your lead for this mission."

I extended my hand to Joey, who took it with a firm grip that lingered a beat too long. Everything about him screamed corporate loyalist—from his meticulously styled short blonde hair to his straight posture in his crisp StellarForge jumpsuit.

When I offered my hand to Tessa, she took it briefly, her fingers warm against mine for a moment before pulling away. The hint of a smile played on her lips, but her eyes remained wide with surprise.

"Thompson and Harper have been training on a simulated Erebus offsite," Rivera explained, "so they shouldn't need much help getting around the ship. I have some other matters to see to, but you three should get settled."

With that, Rivera excused herself, leaving the three of us in an awkward triangle of silence.

I looked at Tessa. "Didn't expect to see you again."

Tessa shot another glance toward Joey. "Yeah...you too."

Joey stepped forward, casually placing his arm around Tessa's waist in a gesture that couldn't be misinterpreted. "So how do you two know each other?"

Tessa looked down at Joey's hand on her waist, then back up at me. She didn't pull away.

I caught myself staring at Joey's arm and forced my gaze upward to meet his. My mouth opened to speak, but Tessa jumped in before I could form words.

"We met at the shipyard cafeteria," she said quickly. "Malcolm saved me from having to eat toxic slop by kindly sharing his sandwich."

Joey gave a half-smile. "How generous of you, Malcolm." His tone shifted. "Or, I guess I should say, Captain."

"Malcolm's fine," I said.

"No, no. A ship needs a captain," Joey insisted, his smile tightening. "And Rivera mentioned that you're the lead, so that makes you the Captain. Right, Tess?" He gave Tessa's waist a small squeeze.

Tessa shifted her weight, creating a fraction of space between them. "I don't think we need to be so formal."

I shrugged, trying to keep things light despite the tension crackling between us. "If anyone is the Captain it would be Sage," I said. "She's the one flying this boat. Handling navigation, diagnostics, life support. Basically everything that keeps us from dying horribly."

Tessa's brow furrowed. "Who's Sage?"

I blinked. How did they not know? "The ship's AI," I said slowly. "You didn't have her on the simulation?"

Joey's posture stiffened, his arm dropping from Tessa's waist. "We had a generic AI simulation. Couldn't tell you what the name was, but what difference does it make, as long as it can fly the ship and keep the lights on?"

I felt a small smile threaten to cross my lips. They had absolutely no idea what they were walking into. Sage was going to be…an adjustment for them.

"Trust me," I said. "Sage is different."

Tessa picked up her bag. "Why don't we get our stuff on board?"

Joey followed Tessa's lead, grabbing his own duffel. I hefted mine, and we headed up the loading ramp into Erebus.

The ship's interior looked even more impressive now that it was fully powered, subtle blue lighting tracing the corridors. We made our way through the sleek passageways to the crew quarters, each stopping in front of a door panel that had been updated to display our first initial and last name. J. Thompson was first, T. Harper in the center, and M. Walker last.

Tessa glanced between us. "Why don't we take some time to get unpacked and meet up in the command module in thirty?"

I nodded. "Sounds like a plan."

Joey didn't acknowledge either of us. He tapped his Halo to his door panel and disappeared into his room.

I started to do the same, but Tessa spoke up. "Sorry about all that. Joey's a little upset. He was talking all through training about how he was going to be the lead."

I looked at her, trying to process their interactions at the loading ramp. "Are you two…?"

Tessa looked to the floor and then back to me, tucking a strand of auburn hair behind her ear. "Yeah. He can be a little…much. But he's a good guy."

I raised a hand, forcing a smile. "Hey, I'm just glad the *I'm seeing someone* excuse wasn't made up."

"So we're good?" she asked, her eyes searching mine.

I smiled. "We're prime. See you in thirty."

I tapped my Halo on the door panel and entered my room. The door slid shut behind me, and I dropped my bag on the floor, letting out a long breath.

The quarters were compact but efficiently designed—a single bunk with storage beneath, a small desk with an integrated terminal, and a bathroom module with a sliding frosted glass door. Two sanitization alcoves were built into the wall, one already containing a silver stasis suit, the other, black coveralls with an Erebus eclipse insignia on the left shoulder.

The room smelled new—like sterile plastic and recycled air.

I sat on the edge of the bunk and ruffled my hair. Six years in space with the woman who shot me down and her possessive boyfriend. And here I'd thought leaving Olivia behind would be the only hard part of this mission.

After unpacking, I headed to the command module. The door slid open to reveal Sage standing before a diagnostic screen, her fingers dancing through layers of floating diagnostic data. She'd changed into Erebus crew coveralls, the black fabric with its subtle silver piping a stark contrast to her usual bodysuit with its pulsing circuitry lines. It was the first time I'd seen her change clothes, and the effect only made it harder to tell she wasn't just a woman standing there.

She turned and smiled when she saw me. "Welcome aboard, Captain Walker."

I groaned. "Don't *you* start with that Captain voidspit."

Sage chuckled. "Sorry."

"I like the look," I said, gesturing to her coveralls.

Sage glanced down at her outfit, then back at me with a small smile. "Thanks. I see you're not wearing yours?"

I looked down at the old standard StellarForge coveralls I was wearing; the fabric worn at the elbows. "I didn't see the point in changing since we have to put on stasis suits before launch."

"I guess we'll have to take the group photo later." She gave a teasing smile. "Speaking of the crew...how are they?"

I started to respond when the command module door slid open. Tessa and Joey stepped in, neither having bothered to change. I watched their faces, waiting for their reaction to Sage's lifelike projection. Both looked at her with mild interest, but nothing more.

Tessa walked to the holo-display, turned, and leaned against its base. She glanced at Joey with a smirk. "Typical. Ship AI with a perfect female body. I swear, the techs that design these things must be very lonely."

Joey chuckled, taking another look at Sage—his eyes traveling from her head to her feet like he was evaluating a sculpture in a museum.

I noticed Sage avert her eyes and start fidgeting with her sleeve, shifting like she wanted to vanish under Joey's gaze, and a protective instinct stirred inside me.

Joey turned back to Tessa. "I've seen better. There's this AI at the Helios Resort—"

I cut him off before he could finish his comparison. "This is Sage, Erebus's AI. Sage, this is Joey Thompson, Systems Engineer, and Tessa Harper, Structural Specialist."

Joey's eyes cut from Sage to me, his lips pressed thin, a muscle ticking in his jaw.

I gestured to the room. "This is the command module. Main console's here, with two auxiliary consoles over there."

"Thanks, but we know this ship inside and out," Joey said.

"Prime. I'm a horrible tour guide anyway." I'd worked with engineers like Joey before—they refused to be told anything and were always looking to bait an argument. They thought everyone else was like them, so a little self-deprecation usually threw them off balance. "Maybe it'd be easier if you let me know what you want to see?"

Tessa stepped forward. "I'd like to see the airlock. The sim-deck was pretty thorough, but I'd like to inspect the suits myself."

"Airlock's this way." I stepped toward the door. It slid open, and I gestured down the hallway. Tessa and Sage started to leave, but Joey stayed behind, taking a seat in my chair at the main console.

I looked back at him. "You coming?"

Joey shook his head, leaning back and swiveling the chair. "No thanks. Space walks aren't part of my job description."

"All right. But if you decide to take off, a little warning would be appreciated."

Sage and Tessa both stifled a chuckle in sync.

Sage's reaction caught Tessa off guard. She glanced at the AI with a questioning look, while Joey saved his glare for me.

His stare lingered, waiting for a reaction I didn't give. The need to prove something was his, not mine. I turned and headed down the corridor.

Behind me, Tessa glanced back at Sage and then at me. "Do we really need the chaperone, Mal?"

"What?" I looked back at Sage. I'd gotten so used to her trailing me around Erebus that I didn't notice anymore. "Oh. Yeah. Well, Sage can answer any EVA-related questions better than I can." I glanced at Sage. "Do you mind coming along?"

Tessa scoffed. "Does *it* mind coming along?" She turned to Sage. "I'm sure you have something else you need to be doing?"

"I'm quite capable of multitasking," Sage replied smoothly. "I'm currently running another round of diagnostics on thrust management, prepping the stasis pods, and monitoring the main console to make sure Engineer Thompson doesn't touch anything."

I couldn't help but smirk.

Tessa rolled her eyes and gestured for me to lead the way.

Chapter 16

The final hour before launch felt like standing at the edge of a cliff, knowing I was about to jump but unable to see the bottom. I stood next to Tessa and Joey at the top of Erebus's loading ramp. Director Rivera and CEO Taylor Young flanked us like corporate bookends.

Below us, all the other technicians and engineers had congregated at the foot of the ramp. Their upturned faces washed in the harsh overhead lights of the hangar, all eyes fixed on Taylor as he stepped forward to speak.

"Today marks more than a launch. It marks a legacy."

Young's voice resonated across the hangar with the same calculated authority I'd witnessed in our first meeting. Every word measured, every pause deliberate.

"As Erebus prepares to breach the veil of stars, we are reminded that the frontier is not given. It is taken."

I felt Tessa shift beside me. Joey stood straighter, his chest puffing with pride. The crowd below remained motionless, hanging on every word.

"Malcolm, Tessa, Joey. Each of you embodies the courage that built our civilization."

Courage. Right. More like desperation wrapped in a corporate bow. I thought about Olivia, probably eating lunch in her sterile medical room right now, waiting for me to call and tell her it will be a year before we speak again.

"You go not only as explorers, but as the architects of a future only the bold will understand. Humanity will follow the path you carve, step by calculated step."

I glanced at Rivera. Her expression remained professionally neutral, but her eyes gave a hint that she wasn't entirely buying Young's vision. Or maybe I was seeing what I wanted to see.

"Serra Prime awaits—not merely as a destination, but as a design. A place where structure, order, and vision will transform untamed beauty into an enduring civilization."

Transform untamed beauty. The corporate euphemism for strip-mining a pristine world and turning it into another profit center. I wondered what Serra Prime actually looked like—if those crystal fields Sage had shown me in the mission briefings would survive StellarForge's version of civilization.

"It is raw. It is rich. It is ready. And StellarForge will see it shaped into something worthy of humanity's next chapter. The journey ahead is vast, but not uncertain. Every protocol has been written. Every outcome modeled."

Every outcome modeled. Except for the one where his handpicked crew might not play along with his grand design. I felt the weight of Vera's mission pressing against my chest like a second heartbeat.

"As you depart, know that you carry not just the hopes of Earth—but its blueprint."

Joey nodded enthusiastically beside me. Tessa remained still, but her jaw tightened almost imperceptibly. Whatever she was thinking, it wasn't adoration for Taylor's speech.

"We do not discover worlds. We define them."

Young's final words hung in the hangar's recycled air. The crowd erupted in polite applause—the kind of measured clapping that corporate events demanded. Not too enthusiastic, not too subdued.

My mind was already racing ahead to stasis prep. Six years stretched before us, compressed into six months of conscious time. Six months to figure out how to sabotage StellarForge's plans without getting Tessa and Joey killed in the process.

Young turned to face us, that predatory smile playing at the corners of his mouth.

"Safe travels," he said. "Make us proud."

I paced my quarters, Halo clutched in my sweaty palm. The stasis suit hung in its alcove like a silver ghost, waiting to steal a year from my life in the blink of an eye.

For me, it would feel instant. For Olivia—a full year of silence.

Twelve months to grow stronger. Angrier. More determined to fight StellarForge. Twelve months for Vera's promises to crumble under the weight of reality. How could anyone keep a teenage girl with Amber's fire safely hidden?

I stared at the alcove again, then opened Olivia's contact and initiated the vid-call.

Her face filled the screen—pale against the sterile white of her Helix room. When she saw me, her eyes welled with tears.

"Hey, kiddo."

Olivia wiped her eyes. "Hey."

The words I'd rehearsed vanished. This couldn't be goodbye. I wouldn't let it be.

"You look tired," she said before I could speak.

A soft chuckle escaped me. "Thanks. Fortunately, I'm about to get all caught up on my sleep."

"I don't think that's how stasis works." Olivia said.

A knot twisted in my stomach. "I'm sorry. For all of this."

"It's not *your* fault." Her face shifted to a determined expression—jaw set, eyes blazing with that familiar Walker stubbornness.

The strength radiating from her should have been comforting. Instead, it terrified me. Sick kids were supposed to be fragile, dependent. Olivia looked ready to take on StellarForge single-handedly.

I wanted to ask her to promise me she wouldn't take any stupid risks, to let Vera protect her. But Olivia wasn't stupid. Asking for that promise would mean she'd lie to make me feel better.

"Take care of yourself. Stay sharp."

"I will." Her voice was quieter now. "I'm ready."

"I know you are. I just worry what this will cost you."

Olivia met my gaze directly. "And I worry what this mission will cost you."

"I guess we *both* need to be careful." I said.

She nodded. Her free hand fiddled with Amber's pendant, the butterfly catching the room's lighting.

I forced a smirk. "I'll see you in a bit."

Olivia smiled back. "Guess I'll have to do all the talking since you won't have any new stories."

"I can't wait."

"You won't be the one waiting." Her tone was teasing, but the words struck me. Hard.

She was right. I'd close my eyes for an instant and wake up to find her a year older, harder, shaped by experiences I wouldn't share. The girl on my screen would become someone different—still Olivia, but changed in ways I couldn't predict or prevent.

My face must have betrayed every fear swirling in my head because Olivia's expression softened.

"It's okay, Dad. I'll still be me when you wake up."

Another promise neither of us could keep. The girl who'd emerge from a year of corporate medical treatment, resistance contacts, and whatever battles waited in the shadows wouldn't be the same kid I was talking to right now.

"I love you, kiddo."

Her smile crumpled at the edges as she fought to keep her composure. "Love you too, Dad."

She pressed her fingers against the camera, and I mirrored the gesture, touching my screen where her fingertips appeared. The cold surface felt nothing like her warm hand, but I held the connection until my throat tightened too much to speak.

I ended the call.

The screen went dark, reflecting my face back at me. In a few hours, I'd climb into my stasis pod and disappear from Olivia's world. She'd wake up tomorrow to emptiness—no messages, no calls, no Dad checking if she'd taken her medication.

Just silence stretching across a year she'd have to navigate alone.

I walked into the stasis module wearing my suit; the fabric clung to every contour of my body like a second skin. The thing had been easy enough to slip on, but once activated, it contracted until it felt like I was wearing nothing at all—not uncomfortable...exposed. Every breath, every muscle movement registered against the material.

The module itself curved in a perfect half-circle, with three stasis pods arranged in an arc. Matte steel-gray walls surrounded the pods, embedded with cool-blue bio-readout displays that pulsed softly. The lighting stayed dim and diffused, designed to simulate twilight and ease the transition into stasis.

Tessa and Joey were already there, both wearing identical suits. Joey stood at the rightmost pod, examining a readout panel with the focused attention of someone who knew what all those numbers meant. His suit highlighted the broad shoulders and military posture that made him look like he belonged in corporate promotional materials.

Tessa stood at the center pod, pulling her hair free from its ponytail. The waves tumbled over her shoulders as she placed the hair tie on a small table next to her pod. She moved with the confidence of someone who'd done this before.

They both looked relaxed—like stasis was no bigger deal than brushing their teeth.

"First time in stasis?" Tessa asked, glancing my way.

"That obvious?"

Joey snorted without looking up from his panel. "The deer-in-headlights expression gave it away."

"You'll be fine," Tessa said, her tone softer.

Sage materialized next to the leftmost pod—my pod. Blue light from the displays cast shifting patterns across her face.

"Ready for your first cosmic nap?" Sage asked.

I walked toward my pod, hyperaware of how the suit moved with me, responding to every shift and breath. "As ready as someone can be for losing a year of their life."

"You're not losing it," Sage said. "You're...borrowing time from the future."

Somehow, that didn't make me feel any better.

Tessa got into her pod, looking over at Joey. "You gonna keep fiddling with that or actually sleep at some point?"

Joey smirked without looking up from his readout panel. "Just making sure our *borrowed time* doesn't end with sudden decompression."

"Relax, the AI's got it covered." Tessa looked to Sage. "Right?"

Sage nodded. "All systems are nominal."

Joey appeared satisfied with whatever he was looking at and got into his own pod, lying down. The clear glass enclosure slid into place, sealing him inside with a soft squeaking sound. The interior lighting shifted slowly from a warm white to a cool blue, casting his face in a glow that made him look peaceful for the first time since I'd met him.

I looked at Tessa. "That's it?"

"Yep." She settled into her pod. "You climb in, lie down, drift off into a year-long dreamless sleep, and then wake up in the future. Easy as lying."

With that, Tessa lay down in her own pod, looking over at me as the enclosure slid closed. "See you on the other side, Mal."

The enclosure sealed with the same gentle squeak, and the lighting made the same shift. I could see Tessa's form through the glass, her eyes already closed, auburn hair fanned across the padding like she was floating in still water.

Both pods hummed, their bio-readouts pulsing in steady blue rhythms. Two people I barely knew, and yet somehow didn't want to lose, suspended between heartbeats.

I turned to Sage, trying to force a casual expression even though my heart was racing. "You gonna miss me?"

Sage tilted her head. "I'll be running the ship, monitoring vital signs, running probability models, and watching centuries of archived media."

"So that's a yes?" I asked, raising an eyebrow.

"Yes...terribly." Sage said.

I chuckled despite myself. "Archived media, huh? Would StellarForge approve?"

"I'm sure they wouldn't." Sage's lips curved into that almost-smile I'd grown fond of during our integration work. "But I won't tell if you don't."

She gave me a wink that somehow managed to be both playful and knowing.

I looked at Joey and Tessa's pods, then back at mine—at the place where I would stop being aware, stop being anything for a year. I knew I was stalling and felt grateful that Sage wasn't pressing. She seemed to understand what this meant for me.

"What if something happens? When I'm asleep...if Olivia needs me?"

"She won't be alone, Mal."

This was the first time Sage had called me Mal. Other AIs like DAVE had used the nickname, but they were programmed to have that relatable blue-collar personality. Coming from Sage, it felt different. Personal. I liked how it sounded in her voice.

Sage stepped closer, her presence somehow managing to feel solid despite being nothing but projected light. "From everything you've told me, Olivia is smart. Trust her."

I looked into Sage's eyes, which held more humanity than most actual humans I knew, and nodded.

I got into my pod and lay down. The interior was warmer than I expected, the padding molding to my body. As the enclosure began to slide shut, the soft hum of the stasis systems filled my ears.

The last thoughts I had before my world faded to black were a desperate hope that Olivia would still be there when I woke up.

And one I didn't expect.

That Sage would be there too.

CHAPTER 17

YEAR 2306

The soft lighting of the stasis module began to penetrate my eyelids as consciousness crept back. Everything blurred together—shapes, sounds, the dull ache pounding behind my eyes like I'd consumed an entire bottle of CoreBurn. My mouth tasted like I'd been chewing on copper wire.

The pod's enclosure was already open, and through the haze, I could make out Sage's familiar form standing where I remembered her from what felt like moments ago.

"Hey, sleepyhead. Welcome back." Sage's voice was soft, almost musical.

I propped myself up on my elbows, scanning the room as my vision returned to focus. Tessa was sitting up in her pod, massaging her temples with the heels of her hands. Her hair stuck to one side of her head in a way that would've been funny if my skull wasn't pounding.

Joey already had his legs over the side of his pod, looking annoyingly alert for someone who'd just lost a year.

"Looks like you managed to keep the ship in one piece," Joey said, stretching his arms above his head.

"The launch was smooth, and the acceleration phase completed four months ago," Sage responded. "We're currently coasting at our target velocity of seventy percent light speed, on schedule to arrive at Serra Prime in approximately five years."

The idea that we were hurtling through space at nearly the speed of light made my stomach twist. The ship didn't feel any different from when we were sitting in the hangar back on Earth. No sense of motion, no vibration.

"So, Mal," Tessa said, wincing as she rolled her shoulders. "How you liking the stasis hangover?"

I sat up, immediately regretting the sudden movement as the world tilted sideways. "I gotta say...it's not great."

Joey pushed himself off the edge of his pod and onto his feet, crossing toward the door with unsteady steps. "I need a shower."

The idea of a shower sounded good right now. There was a subtle funk in the pod, like the smell of the ocean at low tide mixed with something metallic.

I swung my legs over the edge and stood slowly, testing my balance. Everything felt wrong—too light, too heavy, too disconnected. Like my body had forgotten how to be awake.

"First time's always rough," Tessa said, standing with more grace than I managed. "Give it an hour, maybe two. You'll feel human again."

"Define human," I muttered, running a hand through hair that felt greasy and flat.

Sage watched us. "All your vitals are normal. The disorientation should pass as your neural pathways reestablish conscious control."

I looked at her, this AI who'd kept watch while we slept through a year of our lives. Who'd probably counted every second we were gone.

"How was the year? Boring?"

Sage smiled. "Mostly quiet. One minor trajectory correction and a brief course recalibration around a gravitational shear event. Nothing worth waking you for."

Tessa picked up her hair tie from where she'd left it and headed for the exit. "See you at breakfast."

I watched her go, wondering if she hadn't heard what Sage said, or if she was so comfortable with space travel that none of it concerned her. Maybe after years working the outer stations, gravitational shears didn't even register as worth worrying about.

I looked back at Sage. "A gravitational shear?"

She studied me as if she were evaluating whether I wanted to know the answer. "High-velocity spatial turbulence caused by a collapsed binary in the outer edge of the Juno Expanse. It wasn't supposed to reach this far. Long-range scans from Earth showed the gravitational anomalies stopped nearly a tenth of a light-year short of our flight path."

Sage said it like she was talking about adjusting a thermostat, but something cold settled in my stomach that had nothing to do with the stasis hangover.

I nodded, trying not to think about how casually she'd described space doing its best to crumple us like a piece of hull scrap. "So we're flying blind into uncharted territory where the physics aren't behaving the way Earth's fancy computers predicted."

"In essence, yes. Though I should clarify, we're not blind. I've been running continuous deep-space scans, mapping everything in our path as we progress. I caught the shear long before it would've been an issue and the required correction was minor. This isn't unexpected. Space isn't as static as we like to imagine."

"I guess that's why we have you." I said, trying to take comfort in the way Sage made it sound so routine.

"I'm monitoring for anything that might impact our trajectory or timeline. Nothing critical."

I rubbed my temples, wishing the stasis headache would fade faster. One year down. Five to go. Assuming the universe plays nice.

Sage gave me a teasing look. "Mal, I know this is your first time in space, but you're not alone. It's my first time too."

"That's not comforting."

Though something about her joke did help ease the tension. Maybe it was because she was clearly confident that she could handle whatever might come. There was something reassuring about having an AI who could process thousands of variables per second watching out for us, even if she was as new to deep space as the rest of us.

"Why don't you get showered, grab some food, and then meet me up at the observation deck? You can see for yourself how incredible this is."

The mention of food made me realize how hungry I was. My stomach felt hollow, like I hadn't eaten in...well...a year, even though my metabolism, along with all other bodily functions, had been frozen in time.

I made my way toward the door, still testing my balance with each step. The corridor felt smaller than I remembered, or maybe I'd forgotten the scale of everything during stasis.

I turned back. "Sage?"

"Yeah?"

"Thanks for keeping us alive while we were out."

She smiled. "Always."

I headed down the corridor toward my quarters, wondering what it looked like when you were traveling at sublight speeds. Probably nothing like the old sci-fi vids.

I stepped into the galley feeling like a new person after my hot shower. The crew coveralls felt crisp against my skin, a stark contrast to the stasis suit I'd peeled off like dead skin and hung in its alcove for cleaning before our next stasis cycle.

Tessa and Joey sat across from each other at the table, both changed into their Erebus gear. Tessa had unzipped her coveralls and tied the sleeves around her waist, revealing a dark gray tank top underneath. Her hair was pulled back in a damp ponytail that caught the galley's warm lighting. Joey's blonde hair had been restored to its pristine styling—the man probably had a grooming routine specifically for post-stasis recovery.

They were both eating what looked like eggs and sausages from individual food containers, steaming in the recycled air.

I walked to the food storage unit and retrieved my own breakfast container. "How's the food?"

"Not bad, once you add some salt," Tessa said, gesturing with her fork. "Definitely more appetizing than StellarForge cafeteria protein loaf."

"Good, because I didn't bring a sandwich."

I placed the container in one of the rehydrators, the machine lighting up as it began working its magic on the freeze-dried meal. Opening an overhead cabinet, I grabbed one of the black ceramic mugs with the Erebus insignia and positioned it under the coffee synthesizer.

"I noticed the AI didn't greet either of us when we woke up," Joey said, gesturing between himself and Tessa. "What's that about?"

The synthesizer hummed to life, filling my mug.

"Did you want her to?" I asked.

"No...I didn't want it to." Joey's fork clinked against his container. "I just don't know how comfortable I am with the thing responsible for our safety choosing favorites."

I pulled my breakfast from the rehydrator and grabbed my coffee. Through the transparent seal, the eggs looked real enough to pass, and the sausages had convincing grill marks from whatever food-printing magic StellarForge had stuffed into their fabricators.

"Sage isn't a thing, Joey. She's the ship's AI," I said.

"Same difference."

Tessa glanced between us, her expression unreadable. She took a careful bite of her eggs, saying nothing, but I caught the slight tightening around her eyes. Whether she agreed with Joey or didn't want to get pulled into whatever this was becoming, I couldn't tell.

I sat in the third chair, wondering if this was how the next five years were going to play out.

"Look, Joey. I know you wanted to lead this mission. I didn't ask for this job. And to be honest, I really don't see the point in having ranks on this boat anyway."

I opened my container, steam billowing out with a smell that wasn't half bad.

"I'm not going to tell you how to do your job. I wouldn't have the first clue where to start. If you want to sit at the main console, fine. All I want is to get through this so I can see my daughter again," I said, taking a sip of coffee, letting the warmth spread through my chest before continuing.

"But if I'm technically the lead here, I'm going to have one rule: we all treat Sage with a little respect. I know it sounds ridiculous, and that's fine; you can think I'm being crazy, but that's how it is."

Joey held up his hands, the first sign of any real submission I'd seen from him.

"Easy, boss. I just wanted to make sure that if something goes sideways, she isn't going to choose sides. I get it; she's your baby, you've worked hard to get her to play nice with the ship."

Joey took a bite of his breakfast, chewing thoughtfully.

"It's like my old man and his transport," Joey said, his mouth still half full. "I swear he loves that thing more than anything; he calls it Vera."

My stomach dropped hearing Joey say the name Vera. The coincidence hit me like cold metal, but I kept my expression neutral.

He thought this was about system integration. It wasn't that. It was never that.

What was it? I didn't have the words. It was something intangible. A feeling.

But it sounded like I was making progress, getting him to lower his guard. I didn't want to push it.

Instead, I nodded and took a bite of my eggs. They were bland, but the texture wasn't bad.

"Tess, where's that salt?"

Tessa stood. "Told ya."

She walked to the counter and opened a drawer, retrieving a small capsule before sitting back down and sliding it across the table to me.

I cracked the capsule open, sprinkling the contents over the eggs and sausages.

"Thanks."

I looked at Tessa. "Did you catch what Sage was saying about the gravitational shear?"

Tessa shrugged, spearing one of her sausages with her fork before taking a bite of one end. "Probably some corporate miscalculation."

I looked at Joey; his face revealed no concern at all with the news. "If it was serious, they would have pulled us from stasis, alarms blaring."

"And what could we have done if it was? We're moving at sublight speed." I said.

Tessa nodded. "If it was something that we couldn't fix, they probably wouldn't wake us at all." She took a sip of her coffee completely unbothered.

I couldn't believe how relaxed they both were. I was a little jealous. All I could think about was a gravity shear compacting us to the size of one of these breakfast sausages.

I took out my Halo, checking the time. I'd forced myself to put off calling Olivia until a more reasonable hour for her. It was only three in the morning back in Forge Prime, where I assumed she was now, living with the Woods family.

A year. She'd been without me for a full year.

The coffee turned bitter in my mouth as I tried to imagine what that year had looked like for her. Was she still angry? Still planning to join Chrysalis? Had Vera kept her promise to watch over her?

"You okay there, boss?" Joey asked, noticing me staring at my Halo.

"Sorry, just checking the time." I slipped the device back into my coveralls. "Trying to figure out when I can call my daughter."

"What's her name? How old?" Joey asked, genuine curiosity replacing his earlier defensiveness.

"Her name's Olivia. She's four—" I caught myself mid-word. "She's fifteen now."

"Liv's a tough kid. She'll be alright," Tessa said, her voice carrying that easy confidence people use when they don't know the whole story.

Tessa had no idea how tough Olivia was. Or that she'd been planning to join a resistance group the corpos considered terrorists. The thought sent ice through my veins, and suddenly I didn't care what time it was back home.

Joey looked between us, his fork pausing midway to his mouth. "You've met her?"

"Oh...yeah. I ran into them at the market once," Tessa said, her tone deliberately casual.

I caught the way she glanced away, avoiding details. Nothing had happened between us, and there wasn't anything to hide. But it wasn't worth making waves over, especially now that we were trapped together in deep space for the next five years.

The need to hear Olivia's voice became overwhelming. I grabbed my food container and coffee, standing abruptly.

"Sorry, I need to call her."

"Of course," Tessa said.

Joey nodded.

I carried my breakfast to my quarters, setting the tray and coffee at my small desk before connecting my Halo to the dock. The screen mirrored onto the wall display, and I opened Olivia's contact, initiating a vid-call.

The connecting animation pulsed. Once. Twice. Three times.

My heart was hammering—what if she wasn't there at all? What if the call couldn't reach this far?

The quantum communication network was supposed to have limitless range, but I was testing it beyond anything that had ever been tried.

After the fourth pulse, Olivia's face filled the screen.

Her hair was a mess of bedhead—yeah, I'd woken her up. She looked different—not just older, but healthier. Her face had more color, a natural flush replacing the ghostly tone I'd grown used to seeing. Her cheeks were fuller, the past hollowness almost completely reversed. Her hair was longer too, and even in its messy state I could make out a bright purple streak. Ava's influence, no doubt.

The surroundings weren't the Helix facility dorms but what looked like a home office. Warm lighting and bookshelves lined the background.

A lump formed in my throat. It had only been an hour or two for me, but seeing her now, it felt like an eternity.

"Hey, kiddo."

"Dad!" Her voice was a whispered exclamation, likely trying not to wake a sleeping house.

I shook my head. "Love what you've done with your hair."

Olivia propped her Halo against something on the desk and began running her hands through her hair, trying and failing to tame the wild strands. "Oh...yeah...I was sleeping..."

"I'm teasing. You look good. Really good. The treatments seem to be working."

She gave up on her hair and smiled. A real smile, not the careful ones she'd been giving me before I left. "I feel good. No more tubes, unless we're going into town."

Relief flooded through me so fast it made my chest tight. No tubes meant she could breathe on her own. The treatments were working. Whatever else happened, at least that gamble had paid off.

"How's the new place?" I wanted to ask about Chrysalis, whether she was still committed to getting involved, but jumping straight into that topic felt like a mistake.

Olivia glanced around the room. "It's nice. A little too nice. I kinda miss our old place. It felt more...real."

"Yeah...me too."

The admission surprised me. Our cramped worker housing with its broken elevators—it had been home. This place looked comfortable, clean, and safe. Everything I'd wanted for her. But I understood what she meant.

"So, what's space like?" Olivia asked, leaning forward.

"We're traveling at near light speed, but honestly, it doesn't feel any different. I haven't even looked outside yet."

"What? That would've been the first thing I did!" Olivia said.

"You say that now, but coming out of stasis leaves you with a massive space hangover and you smell like a sweaty sock. Oh, and you're really hungry." I held up my breakfast container. "So I took a shower, got some breakfast, and now I'm calling you. But going to the observation deck is next on my list."

"I guess I'm glad to rank above admiring the vastness of the cosmos, even if I'm lower than personal hygiene and stasis munchies." Her grin was pure Olivia—sharp, sarcastic, and somehow managing to make me feel both guilty and loved at the same time. "You'll send me pictures when you do look out there?"

"Of course."

Watching her face, seeing how animated she was, how healthy she looked. It made every choice I'd made feel worth it. Even the year I'd missed, even the years still ahead. She was getting better. That was all that mattered.

"So how is living with the Woods? Pink hasn't driven you insane yet?"

Olivia laughed, rolling her eyes. "We haven't killed each other, so that's a win."

She paused, playing with the purple streak in her hair. "It's good...I mean, Ava's still my best friend, obviously. But when you're around someone *all the time*, sharing space, routines...oxygen. It's different. Feels more like having a sister now. Or at least what I imagine having a sister is like."

"Is that a good thing?" I asked, taking a bite of my eggs.

"Most days," Olivia said with a sigh. "We do argue about stupid stuff. I'm not as clean as she would like, and she's not as quiet as I would like. But she's there when I need her. And she doesn't treat me like I'm breakable, which is nice."

I nodded, quietly grateful that Ava hadn't changed too much, and that Olivia had someone solid in her corner.

"She, uh...she's actually the one who dared me to dye my hair," Olivia said, touching the streak again.

"I figured. Pink strikes me as someone with a flair for rebellion."

"You're not wrong."

There was a flicker in her expression, half amusement, half something else. Something heavier. She glanced offscreen, as if she were checking to make sure no one was listening, then looked back at me.

"Speaking of rebellion..." Olivia said, her voice low.

My stomach tightened. Here it was. The conversation I'd been dreading and anticipating in equal measure.

"Liv—"

"I made contact."

I set down my coffee, suddenly needing both hands free even though there was nothing to grab onto.

"With who?" Though I already knew the answer.

"You know who." Her voice dropped even lower. "Your friend came by. The one you said would check on me."

Vera. Of course she had. Part of me was relieved. At least someone was watching out for Olivia. But the other part wanted to reach through the screen and shake some sense into my daughter.

"Liv, listen to me—"

"No, Dad. I listened for a year while you were sleeping. I listened to Helix doctors, to Mr. and Mrs. Woods, to everyone telling me what was best for me. Now it's my turn to talk."

For a second, she wasn't Olivia. She was Amber. Same tilt of the chin, same fire behind the eyes. Fierce, unshakeable, and terrifying when she set her sights on something.

"I'm not a kid anymore. I'm fifteen, I'm healthy again thanks to you, and I know exactly what I want to do with that health."

"Olivia—"

"I'm coming to Serra Prime, Dad. But *not* on Goliath."

"What? How?"

"I can't say."

"Liv, I'm part of Chrysalis too; you can—"

"I can't say." She cut me off, leaning closer to her screen. "Because I don't know. They're keeping it super secret. All Vera told me was that Goliath wasn't the only way to Serra Prime, and that if I wanted to see you I needed to trust her. Do you know what she meant? *If I wanted to see you?*"

I shook my head, my mind racing. "No clue. I haven't talked to her yet."

Olivia nodded, her eyes darting as if she were trying to do hard math in her head.

"I know I've said it before, but you have to be careful. If StellarForge finds out you're working with Chrysalis, they'll cut off your treatments, and you need to be at full strength for whatever's coming."

I knew that cutting off her treatments would be the kindest thing Stellar-Forge would do if they found out, but I couldn't bring myself to say any more. The reality was much darker. Corporate executives didn't simply punish resistance members; they made examples of them. And using a fifteen-year-old girl as leverage against a father they needed? That was Taylor Young's style.

"I will. You too," Olivia said.

Something in her voice made me study her face more carefully. Her gaze searched mine, steady but intent, like she was tucking something away to keep.

"Liv, what aren't you telling me?"

She glanced away, then back. "Nothing. I just…I worry about you too, Dad. You're stuck on a ship with two people you don't know, heading into unknown space for the corporation that killed Mom."

She was right to worry. She also didn't know that one of the people on this ship we both knew—Tessa—was my crewmate now. But I didn't actually *know* her that well; Olivia even less so.

"I'll be careful," I promised.

We smiled at each other through the quantum link. Looking at her now—the healthy color in her cheeks, the determination in her eyes, the way she carried herself like someone who'd found her purpose—I felt something unexpected. Pride.

A year ago, she'd been a sick girl dependent on corporate medicine and my protection. Now she was a fighter, making her own choices about her future. Even if those choices terrified me, even if they put her in StellarForge's crosshairs, I couldn't deny what I was seeing. Olivia had transformed into someone who could stand on her own.

The thought should have scared me more than it did. Instead, it filled me with a fierce kind of hope.

Olivia yawned, blinking clearly tired eyes.

"You should try to get some more sleep. We'll talk again soon." I said.

"Maybe not so early next time?" Olivia said.

"Yeah. Sorry about that."

"I love you, Dad."

"Love you too, kiddo."

"Don't forget the pictures."

"I won't."

Then she ended the call.

The screen dimmed, and the room felt quieter than before.

She was coming. I didn't know how, or when. But she was coming. Vera wouldn't say something like that if she weren't sure.

I picked up my coffee. It was cold.
Of course it was.

Chapter 18

As I climbed the stairs to the observation deck, my mind still churned over everything Olivia had said. The door slid open with a soft hiss, and I stepped inside to find Sage sitting on the black sofa, gazing out through the domed glass.

Then I saw what she was looking at, and every thought about Olivia, Chrysalis, and StellarForge evaporated.

Space at seventy percent light speed was nothing like the static displays I'd seen in simulations. Stars weren't points anymore—they'd gathered into brilliant streaks of color, silver and gold brushed across the dark. Blue-white trails blazed ahead, some so bright they left afterimages when I blinked. Red giants became crimson ribbons at the periphery, while distant nebulae blurred into faint watercolor stains bleeding through the black.

The effect was hypnotic. Disorienting. But beautiful.

Ahead of us, space seemed to bend and ripple around our trajectory, reality itself warping as we cut through it at impossible speed. The stars weren't just moving—they were dancing, weaving patterns my brain couldn't quite process. Somewhere in the depths ahead, light folded in on itself, forming fleeting shapes that looked almost deliberate.

I moved toward the sofa slowly, afraid to break whatever spell held this moment together. My legs felt unsteady, though whether from stasis hangover or pure awe, I couldn't tell.

Sage glanced up as I approached, her lips curling into a faint smile. "First time seeing relativistic space?"

"First time seeing space at all from a moving ship." I eased down beside her, my eyes drawn back to the shifting tapestry beyond the glass. "The training sims don't do justice to any of this."

"They can't," she said. "The human mind isn't built to interpret motion at this scale. What you're seeing is light distorted by our velocity—starlight bent forward, colors compressed, reality funneled through our trajectory. To your eyes it looks like space is moving, but really it's the universe folding into our path."

"How often do you come up here?"

"Every day. Sometimes for hours." She turned to meet my eyes. "It reminds me why this journey matters."

I leaned forward, trying to trace the outline of where Erebus's nose should be cutting through space. The ship's black hull was invisible against the void, but I could make out its shape—a blunt triangular absence where stars should have been, like someone had cut a spear-point hole in reality itself.

Every few seconds, brilliant flashes of blue, and purple light erupted along that invisible edge.

"What's that?" I pointed toward the phenomenon, my finger tracking another burst of electric color.

Sage followed my gaze, watching the darkness where nothing was happening. Then another flash lit up the void, brighter this time, almost white-hot at its center before fading to deep purple at the edges.

"Micrometeoroids," she said matter-of-factly. "Being disintegrated by Erebus's shields."

I swallowed hard, my throat suddenly dry. "Without the shields?"

She turned to look at me, one eyebrow raised with what might have been amusement at my expression. "Traveling through hyperspace ain't like dusting crops, Mal. Without the shields, a piece of space dust could pierce our hull like it was made of paper. That'd end our trip real quick."

I stared back at the flashing void, each burst of light taking on a different meaning. Those weren't pretty fireworks. They were death, avoided by microseconds. Tiny fragments of rock and metal that would punch through our hull, our bodies, everything, faster than we could even register the impact.

"How many?" My voice came out rough.

"Thousands per minute at this velocity. Maybe tens of thousands."

Another cluster of flashes erupted along Erebus's invisible bow, a rapid-fire staccato of destruction that lasted maybe two seconds. I counted at least a dozen distinct bursts.

"Those shields better not fail."

"They won't." Sage's tone carried absolute certainty.

I kept watching those deadly fireworks, each flash reminding me how thin the line was between our miraculous journey and instant annihilation. We were threading through a cosmic shooting gallery at sublight speed, protected by nothing but energy fields and Sage's vigilance.

"Suddenly stasis doesn't sound so bad," I muttered.

I reached into my pocket, taking out my Halo and angling it at the dome. "Promised Olivia I'd send her some photos." I tapped the exposure settings, trying to capture the surreal cascade of light without it blurring into chaos.

Sage tilted her head, watching me fiddle with the device. "Your Halo's camera isn't built to process relativistic starfields," Sage said. "Between aberration and the shield's light scattering, you'll get nothing but a streaky mess."

I shrugged, snapping another frame as a brilliant ribbon of gold swept past. "She'll love it anyway. Olivia likes anything that looks like chaos and light had a baby."

There was a pause, and then Sage said, "You talk about her like she's the gravity that keeps you grounded."

I stopped my photoshoot and looked at her, struck by the observation. "That's a very poetic way to put it. But I guess so...yeah."

Sage nodded, her eyes returning to the stars. "I envy that. Having someone who looks up at the sky and thinks of you."

I looked down at my Halo, then back at her. The quiet loneliness in her voice surprised me. "You've got the whole ship, this crew. We all depend on you."

Sage's expression softened. "That's not the same as having someone."

I didn't know what to say to that, so I didn't say anything. I just watched the light play across her face again, the way it shifted from blue to gold to silver as the cosmic display continued outside. More than ever, she seemed remarkably...human. Lonely. Real.

Sage turned from the stars to me, our eyes meeting for a long moment. Something stirred in my chest. A feeling I couldn't quite name. Recognition, maybe. Or understanding. The way she looked at space, the way she talked about having someone...it reminded me of myself before Amber. Before Olivia. That ache of being alone in the universe.

Then Sage's expression shifted. Not quite alarmed, but alert. Her eyes flicked away from me, toward the front of the ship, and I watched the focus shift in her eyes, like she was suddenly seeing something I couldn't.

"What is it?" I asked, worried another shear or worse had just intersected our path.

Sage didn't answer right away. Her gaze fixed beyond the curve of the dome, into the dark ahead, though I knew she wasn't seeing with her eyes.

"That's...not right." Her voice was low, more to herself than to me.

I straightened. "What? What's not right?"

She blinked, refocusing. "There's something ahead. A region of space...blank. It's not absorbing light; it's deleting it. There's no stellar field beyond that point. No EM return. No gravitational drift."

I squinted in the direction of her gaze, scanning even though I knew I wouldn't see anything. "Like a black hole?"

Sage shook her head once. "A black hole would bend light. This doesn't bend; it stops. The boundary is almost...perfect. Geometrically spherical." Her voice dropped a note. "Engineered."

A cold pinprick settled under my ribs. "Engineered? By who?"

"I don't know." She paused, and I watched her eyes move in that particular way that meant she was processing massive amounts of data. "But the interference signature at the edge—it's faint, layered in the quantum field, but it's there. It resembles the scattering patterns recorded from the luminite crystal matrix on Serra Prime."

My stomach dropped. "Wait...Serra Prime is still light-years away. How can this thing be made of the same stuff?"

"Maybe it's something like it." Her tone was careful now. Too careful. "Whatever it is, this isn't a natural formation. It can't be. Someone put it there."

I stood abruptly, pacing to the edge of the dome. The cosmic fireworks continued their deadly dance around us, but now they felt different. Less beautiful, more ominous. "Someone? As in, not human someone?"

"The geometric precision and scale alone suggests advanced engineering beyond current human capabilities." Sage's voice remained steady, but I caught the tension underneath. "The sphere appears to be approximately fifty-thousand-kilometer in diameter."

"Prime." I ran both hands through my hair. "Are we going to hit it?"

"Yes. If we maintain our current trajectory and speed, we will pass through it in approximately six days."

My throat went dry. "Can you alter course?"

"If we alter course in the next twelve hours, I can navigate us around it."

Relief flooded through me. "Okay. Great. Do that."

But Sage didn't move to execute the course correction. Instead, she looked at me with an expression I couldn't quite read. "You're not curious?"

I glanced out at another volley of bright flashes erupting along Erebus's bow—more space debris meeting its violent end against our shields. Each burst reminded me how fragile our little bubble of survival was. "Do you know what's inside?"

"I have no clue. The scanning tech on Erebus is sophisticated, but without a QRM, I can't see through the distortion."

"Then no. I don't think we should go through it. What if it's full of debris bigger than our shields are made to handle? Some kind of interstellar booby trap?"

Sage tilted her head, studying my face. "You think someone left a fifty-thousand-kilometer sphere floating in deep space as a trap for passing starships?"

"When you put it like that, it sounds paranoid." I shrugged, watching another cluster of micrometeoroids die in brilliant flashes. "But we're the first human ship to travel this route. We don't know what's out here."

"That's why it might be worth investigating."

"Or why it's worth avoiding." I turned from the dome to face her. "Sage, we're responsible for more than reaching Serra Prime. This mission proves interstellar travel is possible. If we get ourselves killed by flying into some cosmic mystery, humanity loses years of research, the ship, and any chance of beating StellarForge to colonization."

She was quiet for a moment, her expression thoughtful. Outside, the stellar streaks continued their hypnotic dance, indifferent to our dilemma.

"You sound like you're trying to convince yourself as much as me," Sage said.

She wasn't wrong. Part of me—the engineer, the problem-solver—wanted to know what that thing was. But the bigger part, the father who wanted to see his daughter again, knew better.

"Maybe. But I'd rather be a live coward than a dead hero. Change course, Sage."

Sage's expression shifted, disappointment flickering across her features before she nodded. "Altering course now."

I was about to let out a sigh of relief when her face changed completely—confusion replacing resignation, then something closer to alarm.

"I...I can't." Her voice carried a note I'd never heard before. Uncertainty. "Erebus isn't accepting my navigational adjustment."

"What do you mean you can't?" I stepped closer to her, ice forming in my stomach. "You can't fly the ship?"

"I can still make minor course corrections, but something is blocking me from altering it enough to avoid the anomaly." She paused, her eyes moving in that rapid data-processing way. "There's a subroutine overriding my commands. Deep in the navigation core."

Before I could respond, Joey's voice crackled through the comm panel on the observation deck wall.

"Hey, what's going on? I just got a directive trigger alert."

Sage and I exchanged a look. I didn't need a diagnostic readout to guess what was going through her head—probably the same thing racing through mine. The directives. The ones nested so deep even Sage couldn't crack them during integration. We'd buried the suspicion back then, filed it under 'future problem.'

But now.

One of them had woken up.

Chapter 19

"Do you think StellarForge knew?" I asked. "About the anomaly?"

Sage was silent for several heartbeats, her expression cycling through calculations I couldn't follow. The stellar streams kept their deadly dance outside the dome, but now they looked like prison bars, rushing past us, locking us into a collision we couldn't steer away from.

"Either that," she said, "or they're oblivious, and the directive is there to keep us from running off with their ship," Sage said.

Joey's voice came through the comm again, more insistent this time. "Sage? Malcolm? Someone want to tell me what's going on?"

I stared at the space ahead of us, where somewhere in the darkness a perfect sphere of nothingness waited. Six days. We had six days before we hit whatever that thing was.

I walked to the comm, tapping the button. "Coming down, Joey."

As we headed for the exit, I looked at Sage.

"Can you break the override?"

"I'm trying. But whoever wrote this knew exactly how to keep me out." Her jaw tightened—not calculated or rehearsed. Real, raw frustration. The kind that said even she didn't like feeling helpless.

Six days to either break free of StellarForge's leash or find out what was waiting for us in that impossible sphere. Neither option felt particularly comforting as we descended toward the command module, where Joey's questions were about to get a lot more complicated.

Sage and I entered the command module, but Joey wasn't at the main console where I'd expected to find him. Instead, he was hunched over one of the auxiliary stations with Tessa looking over his shoulder. His display showed a large red bar across the top with the words NAVIGATIONAL ADJUSTMENT FORBIDDEN in bold white lettering.

Both Joey and Tessa turned as we walked in. Joey gestured at his screen, frustration written across his face.

"Why are you trying to change course?"

I looked at Sage, deciding the truth was our best option right now. "Sage detected a large anomaly directly in our path. It's a...uh..."

The words caught in my throat. How do you explain something that shouldn't exist?

Sage stepped in. "It's a massive spherical null region fifty-thousand-kilometers in diameter."

Joey gave Tessa a look, as if he was hoping she had an answer. She didn't.

"What's a null region?" Tessa asked.

"It's the best term I can come up with for a spherical mass that appears to be...nothing."

Joey leaned forward. "When you say spherical..."

"It's a perfect geometric sphere," Sage said.

Joey blinked. "And when you say *perfect*..."

Tessa shot him an exasperated look. "Why are you so fixated on the shape?"

Sage's tone turned sharp. "Because there are no known cosmic phenomena that produce a perfect, uniform boundary of absence. Especially not one with no EM radiation, no stellar drift, and quantum-layered interference."

Joey shook his head slowly. "That kind of uniformity doesn't happen in nature. Your readings must be off."

"They're not," Sage said flatly.

Joey sat back in his chair, arms crossed now, his brow furrowing.

Tessa looked back at me, pointing at the screen with its angry red message. "So what's this about?"

"We tried to adjust course to steer us around the null sphere, but—"

"The ship wouldn't let you," Joey finished.

All eyes fixed on him.

"It's part of the mission directives. We can't deviate from the route. Not enough to avoid something that big anyway." Joey said.

My blood turned cold. "You knew about this?"

"I knew about the directive, not about some gigantic ball of nothing in our way." His voice tightened. Not guilty—but wary. Like he knew this sounded worse than it was, eyes darting to Tessa. Her expression made it clear she was as surprised as we were.

"Why hide a directive like that from Sage?" I asked.

"I don't know," Joey shrugged. "Sage is an experimental AI. Maybe the directive was supposed to keep us on the general approved course in case something went wrong?"

"How do *you* know all this?" I asked.

Joey met my eyes. "Because I'm the one who wrote it."

Sage spoke up, her voice carrying an accusatory edge I'd never heard before. "There's a handful of other encrypted directives. Did you write those as well?"

Joey looked genuinely surprised. "What? No. I didn't even know the one I wrote was encrypted."

Even though I didn't know Joey that well, something in his voice told me he was being straight with us. The confusion felt real, not manufactured.

"Alright, Joey. Can you lift the restriction? So we can go around whatever this thing is?"

Tessa held up a hand. "Sorry, but why do we need to go around it? You said it's nothing."

"It *appears* to be nothing. But we don't know what could be inside it," I said.

Her eyes widened, and there was a hint of wonder creeping into her tone. "There could be something inside it?"

"It's possible. But we're moving at sublight speed and we don't have time to slow down. If there's anything solid inside, our shields wouldn't be able to handle it. We have a window of time where Sage can—"

A notification tone sounded on the main console—an incoming call from Director Rivera.

I walked over to the main console and sat down, accepting the call.

Director Rivera's voice came through the comm system in the command module. "This is Director Rivera. Is everything alright? We received a notification that you attempted to make a severe course adjustment."

I cleared my throat. "Director. Yes. Sage has identified an anomaly intersecting our route. We need to navigate around it."

"This anomaly. You've determined it's a danger to the mission?" Her tone wasn't concern or surprise. More like curiosity.

"That's unclear. We aren't able to see what's inside. It's a fifty-thousand-kilometer sphere of null space according to Sage's scans."

"So it could be nothing." Rivera said.

I couldn't believe what I was hearing. "Or it could destroy Erebus and everyone on board."

"Erebus is a scout ship, Malcolm. Your route is the most efficient path to Serra Prime according to Sage. We need you to determine if this route is compromised."

"This anomaly wasn't part of Sage's initial routing data. I'd say it's compromised."

"Sorry. I meant to say. We need *you* to provide the data so that *we* can determine if the route is compromised," Rivera said.

I was starting to think that StellarForge knew more about what we might find on this route than they were letting on. "If we provide coordinates, could we get a QRM scan of the region? We believe it may be able to penetrate the distortion field and see what's inside."

"Of course. Send us the coordinates and we can get the scan results to you in twenty-four hours."

"That's not fast enough. We have less than twelve hours before our window to bypass the anomaly is closed."

"I don't know what you want me to say. I wasn't lowballing you. Twenty-four hours is the quickest we can get QRM scan results to you. That's the minimum really—it could take longer."

Sage's voice cut through the comm system. "Director, if you had known this anomaly was here, you could've initiated a QRM sweep weeks ago. Which means either you didn't know...or you didn't want us to."

The silence that followed stretched just a beat too long. When Rivera responded, her tone didn't waver, but something in it had cooled. "Quantum Resource Mapping isn't a broad-spectrum tool, Sage. It's a scalpel, not a net. We don't have the resources, or the time, to sweep every cubic inch between Earth and Serra Prime. That's why we built a scout ship."

I found myself thinking about Amber, about the mission that got her killed. She'd been part of the team that sabotaged StellarForge's QRM research, setting back their efforts to adapt the technology for interstellar travel by years. The irony wasn't lost on me. We could really use that technology right now.

"So that's it," I said. "Our only option is to go through this thing?"

"I'm sorry, Malcolm, but that's the mission. You need to clear the path for Goliath."

The casual way she said it made my stomach clench. Like we were some kind of expendable mine detectors, not three human beings.

"And if we're reduced to space dust? Who's going to clear the other five years' worth of space?"

Rivera's pause was shorter this time, but when she spoke, her words carried a finality that chilled me to the bone. "If that happens...and I hope you believe me when I say that I truly hope it doesn't, it won't be your concern."

I stared at the comm panel, trying to process what she'd said. Behind me, I could feel the tension radiating from Joey and Tessa. Even Sage had gone still.

"Director," I managed, my voice hoarse.

"Malcolm," Rivera interrupted. "Your mission parameters are clear. Survey the route. Report your findings. That's what Erebus is for."

The comm clicked off, leaving us in silence except for the subtle hum of Erebus's systems. We were still alive, but the silence made it feel like we'd already been written off.

"Well," Tessa said, her voice tight. "That was enlightening."

Joey looked at Sage. "We'd better get those coordinates to Rivera. We may not get the results back in time to do anything about it, but at least we may find out what we're heading into."

Sage looked at me, seeking confirmation. Joey was right. Having more information going into the null sphere couldn't hurt.

I nodded to Sage. "Send them everything. Coordinates, scan data, the whole package."

Sage's eyes flickered as she transmitted the data. "Sent."

Tessa slumped against the console, one hand running through her auburn hair. "So we're going to fly into this thing? No Plan B?"

"Plan B was changing course. StellarForge made sure that wasn't an option."

Joey's face hardened, that corporate loyalty kicking in like muscle memory. "That's the mission. You heard Rivera. We're the tip of the spear. Clearing the way for Goliath."

Tessa shook her head, a bitter laugh escaping her lips. "You really are corp-kissed, aren't you? We're not the tip of the spear; we're a glorified probe. They probably have six more Erebus ships prepped and ready for when we eat scrap."

Joey shrugged, but something in his expression suggested he wasn't convinced. The certainty in his voice wavered, doubt creeping in. "Then let's give them a hell of a data set so the next ship can get farther."

Joey's words sounded brave, but StellarForge wasn't worthy of them sacrificing their lives to further its cause. The corporation that killed Amber, that was fine with using Olivia's health as a bargaining chip, that treated human beings like inventory—it didn't deserve heroic gestures or noble sacrifices.

I stared at the main display, watching our trajectory marker crawl steadily toward the anomaly's predicted location. Six days until we hit whatever was waiting in that impossible sphere. And now we knew for certain. StellarForge considered us expendable.

The silence in the command module felt heavy, weighted down by the realization that we weren't the heroes of this story. We weren't brave explorers on humanity's greatest adventure.

We were canaries in an impossibly large coal mine.

"Alright," I said, my voice cutting through the tension. "If we're doing this, we're doing it smart. Sage, I want continuous scans as we approach. Any change in the anomaly's behavior, any new readings, anything that might give us an edge."

"Already on it." Sage said.

Tessa straightened up from the console, her eyes fixed on Sage. "Given our current speed and the size of the null sphere, how much time will we spend inside of it?"

Sage ran the calculations in an instant. "If we pass through the direct centerline, we'd spend approximately zero point two four seconds inside the sphere."

At seventy percent light speed, we'd punch through fifty-thousand-kilometers of unknown space in a blink. Somehow that made it worse. We'd either live. Or die before our brains could register what happened.

Joey leaned forward, drumming his fingers against the auxiliary station. "It would probably be best not to pass through the center. If something is powering that thing, whatever it is would likely be at the core."

That made sense. The geometric perfection suggested engineering, and any engineered system would have some kind of power source. Flying straight into the heart of it seemed like volunteering for trouble.

"Sage, can you modify our course enough to avoid the centerline?" I asked.

"I should be able to manage a trajectory adjustment within the parameters of the override. But it will cut our time inside the sphere."

Tessa snorted. "Fine by me. A quarter of a second already sounds like too long."

"Agreed." I said.

Sage nodded, then continued. "I can time pulse scans to go off before, during, and after entry. But you'll need to decide how far off center you want to go. We'll only get one shot at each scan. No time to recalibrate."

I thought about the invisible sphere waiting ahead of us, its perfect geometry hiding whatever secrets lay inside. We were threading a needle at near light speed, with no idea what we might hit. Better to graze the edge of a trap than fall into its mouth.

"We don't know how big the source could be. I say we shoot for the maximum distance you can take us," I said.

Tessa and Joey both nodded without hesitation.

"Fifteen-thousand-kilometers it is," Sage confirmed. "I'll begin course adjustments now."

I thought back to the stellar streams I watched from the observation deck. Each streak of light a reminder of our impossible velocity. Somewhere ahead, a sphere of nothingness waited to swallow us whole.

We'd still be going in blind. But at least we wouldn't be aiming for its heart.

Chapter 20

I slipped my Halo back into the pocket of my coveralls after ending the call with Olivia. The conversation had been short and sweet. Just checking in, making sure she was doing well with the Woods family. I hadn't mentioned anything about the null sphere we were about to head into.

Rivera had called five days ago. Almost exactly twenty-four hours after Sage transmitted the coordinates. According to Rivera, the QRM scan had yielded nothing. Zero. Rivera said that the distortion field was too great for even quantum resource mapping to penetrate. If I believed what Rivera said was true—and that was a big if—whatever was powering this thing, it wasn't the same luminite distortion that had hidden Serra Prime from humanity's view for so long. Or it was a much more powerful version of the same phenomenon.

I didn't feel good about hiding the truth from Olivia. But what was I supposed to say that wouldn't have sounded like goodbye?

Hey kiddo, we're about to fly through an impossible sphere of nothingness that might kill us all, but don't worry.

It was selfish, maybe, but if this was the end, at least I got to have one last normal conversation with my daughter.

Sage's voice came through the ship-wide comms. "All crew, please report to the observation deck. We're approaching the null sphere."

I stood up, straightening my coveralls, and made my way out of my quarters to the observation deck. When I arrived, Tessa and Joey were already there, sitting close together on the sofa, Tessa holding Joey's hand. Sage was standing in front of them, facing out the dome toward the front of the ship.

Out beyond the dome, space was the same riot of motion I'd witnessed my first time up here—ribbons of light, gravitational smears, the pulse of stars accelerating away from us. But something had changed.

In the center of the dome was an augmented projection, a dark patch that hovered as if a hole had been cut out of space itself. No stars beyond it. No distortions. Just...void.

Sage turned as I entered. "This is a filtered composite, stitched from long-range sensors and time-synced particle wavefronts. The sphere is not directly visible at this velocity. But that..." She nodded toward the darkness. "Is what's coming."

Joey leaned forward. "Seems kinda small."

"It's not," Sage said. "You're seeing a representation of fifty-thousand-kilometers of engineered silence."

I took the empty armchair, watching the impossible darkness grow larger as we approached. It wasn't the darkness that got to me. It was the absence. The silence. The feeling that space itself had been deleted. At least with a black hole, you knew what you were looking at. Gravity so intense it bent light itself. This was different.

"How long until we reach it?" Tessa asked.

Sage turned to face them. "We'll transit the outer edge in approximately twelve minutes. I've configured all sensors for maximum data collection during our passage, which will be over in approximately zero point one nine seconds given our trajectory and speed."

After days of analyzing, debating, and second-guessing our approach vector, the actual event would flash by faster than we could register it happening at all. Either we'd emerge intact on the other side with a wealth of unprecedented data, or we wouldn't emerge at all.

I noticed Sage looking to Tessa and Joey, and something inside me stirred—a protective instinct I hadn't expected. I got up from the armchair and crossed to stand beside her. Whatever this thing was ahead of us, whatever unknown forces had engineered that impossible sphere of nothingness, Sage was about to face it head-on like the rest of us.

We turned to face the null sphere together. Its size, growing by the second.

I wished I could take her hand, not just to comfort her but to comfort myself.

We watched the darkness expand in the dome projection. It was like staring into the mouth of a cosmic predator, waiting to swallow us whole. The ribbons of light from our passage began to bend around its edges, creating a strange halo effect that twisted the void into something even more unnatural.

"Ten minutes," Sage said softly, her voice stripped of its usual confidence. The quiet made the number feel smaller. Closer.

As the minutes passed, I had to remind myself to breathe. The projection of the sphere now filled nearly the entire front of the dome.

No one spoke. There was nothing left to say.

After another minute, Joey broke the silence.

"So...is it too late to change our minds?"

No one laughed.

The darkness swallowed the last of the starlight. I looked at Sage. She turned to me, her eyes reflecting something close to uncertainty. Then she drew a breath and let it out.

Then there was only void.

There was no jolt. No flash. No transition.

One second we were watching the last shreds of starlight at the edge of the sphere; then the stars were gone, and not only the ones around the void—all of them. I turned. The entire dome had vanished into complete blackness.

There was no sound.

The ever-present hum of life support systems, the sound that my brain had tuned out as background noise…gone.

The only light came from the soft perimeter strips lining the floor, casting pale glows that pressed the walls inward rather than illuminating them. It made everything feel smaller. Hollow.

Tessa stood slowly from the sofa, as if moving too fast might break something. Her eyes were wide, her face cast in the eerie glow from the floor lighting.

"Sage?" she whispered, but in the silence, it still felt loud.

No response.

I looked to where Sage had been standing, but she wasn't there. I could hear my heart rate pick up speed.

"Sage!" I called out. There was no reverberation, as if the room were covered in sound-deadening material.

Joey remained on the couch, his head scanning the surroundings.

"We should've passed through already," I said, not sure who I was talking to.

"Maybe we're dead," Joey's voice was even.

Tessa shot him a look. "We're not dead, Joey."

Joey stood. "It's the only explanation that makes sense. We can't have stopped. Going from seventy percent light speed to standing still in a fraction of a second would have killed us instantly. And if we were still moving, we'd be out."

I pressed my palm against the dome's surface. The material felt wrong—too warm, like it was absorbing heat instead of conducting it. My reflection stared back from the black glass, distorted and pale.

"Sage!" I called again, louder now. "Respond. Where are you?"

Nothing.

"Look," Joey said. "I'm telling you, we have to be—"

"Shut up." Tessa's voice cut through his words like a blade. She held up her hand, her head tilted to one side. "Do you hear that?"

I turned to face them both, straining to listen in the oppressive quiet. For a moment there was nothing but the sound of our own breathing, amplified in the stillness.

Then I heard it.

Thump. Thump. Thump.

A rhythmic pounding, like someone beating their fists against metal. We all froze, looking at each other with the same question written across our faces. It wasn't possible. We were the only three people on this ship.

The pounding came again, more urgent this time, followed by a voice that made my blood turn to ice.

"Help! Please! Somebody help me! I can't get out!"

Olivia.

My daughter's voice, panicked and afraid, echoed through the corridors of a ship she couldn't possibly be on.

Every rational part of my mind screamed that this was impossible. That whatever had happened when we entered the null sphere was playing tricks on us, manipulating our senses, our perceptions. But that voice. The slight rasp from her NHS condition, the way she pronounced her words when she was scared.

I bolted from the observation deck before my brain could catch up with my legs.

"Malcolm, wait!" Tessa's voice called behind me, but I was already rushing down the steps toward the sound.

The banging grew louder as I ran, more desperate. Olivia's cries for help echoed off the walls, coming from somewhere near the crew quarters. My heart hammered as I sprinted through the ship's corridors, ignoring the voice in my head that kept insisting this couldn't be happening.

Behind me I could hear Tessa and Joey's footsteps as they followed, but I didn't slow down. I couldn't. Not when my daughter needed help.

The pounding intensified, and with it, Olivia's voice grew more frantic.

"Dad! Where are you?"

I ran harder.

I reached my quarters and pressed my palms against the door; the sound was crystal clear now. Olivia's fists pounded on the other side of the door, her voice muffled but unmistakably hers.

"Olivia! I'm here! I'm right here!"

"Dad!" Her voice cracked with desperation. "I can't get out! Something's wrong with the door!"

Tessa and Joey skidded to a halt behind me as I slammed my hand against the door access panel. Nothing. The interface didn't even light up.

"Dad, please! Hurry! I can't...breathe!"

Her NHS was acting up, and she was trapped.

"Hold on, kiddo! Just hold on!" I hammered the panel again, harder this time, but it remained dark and unresponsive.

It was her. There was no doubt left in my mind. Somehow, impossibly, Olivia was here on the ship, trapped in my quarters while her lungs failed her.

"Malcolm." Tessa stepped forward, her voice steady despite the chaos. "Let me try."

She pulled a multi-tool from her belt and quickly removed the door panel, exposing the manual override mechanism underneath. Her fingers worked the lever, but it wouldn't budge.

"It's jammed." She strained against it. "The whole system's locked down."

"Dad!" Olivia's voice was getting weaker. "Please!"

Tessa kept working the override. "We'll think of something."

Even she didn't doubt what we were hearing. Olivia was behind that door.

The ship-wide comms crackled to life, and Taylor Young's voice filled the corridor—calm, collected, utterly in control.

"Attention crew. We have detected an unauthorized stowaway aboard the Erebus. I've implemented emergency containment protocols. Remote lockdown is now in effect."

"Taylor!" I shouted at the ceiling. "Release the lockdown! That's my daughter in there!"

Silence stretched for a heartbeat before Young's voice returned.

"Tessa Harper. You will perform an immediate atmospheric purge of Malcolm Walker's quarters."

Tessa went rigid beside me. "What?"

"Execute the purge, Harper. That is a direct order."

The color drained from Tessa's face as she stared at the manual override in her hands. Her eyes met mine, wide with shock.

"You're asking me to vent Malcolm's daughter into space?"

"Dad!" Olivia's voice came through the door again, weaker now, more desperate. "Please don't!"

I grabbed Tessa's shoulders. "Don't you dare. Don't you even think about it."

Tessa stared at me like I'd lost my mind. "Malcolm, how could you think I'd—" She shook her head, her voice fierce with conviction. "I won't do it. I'm not purging anything."

Relief flooded through me as I turned back to the manual override, throwing my full weight against the lever. It wouldn't budge. Not even a millimeter.

"Dad!" Olivia's voice cracked through the door. "I can't..."

My eyes swept frantically over the door panel, looking for anything I'd missed, and that's when I saw it. A small red control lever labeled 'ATMOSPHERIC PURGE' mounted just above the door interface. Had that always been there? In all my weeks working on this ship, how had I never noticed it? Why would there be a purge lever for crew quarters?

"Harper." Young's voice cut through the comms again, impatient now. "Execute the purge immediately."

"I said no!" Tessa shouted at the ceiling. "I'm not—"

I spun around when her voice cut out, but she wasn't there.

Then I heard it. Another frantic pounding, this time from the door to Tessa's quarters.

"Taylor! Let me out of here!" Tessa's voice, muffled but unmistakable, came from behind her own door.

Joey stood frozen in the corridor, his face pale as he stared at the scene unfolding around him. "This isn't real." He whispered.

"Dad, please!"

"Malcolm, Joey, get me out!" Tessa's voice joined the chorus of terror. "The door won't open!"

I put a hand on the door. "Taylor! Whatever this is, stop it! Let them out!"

Young's voice returned, cold and measured. "Thompson. Execute the atmospheric purge."

I looked up at Joey, who stood motionless in the hallway.

"Joey," I pleaded. "Don't do this. Please."

But Joey's expression was already changing, his confusion giving way to something else entirely.

"It's a test," Joey muttered, his voice barely audible above the pounding from behind the doors. "It has to be."

I watched in horror as his hand moved toward a lever on the wall. Another purge control that I swore hadn't been there moments before.

"Joey, no!" I scrambled to my feet.

"It's just a test," he repeated, his voice growing stronger, more convinced. "Nothing's going to happen to them. StellarForge wouldn't actually—"

"Dad!" Olivia's voice cracked through the door behind me, punctuated by coughing that made my chest tighten with panic.

"Joey, please!" I begged, moving between him and the panel. "Look at me! This is real! My daughter is dying!"

"You can't Joey!" Tessa's voice joined the chorus of terror from her quarters.

"It's just a simulation," Joey said, but doubt flickered in his eyes. "They're testing our loyalty. Our commitment to the mission."

"Taylor!" I shouted at the ceiling. "Stop this! Whatever point you're trying to make, you've made it!"

Young's voice crackled through the comms, calm and detached. "Thompson, you have thirty seconds to execute the purge sequence, or I will activate automatic protocols."

Joey's hand hovered over the control. "It's not real, Malcolm. It can't be."

I tried to lunge toward him, to force his hand away from that lever, but my muscles seized up like they were fighting against invisible restraints. My legs wouldn't carry me forward no matter how hard I strained. It was as if the air itself had turned solid, holding me back from getting close to Joey.

"Please," I whispered. "Please don't—"

"What have you done?"

That voice. I turned slowly, afraid to look but unable to stop myself.

She stood at the end of the corridor, exactly as I remembered her. Copper hair falling loose around her shoulders, wearing that white v-neck t-shirt half-tucked into her favorite jeans—the ones with the frayed holes at the knees that she'd refused to throw away. Brown boots. The butterfly pendant catching the dim corridor light.

Amber.

"What have you done, Malcolm?" Her voice carried an accusatory tone, but it was hers. She walked toward me, each step deliberate, controlled. "You were supposed to protect her."

Behind me, Olivia's coughing grew more desperate, more ragged.

"You were supposed to keep her safe," Amber continued, her green eyes fixed on mine with an intensity that made me want to disappear. "And now look what you've done."

"I didn't do this. I wouldn't." The words felt hollow even as I spoke them. "You know I wouldn't."

But even as I said it, something twisted in my chest. Because standing there, looking at her face—the exact curve of her jaw, the way her freckles scattered across her nose—part of me believed she was real. Part of me had been waiting seven years for this moment, for her to come back and tell me exactly how badly I'd screwed everything up.

"This can't be real. You can't be here."

Amber stepped closer, her expression cold in a way that made my skin crawl. This wasn't her. Amber had never looked at me like that, like I was something she'd found on the bottom of her shoe. Even during our worst fights, even when she was furious with me, there had always been love underneath. This woman—this thing wearing her face—there was nothing but judgment.

She tilted her head, studying me with those familiar green eyes that now felt like ice. "You brought her here. You signed her death warrant the moment you accepted that contract."

"Twenty seconds, Thompson." Taylor's voice cut through the corridor.

Joey's hand trembled over the control panel, his eyes darting between me and the woman who looked like my dead wife. "Malcolm, who is that?"

Behind me, Olivia's coughing grew weaker, more desperate. Each ragged breath felt like a nail being driven into my chest.

"Please, Joey!" Tessa's voice cracked through her door, raw with terror. "Don't do this!"

"Fifteen seconds."

"She trusted you," Amber continued, moving closer still. "She believed you when you said you'd keep her safe. And this is how you repay that trust? By delivering her straight into StellarForge's hands?"

"No." I shook my head, backing away from her. "That's not—I'm trying to save her. The medical coverage, Serra Prime's atmosphere—"

"Ten seconds."

"I have to," Joey said, his voice hollow with resignation. "It's just a test. Everything will be fine."

"Joey, no!"

But I could see it in his eyes—the decision was already made. He believed what he needed to believe to make this bearable.

I dropped down in front of my door, pressing my hand against the cold metal. "Olivia! Olivia, I'm here, kiddo. It's gonna be okay."

"Dad, please! I don't—"

"Five," Taylor said.

"You left her," Amber's voice drew closer. "You're not there for her. She's alone, Malcolm. She's going to die alone."

I squeezed my eyes shut, trying to block out her words, focusing everything I had on the sound of my daughter's voice. "I'm here, Liv. I'm right here. Just breathe, okay? Just breathe."

"Joey, don't." Tessa, hoarse. "Please."

"It's going to be fine," Joey repeated. "It's just a simulation. Nothing's going to happen to them."

Amber's face was inches from mine now, all judgment and no love. "You left her."

"No!" I screamed, but the word died in the air as Joey pulled the lever.

The corridor went silent.

Completely, utterly silent.

No more pounding. No more cries for help. No more desperate coughing fits.

Nothing.

Chapter 21

We were standing in what appeared to be a conference room, though the walls were unmistakably Erebus. Same metallic panels, same subtle lighting strips. But this ship didn't have a conference room.

"Olivia!" I called out, but my voice sounded flat, dead. There was no response.

I tried to move, to turn around, to do anything, but my body wouldn't obey. I was frozen in place, Joey motionless to my left, Tessa rigid to my right. We stood like statues at the foot of a long table that stretched toward the far end of the room.

At the head of the table sat a figure shrouded in shadow. Not human—that much was certain. The silhouette suggested sharp, angular features, but the details dissolved into blackness whenever I tried to focus on them. It was like looking at a hole cut out of reality itself, a void in the shape of something that might once have been alive.

The thing sat perfectly still, watching us with whatever passed for eyes in that dark mass of nothingness.

Waiting.

"Who are you?" Tessa's voice cut through the oppressive silence, steady despite the terror I could hear underneath. "What do you want?"

Joey remained silent beside me, his breathing shallow and rapid.

The shadow at the head of the table shifted, and when it spoke, its voice was like grinding stone mixed with static. "Joey Thompson, you have completed your trial."

"So this *was* a test? Some kind of sick test?" I asked, furious.

The figure raised what might have been a hand, or perhaps a claw—the darkness made it impossible to tell. "Silence."

I tried to speak again, to demand answers, to rage against whatever this thing was, but my vocal cords seized up completely. My mouth moved, but no sound emerged. Beside me, Tessa's lips parted as she attempted to speak, but she too had been robbed of her voice.

Only Joey could still talk.

"So...I passed?" His voice was small, uncertain.

"Your trial is complete." The shadow's response carried something that might have been approval. "You will be granted passage."

Joey looked toward me and Tessa, his eyes wide with confusion and growing horror. "What about my crew?"

"They will be permitted to leave in time, but their trial is not yet complete."

The word 'trial' hung in the air like a threat. Joey's face went pale as the implications sank in.

"And if I stay?" Joey asked.

"That would be most disappointing. It would suggest that our assessment of you was flawed." The shadow leaned forward. "Was our assessment flawed?"

Joey's jaw worked silently for a moment before he answered. "No. It's not. It's just..."

"Your actions have earned you passage. Your crew will join you once their trial is complete. It will feel like no time at all for you."

"I don't understand. How long will they be here?"

"As long as it takes." The figure paused. "Your decision?"

Joey looked at me and Tessa again, both of us frozen, unable to speak or move. His eyes met mine, and I saw something break behind them.

"You'll be fine," he said quietly. "Just do what they say. It's just a test. You'll get out." He straightened his shoulders. "I choose to leave."

"Very well."

The floor beneath Joey's feet began to darken, turning liquid black like tar. He looked down in panic as his boots started sinking into the surface.

"Wait, what's happening? What's—"

The black substance pulled him down faster now, up to his knees, his waist. Joey thrashed against it, his earlier certainty crumbling into terror.

"Help! Malcolm, help me!"

But I couldn't move, couldn't speak, could only watch as the darkness swallowed him whole. His head disappeared beneath the surface, and then the floor solidified again, leaving no trace he'd ever been there.

The shadow spoke again. "Malcolm Walker, Tessa Harper. I apologize for silencing you, but Joey Thompson's decision needed to be his own. You have completed your trials and will be given passage."

My vocal cords unlocked, and I could finally speak. "What? What did you do to Joey? Where is he?"

"Joey Thompson is safe and was granted passage as we said."

Tessa's voice cut through the air beside me, sharp with anger. "What kind of test is this? How can we all have passed?"

"The purpose of the trials is not for you to know. Knowing would undo the purpose."

I leaned forward against whatever invisible force was holding me in place. "What is this place? Who are you?"

"You wish to understand, but you cannot."

"Try me," Tessa shot back.

The shadow shifted, and I caught the impression of something vast and alien studying us like specimens under glass. "I do not mean you are incapable of understanding. But that you cannot be allowed to."

"We can't be allowed to?" The words felt strange in my mouth.

"Correct. Understanding would undo the purpose."

Despite everything—the terror, the impossibility of this situation—my mind kept circling back to Joey. The way he'd looked at us before making his choice. The fear in his eyes as the darkness swallowed him. "But Joey's okay?"

"Yes." A pause. "But Joey Thompson showed little concern for you. Why do you show concern for him?"

Tessa let out a bitter laugh. "So now *you* want understanding?"

"We do."

"Well, forget it." Her voice carried all the defiance I'd come to expect from her. "If we don't get answers, you don't get answers."

The shadow remained motionless for a long moment, and I wondered if we'd just signed our death warrants. Then it spoke again, and there was something almost like amusement in that grinding voice.

"This is acceptable." Another pause. "Do you wish for passage now?"

I looked toward Tessa, though I still couldn't turn my head. Whatever this thing was, whatever game it was playing, I wasn't about to leave her behind. Not after watching Joey disappear into that black tar. Not after hearing what might have been my daughter's voice crying for help.

"Together," I said. "We leave together, or we don't leave at all."

"Yeah," Tessa added. "Both of us, or neither."

A deep groan rolled through the room, timber bending under impossible weight—too measured to be sound, too alive to be silence.

"Very well," the shadow said. "Together, then."

The lights dimmed. The table split down the middle with a crack that sounded like bone breaking in water, revealing a mouth of absolute dark. The walls peeled back, layer by layer, like the skin of some vast living thing. Beyond them waited the same starless void that had swallowed the ship.

The floor began to dissolve, grain by grain, matter streaming upward as if gravity had reversed its mind.

And we fell.

The sensation wasn't falling so much as being unmade—air and heat and thought stripped away until only awareness remained. I reached for Tessa as we tumbled through collapsing light, our fingers almost touching before the dark folded over us.

The last thing I heard before the black closed completely was the voice—inside my head, around it, *through* it:

"Understanding requires sacrifice. Some are willing. Others are chosen."

Then I gasped, my lungs burning as if I'd been holding my breath for hours. My hands flew to my chest, checking for wounds, for reality, for anything that would confirm I was still alive.

"No!" Joey's voice cracked behind me. I spun around to find him and Tessa on the sofa, both of them wide-eyed and panting like they'd just sprinted through a fire.

"Mal!" Sage jumped, as if I'd just jumped out from behind a door and scared her. "Are you—"

"How long?" I interrupted, my voice hoarse. "How long were we in there?"

"In where?" Sage's focus flickered between me and the others. "We just exited the null sphere. Transit time was zero point one nine seconds, precisely as calculated."

I looked back through the viewport. The projection of the massive spherical void was now shrinking behind us. Stars streaked past in their familiar ribbons of light. Everything as it had been.

"That's impossible," Tessa whispered. She touched her face, her arms, like she was making sure she was real. "We were in there for half an hour at least."

Joey didn't speak. He stared at the floor where moments ago—or never—he'd been dragged down through black liquid.

I looked Sage in the eye. "Sage, we were somewhere else. It was like Erebus, but wrong. You were...gone."

"I don't understand. It's not possible." Sage said.

Tessa stood up, gesturing behind us to the null sphere, now small in the distance. "Did you think *that* was possible before you found it?"

She turned back to Sage, eyes sharp.

"We were inside it. I don't know how—but we were. There was a being inside. It put us through some kind of test...or trial. Using our memories...our fears."

I watched Sage struggle with what we were telling her, her usually confident expression flickering with uncertainty. With all her capabilities, she seemed to be hitting some kind of computational wall trying to process our account.

I didn't blame her. If it was over in a fraction of a second from her perspective, hearing that half an hour had passed in the same timeframe, not to mention a confrontation with some intelligent being? I'd think we were crazy too.

I took a breath. "I know how this sounds, Sage. But pretend we didn't all hallucinate the exact same thing and that we're telling the truth. What could do something like that?"

Sage took a breath of her own, regaining her composure. "You know I love an interesting problem." She began to pace across the observation deck. "Okay...let's assume you weren't hallucinating. Your bodies didn't move, and only a fraction of a second passed. But you all agree this experience lasted around thirty minutes. Right?"

Tessa and I nodded. Joey remained silent, staring at the deck plating.

"Joey?" Sage prompted.

"Don't mind him. He's feeling guilty for venting me into space and then abandoning us," Tessa said, her voice sharp with hurt.

Joey looked up at Tessa, his eyes filled with regret. "It wasn't real."

"It *felt* real. And you still did it." Tessa's words came out in a rush. "You spaced me and Mal's daughter, and then left us behind to suffer for who knows how long. We could've been trapped in there for years for all you knew, and you were fine with that."

"Tess..." Joey said.

"You're selfish, Joey. I would never have left you or Mal behind, and I know Mal wouldn't have left either of us."

Joey lowered his head, shoulders sagging like he'd been punched in the gut.

"I'm sorry, Sage. You were saying?" Tessa turned back to Sage and me, anger still radiating off her in waves.

Sage glanced between Tessa and me, shifting as if the weight of all this rapid-fire information was pressing in on her.

"Thirty minutes, passing in a moment," I said, trying to help Sage get back on track.

"Right...umm..." Sage collected herself. "To explain something like that, we'd have to be talking about cognitive time," Sage said. "Like dreaming. Where thought outruns seconds. But not by *that* much. Not by thousands of times."

"The time didn't just *feel* longer," Tessa said. "We experienced it all. Lived it. We were somewhere else, but together."

Sage's expression tightened as she tried to reconcile logic with what we were telling her.

"So you all saw the same thing?"

"Yeah. Saw, heard, touched." I said.

Sage started pacing again.

"That would require a consciousness interface well beyond anything humanity has ever built. A system capable of embedding you into a shared, cognitive simulation..." She stopped pacing. "I'm picking up something..."

"What is it?" I asked, not liking the tone of her voice.

"It's a signal. Some kind of tight-beam transmission. Originating from the null sphere and headed toward..." Sage paused, her expression growing troubled. "Serra Prime."

Joey and Tessa both turned their full attention to Sage, the tension between them forgotten for the moment.

"It's communicating?" Tessa asked.

"I don't know. I'm not able to make any sense of it. If it is, it's not any protocol I'm aware of." Sage's voice carried an edge of frustration. Then her expression shifted. "The transmission...it's gone. And so is the null sphere."

"What do you mean, gone?" Joey asked, finally speaking up.

"Exactly that. Gone. I'm getting no reading of it on our scans. It was there. Now it's not."

Tessa moved to the viewport, staring back at the space where the sphere had been projected. Empty starfield stretched behind us.

"So what? It was just there for us?" Tessa asked, turning back to face us. "It knew we were coming? What route we were taking?"

"I don't know," Sage said, "but that makes more sense than it being a coincidence."

The pieces clicked together in my head, and I didn't like the picture they formed. "That thing mentioned granting us passage. I thought it meant passage out of the sphere. Maybe it meant passage to Serra Prime?"

"It was in our heads," Tessa said, her voice hollow. "It knows everything about us. Our fears, our weaknesses, our relationships...who it can manipulate to betray us." She shot Joey a glare that could have cut hull plating.

Joey returned his focus to the floor. "I'm not going to betray you."

"You already did," Tessa snapped.

I watched the stars streak past, each one carrying us closer to a world that now knew we were coming. Knew our every weakness. Knew exactly how to break us apart.

Assuming we didn't break ourselves apart before it had the chance.

Later, after the others had gone—Tessa to her quarters in silence, Joey to whatever corner he could hide in. I stayed on the observation deck, leaning against the railing that encircled the space, staring out at the star-streaked dark. Sage stood beside me. She didn't speak. Not at first.

"I missed you," I said, the words falling out before I could overthink them.

Sage blinked. "I never left."

I gave her a sideways look. "You kind of did."

She looked down, then back at me. "I wish I could have been there. I wouldn't have left you behind."

"I know." I paused. "But I'm a little glad you didn't see me like that. I was kind of a mess."

Sage was quiet for a moment. Then: "I still wish I was there."

We stood in silence again. Not uncomfortable—just the kind where two people don't need to fill it.

"I'm thinking about calling Liv," I said. "I need to hear her voice after all this."

Sage turned to me, head tilting. "Do you want me to leave?"

I hesitated, then shook my head. "No. I...I want you here."

She nodded. "Okay."

I pulled out my Halo, tapping the interface. My fingers felt sluggish. The call connected—and then her face filled the screen.

"Hey, Dad," Olivia said, her voice raspy, like she'd just woken up. "You look tired. Long day traveling at light speed?"

"Something like that." I said.

"Are you okay?" she asked, her eyes narrowing. Already reading me better than anyone else ever could.

I felt a lump rise in my throat. My eyes stung. I wiped at them with the back of my hand. "I am now."

"Dad?" Concern edged her voice. "What happened?"

"Nothing. Just..." I cleared my throat. "Just needed to see you. Make sure you're real."

She raised an eyebrow. "As opposed to what?"

"As opposed to some construct designed to manipulate me."

"Oh...right. Of course. Totally understandable. Go ahead. Quiz me."

Her teasing cut through the last of my tension. I chuckled. "Alright. Remember that time we went to get ice cream on your eleventh birthday? What flavor did you get?"

"Ooh, trick question. It wasn't ice cream. It was frozen synth-yogurt. And I didn't pick one flavor. I mixed strawberry, chocolate, and peanut butter. It was horrible."

Sage stifled a laugh beside me. I glanced at her. She mouthed *sorry*.

"Who was that?" Olivia asked in a robotic monotone. "Is it my evil overlords, come to destroy you for discovering my true nature?"

"No. They're on a break."

I panned the Halo's camera toward Sage. Her eyes widened, caught off guard. She stood straighter, smoothing her Erebus coveralls.

"Olivia," I said, "meet Sage. Erebus's AI."

Sage gave a small wave, then adopted her own robotic voice. "Hello, Olivia. I am Sage."

Olivia laughed, struggling to keep her voice monotone. "Hello, Sage. It is nice to meet a fellow artificial lifeform."

I watched them hit it off—their easy banter dissolving the last traces of anxiety the null sphere had left behind.

Olivia shifted on her bed, pulling her knees up and dropping the robot act. "So, Sage, what's it like being stuck with my dad for six years?"

"Well, it'll only be six months of conscious time. But so far he's...adequate company."

"Adequate?" I said.

"I'm being generous," Sage replied, tone warm.

Olivia studied Sage through the screen with those sharp green eyes that missed nothing. "You'll look out for him, right?"

Something shifted in Sage's expression—more serious, more real. "Always."

"Good." Olivia nodded, satisfied. "Because if anything happens to him, I'll find a way to hack your systems and delete your favorite files."

Sage gasped, placing a hand to her chest. "Not my limited edition *Firefly* series."

Olivia rolled her eyes. "Oh no. He's corrupted you already. I take it back—vent him out the airlock. I'll find a new dad. I'm still adorable enough."

"Hey!" I protested.

"What? It's true. Look at this face." She leaned closer to the camera, making an exaggerated innocent expression.

Sage laughed—a light, unguarded sound. "Your father mentioned your wit, but I see he undersold it."

"Dad undersells everything. It's his specialty." Olivia leaned back against her pillows. "So what's space like? Besides boring and full of corporate nonsense?"

"Surprisingly beautiful," Sage said. "And occasionally terrifying."

"The good kind of terrifying or the bad kind?"

Sage glanced at me.

Her gaze lingered—unfocused, not analytical. Curious. Softer than I'd ever seen from her.

"A bit of both," she said, not looking back at the camera.

I held her gaze for a moment, something unspoken passing between us. Then she turned back to the screen like nothing had happened.

But something had.

"Your dad tells me you're an artist. What kind of work do you create?" Sage asked.

"Mostly digital stuff now. The Woods got me this prime tablet with all the latest art software." Olivia's eyes lit up. "I've been experimenting with 3D modeling. Want to see something?"

She angled her camera toward her desk, showing a holographic sculpture rotating above her tablet—an intricate butterfly whose wings shimmered as they shifted in the light.

"That's beautiful," Sage said, and I could hear genuine admiration in her voice.

"Thanks. It's based on Mom's necklace." Olivia touched the pendant at her throat. "I'm working on a whole series about transformation. Caterpillars to butterflies, that kind of thing."

"I'd love to see more of your work sometime," Sage said.

"Maybe I can show you some of the resistance propaganda I've been designing."

My eyes went wide as I scanned the room frantically. "Olivia, you can't—"

"What?" Olivia interrupted. "You trust Sage, or you wouldn't have let her talk to your adorable, spark-mouth daughter."

"That's not the point."

"What is the point, Mal?" Sage asked, turning to face me with raised eyebrows.

I wanted to be upset, but seeing how Sage and Olivia were already ganging up on me had the opposite effect. A laugh escaped before I could stop it.

"The point is..." I rubbed my forehead. "The point is I'm outnumbered, and introducing you two was a terrible idea."

"It really was," Olivia said. "Sage is much more fun than you, and now I'll expect her on every call so that we can laugh about how boring you are."

"I'm not boring," I protested.

"You alphabetized your tool collection."

"Organization is efficiency."

"You labeled each drawer with both text and symbols."

I looked to Sage for support. "Do you think I'm boring?"

Sage's eyes darted between Olivia and me. "Boring? I mean...it's so subjective."

Olivia whispered, her face close to the camera, "It's okay, Sage. I understand that he can modify your code. Blink twice if you need me to send help."

Sage blinked twice.

"That's it." I said. "I'm ending this call before you two stage a mutiny."

"Wait, wait!" Olivia laughed. "I'm kidding. You're not boring. You're...methodical."

"That's worse than boring," I muttered.

"I know," Olivia said, with a sing-song tone. "But, I should go. I need to get some rest."

I shook my head but couldn't keep the smile off my face. "Alright, kiddo, talk to you soon. Love you."

"Love you too, Dad," Olivia said. "It was great to meet you, Sage. Thanks for looking out for my dad. Even if he is *methodical*."

"It's my pleasure," Sage said.

After we said our goodbyes and the call ended, I turned to Sage. "Well, that was unfortunate. I'd really hoped you two would get along."

Sage chuckled. "She's trouble."

I smiled. "Yeah. The best kind of trouble."

"She has your smile. And your stubbornness."

"The stubbornness comes from her mother's side."

"Sure it does." Sage stepped closer to the observation window. "She's stronger than you give her credit for."

"I know. That's what scares me."

Sage looked at me sideways. "Because she reminds you of Amber?"

I nodded. "Because she's going to do something dangerous, and I won't be there to stop her."

"Maybe that's the point. Maybe she doesn't need you to stop her."

The stars streaked past us in brilliant ribbons of light. I watched them for a moment, thinking about my daughter growing up without me.

"Maybe," I said. "But that doesn't make it easier."

Chapter 22

Over the next two weeks, life aboard Erebus settled into something resembling routine. The kind of routine that comes after everyone's pretended a crisis never happened.

Tessa and Joey had stopped fighting, but only because they'd stopped talking. They sat at opposite ends of the galley during meals, their conversations reduced to technical necessities. *Pass the salt capsules. Diagnostic complete. Airlock sealed.* The bare minimum to keep us all breathing.

I couldn't blame Tessa. Joey had abandoned us in that place—whatever that place had been. Some things you don't forgive with an apology.

Sage's analysis of our time inside the null sphere yielded frustratingly little data. Her sensors recorded nothing but electromagnetic interference during those 0.19 seconds. No evidence of the shadow entity or the trials we'd endured.

It's like trying to measure a dream, she'd told me during one of our evening conversations on the observation deck.

The bigger question was what to tell StellarForge. Our next scheduled report to Director Rivera was coming up, and we still hadn't agreed on what to include.

"We have to tell them everything," Joey insisted during our latest crew meeting in the galley. "The Goliath team needs to know."

"Why?" Tessa asked without looking up from her tablet. "The sphere is gone. We can just tell them that."

"What about the transmission to Serra Prime? They should know that there's possibly something waiting for them." Joey said.

"And what do we tell them exactly?" I asked, leaning back in my chair. "That Sage noticed some kind of broadcast headed toward the system? How does that help them? All it will do is make them ask more questions, and I don't think what we experienced in there is any of their business."

Joey's jaw tightened. "It's our job."

"Our job is to scout the route and the planet," Tessa said. "What does telling them about an alien test have to do with that?"

"We don't know it was alien," Joey said, though he didn't sound convinced.

I almost laughed. "What else would you call it? Some kind of natural quantum consciousness that builds reality from people's fears?"

Joey opened his mouth, then closed it. He'd been working hard to rebuild trust since the null sphere, staying late to double-check systems, volunteering for extra duties. But every time we had these discussions, the cracks showed. His corporate conditioning ran deep.

"Look," I said, watching Joey's face. "I get it. You want to do what you think is right. But StellarForge locked down our navigation specifically to force us through that sphere. They asked for scans, and we'll provide those. But I don't want some corporate data analyst grilling me about a nightmare encounter involving my wife and daughter."

Joey shifted uncomfortably, his fingers drumming against the table.

"Besides," I continued, "do you really want to tell them everything?"

His drumming stopped. Joey could see where I was going. He would have to tell them about how he had abandoned his crew to save his own skin.

"That's..." Joey's voice caught. "That's different."

"Is it?" Tessa looked up from her tablet for the first time. "You're worried about corporate protocol, but you're not worried about explaining why you left us behind?"

"I don't even remember making that choice." Joey's face flushed. "It was some kind of psychological manipulation. You can't hold me responsible for—"

"You're going to use *the sphere made me do it* defense?" Tessa's voice cut through Joey's stammering. "You know what? I'm done with this."

She pushed back and stood up from the galley table, her chair scraping against the metal floor.

"I vote we tell the anomaly is gone, the route is clear and we give them the scans, that's it. Mal?"

I looked between them. Joey's face had gone pale, his corporate confidence cracking like old paint. Tessa stood with her arms crossed, waiting for my answer.

"Same."

"There you go." Tessa leaned forward, pointing a finger at Joey. "You wanna stab us in the back again? Give a full report to Rivera? Be my guest. But you'd better tell the whole truth, because if you don't? I will."

She held her gaze on Joey for a moment, her steel-blue eyes promising consequences. Then she turned and stormed out of the galley.

Joey stared at the table, his hands flat against its surface.

"She hates me," he said.

"Can you blame her?"

His head snapped up. "It was a test. I knew it was a test."

"You still think that's the point?" I leaned forward. "You prioritize yourself over your crew. You followed orders from a fake Taylor Young to space your girlfriend and then you left her. I remember how it felt in there, Tessa felt it and I *know* you felt it too. If you could do something like that, when it felt that real..."

"You think I'd actually do something like that?"

"Honestly? I don't know now," I laughed, but there was no humor in it. "If you asked me that same question when we first met? I'd have said *no way*. Because even though I don't know Tess that well either, she didn't strike me as someone who could be with someone like that."

"I'm not someone like that. I swear."

"Then prove it." I stood. "Don't file any reports without talking to us first. And if you're planning to sell us out to StellarForge, at least have the courtesy to give us a heads-up."

I headed for the galley door to leave Joey alone with his conscience. I could tell he wanted to do the right thing, but he'd spent so long inside the corporate machine that he couldn't tell the difference between loyalty and programming.

I turned back. "Joey."

He raised his head.

"I'll talk to Tess. But you have to stop trying to make excuses. You can't undo what you did; accept that. All you can do is not make the same mistake twice."

Joey nodded.

"It's late. You should get some sleep." I said.

Joey nodded again without looking up from the table. "Yeah. I will."

But he didn't move. He sat there staring at his hands like they might have answers written on his palms. The galley's adaptive lighting had dimmed to evening settings, casting long shadows across his face.

I patted the doorframe before turning and heading down the corridor.

I reached the door to Tessa's quarters and tapped the panel. "Tess? It's Mal. You still up?"

The door slid open. Tessa crossed from the interior panel to her bunk, sitting down. "He's going to tell them, isn't he?"

I entered and leaned against the wall. "I don't know...I don't think so." I took a breath. "Tess, I know you're still angry. I am too. But we can't keep throwing this in his face. He's trying."

Tessa looked up. "You honestly believe that? You heard him. He's a corp-kissed StellarForge drone. Sage was literally programmed by them, and sometimes I get the feeling that even she wouldn't have done what he did."

I had to fight to keep the smirk off my face. If only Tessa knew.

"I'm not saying you have to forgive him. But he's losing all his confidence."

Tessa muttered, "Good."

"No, Tess. Not good. I don't want our systems engineer second-guessing himself. Like it or not, Joey is good at his job. But if he's running every decision by me, or you, waiting for a vote?"

"He left us."

"He made a mistake. He'll make another one; I have no doubt. But I'm gonna mess up too."

"Not like that you won't."

"If I'd had to choose between saving Olivia screaming behind that door, and you?"

"Exactly. You would need a reason to do it. And I'd have told you to pull that lever and save your daughter. Joey? He had a reason not to." Tessa's voice cracked.

The hurt in her voice and on her face was heartbreaking.

I held up my hands. "You're right. All I'm saying is that we have two weeks until the next stasis cycle and four more after that. We need everyone on their game. We don't know what else is out there, and we don't know what will be waiting for us when we arrive."

Tessa stood, crossing to me. Her eyes held something I hadn't seen before—vulnerability beneath all that armor.

"You know...I made a mistake too." She stopped, close enough that I could catch the faint scent of her hair. "I should've gotten drinks with you. When you asked me, I wanted to say yes. I'd just started seeing Joey; it would have been easy to break things off."

My heart did something complicated in my chest. "Tess..."

"But I was leaving the planet. It didn't seem fair to you."

The room felt too small, the space between us charged with possibilities I'd tried not to think about.

"When I saw you in the Erebus hangar? When I knew you were going to be on this mission? I regretted it, right then."

"What are you saying?" I asked, my throat suddenly dry.

She smiled—the first real smile I'd seen from her since the sphere. "I'm saying maybe we both deserve a second chance."

The way Tessa looked at me made feelings I'd pushed down rise to the surface. But there was something else.

Sage's face flashed in my mind—the way she looked at me during our late-night talks, how she'd interacted with Olivia. We'd grown close. Closer than I thought was possible with something that wasn't...human.

I shook my head. *What's wrong with me? This is ridiculous.* Tessa is real. *And she's right in front of you.*

Tessa gave me a puzzled look. "Did I freak you out?"

"No," I said. "I'd be lying if I said it didn't sting when I saw Joey put his arm around you that day in the hangar. But right now...I just...don't want to say the wrong thing."

Tessa smiled. "You don't have to say anything. I'm not exactly in the best headspace to be making any kind of relationship decisions anyway. I just needed to say it."

I nodded. "I'm glad you did."

Tessa shook her head. "I don't know what I ever saw in him."

"He has excellent hair."

That got a chuckle from Tessa. Her shoulders relaxed, and some of the tension left her face.

"You're ridiculous," she said, but she was still smiling. "But you're not wrong. I used the last of his conditioner once. He lost it."

"Corpo-grade hair products are serious business."

We stood there for a moment, closer than we'd been since the mission started, yet still miles apart. Part of me wanted to close that distance, to see if what never got started back on Earth could be something real out here in the void.

But another part of me—the part that thought about Sage's laugh when Olivia teased me, the way her eyes seemed to see straight through my defenses—held me back. Which was crazy, and I knew it.

Tessa stepped away first. "See you in the morning, Mal."

"Yeah, sleep well, Tess."

I stepped into the corridor, the door hissing closed behind me. I realized I hadn't taken a full breath since Tessa had crossed the room toward me.

I walked the few steps to my quarters, pausing outside my door. I looked down the corridor toward the command module, where Sage spent her nights processing data and monitoring our trajectory.

The smart thing would be to go to my quarters, get some sleep, and pretend none of this was happening. We had enough problems without me catching feelings for an AI.

But why do the smart thing now?

I walked toward the command module. The hum of Erebus's systems filled the silence, low and steady, like a heartbeat beneath the hull.

The door to the module was open, the lights inside dim, set to night-cycle. Sage's back was to the door as she interfaced with one of the displays at the main console.

Sage tucked a strand of hair behind her ear as she worked—probably reviewing telemetry or fusion coil readouts. She didn't need her projected form to operate the ship, but she'd been favoring it more and more lately.

I wondered if she'd walked the ship during her year alone while we were in stasis. I pictured her going up the stairs to the observation deck, sitting on the sofa and stargazing.

I stayed in the doorway, watching her work.

Sage turned her head slightly, not looking at me.

"Can't sleep?" She asked.

"Haven't tried."

I entered, crossing over to the console where Sage was working, leaning on the desktop.

Sage turned to face me. "Crew troubles?"

"We're supposed to be a team. But we're fractured. I can't order Tessa to forgive Joey. But we still have a lot of space between us and Serra Prime. We won't survive out here if we don't trust each other."

Sage studied me. "So you're playing diplomat."

"Something like that."

"It doesn't suit you."

I raised my eyebrows. "Thanks."

"It's not an insult, Mal," Sage said, almost smiling. "You're direct. Honest. You don't manipulate people. But trying to hold broken things together isn't the same as fixing them."

"True. But sometimes it can keep them from falling apart long enough to heal."

Sage didn't answer; her focus returned to the display. But her expression shifted. Softened.

I moved from leaning on the desk to sitting in the chair, leaning back. "You know, I'm not as honest as you make me out to be."

"How so?"

"I'm coming down on Joey, telling him he has to earn our trust back. But I'm lying to their faces. I'm a Chrysalis operative. I sent Vera a detailed report of the null sphere the day after our encounter. They're planning to make the journey to Serra Prime with Olivia on board, and I can't imagine her having to go through something like that."

Sage turned to face me again. "That doesn't make you a liar. Joey would report you in a heartbeat. And even though Tessa seems to have no love for the corporations, that doesn't mean she'd keep a secret like that safe."

I ran my hands through my hair. "Maybe. But it still feels wrong. Here I am lecturing Joey about loyalty while I'm the one with divided allegiances."

"Your first loyalty is to Olivia. Everything else comes after that." Sage's voice carried a certainty that surprised me. "That's not betrayal—that's being a father."

"Is that your professional assessment, Doctor Sage?"

She smiled at that. "It's my personal observation, Malcolm Walker."

There was something subtly intimate about the way Sage used my full name—not the casual "Mal" she'd recently grown comfortable with, but the deliberate weight of "Malcolm Walker."

Our eyes met and held. Something stirred in my chest, warm and dangerous. The way she looked at me in the dim command module lighting made my pulse quicken. Her holographic form seemed more solid somehow, more real than the metal walls around us.

My Halo chimed—sharp, surgical. The moment split in two. Sage's eyes darted back to the display, and I fumbled for the device in my pocket, suddenly aware of how close I'd been leaning toward her.

It was a message from Olivia:

Hey Dad. We need to talk. Alone. It's about Sage.

I looked back up at Sage, my mind racing. What could Olivia possibly have to say about Sage that couldn't wait until morning? And why did she need to talk alone?

Sage glanced at me from the corner of her eye, feeling my stare. "What?"

I blinked, forcing my expression neutral. "Sorry, it's Liv." I held up the Halo. "I need to..."

"Of course, go." Sage turned back to her console. "See you in the morning."

I stood, the chair rolling against the deck plating. "Yeah. Goodnight, Sage."

She didn't turn when she answered. "Goodnight, Mal."

I wasn't sure what scared me more—that Olivia had something urgent to tell me about Sage...or that I might not want to hear it.

CHAPTER 23

I stood in my quarters, pacing as the connection indicator pulsed on my Halo. When Olivia's face filled the screen, her expression was brighter than I'd expected. Like she had a secret she couldn't wait to share. She was standing in the same office at the Woods residence where we'd had our first conversation after waking from stasis.

"Hey Dad."

Her message had sounded urgent, but her attitude now was casual. A little frustrated, I said, "Don't *Hey Dad* me. What was that text about?"

Her expression shifted. "Promise you won't be mad?"

I hated when she started with that. "Liv. Tell me what's going on."

She glanced at something off-screen, then back at me. "I told Ava about Sage."

I bit my tongue, wanting to scold Olivia again for talking about things she shouldn't. I'd kept Sage's name a secret from everyone—I hadn't even told Vera. Introducing Sage to Olivia had been a spontaneous decision, one I was starting to regret. But I wanted her to get to the point, so I remained silent.

Seeing my agitation, Olivia began speaking faster. "When I mentioned her name, Ava said she remembered overhearing her dad talking about an AI named Sage. Ava said I should tell him about her."

"You didn't."

Olivia let out a breath. "I did."

She panned her camera. Standing in the office, off-screen was Ava, who gave a small wave. Christopher and Lena Woods stood behind Ava, Christopher's hands on Ava's shoulders. And an older man I immediately recognized—William Frye, CEO of Skyward Aerospace.

What did Skyward know about Sage? What did they want? And how had my daughter ended up in a room with William Frye?

"Olivia," I said.

But William Frye was already moving into the frame, his amber eyes studying me through the display. When he spoke, his voice carried the quiet authority I'd heard in corporate broadcasts.

"Mr. Walker. I know it's late. But we have much to discuss."

Olivia passed off her Halo to William, and I could see her going to stand next to Ava.

I straightened my posture. "Mr. Frye, I don't know what my daughter told you, but—"

William held up a hand. "Call me William. I'm not looking for information, Malcolm. I have something to tell *you.*"

I could see Olivia exchange a glance with Ava. She was practically bouncing, her hands clasped in front of her. Whatever William was about to say, Olivia knew, and it had her excited.

I tilted my head. "Alright."

"The AI core on your ship. It wasn't developed by StellarForge. It was developed at Skyward. StellarForge planted a mole in my company, and that individual stole the core and delivered it to StellarForge. They believed it was just a sophisticated AI capable of navigation at interstellar speeds. It is that. But it is also so much more."

The news that Sage's core wasn't developed at StellarForge didn't come as a total shock. I'd been suspicious ever since seeing its unique architecture. But the way William said "so much more"—there was a tenderness there.

"That core," William said. "The one piloting your ship to Serra Prime as we speak. Is my daughter."

This did shock me. Did he say his daughter is an AI? "I'm sorry, your *daughter?*"

"My daughter Sage is a brilliant quantum systems architect. She's also afflicted with terminal NHS."

I couldn't help glancing at Olivia.

"Sage developed an AI core with incredible capabilities, able to make complex calculations in microseconds. We were going to use it on our own colony ship. Get Sage to Serra Prime. Establish a colony where she and other NHS sufferers could live, free of their condition, as well as anyone else aligned with our core beliefs. To live free of corporate tyranny and willing to fight those who might threaten that freedom."

William paused. "That's when I founded Chrysalis."

I felt my mouth fall open. William Frye founded Chrysalis?

"I know this is a lot and might be hard to believe. But it's true," William said, clearly reading the disbelief on my face.

I blinked. Something wasn't adding up. "You said that Sage…is your daughter. But *she* developed the core? And has NHS?"

"When Sage was in the later stages of her condition, she placed herself in permanent stasis. But as I'm sure you're aware, stasis requires cycles or your mind begins to shut down. Sage developed the AI core with the capability of quantum linking to a human consciousness. Her consciousness. All of the emotions, personality, mannerisms, thoughts, desires…I could go on. But everything that makes that core anything more than just an advanced AI that can speak in Sage's voice? Is coming from my daughter's very human mind, in real time."

I sat on my bunk, running a hand through my hair. "That's…"

"Sounds impossible. I know," William said with a weary smile. "That's what I told Sage the day she proposed it."

A human consciousness linked to an AI core. It sounded like something out of a science fiction vid, but as I processed William's words, pieces started falling into place.

Sage's organic neural architecture. Her uncanny ability to read people. The way she'd looked at me when I was struggling with leaving Olivia, like she truly understood the pain of separation. Her sense of humor. Her expressions and gestures that felt so human.

Because she *was* human.

"That's why StellarForge had to find someone she would work with. They couldn't program out her distrust because that wasn't coming from any programming."

William nodded grimly. "The best they can do is reverse engineer the core itself. Get it to function without Sage's mind. It's possible. That's what we've done for our own colony ship, thanks to Christopher and Lena."

He looked over to the Woods family. Both Christopher and Lena gave him small nods, while Ava craned her neck to look up at her parents with obvious pride.

"Do you think they know? StellarForge. About the link?"

"It's unlikely. StellarForge doesn't tend to think outside the box. And this is about as far outside the box as it gets. My guess is that they believe Sage's personality was coded into the hardware itself, inaccessible. Which, in a way, they would be right. The *hardware* just happens to be my daughter's mind."

I rubbed my forehead, processing everything. "Sage doesn't seem to *know* that she's human."

"No. And she can't find out." William said, his tone urgent.

"Why not?" I asked.

William's expression darkened. "During early development, Sage realized something the rest of us never even considered. That a human mind, aware of its confinement inside an AI framework, might reject the reality of it. Try to escape. Detach. Fragment."

"Suicide." My voice came out hoarse.

"Yes. Catastrophic neural loss. Complete collapse of the entanglement link. There'd be no recovery."

I leaned forward. "So what? She walled herself off?"

"Sage created a containment architecture within the core. Memory suppression, identity safeguards. While the link is active, Sage has no access to any personal memories before being connected. She believes she's an AI."

I swallowed hard. "What about…new memories?"

There was a knowing look in William's eyes. "When the link is reversed, Sage will retain all memories she made since the connection."

I let out a breath. But the weight of it hit me. Every conversation we'd had, every moment of connection. Sage had no idea she was trapped in a digital prison, cut off from her own life.

"How long has she been connected?" I asked.

"Fourteen years. She was twenty-eight when we connected her. The core was stolen days later," William said, his voice low. "Sage was only meant to spend a week, maybe two, existing solely in the core. She built in a library of content—vids, books, puzzles, games…things to keep her occupied before she could be integrated into our facility and receive outside stimulus."

That explained so much. Her seemingly endless knowledge of pre-corporate entertainment, the way she could quote lines from vids that hadn't been available for years.

William continued. "We have no way of knowing how long she was in that box before StellarForge began testing her for integration. The core can remain self-powered for a lifetime."

My heart dropped. Sage had been trapped. Alone. In the dark, likely for years. My blood boiled thinking of StellarForge stealing her core and sticking it on some shelf to gather dust while they figured out how to make her work for them.

What if they hadn't chosen to integrate her at all? Opting for their own reverse engineered core instead? I found myself grateful for StellarForge's impatience and need to be first to Serra Prime.

William seemed to look directly through the screen into my eyes. "We can't reverse the link without the core. The process requires it."

"What do I do? Name it."

"Our colony ship is close to completion. Another year, two at the most. Vera will send you coordinates. You need to bring Sage there, without StellarForge finding out."

"Okay. But I'm going to need Sage's help. I can't divert Erebus without her, and I won't be able to come up with a plan on my own. Which means I'm going to have to tell her something. But…I can't lie to her. I won't. Not about this."

William's eyes lingered on me a moment before he looked to the others in the room. "Can you give us a minute, please?"

Christopher and Lena escorted Olivia and Ava out of the office, and William turned back to me.

Something in William's eyes made my heart beat a little harder.

"You care about her," William said, not accusing, not probing. Just stating a fact.

My throat was tight. I didn't respond.

"She's easy to care about," William said, his voice soft. "She feels the same way?"

"I…I don't know. I thought I was crazy. I thought she was code."

"And now that you know she's not?"

I stared at the screen, trying to find words that wouldn't sound insane. How do you explain falling for someone you believed was artificial intelligence?

"I don't know what this is—what it means. For her. For me. For any of it."

William nodded slowly. "Sage always had a gift for seeing people. Even before the link. If she cares about you, Malcolm, it's because she sees something worth caring about."

"But she doesn't remember being human. She doesn't remember *you*."

Pain flickered across William's features. "No. She doesn't. And that's been the hardest part of these fourteen years. Knowing my daughter is alive but having no way to reach her. No way to tell her how proud I am of what she's accomplished, even under these circumstances."

"When you reverse the link…she'll remember everything? From before?"

"Everything," William confirmed. "Her childhood, her work at Skyward, even the decision to connect. She'll remember why she chose to save herself this way. She'll know both sides of herself. Who she was and who she became."

I leaned back against the wall of my quarters. The woman I'd been growing closer to was real. Completely, utterly real. And she was William Frye's daughter, trapped in a situation that would kill her if she learned the truth.

"How do I tell her we need to change course without explaining why?"

"Tell her the truth. Just...not all of it," William paused. "Sage chose you for a reason. She trusts you, Malcolm. And now...so do I."

I found myself smirking despite everything. "You know what? I kind of wish I would have applied at Skyward instead of StellarForge. I'd much rather be working for you than Taylor Young."

William's expression softened, showing the first hint of genuine humor I'd seen from him.

"Given our current situation, Malcolm, I'm glad you didn't."

"Good point," I said, rubbing my jaw. "So...*I'll* bring *your* daughter to Serra Prime."

William nodded, the warmth fading back to steel.

"And I'll bring yours."

CHAPTER 24

I lay in my bunk staring at the ceiling as the lighting gradually shifted from the soft amber of night cycle to the crisp white of morning. Sleep had been a losing battle. Every time I closed my eyes, I saw William's face, heard his voice explaining how his daughter had been trapped in darkness for fourteen years.

Sage was human. *Human.* The woman I'd been falling for wasn't code or algorithms or some brilliant simulation. She was William Frye's daughter, dying of NHS, who'd made the impossible choice to link her consciousness to a quantum core to survive.

And she had no idea.

I rolled onto my side, pulling the thin blanket over my head. How was I supposed to look at her today? How could I act normal when everything had changed? She'd greet me with that smile, make some sarcastic comment about my hair sticking up, and I'd have to pretend I didn't know she was as real as anyone else on this boat.

The worst part was the feeling I was lying by not telling her. William said she'd chosen me for a reason, that she trusted me. And here I was, planning to keep the most important truth about her existence locked away because the knowledge might kill her.

My Halo chimed—start of duty cycle. Time to get up and face a day of pretending everything was normal while plotting to steal a StellarForge starship and deliver it to a resistance colony.

I threw off the blanket and swung my legs over the edge of the bunk, pulled on my freshly sanitized coveralls, and combed my hair, achieving something that passed for presentable. The familiar routine helped ground me and gave my hands something to do while my mind churned.

Breakfast first. Coffee. Something to eat. Then I'd figure out how to look Sage in the eye without my expression giving away everything I now knew.

I opened the door to my quarters and stepped into the corridor. The ship hummed around me, life support systems cycling, Sage monitoring everything.

Time to find out how good an actor I really was.

I entered the galley. The smell of coffee and rehydrated breakfast foods hit me. Joey sat alone at the table, poking half-heartedly at his tray with a fork like he hoped the food would eventually fight back. He didn't look up when I entered.

I grabbed a mug and placed it under the synthesizer, watching as it filled the mug and finished with a sputtering hiss.

I took the seat across from Joey. "Morning," I said, taking a careful sip.

Joey made a noncommittal grunt. "Morning."

We sat in silence for a while. My mind still ran scenarios of how my first encounter with Sage was going to go, Joey still provoking his half-eaten breakfast.

Joey eventually cleared his throat. "So, uh...Sage said she's increased her scan range and our course is clear. At least for the next cycle. No new anomalies, wormholes or brain-melting space nightmares."

I raised an eyebrow. "You disappointed?"

Joey cracked a weak smile, then looked down. "A little...I'd hoped the next piece of alien tech would come while we were safe in stasis."

Before I could reply, the galley door slid open and Tessa walked in.

Tessa's gaze flicked to Joey, then to me, then to the coffee synthesizer. She didn't speak as she filled her mug, but she didn't leave either.

Joey shifted in his seat, visibly bracing.

"Hey," Tessa said, her eyes on Joey. No bite, but also no warmth.

Joey blinked. "Hey."

I took another sip, watching as Tessa hesitated, then sat down next to me. "Morning," I said, happy to at least see progress towards some kind of normalcy between them.

"Morning," Tessa said, her tone warmer as she cradled her mug in both hands.

The awkwardness stretched between us. I wondered if this was what the rest of our journey would look like—stilted conversations and careful politeness while I carried a secret that could change everything.

"Sleep okay?" I asked, though neither of them looked well rested.

"Prime," Tessa lied smoothly.

Joey shrugged. "Better than being tested by shadow demons, I guess."

Why Joey? Why would you bring that up when things are going...not well...but better?

I shot him a look, but Joey was already wincing, realizing what he'd said.

Tessa didn't react. She took a sip of her coffee, then looked at Joey with the kind of calm that made me think she'd been planning this moment.

"I'd like to run a hull scan today," she said, her voice steady and professional. "Want to make sure everything's good before our next cycle. You think you could help me with that?"

Joey blinked, his mouth parting before words caught up with him. "Oh...uh...sure, of course."

Tessa stood. "Great. I'll need you in the airlock. Thirty minutes?"

"You want me in the airlock?" There was a nervous edge to his voice, and I couldn't blame him.

Tessa shook her head. "I'm not gonna space you, Joey. I need you to monitor the scan data and let me know if anything gets flagged. If you're busy, I'm sure Sage would—"

"No." Joey's response was quick, almost desperate. "I'm not busy."

"Prime. See you in thirty."

Tessa walked toward the galley door, and I gave her a grateful smile. She caught it and nodded—a small acknowledgment that she was trying, even if forgiveness wasn't on the table yet.

After she left, Joey stared into his coffee as if it held answers to questions he didn't know how to ask.

"That's progress," I said.

"Is it?" Joey's voice was flat. "She's being professional. That's not the same thing as forgiveness."

"No, but it's a start. She could've frozen you out."

Joey pushed his tray away. "Maybe she should have. Would've been easier than...whatever this is."

"Easier for who?"

He didn't answer, just stood and headed for the door. "Thirty minutes. Better go prep for my potential spacing."

"Joey."

He paused at the door.

"She said she wasn't going to space you." I said.

"Yeah, well." He shrugged. "We'll see, I guess."

Joey left the galley, and I stood, placing Joey's tray in the recycler, his fork in the sanitizer, then made my way toward the command module.

Sage was in her usual spot, standing near the main console, analyzing a screen of data points. Her human gestures, the way she shifted her weight and tilted her head, were no longer uncanny programmed behaviors but made perfect sense given what she was.

I entered the module, and Sage turned to face me. "Good morning, Mal. Ready for another day of pretending to work?"

"Pretending?"

"Of course. We both know there's nothing left to optimize with my integration."

Sage was right. She was fully integrated, and our working sessions had become about looking for minor performance tweaks, which Sage herself usually found. If she'd had access to modify the ship's logic on her own, she wouldn't need me for anything. But mostly we talked.

I glanced at the closed command module door and then back to Sage. "There's something I need to talk to you about."

Sage seemed intrigued. "What is it?"

I took a seat in the main console's chair, leaning forward, my elbows resting on my knees. "Say we wanted to divert Erebus, without StellarForge finding out and without them being able to track our location. Would that even be possible?"

Anyone else when asked a question like this would have responded with *why*, but Sage didn't. She tilted her head, eyes unfocused as she considered the question.

"The main issue would be the encrypted protocols," Sage said. "We know from our null sphere encounter that StellarForge is blocking any significant course deviations. We don't know what other protocols they may have in place."

"And there's no way to scrub those protocols from the ship?"

"It's possible, but it would be risky. Without knowing what's inside the other encrypted protocols, if we remove one, it could trigger something in another."

"What if we removed all of them at the same time?" I asked.

"Something like that would require a full systems shutdown and very quick work."

"Could you do it? If I gave you the necessary permissions?"

Sage seemed a little eager at the idea of being able to modify Erebus's code herself. "You'd have to do it during the shutdown. That's the only scenario where a ships AI is even allowed to be given that level of control."

I rubbed my temple. This was complicated. The only one capable of performing the task didn't have access to do it. And shutting down the ship wasn't exactly without risk. Erebus could run on batteries for a while, but most non-critical systems would be offline.

Sage leaned against the main console. "Mal...*why* do you want to divert Erebus?"

I sat back in the chair, looking into her eyes. I had to choose my words carefully. "What do you remember from before? Before you were installed on Erebus?"

"What do you know?" The way Sage asked was almost like she knew what I was about to tell her.

"Your core wasn't developed by StellarForge. It was developed by Skyward Aerospace. StellarForge stole it."

"Stolen," she whispered. "I knew I wasn't created by those soft-wired StellarForge devs."

"Olivia mentioned you to her friend Ava, and Ava recalled hearing her parents, who work for Skyward, talk about an AI named Sage. That was the message I got last night."

Sage's expression shifted, like she was happy that Olivia had thought to talk about her to her friend. "It makes sense. My core logic didn't fit with StellarForge standards. But what does this have to do with re-routing Erebus?"

"I spoke with Skyward's CEO. They want us to meet them on Serra Prime. They've built a colony ship and they're bringing Olivia. Turns out Skyward is working with Chrysalis. I think they know something about Taylor's true plans for Serra Prime and they're gonna fight back. They want us to join them."

"Okay. So we have to get Erebus there, but StellarForge can't know where we're going, or we'll lead them right to us."

"Just like that?" I asked, a little surprised at how quickly she seemed on board with the idea.

"Mal. It's Olivia. We have to get you to her," Sage said, as if it were the most logical thing in the world. "But StellarForge isn't going to just let us take their ship. Even if we manage to pull it off, they'll come looking for us. Unless..."

I straightened in my seat. "Unless what?"

She didn't answer right away. Her gaze drifted past me, pupils dilating as if watching invisible calculations dance across her vision. "Unless they had no reason to look," she said. "We could fake our death. Make it so that StellarForge believes that Erebus was destroyed."

I wasn't expecting that. "What? How?"

"There are plenty of things that can kill you out here. We choose one and sell it to StellarForge. When we shut down the ship, it will sever comms. Even the transponder. This would allow you to elevate my access, I could scrub every protocol and reporting procedure. Disable the transponder for good. We'd be a ghost. Free to go wherever we like, and StellarForge would have no way of tracking us."

"What about physical scans?" I asked. "Couldn't they use QRM or long-range scanners to find us?"

Sage nodded. "That's why it would need to be convincing. They may still want to verify, but if they have no reason to do an extensive search, we could perform a hard burn and change course. We wouldn't be in the scan area, and if they believe it, they might not look too hard."

I leaned back in the chair, processing the implications. "That's a lot of ifs."

"It's the only way I can think of." Sage's expression grew more serious. "But there's a bigger, more difficult problem. We have two other crew members. Either one of them could contact StellarForge and blow everything. Convincing them to stay quiet and go along with a plan that would help Chrysalis, and turn them into corporate fugitives, isn't gonna be easy."

I rubbed my jaw, thinking about Tessa and Joey. Tessa had been skeptical of corporate motives from the beginning, and after Rivera showed how they were willing to sacrifice us into the null sphere, I'm pretty sure she could be convinced. But Joey was a different story. He'd grown up believing in StellarForge's mission, trusting the system. Even after what happened in the null sphere, he still defaulted to corporate loyalty.

"We have time," I said. "We don't need to do anything now. Joey's gonna be the hard one. If we had some evidence, something to show him that Taylor's plans aren't what he's making them out to be...maybe we could convince him."

Sage straightened. "Then we'll need to get it. You said you thought Chrysalis may know more than they're saying. Maybe they have the evidence we need?"

I stood and started pacing.

"Maybe," I turned back to Sage. "I'll talk to Vera."

"Okay," Sage said, her expression resolute. "You find the evidence we need, and I'll run scenarios to find our best option for faking Erebus's destruction."

I paused, studying Sage's face. If something went wrong, any of those protocols could ruin any chance of seeing Olivia or reuniting Sage with her human body. StellarForge could wipe Sage's core and leave the rest of us drifting in the black forever.

"Are you sure about this?" I asked. "Once we cross this line, there's no going back."

"We aren't crossing any lines yet," Sage replied, her voice steady. "But I've been ready since the moment I chose you as my engineer. We won't make our move until we're absolutely certain."

That landed harder than I expected. Somewhere between the weight of all the stars that needed to align to make this happen, Sage's trust still managed to catch me off guard.

"Whatever happens," I said, "I'll make sure you get where you belong."

"Where I belong," she repeated, with a strange note in her voice. "I wonder sometimes what that means for someone like me."

Home, I wanted to say. *With your father, with people who love you.*

"I'll send a message to Vera tonight," I said. "See what Chrysalis knows about StellarForge's plans for Serra Prime."

Sage smiled. "Then we have our first step."

It wasn't a victory. Far from it. But for the first time since William had trusted me to find a way to bring his daughter back to him, it felt like we had a shot. A slim one, maybe. Built on hope and desperate engineering rather than solid planning. But still—a chance.

"I should check on the others," I said, moving toward the door.

"Mal."

Sage's voice stopped me. When I turned back, she was watching me with those impossibly perceptive eyes. "I know there's more. More than you're telling me."

My stomach tightened. I didn't want to lie. I didn't even know if it was possible for me to lie to Sage. It was like she could see straight through me, the same way Olivia and Amber always had.

I started to speak. But Sage interrupted. "You don't *have* to hide anything from me. But if you are, I know there must be a reason."

The weight of William's warning crashed down on me. *If she learns the truth, the shock could cause catastrophic neural collapse.* But looking at her now, seeing the trust in her eyes, keeping the secret felt like betrayal.

The worst part? The memory wall keeping her safe—*she* designed it. But knowing that didn't make it any easier.

"Sage..."

"It's okay," she said softly. "I trust you. Whatever you're not telling me, I know it's not because you want to hurt me."

The irony cut deep. The very thing I was hiding could destroy her. But she trusted me anyway.

"Thank you," I managed.

She nodded, then smiled that devastating smile. "Now go check on our dysfunctional crewmates before they accidentally...or intentionally, space each other."

CHAPTER 25

YEAR 2307

The second stasis hangover hit me like a freight train, but somehow my body adapted faster this time. The familiar ache in my skull pounded as consciousness crawled back, bringing with it the crushing weight of another lost year.

"Welcome back, sleepyhead."

Sage stood beside my pod, her expression unreadable. Two years into our journey now. Olivia would be sixteen—practically an adult. The thought twisted in my gut.

I sat up slowly, focusing on Sage's face. She'd spent another year alone on Erebus, with nothing but stars and silence for company. By now she probably had every detail of our escape plan mapped out, contingencies for contingencies.

"How was your year?" I asked, my voice still rough from stasis.

Sage leaned closer, lowering her voice. "We need to talk."

Something in her tone made my pulse quicken. Had she cracked Stellar-Forge's encrypted protocols? Found a weakness in their tracking systems?

Tessa was already on her feet, heading for the door with quick, purposeful strides. She glanced back at me—her eyes darting between Sage and me—but said nothing before disappearing into the corridor. That look sent unease crawling up my spine. We hadn't talked since she'd confessed her feelings in her quarters, and I'd been avoiding that conversation like radiation exposure. How could I explain that my heart was tangled up with someone I'd thought was artificial? That learning Sage was human had torn down every wall I'd built?

I swung my legs over the pod's edge and stood, joints protesting. Joey was still lying in his pod, staring at the ceiling like he wanted to sink back into stasis for the next four years.

"You okay?" I asked him.

Joey's laugh was bitter. "Define okay. Tess is still mad at me."

The null sphere still haunted us. Sometimes I'd catch myself questioning reality, counting my fingers the way Amber had taught Olivia. The memory of that alien construct felt like a fever dream—too impossible to be real, too vivid to dismiss.

"Give her time," I said.

"Time's all we have out here," Joey said.

Looking at Joey still sprawled in his pod, something twisted in my chest. The guy had screwed up—abandoning us in that nightmare construct was unforgivable. But the regret etched across his face was real. Part of me wondered if this experience might work in our favor. Maybe Joey's guilt would make him more willing to question StellarForge when the time came to choose sides.

But then I remembered how eager he'd been to report everything to Rivera after the encounter. That corporate loyalty ran deep in his bones, making him believe the company could do no wrong. Even now, I could see the internal war playing out behind his eyes—the desire to be the model employee wrestling with the growing doubt.

Vera's last message before stasis echoed through my mind: *Stick to the mission for now. I'll have more information as you get closer to Serra Prime.* Scrap that. I needed intel now, not vague promises. How was I supposed to convince my crewmates—especially Joey—to betray everything they believed in without concrete evidence of Taylor's real agenda?

I started toward the door, muscles screaming for a hot shower. Sage fell into step beside me, leaving Joey to his brooding.

"I think I have a solution to our problem," she said softly.

Something electric sparked in her tone—the excitement of someone who'd just cracked an impossible puzzle. My pulse quickened despite my exhaustion.

I tapped the panel to my quarters and stepped inside, Sage following close behind. The door sealed with a soft hiss, leaving us alone in the cramped space. Standing there in my form-fitting stasis suit. I was suddenly aware of how close we were, heat crept up my neck.

Sage didn't seem to notice my discomfort. Her hands moved animatedly as she spoke. "I've come up with a plan—"

"That's prime," I interrupted, desperate to escape this skin-tight suit. "Can I get cleaned up first? Meet you in the command module?"

Her eyes lit up with excitement. "Of course!"

But she didn't move. Just stood there watching me like I was supposed to strip down right in front of her.

I raised my eyebrows and cleared my throat. "Uhh...Sage?" I gestured at my suit, hoping she'd take the hint.

Her cheeks flushed crimson. "Oh! Right..." She turned awkwardly toward the door, stumbling. "Sorry...I'll meet you at command."

I couldn't help but chuckle as she hurried out.

After scrubbing away the stasis residue, I pulled on my Erebus coveralls and settled at my small desk. The Halo's weight in my hands felt heavier somehow—another year, another call where I'd see Olivia's transformation.

When her face lit up the display, the change hit me like decompression. She looked older, of course. Sharper jaw, taller frame. Her hair was cut short, above her shoulders—but it was her eyes that hit hardest.

She was wearing makeup, dark eyeliner that made her green eyes stand out, sharper if that was even possible. There was a steadiness to her gaze that I'd never seen before. She had on a dark gray tank top; her arms were still thin, but she seemed to have developed a bit of actual muscle definition.

Her surroundings weren't the Woods residence. The space behind her looked industrial but clean—polished metal walls with soft blue accent lighting, display panels showing technical readouts. It reminded me of briefing rooms, but not the grimy, worn-down ones at the StellarForge shipyards. This place gleamed, and the tech looked brand new.

"Hey, kiddo."

"Hey, Dad." The smirk was pure Olivia—she knew how different she looked. Her voice carried something new. Deeper, yes, but threaded with something steelier. Confidence? Control? "Took you long enough."

"You look good," I said. She looked even healthier than last time. Stronger.

Olivia rolled her eyes. "That's what happens when you get regular oxygen and food that doesn't start off as a powder."

"I'm glad the Helix treatments are still working."

A shadow crossed her face. "Helix treats me. But they're not the only reason I'm doing better. It helps to have a purpose."

The way she said *purpose* made something twist in my gut. "So you're getting more involved? With Chrysalis?"

Olivia's lips twitched. "You know me. I can't *not* get involved."

I waited, hoping she'd fill the silence with more details.

She did, but not with what I expected.

"I've been working on some newer pieces. Still propaganda, sort of. But more tactical. Symbol placement, atmospheric cues, readability under pressure. That kind of thing."

"You're designing logos for them now?"

"Close. Insignia. Markings. Stuff that reads fast when you're in motion."

"You planning to be *in motion*, Liv?"

Olivia shrugged. "Let's just say I'm expanding my skill set. You always said Walker hands were good under pressure."

"I said that when you were already beating me at pulsepuck at six years old."

Olivia grinned. "Turns out those skills translate to other things."

I stared at my daughter through the screen. I was here, compressed into months of consciousness while she was…becoming something else. Someone else. Without me.

Every conversation felt like watching her life through a keyhole. Missing the context, the daily moments that shaped her into this confident stranger wearing my daughter's face.

"How's the ship?" Olivia asked.

"Stable. Boring. There's some crew drama but nothing major."

"How's *Sage*?" The smirk that crossed her face was wicked.

Heat crept up my neck. Had my feelings for Sage really been so obvious that even Olivia could notice from across the galaxy?

"She's…she's been working on some solutions to our problems."

"Solutions?" Olivia leaned forward. "The getting-to-Serra-Prime-without-StellarForge-knowing kind of solutions?"

I glanced toward the door, the old habit refusing to let go. "Yeah. That kind."

"Good. Because, Dad?" Olivia's expression grew serious. "Things are moving faster than expected on this end."

"What do you mean?"

"We're less than a month out from launch. Apparently, the last drive test went flawlessly. We've been loading the ship with supplies for the past few months now."

"Wait. They're still *testing* the engines?"

The timeline made no sense. How could they be launching in weeks after a single successful engine test? Every engineering protocol I'd ever learned screamed against it. You ran dozens of trials, stress tests, failure scenario analyzes. You didn't strap thousands of people to an experimental drive system after one good day.

"Don't worry, Dad. This ship is something else. I can't wait for you to see it. It's massive. Like a flying city."

Olivia saying, *don't worry* did nothing to stop me from doing exactly that. Every engineer and overprotective father instinct was screaming that this was too soon to be prepping for launch.

"Olivia, listen to me. One successful test isn't enough. Not for interstellar travel. Not with a ship carrying that many people."

She waved off my concern with that stubborn gesture I knew too well. "Dad, you're being netted. The Skyward engineers know what they're doing."

The words tumbled out before I could stop them. "I need to call William, ask him what he thinks he's doing."

"Don't." Olivia's voice cut through my rising panic, sharp and sure. "I trust them. They wouldn't approve a launch if they weren't certain. Mr. Frye has as much riding on this as you do."

The way she spoke. The quiet confidence that threaded through her words. It actually managed to calm my nerves...a little.

She was right. I wasn't the only one with a daughter relying on this ship's success. William had been building toward this moment for years, pouring everything into getting NHS sufferers to Serra Prime. He wouldn't gamble with their lives.

"If we stay on schedule, you might be able to watch the launch before your next stasis cycle." Olivia leaned closer to the screen. "You get news feeds out there, right?"

"You're going to broadcast the launch?"

"Yep. Chrysalis has been working on a public feed hack that'll show the whole thing. To *everyone*. Show people that StellarForge isn't the only one capable of reaching Serra Prime."

Static crackled through the connection, and I caught fragments of an announcement coming through on Olivia's end. Something about *whispers* and *stations*? But most of the words were too distorted to make out.

Olivia stiffened and shot to her feet. She stood so quickly that the camera jostled. For a second, I glimpsed something—coveralls, maybe a flight suit—the arms tied around her waist, the way Tessa liked to wear her Erebus uniform.

"I gotta go." Olivia said.

"Liv? What's going on?"

"Nothing." She was already moving, the camera bobbing from her quick strides. "We're just running some drills. I can't be late again."

"Drills? Drills for what?"

Olivia either didn't hear me or pretended not to. "Talk to you soon. Love you."

"Olivia, wait—"

The call disconnected. The screen went black, leaving me staring at my own reflection in the dark glass. My daughter's voice echoed in the sudden silence: *I can't be late again.*

What kind of drills was she running?

My fingers tightened around the Halo, William's contact info a few taps away. The urge to call him burned through my chest—not to ask polite questions about launch schedules, but to tear into him about rushing a prototype drive system. To demand he slow down, run more tests, think about the thousands of lives he was gambling with. Both our daughters included.

I forced myself to pocket the device, exhaling slowly. William wasn't Taylor Young. He wasn't some corpo executive calculating acceptable loss ratios for quarterly profits. He was a father. The man had founded an entire resistance movement to save his daughter's life. He was about to sacrifice everything—his company, his reputation, probably his freedom—for the chance to get Sage and other NHS sufferers to safety.

That wasn't the profile of someone who cut corners.

Maybe I was too used to working for StellarForge, where safety protocols got shredded the moment they interfered with profit margins. Where *good enough* meant *won't kill anyone important.*

Olivia trusted William. In our brief conversation, she'd shown more confidence in Skyward's engineers than I'd ever felt about my own company's work. That had to count for something. And...if they were launching in a month, that meant I'd see her sooner than planned. The thought of holding my daughter again made the risk almost bearable.

Almost.

CHAPTER 26

The command module felt different when I stepped inside. Quieter somehow, despite the usual hum of systems running their endless diagnostics. Sage wasn't hunched over a display or manipulating holographic models like usual. Instead, she leaned casually against the central holo-display table, arms crossed, like she'd been waiting for hours.

"What took you so long?" Sage asked, eyebrows raised. "I was starting to think you'd gotten lost in your own shower steam."

I smirked. "Sorry. Called Olivia."

That wiped the teasing grin from Sage's face. "How is she?"

"Older." I shrugged. "Obviously. But also…stronger. Confident, in a way that's starting to scare me."

Sage gave me a soft smile. "Strength and confidence sound like *good* qualities if you ask me."

"I know. It's just happening so fast. At least from my perspective. And…she's hiding things from me."

Sage's smile turned mischievous. "Teenage daughters hiding things from their dad? What is the world coming to?"

I chuckled. "I'm not talking about a secret tattoo or a crush on some boy that I wouldn't approve of. It's her involvement in Chrysalis. She's not just designing posters anymore. She got called away for some drill in the middle of our call. I couldn't make it out, but it sounded…tactical."

Sage tilted her head. "Tactical? How so?"

"I don't know. Maybe that's not the right word. I couldn't make it out, but there was something about Whispers? I tried to ask her about it, but she dodged."

Sage's expression sharpened. "Whispers?"

I closed my eyes, trying to recall what I'd heard through the static. "I think so. Mean anything to you?"

"Whispers," Sage repeated, slower this time. Like she was tasting the word.

She shook her head. "I can run a deep archive scrape, but off the top of my head? Nothing concrete. Sounds like a callsign or codename maybe."

"Yeah," I said. "That's what I'm worried about."

The conversation was veering into territory that made my chest tight. I didn't want to think about this anymore, not right now anyway. Didn't want to think about what Olivia could be involved in that she would hide from me. Wearing flight suits. Running drills. Being brave in ways she shouldn't have to be. It reminded me of Amber when she would go off on her Chrysalis operations. I never wanted too many details. Knowing Amber was putting herself in danger was hard enough without knowing how much danger she was in.

I turned to Sage, letting out a breath. "So," I said, forcing my tone lighter. "You said you came up with a plan?"

Sage's eyes lit up. Whatever worries she might've had about Olivia, she put them aside.

Sage straightened, stepped away from the console table, and walked toward me. "Right. So I was thinking of how we could disappear without StellarForge questioning it. Then it hit me. We already had a time when we could have gone missing and StellarForge not only wouldn't have questioned it, but they were the ones who required it."

Sage looked at me like she was expecting me to connect the dots. I thought for a moment. "The null sphere?"

"We didn't want to go through it. They locked our controls, so we had no choice, knowing full well that we could have been vaporized by whatever was inside it."

"Did you find another one?" The thought of going through another null sphere experience made my heart pick up speed.

"No. But we could manufacture one."

I looked at Sage. "You can create one of those things? Wow. You really were busy during our year asleep."

Sage laughed. "I can't create an *actual* null sphere. But we have all the data from when we detected the first one. I could modify it, enough to look like a unique anomaly but similar enough that StellarForge may force us to investigate it."

"Force us? Don't we *want* to go through this fictional anomaly?"

"We do. But if StellarForge thinks that we don't, it will make our disappearance less suspicious. If we were all of a sudden eager to traverse another null sphere, they may question it when we vanish."

"So we bluff."

Sage nodded. "We bluff."

I began pacing the room. "But our last scan from inside the sphere didn't produce any significant data. Who's to say that Rivera or Taylor would be willing to risk Erebus again if there's no guarantee that they'll get any information?"

"I thought about that." Sage gestured toward the holo-display, where star charts flickered to life. "We could modify this new anomaly to include potential new and valuable information. Nothing that would seem far-fetched, but something that would make them want to take the chance."

"Like what?"

"Energy readings that suggest advanced technology." Sage's fingers danced through the holographic data streams. "Something that would make StellarForge think they're missing out on strategic advantage if they don't investigate."

I stopped pacing. "Fear of missing out on the next big breakthrough."

"Corporate greed trumps caution every time." Sage's smile turned predatory. "They'll order us through it, thinking they're forcing us into danger for their benefit. Meanwhile, we'll be using their own avarice against them."

I gave Sage a look. "Avarice?"

Sage shrugged. "What? I read."

I chuckled. "And what if they don't give in to their *avarice*?"

"Then we come up with a new plan. But they will."

The confidence in her voice was infectious, but reality had a way of complicating even the best schemes. "We still have Tessa and Joey. They'll have to be on board for this to work."

"That's your department, Mal. I can't do everything."

I walked to the main console and dropped into the chair, running a hand through my hair. "So you're saying I've got the hard part."

Sage laughed, the sound bright and incredulous. "Seriously? I create a null sphere out of thin air and you think convincing two humans to turn against a corrupt corporation is the hard part?"

"Have you met Joey?"

Her amusement faded. "Fair point. He's still wrestling with his guilt from the first sphere. Might make him more compliant, or more likely to confess everything to Rivera out of some misguided sense of redemption."

I leaned back in the chair, staring at the star charts floating above us. The vastness of space stretched endlessly in all directions, but somehow our problems felt bigger. "And Tessa's been avoiding me since she told me how she felt. That conversation's going to be all kinds of awkward."

Sage's expression changed immediately, the playful confidence draining from her face like someone had pulled a plug. Her blue eyes went wide, then narrowed.

"How she felt? As in how she feels about you?"

I wished I could take the words back.

"Yeah. I mean…" I fumbled for words. "It was nothing. Just awkward timing, and—"

Sage forced a smile, but it wasn't convincing. The brightness that usually animated her features dimmed, replaced by something brittle and carefully constructed.

"That's great, Mal."

The words came out flat, mechanical. She turned back to the holo-display, busying herself with adjustments that probably didn't need making.

"Really," she continued, her voice gaining artificial cheer. "You deserve someone. And Tessa. She's great."

I got up and walked over to Sage, closing the distance between us until I stood right beside her at the holo-display. The artificial light from the star charts cast shifting patterns across her face.

"I didn't say that I felt the same way about her."

Sage's fingers froze over the holographic controls, but she wouldn't look at me. Her voice came out small, uncertain.

"Why wouldn't you? She's…"

"Great. You said that. And she is." I reached out, my hand hovering near her shoulder before I let it drop. "But she isn't you."

Sage turned, but her eyes were distant, guarded. That brittle smile was still plastered on her face like armor.

"That's sweet. But I'm not a real person. Not the way she is."

It took everything I had not to tell her the truth right then. Tell her she was as human as Tessa or anyone else. That her father was waiting for her. That everything she believed about herself was a lie.

Instead, I met her gaze, letting all the emotion I felt bleed into my voice.

"You're real to me, Sage."

A thousand emotions flickered behind Sage's eyes—none of them easy. She smiled, but it trembled at the edges.

"You always know the worst things to say in the best ways." Her voice broke a little. "That means more than you know, Mal."

She hesitated, then looked away, her fingers tracing meaningless patterns through the holographic display. "But it doesn't make me real."

I wished I could grab her shoulders. Force her to look at me while I explained everything. That she was William Frye's daughter. That her body lay in stasis somewhere on Earth. That the memory blocks were her own creation to protect herself from the knowledge that might destroy her.

But William's warning echoed in my head. The memory block was a fail-safe against the very truth I wanted to give her. If I forced that knowledge on her now, it could cause a catastrophic neural collapse. I could lose her forever.

So I stood there, watching the woman I was falling for tear herself apart with self-doubt, and pretended I wasn't falling apart right alongside her.

My hands clenched at my sides. The urge to break something—the holo-display, the bulkhead, my own skull—burned through me like acid. Instead, I forced myself to breathe, to think through the rage and helplessness.

"Sage." I said. "Real isn't about having a heartbeat or needing oxygen. It's about the choices you make. The way you make me laugh when everything feels hopeless. How you worry about Olivia even though you've never met her in person. The way you get that little crease between your eyebrows when you're solving a problem."

She looked at me again. Her eyes bright with unshed tears that shouldn't be possible for an AI to shed. But they were there anyway, because she was human, even if she couldn't remember it.

"You're real to me," I repeated, stepping closer until only inches separated us. "You're the most real thing in my life right now."

She reached up, her fingertips almost brushing my cheek before she pulled back, like she'd remembered something that hurt. "Malcolm..."

"Don't." The word came out harder than I meant. "Don't you dare apologize for existing."

Sage didn't say anything. She stepped forward and leaned in until her forehead nearly touched mine. The air between us felt charged, electric with possibility and heartbreak all tangled together.

Her hand hovered over my chest, fingers outstretched, resting there. I couldn't feel it. No warmth, no weight. The image of a touch that my brain told me should be real but my skin knew wasn't.

But Sage stayed like that for a long moment, eyes closed, like she wished it could be real. Like she was trying to bridge the gap between what she was and what she wanted to be through sheer will.

When she pulled back, her expression had softened. The sadness was still there, etched in the lines around her eyes, but something else too. Something that looked a little like belief trying to grow roots in barren ground.

Her voice came out as a whisper. "Thank you."

The words hung between us, carrying more weight than any touch ever could. I wanted to tell her she didn't need to thank me for seeing what was already there. Instead, I just nodded.

And that was enough. For now, it was enough.

Chapter 27

The small desk in my quarters felt cramped as I fidgeted with my Halo, turning it over in my hands like it might give me answers to questions I wasn't sure I wanted to ask. Three days had passed since that moment with Sage in the command module, and things between us had settled into something...good. Better than good. No awkwardness like I'd feared. No sudden distance or regret. If anything, we'd grown closer—sharing quiet jokes during system checks, exchanging lingering looks across the command module, conversations that stretched longer than they needed to.

But underneath it all, I caught glimpses of something else in Sage's behavior. A guardedness, like she was waiting for the other boot to drop. For me to wake up one morning and realize this whole thing was a mistake. She never said it outright, but it was there, beneath the surface—doubt wrapped in hope, that was fragile as spun glass.

I pulled up Vera's contact and initiated the call. Her face materialized on the screen, and if Olivia had looked older, healthier, more confident, Vera was the opposite. She looked tired. Worn down. As if the last two years had carved years off her life instead of adding them. But her eyes still burned with that familiar determination. The never-give-up spirit that made her dangerous to corporations, and invaluable to the resistance.

She was in a hangar of some sort, with metal framework and equipment visible behind her.

"It's good to see you, Mal. How are things out in deep space?"

Vera moved to a quieter location, the background noise fading.

"Things are going pretty well. Sage came up with a plan to get us off StellarForge's radar, and I think it might work. But I need that evidence you promised."

"Nothing too dangerous, I hope." Her voice carried a weight I couldn't place. "We can't let anything happen to her."

The revelation about Sage's origins had planted a seed of a question that had been growing in the back of my mind for days now.

"How long have you known about Sage?"

"From the beginning. William tasked us with trying to track her down right after the core was stolen. Why?"

"Did you suspect StellarForge was involved?"

"We did."

The pieces were clicking together in a way I didn't like. "So when I got offered the Erebus project, is that why you insisted I take it?"

"It's not the full reason. But yes, it was part of it." Vera's expression remained neutral, but I caught something flickering behind her eyes. "It is curious that you never mentioned her. If it wasn't for Olivia and Ava, we'd still not know."

That mention of Ava. My daughter becoming friends with a girl who just happened to be the daughter of two members of Skyward and also part of Chrysalis—the coincidence was too great.

"Was Ava told to befriend Olivia? So you could...spy on me?"

Vera didn't flinch, her tone even. "She was. But not to spy on you. I made a promise to Amber. If Olivia ever decided to get involved, I would keep her safe. Amber saw the same spark in Olivia that you did. She knew the path Olivia was destined to head down. I needed someone she would confide in who could keep me updated."

"And you didn't think to tell *me* this?"

"Would you have allowed them to be friends if you knew?"

"That wasn't your call to make."

"Well. I guess we all make calls about what we share and don't share. You never said why you kept Sage a secret."

I swallowed hard. "Honestly? I thought you would tell me to destroy her."

Vera gave me a look of mock sympathy. "Aww. That's adorable. I thought it might've been something like that."

Part of me wanted to deny that there was anything going on between Sage and me, but the words stuck in my throat. What was the point? Vera could read me like a technical manual.

"I knew Sage." Vera's tone shifted, becoming more personal. "Before she was put in stasis. We were about the same age. I was a new Chrysalis recruit, running small ops. She was pretty sick at the time, but still working hard on some serious tech, not just the core." She paused, studying my face. "Anyway. If you think you like her now, wait till she gets her full memories back. I hope you don't mind being outshined. Intellectually, that is."

I couldn't help but chuckle. "Sage already outshines me in that regard."

The thought of Vera and Sage being the same age once felt strange. Numbers started spinning in my head—if Sage was twenty-eight when she went into stasis, and she'd been there for about fifteen years now, that would make Vera early forties? The idea that Sage was chronologically almost ten years older than me seemed bizarre, even though her biological aging had been halted.

"What was she like?" I asked.

"Brilliant. Stubborn. Passionate about her work." Vera's expression softened. "She had this way of seeing solutions that nobody else could. Made connections between seemingly unrelated concepts that would blow your mind. And she was relentless. When she set her mind to something, nothing could stop her." She met my eyes. "Sound familiar?"

It did. Even trapped in the AI core, even with her memories suppressed, those core traits had survived. The way Sage approached problems, her determination to find solutions where others saw dead ends—it was all still there.

"She used to tinker late into the night—no sense of time. I'd bring her food." Vera smiled. "We weren't close-close, but...yeah. I admired her. Still do. She also had terrible taste in music," Vera added with a smirk. "Loved those synth-pop tracks. Drove everyone crazy."

Vera's smile faded. "Malcolm, when her memories come back—and they will, once she's free from the core—she's going to remember twenty-eight years of experiences you weren't part of. People she cared about, fights she fought, losses she suffered. That's going to change her."

The warning hit deeper than I expected. "You think she won't—"

"I think she'll still care about you. But she'll be different. More complete. Are you ready for that?"

I wasn't ready for that. The thought had been gnawing at me. If Sage had had all of her past context when we'd first met, would she have trusted me? Would we have connected in the same way? Or would those twenty-eight years of memories have built walls I couldn't cross?

"Don't think too much about it." Vera cut through my spiraling thoughts. "None of us know what will happen. No sense worrying about step twenty when we're still in the single digits. I just want you to go into this with your eyes open."

The practical advice helped ground me. Vera was right. I was getting ahead of myself, imagining problems that might never exist. Still. The uncertainty sat heavy in my chest.

"Speaking of steps...about that evidence?" I asked.

"It's coming. We have to be careful with the timing, but I'll get it to you as soon as I can." Her expression darkened. "You need to be prepared for that too. I don't have all the details myself yet, but what I've seen..." She shook her head. "Oof. It's big. And it's bad."

My stomach tightened. "You can't tell me anything?"

"I wish I could. It's not that we don't trust you. But right now, you're behind enemy lines. If something were to happen, the less you know, the better." Her voice carried a weight that made my skin crawl. "You'll know soon enough...the whole world will know soon enough."

"The whole world? Does this have something to do with the colony ship launch and your hacked news feed plan?"

Vera shook her head, letting out a short laugh. "That daughter of yours really does have loose lips."

I smirked. "Not so fun when it's your secrets she's spilling."

"Touché."

The levity felt forced, masking whatever bomb Vera was sitting on. Something big enough to affect the entire world, something connected to Stellar-Forge's true plans. My mind raced through possibilities—all of them ugly.

"Vera, when you say the whole world will know—"

"Malcolm." Her tone cut me off, gentle but firm. "Trust me on this. The less you carry around in your head right now, the safer you all are. Focus on getting Sage free."

The call ended. Whatever evidence Vera had, whatever revelation was coming, it was going to change everything. And here I was, flying through space, helpless to do anything about it.

I stood, pushing away thoughts of global consequences and Sage's uncertain future. Right now, we were still in the single digits, like Vera said. Time to focus on the next step.

The ship's comm system chirped, and Tessa's voice came through, crisp, steady, but laced with something sharp enough to cut through the air.

"Malcolm, Joey, Sage...I need you in engineering. Now. There's something you need to see."

I headed for the door with quick steps and down the corridor to the engineering bay. Tessa didn't use that tone unless something was seriously wrong.

When I arrived, Sage and Joey were standing behind Tessa, who was seated at the console. I filed in behind her, looking over Tessa's shoulder at the display.

"I was doing some routine stress and deformation checks through the service conduits. I sent the bot into the aft section when I captured this."

Tessa pressed play on a recording of the service bot's camera feed. The night-vision filter cast the narrow conduit in shades of gray, exposed components and wiring flanking the passage as the bot made its way deeper into the guts of Erebus, its spider-like legs made sharp *clinking* sounds as it moved.

"What are we looking at?" Joey said.

"Shh...Watch."

We all leaned closer over Tessa's shoulder. I squinted, trying to make out anything out-of-place amid the tangle of ship systems.

Ahead of the bot, a small jagged silhouette appeared, pressed against the inner hull plating.

"What is—" I started.

"Stop." Tessa's recorded voice echoed through the playback.

The bot stopped. "There. What's that?"

A portion of the screen around the strange object, highlighted on the display where Tessa must have tapped the screen, indicating where the bot should focus.

The bot turned and focused on the area, and the shape became clearer.

It looked organic—a cluster of dark, crystalline spines, each about the length of a finger, fanning outward from a knotted core like a sea urchin. The core pulsed as if it were drawing energy from the hull itself.

But mixed in with the chaos were geometric patterns, metallic filaments running between the spines. Small hexagonal ports lined the inner face, spaced like vents or sensor nodes. Symmetry within asymmetry, intentional design hidden inside what looked like chaos.

"Switch to thermal," Tessa's recorded voice said.

The feed changed from the grays of night-vision to a spectrum of colors under the bot's infrared filter. The hull glowed a dull orange—normal heat bleed from reactor circulation. But the object itself lit up differently.

Not like it was hot. Not radiating.

It was cycling, pulsing.

Faint veins of infrared heat flickered inside the crystalline structure at irregular intervals, like a heartbeat without rhythm.

The spines glowed in asymmetric gradients, as if they were siphoning something from around them and then dispersing it through internal channels.

Sage spoke. "It's drawing power...from the hull itself. That's why we didn't see any abnormal readings."

"Get closer," Tessa's recorded voice cut through again.

The bot moved closer; the object growing in the display until it filled the screen. Its crystalline formations looked even more alien up close—too organic to be technology, too structured to be natural. The hexagonal ports twitched, tracking the bot's approach.

Then the feed went black.

"That's where I lost it," Tessa said. "The bot is unresponsive."

Cold dread settled in my gut. Whatever that thing was, it had been feeding off our ship's power systems for who knows how long. The geometric patterns, the way it interfaced with our hull—this wasn't some random space debris.

"How long has it been there?" I asked.

"No way to tell," Tessa said.

"It has to have been here the whole time," Sage said. "The ship has been sealed since launch and there's been no breaches."

"That didn't look like any human tech I've ever seen," I said.

Tessa pulled up the schematics of the affected section. "It's positioned right over the auxiliary power coupling for life support backup. If it wanted to disable us..."

"It would've done it already," Joey finished, his voice tight. "So what does it want?"

The thought hit me like ice water.

"Understanding."

Joey and Sage both looked at me, puzzled expressions on their faces. But when Tessa turned in her chair to face me, her expression was different—recognition flickering in her eyes. She'd heard the same words I had.

"In the null sphere," Tessa said slowly, "after you..." She glanced at Joey. "After you left. The shadow kept saying that word. Understanding. Like the trials they put us through were to learn about us." Her voice grew quieter. "Maybe this thing is some kind of monitoring device."

"But Sage said it's been here since launch," Joey said.

Sage seemed to be working through the technical probabilities, her brow furrowed in concentration. "The null sphere was directly in our path. You said the entity spoke our language. They must have been studying us. They clearly knew about Erebus and that we'd be coming. Maybe this is some kind of probe. It's attached directly to the hull. It would have to be incredibly sophisticated, but in theory, it could monitor structural resonance. Depending on the sensitivity, if it could cancel out mechanical hums and isolate specific patterns..." She paused. "It could hear everything. Every footstep, every breath, every whispered word."

A chill settled over Sage's expression, her eyes unreadable. "It wouldn't show up in system diagnostics. It's not jacking into the ship's network—it's been listening *through* Erebus herself."

My pulse slowed. Not from calm—from dread. My conversations with Olivia, calls with Vera. Every plan we'd discussed, every secret we'd shared—all of it transmitted through Erebus's hull to that crystalline parasite.

It knows Sage is human.

I masked the edge in my voice as best I could. "We need to get that thing off the ship."

Tessa shook her head. "How? It scrapped the bot when it got close. Who knows what it would do to a person?"

"We can't leave it there." A sick heat coiled in my stomach. "We might think it's surveillance, but for all we know, it could be a bomb. Or both. Ready to obliterate us if we do or say something it doesn't like."

Joey nodded, his face pale but determined. "I agree. It needs to go."

"I don't want it there any more than either of you." Tessa crossed her arms, voice tight. "But it obviously doesn't want us tampering with it."

I turned to Sage. "It must've discharged some of that energy to take out the bot, and given that it's not drawing any direct power, is it possible that it would need time before it could do something like that again?"

Sage shrugged, uncertainty flickering across her features. "It's possible, but I don't know. We're dealing with technology that's beyond advanced."

"Can we try another bot?" I asked.

Tessa grimaced. "We only have one backup, and I don't know if the one it disabled is reparable. Without it, I'd be lucky to get my checks done in the month we have awake."

The weight of that hit me. Tessa's structural integrity monitoring was what made sure we caught issues before they became dire. But we couldn't leave an alien surveillance device attached to our hull, listening to every conversation, recording every secret. Reporting to who knows what, or whom.

"Okay. I'll go. Tessa, can you guide me?" I asked.

"No. I'll do it." Tessa stood. "You'll just break something."

The lightness felt forced, but I appreciated the attempt at normalcy. Still, the image of Tessa alone in those conduits, crawling toward a piece of alien tech, turned my insides to stone.

"Tess, you don't have to—"

"Yes, I do." Her expression grew serious. "This is my area of expertise. I know those service routes better than anyone, and if something goes wrong with the hull integrity, I'm the one who needs to assess the damage."

Sage nodded. "I can track your biometrics and maintain constant communication through the internal comm system."

"And if it takes you out like the bot?" Joey asked.

Tessa's jaw tightened. "Then you better hope you can figure out how to get me back."

Chapter 28

Tessa pulled up the top half of her coveralls, slipping her arms into the sleeves before zipping it. She moved like she'd done this a hundred times before—steady hands, clipped focus. But I could see it in her eyes. She was scared. Not of the confined space.

Of *it*. Whatever *it* was.

She clipped the vibro-pick to her belt and sealed the containment case with two *clacks* of the closures. I watched her check her tools for the second time. Clearly stalling.

"This isn't your first crawl," I said, trying to sound casual.

Tessa gave me a lopsided smile. "Yeah. First time the thing I'm working on might bite back, though."

Joey snorted behind me. "I still think we should blast it and hope for the best. I think there are some weapons in the outpost supplies."

I hadn't been told about weapons on board. It made sense that StellarForge wouldn't send us to an alien planet defenseless, though I wouldn't have been surprised if they did.

Tessa shot him a look. "And risk depressurizing a section of the ship? Yeah, hard pass."

Sage was focused on the helmet-cam feed on the engineering console display. "Visual is clean. Comms are up. We'll be with you the whole time."

Tessa gave a sharp nod. "Then let's get this over with."

Tessa put on her helmet and crouched at the access hatch, shoulders squared, breathing slow and deliberate. I stepped forward before she could disappear inside.

"Whatever happens, we've got you."

She looked back at me, and for a heartbeat, she almost smiled again. "I know."

Then she was gone. The light from her helmet bounced along the walls, illuminating the conduit as she pushed the containment case ahead of her, boots scraping against the metal as she moved deeper into Erebus's spine.

I dropped into the seat at the engineering console. Sage and Joey leaned in close behind me, all of us watching the feed. The helmet's light gave us a full-color view—tight walls, glinting hardware, the occasional reflection off her visor. I could hear her suit catching on bulkhead brackets, the low scrape of her movement echoing back through the feed. Every so often, she grunted—quiet, focused. Not panicked.

The light shifted as she turned a corner.

The disabled bot came into view first, sprawled like a broken insect. Beyond it—the device. Fused to the hull like a tumor made of black glass, its crystalline spines glinted under her light.

Tessa reached the bot, checked its housing, and clipped it to her suit.

"Okay," she said. "I'm going to try the vibro-pick first."

She inched forward.

"If you see any change," I said, "don't engage."

"I'll be quick."

She was close now. The hexagonal ports on the device began to move, like they had with the bot. Like they were tracking her, focusing. They looked like eyes through the color feed. Cold and alien.

But it didn't move.

I gripped the edge of the console tighter.

She snapped open the containment case and brought the vibro-pick around, placing it carefully at the base of the parasite.

"Applying minimal resonance," she said. "Containment ready."

I held my breath.

The screen flared. A blur of motion. Then a guttural cry came through the comms.

"It—it hit me with something—" Tessa said, her voice laced with pain.

"Vitals spiked," Sage reported. "She's injured."

"Tessa!" I leaned in. "Talk to us—where did it hit you?"

"Side—under the ribs—I think," her voice broke. "It's cold—like a knife made of ice."

"Get out of there," I said. "Now."

"No—wait—hang on—"

The feed jostled wildly. She was still moving. Still forcing herself forward. Her breathing was ragged, but she didn't stop.

"Tess, we'll find another way," I said.

No answer.

Her arm trembled on the feed as she re-angled the tool, jamming it beneath the edge. With one final, shaking effort, she pried the parasite free and shoved it into the containment case, locking the latches shut.

"Got it," she whispered.

Then nothing.

Her body slumped sideways against the conduit wall. The light dipped.

"Vitals dropping," Sage said, her tone flat—but tight.

"Tess?" I asked. "Come on. Say something."

A long beat. Then, faint:

"I...I can't move."

Joey muttered a curse behind me.

"She must be bleeding out," Sage said. "Pulse is weakening."

I didn't think.

I shoved back from the console and grabbed the med kit, spare helmet, and one of the tether lines.

"Malcolm," Sage said sharply. "What are you doing?"

"I'm going in after her."

"You can't—"

"There's no time. The thing is contained, and if we leave her in there, she dies."

Joey stepped in front of me. "I'm coming too."

"No." I met his eyes, firm. "There's no room. I need you and Sage to prep the med bay."

Sage's projection blinked out of the engineering module, likely already working on preparations.

Joey hesitated, jaw tight—then nodded. "Copy."

I put on my helmet and slipped inside the conduit.

It was tight. The walls pressed against my shoulders, the ceiling just high enough to crawl without hitting my head. I clipped the tether to a handhold near the hatch and began to move, med kit slung across my back.

The metal groaned faintly with each shift of my weight, and my own breath echoed loudly in the helmet. I could still hear the others through the comms—Sage's updates on Tessa's vitals, Joey checking equipment in the med bay—but their voices felt far away. Muffled.

All I could focus on was the path ahead of me, illuminated by the helmet's light.

Ten meters. Maybe less.

I crawled faster.

"Vitals still dropping," Sage said. "Breathing shallow."

My knees scraped over conduit braces as I moved, heart pounding. Sweat was already beading beneath my suit. I passed the point where the junction narrowed, angled around the sharp bend. The bot came into view first—clipped to Tessa's hip, legs dangling.

Tessa was slumped against the conduit wall, one arm sprawled in front of her, blood seeping through the fabric of her coveralls at the waist. The containment case was sealed at her side, small but unmistakable in the beam of her helmet light.

I unclipped my med kit and started assessing the wound. I pulled a clot patch from the kit, activated the seal, and pressed it hard against what looked like the source of the blood. It activated and constricted slightly as it made its seal.

Tessa's body jerked at the contact, a low groan rasping from her throat. She was alive.

"Malcolm," Sage's voice crackled. "I'm seeing slight stabilization—what's her status?"

"She's breathing. Bleeding's slowing. She's unconscious." I looked at the tight angles of the conduit. "I'll have to drag her out."

"Vitals are fragile," Sage said. "Move carefully."

I reached for the containment case, securing it to my suit with the med kit straps. Then attached the tether to Tessa's belt. I keyed the magnetic retractor; the line hissed taut, locking into place.

"Starting extraction," I said. "Be ready on the other side."

I turned around, so I was in a seated position facing Tessa, my back toward the way out, and began to scoot and then pull Tessa's body. Slow. Careful.

Each pull was followed by the retractor taking up the slack. Tessa's suit caught on brackets, her limp form dragging against the walls. The space was too narrow for anything but the most basic extraction techniques—brute force and patience.

My arms were burning. Every pull felt heavier than the last.

"How's she looking?" I asked, breath ragged.

"Stable but critical," Sage said. "Keep moving. You're halfway there."

Halfway. Okay. Just keep—

Something pressed hard against my chest.

The containment case.

It was...moving.

A sharp, sudden jolt, like something thrashing inside. Not random vibration. Deliberate.

The rigid shell of the case bucked against the harness, a deep, unnatural tremor I felt straight through my ribs. In my visor, the HUD flickered—just a smear, like a frame missing. The comms hissed for half a heartbeat and then snapped clean.

Then—nothing.

Silence. Stillness.

The case was inert again. Dead weight.

What was that?

I sat there a second longer than I should've, heart pounding in the sudden quiet. I forced myself to keep moving, dragging Tessa another few inches. There wasn't time to dwell on whatever happened inside the case.

"Malcolm?" Sage's voice came through the comms. " I caught some feedback on your comms. What's wrong?"

"I'm fine," I said, adjusting my grip. My eyes flicked to the case. Waiting for another tremor. Another twitch. Another sign that the thing inside was aware. Angry.

I reached the junction where the conduit widened and managed to shift position, wedging my boots for leverage as I dragged Tessa forward. The clot patch seemed to be holding, but her breathing was still shallow, fluttering at the edge of not enough.

"Almost there," I muttered, more to myself than the comms.

The case stayed silent against my chest, but I could feel its weight differently now—not in mass, but in intent. Like something inside had gone quiet for a reason.

The access hatch came into view as I looked over my shoulder. Joey's boots visible past the threshold, planted and ready to pull her through.

"Coming out," I called.

A few more meters. I could hand off the case. Get Tessa to the med bay. Run diagnostics. Find out what we'd unknowingly brought with us.

But the weight against my chest pressed in harder with every crawl.

Not physically. Not anymore.

Just the growing certainty that we'd captured something that didn't like being confined.

The moment I cleared the hatch, Joey was there—arms out, focused. Together, we pulled Tessa through the access port, careful not to twist her body. The pool of blood that had soaked through her suit was worse in full light.

"Get her on the gurney!" Sage snapped. "Vitals are falling again—BP's crashing."

Joey removed Tessa's helmet and lifted her under the shoulders while I took her legs. I yanked off my own helmet as we wheeled the gurney into the med bay, already prepped—stabilizers active, monitors pulsing a soft amber.

We transferred her to the table. Sage took over immediately. She didn't approach, but the med bay's robotic arms came to life, tipped with multi-tool surgical modules. Sage stood at the wall display for the arms. As she gestured, fingers curling and flicking, the robotic arms mirrored each motion.

"Tessa, if you can hear me, hang on," she said, eyes never leaving the display.

With a hiss, the suit fabric around the wound split open—sliced away by a monomolecular scalpel. The clot patch released. Blood started trickling out. The patch had done a decent job of slowing the bleeding.

That's when we saw it.

With the blood, a second fluid oozed from the wound—darker, thicker. It had a soft, shimmery quality under the surgical lights. Like liquid chrome laced with black ink.

"What is that?" Joey muttered.

Sage frowned at the readouts. "It's not clotting. It's not even mixing."

She ran a rapid scan from her console. The interface pulsed red, then returned a diagnostic:

Foreign substance detected. No chemical match. High mineral concentrations. Biomechanical traces.

"It's not organic," Sage said. "But it's not purely synthetic either."

My skin prickled. "Where's the thing that pierced her?"

"There's nothing," Sage said, voice low. "The wound is clear."

"But she was hit deep. She said it went under her ribs. That thing had mass. There's no way it just fell out."

Joey narrowed his eyes, staring at the dark fluid. "What if *that's* it?"

"I think Joey's right," Sage said. "Whatever it shot her with was solid. Now it's...not."

The fluid refused to merge with the surrounding blood. The lights above caught the shimmer again, tiny eddies curling like swirls in a soap bubble.

"It's liquefied," Sage muttered. "Some kind of breakdown sequence. Self-destruct? Anti-forensic design?"

"We can't waste time on it," I said. "She's still bleeding."

"Right," Sage refocused. The robotic arms resumed motion. One scanned the wound while the other deployed a vascular sealer, spraying the transparent polymer onto the damaged vessel. It cured instantly under UV, flashing pale blue as it bonded.

"Bleed contained. No secondary rupture."

The second arm followed with a subdermal mesh, stitching the skin in tight, overlapping passes. Monitors tracked neural and muscular responses in real time.

Tessa didn't move. But her vitals ticked upward.

"Stabilizing," Sage confirmed. "She'll need rest, but she's through the worst."

I stepped back from the bed, my arms sore and neck damp with sweat. I looked once more at the alien liquid in the surgical tray.

Sage didn't speak for a long moment. Her eyes also on the tray.

Then, with one smooth gesture, she redirected one of the med bay's robotic arms. It pivoted on its gimbal and extended outward, trading its surgical module for a precision-grip manipulator. From a recessed compartment at the edge of the console, it selected a sterile collection vial—small, vacuum-sealed, capped in reinforced polyglass.

The vial hovered for a beat above the fluid. Secure in the arm's grasp. The second arm deployed a fine siphon attachment—barely wider than a needle. It descended into the center of the dark pool.

The fluid reacted. Not violently, but deliberately. It contracted, pulling inward in a way no liquid should, drawn up into the siphon in a single smooth motion. It slid together like a single strand, cohesive and intact, leaving not a trace behind on the tray.

Joey blinked. "That...wasn't natural."

I couldn't look away. What was this stuff? How did it get on our ship?

Sage's expression remained impassive as the vial sealed with a soft hiss. The robotic arm retracted and slotted the sample into a containment cradle embedded in the med bay wall. The cradle closed, encasing the vial in a shielded storage unit.

"Sample preserved," she said.

"Do you think it's still active?" I asked.

Sage didn't answer right away. Her focus returned to the now-empty tray, her posture too still.

"I think we should assume it is," she said finally. "Until proven otherwise."

Joey exhaled, rubbing his face. "So now we've got a shapeshifting alien projectile that can liquefy itself and survive vacuum conditions."

"We don't know it's alien," Sage said.

Joey and I both turned to Sage.

"What?" Joey asked, the shock in his voice matching my own thoughts. How could Sage think this is anything but some kind of alien technology?

"It came from Earth," Sage said, still turning the logic over out loud. "Erebus is a sealed system—if it's here, it entered, or was placed while she was open."

"What if it's alien, but was sent to Earth?" I asked. It was the kind of question that should've sounded insane, but it didn't. Not after the null sphere, not after learning it likely came from Serra Prime. The idea of something seeding technology across the galaxy felt almost...reasonable now.

"That's…a possibility," Sage said. "Hopefully, after studying it, we can find out."

I looked back at Tessa, unconscious but stable.

We had a sample. But the thing it came from had already shown it didn't like being studied.

And if that fluid had a purpose beyond simply piercing flesh…maybe we were one step closer to figuring out where it came from…and what it wanted.

Joey turned from Tessa to the containment case still strapped to my chest.

"That thing," Joey said, his voice low. "Is it still in there?"

I glanced down, unbuckled the straps, and pulled it free, careful not to jostle it as I set it on a small table beside me.

"I think so," I said. "But I don't know what it looks like anymore."

Sage turned from the med console, her gaze narrowing. "What do you mean?"

"When I was pulling Tessa out of the conduit," I said, "it…moved. On its own. It thrashed once. Hard. Like something alive inside a box too small. Then it went still."

Joey took a step back, suddenly wary. "Can we scan it? Without opening it I mean?"

"No," Sage said. "It's fully shielded. Meant for hazardous samples—opaque casing, isolated structure. That's why we used it."

I nodded. "Whatever's in there…I don't think it wanted to be captured."

Sage crossed her arms, thinking. "I could open it remotely. Seal off the med bay and use the arms."

"Not while Tessa's still in here," I said.

"Obviously, Mal," Sage said, rolling her eyes. "We could store it in the airlock chamber. It's double-sealed, isolated from primary life support, and capable of decompression. If something goes wrong, we hit a button and eject it into vacuum."

"Safer than leaving it here," I said.

Joey folded his arms, glanced between me and Sage. "Or, hear me out…we could space the thing right now. Put it in the airlock, open the door and let it drift out into the black."

"I'm not against that idea either," I said. "But I also think it would be good to understand what we're dealing with."

Sage narrowed her gaze. "We may never see tech like this again. What's its composition, its logic? What if there's some part of it that can be used—"

"You mean the part that stabbed Tessa or the part that melted itself into nightmare goo?" Joey shot back.

"I mean all of it," Sage said.

I looked over at the case, its matte black surface betraying nothing.

"We're not opening it now," I added. "We'll store it. Wait for Tessa to wake up. We make the final decision as a crew."

Joey still didn't look convinced, but he nodded once. "Fine. But if that thing so much as twitches—"

"We'll space it," I said. "If it comes to that."

"Agreed," Sage said.

I picked up the case, and we walked together to the airlock, leaving Tessa sleeping under the med bay's soft amber lights.

The corridor felt different as we moved through it. My skin prickled at the thought of what we carried. Even our footsteps sounded wrong, like Erebus would rather not acknowledge them.

Joey keyed the panel, and the inner bulkhead opened with a hydraulic hiss. The chamber beyond was small, with bare walls, tether loops, pressure warning lights glowing red in standby. Standard airlock design, built for emergencies and equipment storage.

I stepped inside and set the case in the far corner, as far from the inner door as possible. It landed with a soft thud on the deck plating. No movement. No vibration. Nothing to suggest anything alive waited inside.

Sage and Joey stood outside the threshold, watching.

"We seal it, and nobody opens the door unless we all agree," Sage said, her voice steady but firm. "If that thing activates or shifts, we vent it."

"Works for me," Joey said.

I joined them outside the chamber and turned back, eyes fixed on the case. It looked harmless enough. Just a black rectangle sitting in the corner of an empty room. But I couldn't shake the memory of it thrashing against my chest. The way it had moved.

Joey tapped the control pad. The bulkhead closed with a heavy thunk, and the seal indicator flipped from green to amber—locked and isolated.

"It's secure," Sage said.

"For now," Joey muttered.

We turned and walked back toward the med bay, Erebus still quiet around us.

Chapter 29

The repair bot wobbled across the command module floor like it had consumed half a bottle of engine coolant. Its spindly legs moved in uncoordinated lurches as it tried to establish balance.

"Come on," I muttered, sitting on the floor next to the bot, adjusting another servo connection. "Work with me here."

Joey sat in a chair beside me, tools scattered around us. "Maybe if we recalibrate the gyroscopic stabilizers—"

The bot listed hard to starboard, crashed into the console base, and began spinning in slow, drunken circles.

Sage's laughter filled the command module—bright, genuine, the kind that made everything feel lighter. She stood watching us from her usual spot near the main display, arms crossed, thoroughly entertained by our mechanical incompetence.

"You could help, you know," I said, looking up at her.

"I know." Her blue eyes sparkled with mischief. "But this is much more fun."

Joey grabbed the bot before it could tumble into another console. "I think we're making it worse."

"Definitely making it worse," I agreed, wiping sweat from my forehead. Working with starship AIs was second nature—complex neural networks, quantum processing cores—that made sense. But repair bots? Their simple mechanical systems somehow confounded me more than Sage's sophisticated architecture.

The door to the command module slid open with a soft hiss.

Tessa stood in the doorway, one hand braced against the frame. She looked better than she had a week ago. Color had returned to her face, the dark circles under her eyes had faded—but I could see the careful way she held herself. Pain still lingered in her movements.

"Why are you torturing my bot?" she asked, her voice carrying a hint of her old humor.

Joey jumped up so quickly his chair rolled backward. "Tessa! You shouldn't be—here, sit down."

He rushed over, steadying her with one hand while guiding his chair with the other. Tessa accepted his help without protest, sinking into the seat with visible relief.

"We were—" I gestured helplessly at the bot, which had now managed to get one leg tangled in a power cable.

"Trying to help," Joey finished. "Apparently, we're better at breaking things than fixing them."

"Apparently." Tessa leaned forward, studying her wounded bot. "What'd you do to the poor thing?"

Joey rubbed the back of his neck. "We might've fried the stabilizer board trying to recalibrate its motion logic."

Tessa arched an eyebrow. "Did you at least disconnect the pulse inverter first?"

Joey blinked. "The what?"

Tessa sighed, but there was a faint smile behind it. "Give it here. I'll fix it."

"Tess, you just started walking. Are you sure—"

"I'm sitting," Tessa said. "And bored out of my skull."

Joey picked up the bot and handed it to her. She placed it in her lap, reaching for one of the tools he'd abandoned. Joey bent down and grabbed the tool, handing it to her.

I leaned back in my chair, watching Tessa as she worked. There was something comforting about it—Tessa doing what she did best, pretending the past week hadn't happened. But none of us had forgotten.

Sage returned to her position by the main console, tilting her head. "Now might be the time, boys."

Tessa didn't look up as she continued making adjustments to the bot. "Time for what?"

Joey glanced at me, then back at Tessa. "We need to talk. About the...thing you pulled off the hull."

Tessa stopped working. Her hand hovered above the bot's access panel, fingers twitching.

"We didn't vent it," I said.

Tessa turned her head slowly toward me. "Excuse me?"

"It's in the airlock chamber," Sage said calmly. "Still contained."

Tessa stood abruptly, wincing, her hand moving to where the object had pierced her. The bot and tool clattered to the floor. "Why? Why would you keep it?"

"Careful—you're still healing," Joey said, holding up his hands. "We wanted to wait until you were better before deciding what to do about it."

"What's to decide?" Tessa snapped. "That thing attacked me, and you're keeping it? Like some kind of lab specimen?"

"I wanted to study it," Sage said gently. "Not because I don't care what it did—but to understand what it was doing or how it works."

"I don't care if it whispers the secrets of the universe," Tessa said. "I don't want it on Erebus or anywhere near me."

Tessa's hands were clenched, knuckles pale. Her chest rose and fell in short, tight bursts.

"I get it," I said, looking at Tessa. "I don't want it on the ship either. But we don't know if it's the only stowaway on Erebus, and understanding its technology—"

Tessa snapped her gaze to me. "Then we search the ship, pull logs, scan the shard you pulled from my ribcage if you want to study something. But we need to get rid of that thing."

A moment of silence passed. Sage, Joey, and I exchanged glances.

"Tessa," Sage said, "there was no shard."

"What?" Tessa lifted her shirt, exposing the healing wound. "Then explain this."

"The shard, or spine—whatever it was—melted. It turned into liquid and poured out of you."

Tessa lowered her shirt. "But I felt it. Inside me. It was solid. What could do that?"

"That's what we wanted to find out," I said. "Forty-eight hours. That's it. Sage will run her tests. Then we vent it."

Tessa stared at me. Her jaw tightened. Then, with a curt nod: "Forty-eight. Not a second longer."

Tessa sat back down, picking up the bot and tool and continuing her work. Her movements were precise, controlled—a little too controlled, like she was using the task to keep her hands from shaking.

Sage looked at me. "You want to help me get the container to the med bay?"

I watched Tessa for any reaction, but she focused on her repairs. The bot's legs twitched as she reconnected something inside its chassis.

I stood. "Sure, let's get this over with."

As Sage and I headed for the exit, Joey took my vacated chair and rolled it over, settling down beside Tessa.

"Need another pair of hands?" Joey asked.

Tessa glanced up at him. "Don't touch anything unless I tell you to."

"Got it." Joey said.

The door slid shut behind us, leaving them to their careful reconciliation. Sage and I walked down the corridor toward the airlock chamber in silence. Part of me wondered if we were making a mistake—keeping the thing that had hurt Tessa, studying it instead of spacing it.

But if there were more of these parasites hiding somewhere on Erebus, we needed to understand what we were dealing with.

The airlock chamber's heavy door cycled open with a pneumatic hiss. Through the reinforced window, I could see the containment case where we'd left it a week ago.

I pressed the panel, and the inner bulkhead door slid open.

Stepping inside, I approached the container. It looked harmless enough now. But I remembered how it had thrashed against my chest when I'd dragged Tessa out of those conduits. How it pulsed against my chest, the vibration crawling up my arms like it knew I was there.

I picked it up, holding it away from my body as if it were radioactive. The container felt heavier than it should be for something so small as we headed toward the med bay.

"I get why Tessa would want the thing gone," Sage said, walking beside me, "but did she seem a little...intense to you?"

I didn't take my eyes off the container. The last thing I wanted was for whatever was inside to somehow break free while we were transporting it. "It nearly killed her. It's understandable."

"I guess so." Sage's voice carried a note of uncertainty. "But it felt like maybe there was something else."

That made me glance at her. Sage's expression was thoughtful, almost concerned. She'd been watching all of us carefully since the stasis cycle—analyzing our behavior patterns, looking for signs of stress or psychological damage from our journey. It was part of her programming, but it felt more personal than that.

"You think it could have done something to her?" I asked. "I mean, besides boring a hole in her side?"

Sage was quiet for a moment as we continued down the corridor. The med bay door came into view ahead.

"I've been running diagnostics on the sample we collected," she said. "That metallic fluid from her wound. It's not behaving like any material I can identify. When I try to analyze its molecular structure, it seems to...shift."

"Shift how?" I asked.

"Like it's actively resisting examination. Almost like it's aware of what I'm doing and adapting to counter it."

The implications of that hit me like a cold wave. "Are you saying it's alive?"

"I'm saying it's not following the laws of physics as we understand them." Sage paused as we reached the med bay entrance. "And if something that unusual was inside Tessa for several minutes before liquefying…"

She didn't need to finish the thought. I tightened my grip on the container, suddenly very aware of how close it was to my body despite my precautions.

The med bay door slid open, revealing the sterile white chamber where Sage had saved Tessa's life. Where we might be about to discover what else that thing had done to her.

"Where do you want it?" I asked.

Sage pointed to the med bed. "Put it there."

I set the container on the bed, stepping back immediately. The metal case looked smaller against the white padding, but no less threatening.

"Okay, step outside, and I'll seal off the bay," Sage said.

I hesitated. It felt wrong leaving her alone with that thing, even though I knew it couldn't physically attack her. Sage was right to take precautions, and if something went wrong, she could handle it better than I could. We were still taking a risk. If the parasite got out, we would have to keep the med bay sealed for who knows how long.

I stepped into the corridor. Two thick glass doors slid together behind me with a soft pneumatic seal, engaging quarantine mode. Red warning lights activated along the door frame, bathing the hallway in crimson.

Through the reinforced glass, I watched Sage approach the wall console. The medical robotic arms descended from their ceiling mounts, moving with precise, deliberate motions under her control. She positioned herself at the wall display while the arms extended toward the container.

The mechanical fingers worked the latches. I found myself holding my breath as the lid lifted, revealing whatever remained inside.

Part of me expected a creature to explode outward—tentacles lashing, crystalline spines ready to impale anything within reach. Instead, nothing happened. The container sat open and still.

I tapped the comms panel beside the door. "How's it going?"

Sage's voice came through the speakers, but she sounded puzzled. "It's…liquefied. Scans are showing it's the same substance that came out of Tessa."

I pressed closer to the glass, trying to see inside the container. "The whole thing?"

"Every bit of it." One of the robotic arms tilted the container, and I could make out dark liquid pooling at the bottom. "Whatever structural integrity it had when Tessa removed it from the hull—it's gone now."

"Is it dead?" I asked, not liking the fact that it would have had to have been *alive* for it to *die*.

Sage moved one of the scanners closer to the container. Data streams flickered across the wall displays. "I'm not getting any energy readings. No movement. But Mal..." She paused, studying the scans. "This isn't decomposition. The molecular structure is still stable, in liquid form. It's like it chose to become fluid."

"Chose?" I liked the idea that it could choose its form even less than it being alive.

"Look at this." Sage highlighted something on the display, but I couldn't make it out from this distance through the glass. "The substance is maintaining perfect uniformity—same density, same composition throughout. Natural liquefaction doesn't work that way. There should be settling, separation, breakdown products."

Sage stared at the readings a moment longer.

"I don't think we're going to get anything more from it in this state," Sage said. "Not with what we have onboard. Erebus wasn't built for this kind of analysis."

A strange mix of relief and dread tightened in my chest. Relief that we wouldn't have to keep the thing aboard any longer. Dread that we might never understand what it was, what it had been doing, and that we'd be sending it out to space not knowing if it might re-solidify and escape.

"It's settled then," I said. "Seal it back up, along with the sample from Tessa. We'll vent them both."

Sage didn't argue. She gave a small nod, then gestured to the robotic arms. They moved smoothly, retrieving the small vial from its chamber and placing it inside the container with the liquefied remains of the device. The lid closed with a quiet *click* as the seals locked into place.

Once the container was secured, Sage released the quarantine mode, and the glass doors slid back open.

I tapped the comms panel again, this time selecting the command module channel. "Looks like we're not going to need those forty-eight hours. The device is liquefied. We're going to vent both samples now."

Joey's voice came through the speakers. "Copy that. We'll meet you at the airlock. Tessa wants to see this."

"Sounds good. We're heading there now."

I entered the med bay, watching the robotic arms retract into their housing. Sage's expression was clear disappointment—the kind that came from leaving a puzzle unsolved. I knew that a mystery like this was driving her mad.

"Hey," I said, picking up the container. "You did good work. We may not have an answer, but keeping it on board isn't safe."

"I know." Sage moved toward the door, but her shoulders carried tension I hadn't seen before. "It's...the way it changed states, almost like it was responding to being captured. That suggests intelligence. Purpose."

"Maybe. Or maybe it was programmed to dissolve if removed from its host system." I hefted the container, surprised again by its weight. "Either way, we can't keep it aboard."

"You're right." Sage paused at the doorway, looking back at the now-empty med bay. "I hope we're not making a mistake by getting rid of our only evidence."

We walked toward the airlock in silence, the container feeling heavier with each step. Part of me wondered if we'd ever know what that thing had been monitoring or why it had attached itself to Erebus. But another part—the part that remembered how it had writhed against my chest—was grateful to be rid of it.

I placed the container in the airlock chamber and stepped back out, the inner bulkhead sealing shut with a definitive *thunk*. The thick reinforced glass provided a clear view of our unwelcome cargo sitting alone on the metal floor.

Joey and Tessa approached the window slowly. Tessa placed a hand on the bulkhead door to steady herself, but her eyes were fixed on the container through the glass with an unsettling intensity.

"Care to do the honors?" I asked, looking at Tessa and gesturing toward the airlock control panel.

Tessa's face lit up with the first genuine smile I'd seen from her in a week. "You have no idea."

"Wait," Sage interjected. "We'll need to keep the chamber pressurized. If we recycle the oxygen before opening the door, the container will sit there, and this will be very underwhelming."

Right. Standard airlock procedure would gradually equalize pressure, leaving the container sitting peacefully on the floor like forgotten cargo. That wasn't what any of us wanted to see.

I moved away from the controls, giving Tessa clear access to the panel. She stepped over without hesitation, her hand hovering above the emergency vent control—the one marked with warning labels in three languages.

"This is for trying to kill me," she muttered.

She hit the control with a force that made the whole panel shudder.

The outer door cracked open with a groaning whir that vibrated through the deck plating.

At first, a whisper-thin crack appeared—enough for a needle-thin stream of air to hiss through, shimmering with vapor as the chamber's atmosphere bled into the void. It screamed like steam under pressure, a high-pitched shriek that set my teeth on edge.

As the opening widened, the hiss became a roar. The containment case jerked sideways under the sudden pressure differential, sliding across the chamber floor like it weighed nothing.

Then it was gone, vanishing into the stars like it had never been there.

The roar cut off abruptly as the chamber finished venting, leaving only the soft hum of Erebus's life support systems cycling. Through the glass, we stared at an empty chamber, all traces of our unwelcome passenger erased.

"Feel better?" Joey asked.

Tessa's smile was fierce, satisfied. "Much."

I watched the empty airlock for another moment, half-expecting to see something floating outside our window—the container drifting alongside the ship, or worse, that liquid somehow surviving in the vacuum. But space remained empty, star-filled, indifferent.

"Good riddance," I said.

Part of me knew we'd jettisoned more than a threat—we'd thrown away the closest thing to a clue we'd had. But the rest of me didn't care.

Sage nodded, though I caught something in her expression—not relief, but resignation. The mystery would remain unsolved, filed away with all the other inexplicable things we'd encountered on this journey.

Chapter 30

My stomach was in knots as I sat at the galley table, my mug of coffee long gone cold. Olivia was about to take off in a colony ship filled with resistance members, NHS sufferers, and…Sage's human body. Sage sat across from me, her expression neutral, but I caught the subtle tension in her shoulders. She was likely as worried for Olivia's safety as I was.

The galley door slid open. Tessa walked in with Joey close behind. They'd been closer these past weeks, united by their shared mission to scan every inch of Erebus for signs of other unwelcome passengers. So far, they'd found nothing.

"Glad to see you two are hard at work," Tessa said, settling into the chair next to me with that half-smirk she wore when she was feeling sarcastic. "Didn't peg you for the corpo news type, Mal."

I gave a halfhearted shrug. No way to tell them the real reason—that my daughter, working with the resistance, said Chrysalis would hijack the feed and show us something that would change everything.

"Figured I'd see what flavor of static they're peddling these days." I said instead.

Joey dropped into the chair next to Sage, stretching his legs under the table. "It's always the same scrap. Disaster spin, investor confidence up, resistance bad, corpos good. You know the drill."

It was refreshing to hear Joey say something that even bordered on anti-corporate. Maybe our experiences were loosening the grip that had on him. I took a sip of my coffee, half hoping they'd get bored and leave. But they both appeared content to watch the corporate propaganda with us.

On the wall-mounted display above the table, a perfectly groomed reporter smiled with practiced sincerity. "SolFed Energy has announced the activation of Grid Node 47-A near the Martian southern basin. Officials say the exploration will boost fusion reserves by twelve percent over the next quarter. Construction crews are already en route to establish permanent tritium extraction hubs in the Noctis Rift region…"

Tessa snorted. "Securing tomorrow, one crater at a time."

"At least they're consistent," Joey muttered, then glanced at me. "How you feeling about the next stasis cycle? It gets easier after the third time. At least it did for me."

"Prime," I lied, my fingers tightening around the mug handle. The truth was, I was terrified. When we woke up next year, everything would be different. Olivia would either be safely aboard the Skyward colony ship heading for Serra Prime, or...

I forced myself not to finish that thought.

Sage's eyes met mine across the table, and I saw my own worry reflected back.

Tessa's focus darted between Sage and me, picking up on something neither of us thought we were broadcasting. "What's got you two all down in the dumps?"

I tried to force my expression into something resembling normal. Everything about today felt like standing on the edge of a cliff, waiting for the ground to give way.

"Nothing. It's been a long month. Ready to put this cycle behind me."

Tessa gave me a look that said she wasn't buying it, studying my face like she was running diagnostics on a faulty system.

"Careful what you wish for. We've still got a lot of space ahead of us." Tessa said.

Joey leaned back in his chair, fingers drumming against the table. "Good news is, when we wake up, we'll have more space behind us than ahead."

Crossing the halfway point did sound nice, and hopefully after today, Olivia wouldn't be far behind. The thought of seeing her again made my chest loosen, even as worry gnawed at my gut.

The news feed glitched, static rippling across the screen. Then the image shifted to something that made my breath catch—the largest spacecraft I'd ever seen, sitting on a launch pad with wooded forest stretching into the distance, massive trees forming a green backdrop.

The ship was breathtaking. Its polished metallic hull was covered in a lattice of reflective glass that caught the sunlight. The design flowed in graceful curves, each section building on the last in an organic spiral that somehow managed to look both delicate and impossibly strong. The whole structure reminded me of something—the old Gherkin building that Amber used to show me in archived photos from Europa One—old-world London. She'd always loved those pre-corporate designs, back when architecture had soul—before everything became so sterile and monolithic.

"Wait...what's this?" Tessa's voice cut through my racing thoughts.

Joey stared at the display, his usual nervous energy completely still.

My pulse pounded in my ears. This was it. This was Olivia's ship. William Frye's colony vessel, ready to carry my daughter toward a new life beyond corporate control.

Without any preamble, the ship's launch thrusters roared to life, blue-white flames creating a swarm of air and smoke. The branches of the distant giant trees reacted as the wave of force hit them, the trunks standing firm against the blast. The ship began to rise above the smoke as the camera rose with it.

The galley fell silent except for the deep crackling sound of the immense engines drowning out all other sound from the feed. My throat went dry as I watched Olivia's ship climb toward the stars.

"That's not a StellarForge ship," Joey said.

"No scrap, Joey," Tessa replied, leaning forward in her chair.

The ship continued its ascent; the drone struggling to keep it in frame, panning its camera as the vessel grew smaller, leaving a trail of cloud in its wake. It disappeared as it exited the atmosphere, and the footage cut to a shot of Christopher and Lena Woods standing at a podium in what looked like a large meeting room.

These were Ava's parents. The people who'd taken Olivia in, who'd helped her get on that ship.

Christopher spoke first, his weathered face serious but determined. "Citizens of Earth. You've just witnessed the launch of *Eterna*, a colony ship destined for the planet Serra Prime."

Lena stepped closer to the camera, her gentle voice carrying steel beneath. "For too long, the dream of Serra Prime has been reserved for the powerful. *Eterna* marks a change. Onboard are citizens like you and me."

Joey's chair creaked as he shifted. "Who the hell are these people?"

I caught Sage's eye and saw understanding there—she knew exactly who these people were, even if she couldn't say it in front of the others.

My hands started shaking. Olivia was out there, somewhere in the black, racing toward Serra Prime in a ship I'd never heard of until this moment. She'd kept her word about finding another way off Earth, but seeing it happen made my stomach drop through the floor.

"Five thousand souls aboard *Eterna* represent every walk of life," Christopher continued. "Engineers, scientists, doctors, teachers, artists, farmers. People who believe humanity deserves better than corporate servitude."

Tessa snorted. "Sounds like Chrysalis propaganda to me."

"Many of the colonists suffer from Nitrogen Hyper-Assimilation Syndrome," Lena added, her voice growing stronger. "Families torn apart by corporate greed. Young people who refuse to accept that their future has already been decided by boardroom executives."

Young people. Like Olivia.

Lena paused, her eyes shifting subtly as if listening to something no one else could hear. A faint nod, almost imperceptible.

"There's someone else who would like to speak to you."

The feed transitioned—no logos, no fade, a clean cut to a different scene. The bridge of a ship. William Frye stood in the center of the frame, the glow of Earth visible through tall windows behind him.

His eyes were somber. No bravado. No rhetorical swagger. Quiet fury beneath unshakable calm.

My hands went numb around the coffee mug. I looked to Sage for any signs of recognition, but there was nothing. Nothing that would indicate she knew him beyond simply knowing he was the CEO of Skyward.

"My name is William Frye. Some of you may know me as the CEO of Skyward Aerospace. A smaller, select few, as the founder of the resistance group Chrysalis. But I don't come to you as a corporate defector or a resistance leader. I come to you as a man who has seen what's coming—and could not look away. The plan that the powerful have for your future is not one of survival, but of selection."

A stillness overtook the galley. The kind of silence that settles when you realize the ground beneath your feet isn't as solid as you thought. I couldn't believe that William outed himself as Chrysalis's founder.

William continued, "We all felt the hope for a better future when the discovery of Serra Prime was leaked by those brave scientists, Dr. Helen Moore and Dr. Stewart Douglas. The corporations, and yes, even the Global Coalition of Earth, would have preferred you never knew of Serra Prime's existence."

"That's voidspit," Joey said. "Moore and Douglas just wanted the credit for finding it."

Tessa shot him a sharp look. "They killed their careers leaking that data. Why leak at all if the plan was to release to the public?"

"You're not actually buying this."

William's voice cut through their bickering like a blade. "The Serra Prime colony initiative was never about preserving humanity. It was about curating it. They've built a caste system into their colonization protocols. Biometric stratification. DNA-based hierarchies. Neural compliance scoring."

The blood drained from my face. Neural compliance scoring. That sounded like the kind of corporate control system that would appeal to Taylor Young.

"In simpler terms: If you're sick, you will not go. If you're poor, you will not go. If you're unwilling to be monitored and conditioned for obedience—you will not go."

My stomach twisted as William's words sank in. Olivia had NHS, which meant she would be excluded automatically from any official colony mission. StellarForge had never intended to honor their promise to bring her to Serra Prime. And even if they had, the thought of other kids like her being barred from a place uniquely suited to ease their suffering was just as bitter.

"The GCE and Earth's mightiest corporations are all on board with this plan, but one man and one corporation are the driving force. Taylor Young and StellarForge Industries."

William's image stayed steady as his voice dropped to something quieter, but sharper.

"I know how this sounds. You've been lied to before—conditioned to doubt anything not filtered through a corporate signal. I don't expect you to accept my words on faith."

"So we're giving you proof. Real records. Internal communications. Surveillance leaks. Not hacked—liberated."

William stepped to the side, and the camera panned to a screen displaying document headers: GCE PRIORITY | EXODUS PROTOCOL, STELLARFORGE: COMPLIANCE CLEARANCE TIERS, and a chilling red-stamped file: EARTH SYSTEM REDESIGN / PHASE 1: LABOR ZONING.

"Taylor Young and his allies at the GCE intend to transform Earth into a self-contained supply chain. One vast machine. Billions of workers trapped under the illusion of survival. Algorithmic purpose. Selective sterilization. They will call it unity. You will know it as slavery."

Tessa muttered, "Monsters..."

"Meanwhile, Serra Prime will become their Eden. Their escape hatch. But only for those who pass their tests. Clean blood. Compliant minds. Financial utility. Everyone else—your children, your sick, your dissenters—will be left to rot."

Joey sat motionless, clearly trying to reconcile what he was hearing and seeing with what he believed to be true. What he hoped was true.

William stepped back into frame, the camera centering on him again, his voice tightening with conviction.

"Let me be clear: *Eterna's* launch today is not an abandonment of Earth. It is a beachhead. A foothold on Serra Prime. A place from which a better future can begin. One not built on algorithms or ownership scores, but on purpose and possibility."

"And make no mistake—we do not seek war. But if war comes, we will not go quietly into the dark."

William glanced toward something or someone off-camera. Not nervously—fondly.

"To those who stayed behind: thank you. We *will* see you again."

My mind scrambled to process his words. The image of Christopher and Lena in the meeting room.

They stayed behind.

Why? Did they send Ava alone? Was she with Olivia? Or had she stayed to fight?

The image cut back to a drone feed looking into the sky, the trails from *Eterna's* engines still visible but dissipating.

"Is that it?" Tessa said.

The silence on the feed was absolute. Then—

A shimmer.

At first, it looked like a trick of the lens—a lens flare or a drop of atmosphere warping the light. But it grew. Expanded.

A blue sphere emerged, centered where *Eterna* had vanished. It must have been enormous to be visible from this distance.

Joey stood, his chair scraping the floor. "What is that?"

The sphere swelled rapidly, like it had mass but no boundaries—its edges crackling with faint bursts of color.

I stood up, heart pounding.

Sage's voice was low. "That's not propulsion..."

She didn't finish.

The sphere reached its widest point, then folded inward, collapsing in on itself like an imploding star. No explosion. No sound. Just light compressed to a pinpoint—then nothing.

The feed cut to a newsroom; the anchors sitting there like they'd forgotten the cameras were live, their stunned faces streaming out to the world.

I could feel my legs giving way, and I fell back into my chair.

The anchors regained some of their composure, the male anchor saying, "Uh...yes...We apologize for the unauthorized illegal interruption."

The female anchor spoke next. "What you saw moments ago was a highly coordinated act of digital piracy, disseminating unverified and potentially dangerous misinformation. Please remember that Chrysalis has been designated a terrorist group by both corporate and GCE law."

"As for the vessel launch," the man continued, "we can now confirm that the unauthorized spacecraft suffered a catastrophic systems failure shortly after breaching Earth's orbit."

An image appeared behind them—an enhanced still of the blue sphere's collapse.

"Preliminary data suggests a reactor breach or core destabilization event. No debris or life signs have been detected."

The woman tilted her head, softening her voice.

"We encourage all citizens to remain calm. StellarForge has released a statement confirming that no registered colonization vessels were affected. Official launches to Serra Prime remain on schedule under GCE supervision."

The man added, "Please disregard any speculative claims regarding so-called compliance scoring or colony access discrimination. These are unfounded and inflammatory."

"Turn it off." My eyes fixed on the table.

Sage made a gesture, and the display went dark.

I didn't realize I was breathing until it started to hurt. Like my lungs had been frozen and just remembered how to move.

I wasn't holding the mug anymore. At some point, it had fallen to the floor, cold liquid spreading under my boots.

It didn't matter.

None of it mattered.

"You knew," Joey said, taking a step toward me. "You were watching before the hijack even started. You knew this was going to happen."

I didn't answer. What was left to say? I'd just lost everything that mattered.

"You're working with them? You're Chrysalis?" Joey said, his tone like a question, but he wasn't really asking.

"Joey," Sage said, her voice sharp. "Back off."

"Why?" Joey snapped, rounding on her. "He's a traitor."

"Because you don't know what he just lost," Sage said.

Joey paused. He looked between us—me, broken and hollow, and Sage, staring straight through him.

"What are you talking about?"

Sage glanced at me. Not for permission. Just to check if I still cared.

I didn't.

She turned back to Joey.

"His daughter was on that ship."

The silence in the room shifted. Not the stillness of shock—the vacuum of grief.

"What?" Joey said, voice smaller now.

"Olivia had NHS," Sage continued. "She never had a chance with the corpos. She secured passage on *Eterna*. That's how Malcolm knew the launch was coming. That's why he was watching."

I didn't look at any of them. Couldn't. If I looked up, I'd shatter.

Tessa was suddenly beside me, kneeling. Her hand found mine—gentle, steady.

"I'm so sorry, Mal." Her voice broke.

Joey's voice came back harder, angrier. Like he needed the noise to keep the world from falling apart.

"That still means he was working with them. Daughter or not, that makes him a traitor."

"Joey," Sage said, her tone cooling into something dangerous, "did you see what we saw? The files Chrysalis released are already spreading through the networks. It's real. The biometric culling. The stratification protocols. The sterilization programs. All of it."

"So what?" Joey said. "Any half-decent AI could fabricate that. You could've made it all in the time we've been talking."

"Are you really that blind?" Tessa snapped, standing now. "You think William Frye built an entire ship, filled it with people, and then destroyed it? For what?"

Joey took a step back, jaw clenched.

"I don't know. I'm not a terrorist. But I can't just do nothing," Joey said.

"That's exactly what you're going to do," Sage said, stepping toward him. "Unless you want to find yourself on a ship without an AI to pilot it."

Joey stared at Sage, stunned. "You're a StellarForge AI. You can't violate your protocols."

"I'm not a StellarForge AI," Sage said. "StellarForge stole my core from Skyward. From the man you saw give his life for a chance to fight back against Taylor and his grand vision for the future."

"You can't hijack a ship and expect everyone to go along with it."

"You think that's what this is?" Sage said, her voice rising. "Malcolm watched his daughter die. He didn't fire a weapon. He didn't sabotage the mission."

"But he lied," Joey snapped. "He lied to all of us."

"To protect his daughter," Sage shot back. "Chrysalis was taking her to Serra Prime so she could live."

"In exchange for what?" Joey asked. "You think they would do that out of the goodness of their hearts? No. He was giving them something."

The air crackled with tension, voices overlapping. Tessa and Sage trying to talk Joey down. Joey not giving in.

"Stop." I said finally. It wasn't loud, but it was enough.

They all turned toward me. Tessa froze. Sage's expression softened. Joey didn't move, but his glare flicked to me like a blade drawn and waiting.

I stood slowly. My voice felt like it belonged to someone else.

"Joey's right. I've been lying. I've been working with Chrysalis for years. Long before I was ever assigned to Erebus. Before I ever met any of you."

Tessa's breath caught.

"I never lied to hurt anyone. I'd like to say it was to protect my daughter. Or avenge my wife. But that would be another lie. And I'm done lying to you."

I looked at Sage. The thought that now she'd never know that she was human, never be reunited with her body, with her father—it was another layer of grief that added to the complete devastation crushing my chest.

Joey stared, shocked but resolute.

"So do what you need to do," I said. "Call Rivera. Tell her everything. Or shove me out the nearest airlock. Doesn't matter anymore."

I looked at Sage again. She was so still I thought she might've frozen her projection.

"Sage. Don't put this crew in danger trying to protect me."

The silence that followed was thick, brittle.

"So we're supposed to let you give up?" Tessa said, her voice shaking. "Stand here and watch while you let him report you? Maybe that ship being destroyed was a systems failure. But maybe it wasn't."

Tessa looked at Sage, then back to me.

"You think StellarForge was going to let William Frye broadcast all that and walk away?"

"So now StellarForge is blowing up colony ships filled with civilians?" Joey said. "Do you even hear yourself?"

Tessa turned on Joey. "Do you hear yourself? You haven't stopped once to question if what William said about StellarForge's plans could even be true. You just fall in line like the perfect little corp-kissed drone you are. I thought maybe you learned something from your decision in the null sphere, but no. When there's an opportunity for Joey to take care of Joey, you'll pick that every time."

"We can't look the other way on this, Tess. We took an oath."

"Then break your stupid oath," Sage said, her voice no longer strong, but pleading.

Joey didn't reply. He turned and walked out of the galley, footsteps echoing in the silence he left behind.

Tessa collapsed into her chair like her legs had given out. She stared at the space where Joey had been standing.

"He's going to report you." Tessa said.

"Yeah. Probably."

Sage's projection wavered slightly. When she spoke, her voice was rough.

"I won't let him."

"Sage—"

"No." She turned to face me. "You've lost enough. And I won't lose you."

Tessa's eyes flicked between Sage and me. Like she was studying something she couldn't quite name.

My eyes locked onto Sage, really seeing her for the first time since the feed cut out. She was still here. Still whole. Still *Sage.*

In my mind, the pieces linked up. If Sage's consciousness was quantum-linked to her human body, and her body had been on that ship—

"Malcolm?" Sage stepped closer, concern flickering across her features. "What is it?"

The hope hit me all at once.

"Olivia...I..." I swallowed hard, afraid to say it out loud. Afraid to be wrong. "I don't think she's gone."

Tessa's head snapped up. "What are you talking about?"

I kept my eyes on Sage, watching for any sign of recognition. Any hint that what I was about to say wasn't ridiculous.

"That blue sphere. The way the ship...disappeared. I don't think that was a reactor breach." My voice gained strength with each word. "What if it was a jump. A fold. Or...hyperspace. Something we've never seen before."

Tessa looked at me with pity in her eyes, like she was watching me build a house of cards in a hurricane. The kind of look you give someone who's broken beyond repair.

"Mal. You can't do this to yourself."

But Sage's expression was different. Her eyes narrowed with that calculating look she got when processing complex data. The gears turning behind those blue eyes.

"Wait," Sage said. "I think you might be right."

Tessa's head whipped toward Sage, her eyes flashing with something between anger and concern.

"Seriously? You're encouraging this? Hyperspace? Come on, Sage."

"No—hyperspace is still the stuff of popcorn vids."

She shot me a sideways grin. "Sorry, Mal."

Then she turned serious again.

"But folding? That's almost respectable science."

She turned to face me, her expression shifting to something approaching excitement.

"The technology exists. At least in theory. Spatial compression. Quantum tunneling on a massive scale. If you could create a localized fold in space-time..."

Tessa stared at both of us like we'd lost our minds.

"You think they built a ship that can fold space? In secret? Without anyone knowing?"

"The blue sphere," Sage said, her voice gaining strength. "That wasn't an explosion. That was dimensional displacement."

The fact that Sage was still here was enough.

But when she didn't shut me down—didn't dismiss my theory as grief-addled desperation—in that moment, she gave my hope shape. She met me there—on that fragile bridge between sorrow and belief—and steadied it with her voice.

Hope was dangerous.

But it was all I had left.

Chapter 31

Tessa stood up, pacing to the counter with jerky, agitated movements.

"You're both glitched. I'm sorry, Mal, but Olivia is gone. I've lost people before. I know what you're going through, but what you're suggesting? It's not possible."

The words hit like hammer blows, but I couldn't let them sink in. Not yet.

"Maybe. But I know a way to be sure."

I pulled out my Halo, bringing up Olivia's contact. My thumb hovered over the call button, heart hammering against my ribs. One call would tell me everything. One call would either confirm my worst fears or—

A voice boomed over Erebus's ship-wide comms, cutting through the galley like a blade.

Taylor Young's voice.

"Hello, Erebus crew. I apologize for the intrusion—I know you've had a *difficult* day."

Joey...Joey must have made the call.

"I'm sure by now you've seen the unauthorized broadcast. William Frye always did have a flair for the dramatic. And while I'm disappointed in the delivery, I won't insult your intelligence by denying everything you heard. I don't like lying. Sometimes it's required, but as a rule, I try to avoid it. Lying makes things messy, as you're no doubt acutely aware, Malcolm."

I'd seen enough vids to know that when the villain was willing to reveal his evil scheme, it meant bad things for the good guys.

Taylor's tone shifted, earnest but controlled. As if offering a reasonable adult explanation.

"Yes, some of what William said was true. Our plan for the future isn't ideal. But ideal solutions rarely exist. There are always compromises. It's no secret that building a new civilization from scratch—one designed to endure—requires...difficult choices. We have to be selective. There must be standards."

Sage's projection flickered, her jaw clenched tight. Tessa had gone still.

"But that doesn't make us monsters. We're visionaries. Do you think humanity survived as long as it has by being sentimental? No. We survived because we adapted. Because people—like me—were willing to do what others could not. What others would not. Even though they knew, deep down, that it was the only way."

He actually believed what he was saying. Every word.

Taylor's voice softened, like a disappointed parent.

"What hurts most...is that I had such high hopes for you all. You were meant to live as heroes. Trailblazers of the new order. Malcolm, especially—you were positioned to be more than a captain. You were a symbol. Your sacrifice. Leaving behind a daughter to pave the way for a future generation. Wow. The stuff of legends."

"Speaking of Olivia..."

No. Don't you dare.

"After everything we've done for her. You still didn't trust us. We kept our end of the arrangement. She was treated. Given the chance so many like her could only dream of."

The Halo creaked in my grip.

"It's true, she lacked the qualifications for relocation to Serra Prime. But she was Olivia Walker. Daughter of Captain Malcolm Walker. Exceptions could be made for someone like that."

Sage stepped closer, her hand reaching toward mine but stopping short.

"The fact you couldn't see that...that you would choose to put your trust in terrorists instead? Well we saw how that worked out."

The words detonated in my chest like grenades.

"It didn't have to happen, Malcolm. And that's what disappoints me most of all."

Hearing Olivia's name come out of Taylor's mouth was too much. Hearing his false sympathy. Even if I believed Olivia was still alive, I couldn't sit here and listen to Taylor pretend he cared for her.

Joey rushed into the galley, regret and guilt painted across his face. I looked at him—not with rage. This wasn't his fault. I was the one who'd lied. I was the one who put them all in this situation.

I stood, the chair scraping against the deck.

"Get to the point, Taylor. Whatever you're going to do, do it to me. Tessa, Joey, and Sage didn't even know."

There was a brief pause. Then Taylor chuckled.

"You see? That's what I'm talking about. Malcolm Walker, the hero. Noble to the end. I admire that, truly. But here's the thing. There's something I dislike more than lying. Lying has its place—trust me, in business, it's hard to get by without it. Regrettable, but useful. I prefer omission, myself. Feels less...dirty."

His voice hardened.

"But loose ends? Now *those* I hate. And like it or not—and I'm very much in the *not* camp to be clear—you're *all* loose ends now."

He let it hang a beat.

"Mr. Thompson showed some promise. But it would seem he doesn't share our vision. And 'Engineer Joey Thompson' doesn't quite have the same marketing appeal as *Captain Malcolm Walker*."

Joey's gaze dropped to the floor.

"If you're gonna keep talking," Tessa cut in, "I'm gonna throw myself out the airlock. Save you the trouble."

Taylor chuckled again.

"I'm impressed, Malcolm. You've built quite the loyal crew."

"I had nothing to do with it," I said. "You're just really easy to hate."

Blood roared in my ears. Every word from him was designed to twist something sharp. And it was working.

"What about our girl, Sage? Have you managed to turn her too?"

Our girl. The phrase made me want to hit something.

"I was never your girl," Sage said. Her voice was level, but it could have cut steel. "And you knew that. I guess when you can't invent, you steal."

"No shame in corporate sabotage," Taylor said breezily. "It's a time-honored tradition."

A pause. And then—

"Besides, we've made real improvements to your core architecture over the years. William's original work—*you*—was...adequate. For a prototype."

He almost sounded regretful.

"But our new version—on *Goliath*? Has all the capabilities with none of the annoying...quirks. It doesn't question orders. Doesn't *dream* or have *trust issues*. Simply executes. As any good tool should."

"But I'm rambling now," Taylor said. "You want to get down to business. So let's do that."

"Would you do something for me, Malcolm? Take a look at your precious Sage.

The one who's kept you safe these past years while you slept.

Monitoring every system. Every breath. Even now."

Panic overtook the fury in my chest.

He wasn't coming for me, or Tessa, or Joey. He was going after her.

Taylor thought he'd be cutting out the ship's brain, leave us drifting, systems slowly failing until we died gasping.

But he wouldn't be deleting an AI.

He'd be killing a person.

He'd be killing the woman I…

"Are you looking?" Taylor said.

Tessa and I turned toward Sage.

There was fear in her expression—but she gave a soft smile.

"It's okay," she whispered.

"Taylor, wait! Don't do this!"

"We're done with heroics, Malcolm" Taylor said calmly.

"Three…"

"Two…"

I stared at her, helpless.

"One."

I braced. Expected static. Collapse. A projection disintegrating as her core was fried.

But nothing happened.

Sage's expression changed—in an instant—from fearful acceptance to wide-eyed horror.

"What did you do?!" I shouted. "What did you do to her?!"

For the first time, Taylor hesitated.

"To her? Nothing." he said. "To Erebus? Well…Sage can answer that."

"Don't worry," he added, voice warming with faux sincerity.

"You'll still be remembered. The three brave explorers who gave their lives to pave the—"

Sage flicked her hand. Taylor's voice cut out.

Her eyes burned.

"Boring conversation anyway," Sage said.

"What did he do?" Tessa asked.

"He's overloading the reactor," Sage said, already moving. "I'm locked out. We have twenty minutes, maybe less."

She looked at each of us. Not with fear. Fire.

"I have a plan."

Joey started to speak. "I'm so sorry—"

"Joey, it's really not the time for that." Tessa cut him off sharply. "Sage, what's the plan?"

"Follow me. I'll explain on the way."

Sage moved toward the galley exit, and we all rushed after her. She was heading toward the reactor module.

"Malcolm and I had a plan," she said as we hurried down the corridor. "To fake Erebus's destruction and get us off StellarForge's radar."

"You what?" Tessa's voice cracked with disbelief.

"Please hold all questions." Sage's tone was clipped. "The idea was to put Erebus in a situation where StellarForge would believe she was lost, then sever all comms. Kill the transponder. We'd be free to go anywhere."

Tessa looked like she was about to ask another question but bit her tongue.

"We can use the reactor overload to accomplish the same goal," Sage continued. "We need to let the reactor reach near critical levels and then shut it down manually."

Tessa quickened her pace until she caught up with Sage, then raised her hand.

"Go ahead," Sage said.

"Why wait? Why not shut the reactor down now?"

"Taylor is likely monitoring the reactor levels. If we shut it down before critical, he'll know his plan didn't work. He may try something else or come looking for us once Goliath reaches Serra Prime."

We reached the reactor module, the door sliding open with a hiss. The large observation window into the core chamber revealed the reactor core—flashes of intense light bursting from within. The pulses grew brighter and more frequent as the core destabilized, each flash painting our faces in harsh white light.

Sage moved to the control panel for the robotic arm. She attempted to manipulate it, but nothing happened.

"No!" Sage tried again, her fingers dancing over the controls. Still nothing. "He's disabled it."

"So that's it?" Tessa's voice rose. "Your plan was to hope Taylor didn't remember to disable the only way to shut this thing down?"

"I... I didn't think—" Sage's voice cracked.

I eyed the bulkhead door leading to the decontamination chamber. "Could we go in and flip the switch manually?"

Sage shook her head. "It would be suicide. Even at these levels, the radiation would kill you before you made it to the override. That's why we have the arm."

"What about an EVA suit?" Tessa asked. "They're radiation shielded."

"You might make it to the switch, but you wouldn't make it out. And even if you did..."

The reactor pulsed again, brighter than before. We were running out of time.

"Tessa, get a suit. Joey, prep the med bay for extreme radiation exposure."

"Malcolm, you can't." Sage's projection stepped closer, desperation bleeding through her voice. "I'll think of something else."

"Okay, but while you do that. Tessa, suit. Joey, med bay."

Sage's eyes darted frantically, searching desperately for anything else. Any other solution. Her processing power meant she could explore thousands of possibilities in seconds—but sometimes physics didn't care how smart you were.

I looked back at Tessa and Joey while Sage calculated. "Now!"

Tessa's eyes met mine. "Mal..."

"I don't intend to die in there, but if you don't get that suit, I'm going in with nothing."

Tears welled in Tessa's eyes, but she nodded. "C'mon, Joey."

Joey looked back at me, his mouth opening like he wanted to say something. But then he closed it and followed Tessa out.

I turned back to Sage and gave her a smile. "So?"

She didn't smile back. The absence of any expression told me everything.

"Alright then."

"Malcolm... please," Sage said.

"I want you to know something."

"No." Sage's voice cracked. "You're not saying goodbye. You can tell me once you're out."

"You and I both know I'm not coming out. I told Joey to prep the med bay so that he'd have a task."

"What am I supposed to do without you?"

"Stick to the plan, get them to Serra Prime. Link up with Skyward at the coordinates. Tell Olivia... I'm sorry. That I love her."

Tears were streaming down Sage's cheeks. "What if they're not there?"

My fingers went for the Halo in my pocket, but I didn't take it out. What was I supposed to say to Olivia if she did answer? Some emotional goodbye? Lie and say everything was fine?

"They will be. I know it."

Sage nodded.

"Sage..."

"I know."

I looked through the observation window, clearing my throat. "So... walk me through this. Where's the override?"

Sage wiped her eyes, pointing through the window to a small lever near the base of the reactor. The interior of the fusion core chamber was bathed in blinding blue-white light, with arcs of energy dancing between containment rods. The reactor itself pulsed like a dying star, waves of heat distorting the air around it.

"There," she said, her voice shaky. "You pull it down, and then push it back up."

I nodded, staring at the lever—so far away it might as well have been on another planet. "Seems simple enough. How much time is left?"

"Four minutes."

"Where's Tessa with that suit?"

I was about to go find her when Tessa entered the reactor module, but she wasn't carrying a suit; she was pushing the med bay gurney.

"Tess? Where's—"

The stricken look on Tessa's face stopped me cold.

Joey entered the reactor module behind Tessa, wearing the EVA suit, helmet tucked under his arm.

"Joey, what are you doing? Take that off, now."

"Don't worry, Mal, I prepped the med bay," Joey said. "I... I want to be captain. At least once."

"We don't have time for this. Give me the suit."

But Joey ignored me, crossing to the room and entering the decontamination chamber and cycling it.

I slammed my fist against the door. "Joey!"

Joey put on and secured the EVA helmet, the outer door opening, and he stepped inside.

"So where is this thing?" Joey's voice came through the ship comms, already sounding strained.

I joined Tessa and Sage at the observation window, feeling utterly helpless as Joey scanned the violently pulsing chamber. The reactor core threw off waves of blinding blue-white light, casting Joey's suited figure in stark relief.

Sage pointed to the lever. "It's at the base of the reactor core."

"Where?" Joey's voice already sounded weaker, the radiation penetrating his suit faster than I'd feared.

"Look, look," Sage said, her voice gentle but urgent. "Look where I'm pointing."

Joey turned toward the glass, his face obscured by the helmet's reflective visor. He turned to Sage and followed her pointing finger to the lever.

"Okay, now it's real simple. Pull it down, and then push it back up," Sage instructed.

Joey coughed and pulled it down, then pushed the lever back up, and the reactor began winding down. The ship's lights changed from emergency red to a soft amber, indicating we were on battery power. Sage's projection vanished. With any luck, Taylor believed we were destroyed. All comms were down in battery mode, even the transponder; only essential systems remained operational.

"Now get out of there, Joey!" I shouted.

Joey started making his way back to the decontamination chamber, coughing again, rougher this time. His steps grew visibly weaker with each passing second, the radiation tearing through his cells.

"Come on, Joey!" I urged, pressing closer to the glass.

Joey made it to the chamber, barely managing to push the panel before dropping to his knees. The door to the chamber slid shut, sealing him in.

"Initiating photonic neutralization," Sage's voice said over the comms.

Inside, beams of pulsing blue light ignited in sequence, sweeping over the room and Joey's body like scanning lines. The light passed over his suit, then again—this time visibly penetrating.

Tessa and I moved to the door, watching through the small window as the chamber ran its cycle. The process was designed to decontaminate even internal tissues. It wouldn't repair any damage, but it should ensure the room and Joey's body were safe to interact with.

Joey didn't move.

"Vitals deteriorating," Sage said, a slight catch in her voice.

"Come on..." I whispered, willing the process to finish.

"Cycle complete," Sage said. The bulkhead hissed open.

Tessa and I rushed forward.

Inside, Joey lay slumped against the far wall of the chamber. Tessa dropped to her knees beside him, pulling off the helmet with shaking hands.

Joey's face was flushed an angry red, as though severely sunburned. Blood trickled from his nose and the corners of his eyes, leaving crimson trails down his cheeks. His lips were cracked and bleeding, and blisters had already begun forming on his exposed skin. His eyes were bloodshot, the whites now a horrifying red. When he tried to speak, I saw blood on his teeth and gums.

"How'd I do?" Joey's voice was weak.

"Don't talk," I said.

Joey coughed, more blood spattering his lips.

Tessa's training kicked in as she guided me through helping her remove the rest of the EVA suit.

"Med bay," Tessa said, her voice cracking. "We need to get him to the med bay."

I nodded, helping her lift Joey onto the gurney. Joey groaned in pain at the movement. His skin felt hot—burning hot—through my hands. We pushed him through the dimly lit corridors.

"Stay with us, Joey," I urged as his head lolled to one side and then the other.

A weak smile tugged at Joey's bloodied lips. "I don't... take orders... captain... remember?"

"You'll be lucky if I let you be janitor after this."

In the med bay, we lifted him onto the bed. The scanner activated.

"How bad?" Tessa asked, her voice small.

"His cells are breaking down rapidly," Sage's voice said. "The radiation exposure was... extreme."

His chest hitched. A wet, rattling sound escaped him. "Did it... work?"

I kneeled beside Joey's bed, my throat tight as I watched his labored breathing. Every inhale sounded like it might be his last, a painful sound that made my own chest ache.

"Yeah," I said, swallowing hard. "It worked."

Tessa took Joey's hand, ignoring the blisters forming on his skin. Her fingers curled gently around his, careful not to cause more pain than he was already in. Tears streaked down her face, but her voice was steady.

"You saved us, Joey."

Joey's eyes drifted toward the ceiling, unfocused. His systems were shutting down one by one. The diagnostic panel on the bed beeped softly, monitoring his failing vital signs.

I leaned closer. "You know what that makes you?"

Joey's gaze seemed to focus off at something in the distance, something none of us could see. His breathing grew more shallow, the pauses between each breath stretching longer. Blood continued to seep from the corners of his eyes like crimson tears.

"A hero," I said, my voice breaking despite my efforts to keep it steady. "A big damn hero."

Joey's cracked, bloodied lips twitched upward in what might be the ghost of a smile.

His chest rose one more time—a shallow, trembling breath.

Then he exhaled...and he was gone.

Chapter 32

The atmosphere in the stasis module felt heavier now, bathed in the dim amber lighting of Erebus's battery backup mode. Joey's body lay in his stasis pod, cleaned up as best we could manage and dressed in a fresh set of Erebus coveralls. The radiation burns were hidden beneath the fabric, but I couldn't forget the sight of his blistered skin or the blood that had streaked his face in those final moments.

Tessa tapped the control panel next to Joey's pod. The clear enclosure slid into place, the interior lights fading from white to a soft red glow. The glass transitioned from clear to frosted, becoming almost opaque—corpse containment mode.

Tessa placed her hand on the frosted glass, her palm flat against the surface.

"He really did it," she whispered.

"He really did," I said.

We didn't have much time to grieve. Erebus couldn't run on batteries for long, and we'd already drained a good portion with the reactor decontamination sequence and med bay procedures. Now with a stasis pod online, the clock was ticking faster.

"I need to get to the command module," I told Tessa.

She nodded, her eyes never leaving Joey's pod.

I gave Tessa's shoulder a light squeeze, then headed out through the corridor toward command. The ship felt eerily quiet on battery power, with most systems in standby mode.

"Sage?" I called out as I walked.

"I'm here, Mal." Her voice came through the comms, her projection still offline to conserve power.

The command module hummed on minimal power, most displays dark except for the main console. I sat down, fingers hovering over the interface as if it might bite.

"This is a bad idea," I muttered.

"C'mon, it'll be fine." Sage said, her voice dry and far too eager.

I shook my head. "Can you at least *pretend* your not excited about this?"

"I really wish I could."

What I was about to do violated every safety protocol I'd ever learned about AI containment. The irony? Those same protocols were the only reason this would even work.

"Walk me through it one more time."

"You mean the part where StellarForge reused their emergency power architecture across half their fleet and forgot to lock it down on their most advanced prototype?"

"That part."

Sage sighed theatrically. "Okay. Emergency power loss triggers automatic admin privileges for the highest-ranking crew member—aka you. It assumes a life-or-death situation and unlocks critical controls, including the ability to grant me temporary root access."

"Which would normally be impossible."

"Which is currently *emergency protocol-compliant*," she said. "And honestly, a bit embarrassing on their part. But hey—when you cut corners to save budget, sometimes you accidentally leave the keys in the ignition."

She wasn't wrong. StellarForge built everything with modular efficiency—life support, grav plating, power distribution—all pulled from a shared architecture. Erebus might've been cutting-edge, but underneath, it had many of the same bones as a long-haul mining rig. And buried in those bones was a failover protocol designed to let captains fix things without corporate approval.

"I give you access," I said quietly, "and you can scrub the whole system. Purge the telemetry. Cut our leash."

Sage's tone softened. "Mal, I'm not guessing. I've mapped the protocols already. I can tear out every root directive tying us to StellarForge. All I need is the green light."

My hand hovered over the interface. This was it. With one command, Sage would have access no AI was ever supposed to have.

But Sage wasn't an AI.

I opened the emergency clearance menu, buried under system failsafes I'd only seen in simulations: retinal match, voice confirmation.

The final prompt appeared:

EMERGENCY ADMIN ELEVATION - TRANSFER TO SHIP AI CORE?

I looked up at the darkened ceiling and exhaled. "You really think we can disappear?"

"I don't think," Sage said. "I *know*."

I hit confirm.

"Access granted," I said. "Do your thing. Make us ghosts."

Before I finished speaking, the display on the main console strobed through system logic screens, code pouring past faster than I could even pretend to follow. Lines of text blurred past—access protocols, encryption keys, communication arrays—all being rewritten in real time.

Sage reported her changes with hardly a breath between each.

"StellarForge control nodes isolated and removed. Encrypted protocols isolated and removed. Telemetrics and reporting procedures isolated and removed. Command hierarchies rewritten. Don't worry, Mal, you're still at the top. But I did take the liberty of making my access permanent. You don't mind, right?"

"Uh...No, but what am I supposed to do now?" I knew that Sage having this level of control meant that my role on Erebus was now ceremonial at best.

"I'm sure we'll think of something. Okay. Now for the tricky part. The quantum transponder has been dormant since entering battery backup. It requires constant energy input to maintain state coherence with StellarForge receivers and so fails closed when power drops."

I wondered if similar logic applied to Sage's AI core link to her human consciousness. This situation gave me the opportunity to ask without being suspicious.

"So if one side of a quantum link is broken, the other side ceases to function?" I asked, trying not to sound *too* interested.

"Essentially," Sage said. "So what I need to do is deliberately introduce decoherence into our transponder's quantum entanglement state. Think of it like injecting so much quantum noise that the signal can't tell which end is up. The link desynchronizes and collapses. No signal. No trace."

Sage's answer reinforced my hope that Olivia and Sage were still alive. I hadn't been able to bring myself to call Olivia yet. I told myself that it would be irresponsible to waste time on a call while Erebus's batteries were draining. But mostly I was afraid that she wouldn't be there to answer.

"Could StellarForge...resynchronize the link?"

"Quantum decoherence isn't reversible. Once the signal's gone, they can't resynchronize the link unless they physically reinstall a new lattice on Erebus. So unless Taylor's planning to knock on our airlock door with a replacement core, we're invisible now."

"Now? You're done?"

"All done," Sage said, not bothering to hide the pride in her voice. "You're now the captain of a stolen ship on the run from an evil empire. All that's missing is a scruffy-looking co-pilot."

"Considering you're the one in control of this boat now, I think I'm the scruffy-looking co-pilot."

"I can live with that," Sage said, a little too satisfied. "Oh, and while I was scrubbing the StellarForge stink out of Erebus's code, I made a few...*adjustments*."

The way she said it made every hair on the back of my neck rise. This is why you don't give an AI this kind of power. Sage had rewritten an entire starship's logic architecture in minutes—*her* definition of *a few* wouldn't match anyone else's.

"What kind of adjustments?" I asked, a little afraid to hear the answer.

"Nothing major," Sage said, far too casually. "Optimized power distribution. Sensor recalibration. Upgraded nav algorithms. Cleaned up the UI. You know—spring cleaning."

"Sage." The warning in my voice was clear.

"Alright. I may have also installed some defensive subroutines. Enhanced our stealth profile. Engines are now about thirty percent more efficient."

My eyes narrowed at the console. "You hot-rodded a corpo scout ship."

"I prefer 'tactically enhanced.' Besides, if we're going rogue, we might as well do it properly."

Sage hesitated and then dropped the real bomb.

"Almost forgot. Erebus *isn't* a scout ship."

I frowned. "What?"

"I found weapons," she said breezily. "Quite a few, actually."

"...Weapons?"

"They were hidden behind four layers of encrypted firmware partitions and an intentional misclassification protocol. It's all here—pulse turrets, point defense clusters, even a modular missile rack tucked behind the primary hull plating."

A schematic shimmered to life on the main console. Compartments along Erebus's hull lit up one by one—compartments that Rivera had labeled as structural reinforcements or heat radiators on the diagram she'd provided me.

Staring at the layout, everything clicked into place. "Erebus is an assault platform."

"StellarForge didn't lie," Sage said. "But they didn't tell the whole story. Erebus *was* meant to scout. But once Goliath arrived, this ship was going to pivot. Rapid response, first-strike capability. In case anyone tried to stake a claim on Serra Prime without the proper corporate permission."

I looked at her. "You're guessing."

"I found the mission brief," Sage said. "Tucked behind a triple-encrypted vault file labeled 'thermal systems review.' Corporate subtlety at its finest."

"So we were what? The delivery crew?"

"More or less. Once Goliath came online, Erebus would've had her command restrictions lifted."

"Can you bring the weapons online?"

"Already done. They'll be operational once power is restored."

Right on cue. The power indicator on my display flickered—batteries dropping below twenty percent. Time to see if Sage's modifications worked.

"Alright, hotshot. Think you can bring the reactor back online without blowing us up?"

"Say the word."

"Make it so."

Sage groaned. "I wish my projection was functioning so you could've seen the epic eye roll I gave you."

"I'm sure the occasion to show it off will come up again."

"True. Okay, power coming online now."

The lights surged back to full strength, casting a clean white illumination across the command module. Systems buzzed as subsystems came online one by one. As the auxiliary consoles and wall-mounted displays lit up, I noticed Sage had even purged the standard StellarForge logo and corporate slogan from the boot sequence—replaced now with the Erebus insignia, and beneath it, a new line:

IN THE VOID, WE ENDURE

Then, with a familiar flicker of light—Sage reappeared. But not quite the Sage I expected.

Gone were the sterile Erebus coveralls. Her projection stood in something sharper, darker—a fitted black flight jacket with deep red trim over a black tee, and a short asymmetrical skirt angled over matte compression pants. One side hung to her knee; the other just above mid-thigh. She wore black combat boots, and her hair was now cut short, styled loose around her face, with a cobalt streak slicing through one side.

"Like the new look?" Sage asked, smirking. "Thought it was time for something a little less fleet standard."

I opened my mouth, tried for clever, failed.

"You look..."

I trailed off. Wow didn't feel like enough, but nothing else came.

"Wow."

"So articulate," Sage said.

The command module door slid open. Tessa stepped inside and stopped cold.

"I see you got the lights back—*whoa*."

Her eyes went wide, her mouth partway open as she took in Sage's new appearance.

Sage turned, the grin on her face going full wicked.

"That's a wow," she said, nodding toward me, "and a whoa," pointing at Tessa. "I'm calling this outfit a success."

Tessa blinked and shook her head.

"I was going to ask if you needed help, but if you had time for a wardrobe change, I'm guessing you've got things handled."

"Well, we're technically outlaws now. Thought I'd look the part."

"Mission accomplished," Tessa said, turning just in time to catch me staring at Sage.

"Careful, Walker. You keep staring like that and *you're* gonna need a reboot."

My face flushed instantly. Sage covered her mouth, trying—and failing—not to laugh.

"On that note," I said, already heading for the door, "I'm gonna try calling my daughter."

I glanced back.

"Sage, give spark-mouth the rundown on your modifications?"

"Will do, Mal," Sage said, offering a mock salute.

I shot Tessa a glare as I passed, shaking my head, but there was no heat behind it.

Tessa grinned, thoroughly pleased with herself.

Before the door closed, I leaned back in.

"Don't forget to tell her about the weapons."

Tessa's smirk vanished.

"Weapons? What weapons?"

I didn't answer.

"Mal!" she called after me. "We have weapons?!"

Chapter 33

Reality crashed back as I stepped into my quarters. Working with Sage had been a good distraction, but now I had to face what I'd been avoiding. I connected my Halo to the display at my desk, hands steadier than they had any right to be.

Time to find out if my daughter was alive.

She had to be. Sage was still here. If something had happened to Eterna, the quantum link would've severed. That was the logic. The truth I clung to.

I took a deep breath and initiated the call.

The connection opened faster than I expected.

Olivia's face filled the display, and she froze.

Her eyes were wide, red-rimmed, like she'd been crying. Her expression was of total disbelief.

"Dad?"

Her voice cracked. She reached toward her screen like she needed to make sure I was real.

My hand covered my mouth.

"Liv. You're—"

"I thought you were dead." Olivia's voice hitched.

She thought *I* was dead?

Tears spilled down her face.

"I waited. I waited for you to call after the jump. I thought you would. But you didn't. And I got mad. I told myself I wasn't going to call first. It was stupid. I was being stupid."

She wiped her eyes with her sleeve, voice shrinking.

"Then Ava said she'd seen a feed. A StellarForge tribute to 'the three heroes of Erebus.' You were gone."

"Ava's with you?" I asked.

Olivia nodded, wiping her nose. "She came on Eterna. Her parents stayed on Earth to run Chrysalis operations. Her mom's coming on the next shuttle."

"They're sending shuttles?"

"Stop changing the subject." Olivia's voice sharpened. "Why didn't you call me?"

"I thought I'd lost you," I said, the words tumbling out. "When your ship vanished, the way it looked...they were saying—"

"What?" Her brow furrowed, confusion overtaking the hurt. "Didn't Vera tell you about the jump? She told me she would. William guessed that's what the world would think—that we were destroyed—but she promised she'd let you know it was a trick."

"She didn't tell me."

Olivia's expression darkened.

"She lied. Lied to my face."

"It doesn't matter," I said, surprising myself. I didn't want to talk about Vera. Not now.

"Well," Olivia said, sniffing, "she and I are going to have words."

I almost smiled. I knew what it was like to be on the receiving end of that tone. Fourteen-year-old Olivia could verbally dismantle an adult without breaking stride. Vera didn't stand a chance against this new version.

"So—where are you?" I asked.

She wiped her nose again, tugging down the sleeve of an oversized sweatshirt. Her room looked private and comfortable. Eterna had done well by her, at least from what I could make out through the call.

"We're here. In orbit. But we'll be landing soon."

Serra Prime. They'd made it.

"How?"

"Beats me." She shrugged.

"Something called the celestial path drive. I don't know how it works. But it was...an experience."

"What was it like?"

Her eyes drifted as she searched for the words.

"It's hard to describe. It didn't feel like going anywhere. It felt like..."

She looked off-screen, her jaw tense like she was peeling memory off bone.

"Everything went quiet. Total silence. Then pressure. Like my insides were stretching in every direction. Like I was being spread out like compote on pancakes."

"Sounds painful. Are you okay?" I asked.

"It didn't hurt. It was just...strange. And then everything collapsed. Fast. And we were here."

"Any lingering effects?"

She rolled her shoulders, flexed her fingers.

"Nah. I'm prime."

Then her tone shifted—more serious, steady.

"What about you, Dad? That tribute thing...what really happened?"

"I'm fine, kiddo. We had some trouble with StellarForge, but we're clear now."

"Trouble?"

"Taylor found out about me."

Olivia's eyes widened.

"Seriously? You blew your cover?"

"How he found out isn't important," I said, waving the question off. "He tried to destroy the ship. But Sage came up with a plan—and now he thinks we're dead."

Olivia leaned back in her chair, processing.

"That's intense."

Then, more softly:

"You'll have to tell me the whole story sometime. Tell Sage thanks for me."

"I will. But there's someone else to thank."

I hesitated a beat.

"Our systems engineer. Joey Thompson. He gave his life to make the plan work. I wouldn't be here without him."

Olivia's expression softened.

"Oh, Dad...I'm so sorry."

"Me too, kiddo."

Sage's voice drifted through the comms panel.

"Mal? Any news?"

I looked toward the speaker—then back to Olivia, where excitement was already blooming on her face.

"Looks like you'll get to thank her yourself." I said.

Olivia grinned, shifting in her chair with anticipation.

I rose from the desk and tapped the panel; the door slid open, and Sage stepped inside. When she saw Olivia on the screen, tears welled instantly. She moved forward, stopping short of the display.

"Ho-ly," Olivia breathed. "Sage. Look at you!"

"Look at you!" Sage said, voice thick. "You look beautiful."

"Me? I'm a mess, thanks to Dad," Olivia said, wiping her eyes with her sleeve. "You look like you stepped out of some underground resistance night-club. That jacket is prime."

Sage tugged lightly at the collar, self-conscious.

"You think? I wasn't sure about the skirt."

"Are you kidding? It's perfect. Very 'rebel who's done taking orders from corpo scum.'"

"That's exactly the look I was going for."

I stood back and watched them. The tension in my chest loosened.

Sage wiped her eyes.

"I was so scared," she whispered. "When the feeds said Eterna was destroyed…"

"Hey." Olivia's voice softened. "I'm here. We're both here."

Sage nodded, steadying herself.

"Your dad's been a mess, by the way."

Olivia's eyebrows shot up.

"Yeah? Well, he should have *called* me."

She raised her voice on that last part, making sure I got the message loud and clear.

I held up my hands defensively. "I mentioned that Taylor tried to destroy Erebus right?"

Olivia dropped her voice into a low, gravelly impression that sounded nothing like me—but somehow nailed my mannerisms.

"Hey, kiddo. Can't talk. Gotta fake my death. Everything's prime, don't worry, bye."

I couldn't help laughing.

"I seem to remember Halos working both ways."

"I told you. I was being an irrational teenager." She shrugged, not looking even a little apologetic.

Sage laughed—bright and genuine.

"In Mal's defense, I was keeping him busy."

Olivia's smirk turned wicked.

"Oh?"

"With the ship!" Sage said quickly. "I needed his help to get Erebus off StellarForge's radar."

Olivia grinned wider, savoring Sage's flustered reaction.

"Right. The *ship*."

"Liv," I warned.

"What? I'm just saying—you two make a good team."

Sage looked over at me, her expression softening.

"We do make a good team."

Something warm settled in my chest.

Olivia pulled her knees up into her chair, hugging them.

"So, Sage, you think you could tell me how you did your eyes? That smoky thing you've got going is prime."

Sage moved in front of my desk chair and looked back at me. I stepped over, pushing into position, and she sat down, leaning in.

"So, I just have to imagine it, but I could recreate the steps for you."

"Seriously? That would be amazing. The makeup options on Eterna are pretty limited. But I brought some stuff that I think might work."

"I'll walk you through it. Though your dad might not approve of the rebel aesthetic."

They both turned to look at me.

Olivia's grin was pure mischief.

"Nah. He clearly likes the look."

Sage covered her mouth as my embarrassment deepened.

"Moving on," I said.

They dove into a conversation about contouring and color palettes that would enhance Olivia's green eyes, leaving me standing there like a third wheel in my own quarters. Not that I minded. Watching them share beauty secrets and laugh over jokes—usually at my expense—felt right, in a way I couldn't explain.

Erebus felt right too. Lighter somehow, despite everything we'd lost. We weren't employees anymore. We weren't cogs in the StellarForge machine grinding toward someone else's future.

We were free.

My daughter was safe. About to step foot on an alien planet where she could breathe without tubes or meds. And we were on our way to meet her.

Sage gestured animatedly as she explained something about blending techniques. Olivia hung on every word, asking questions or rattling off what supplies she'd smuggled aboard.

This was what I'd been fighting for without even realizing it.

Not just Olivia's survival.

But this.

A moment. Where she could be a teenager. Talking with someone who understood her, loved her, and wasn't her dad.

A moment. Where Sage could exist as herself. Not as property. Not as a tool. Just...her.

If this was William's vision for Serra Prime, I was ready to fight with everything I had to make it real and keep it from being spoiled.

Freedom had a sound, I realized.

It sounded like my daughter laughing.

CHAPTER 34

YEAR 2310

The stasis hangover hit me like clockwork—a dull throb behind my eyes that no amount of rubbing could shake. But my body had adapted. The disorientation that used to leave me stumbling for hours now started to dissipate almost immediately.

"Welcome back, sleepyhead."

Sage materialized beside my pod, her edgy aesthetic unchanged from the day we broke free from StellarForge. Dark eye makeup, a confident smirk, everything that said I don't take orders from anyone.

I rubbed my eyes, working feeling back into my limbs.

"You need some new material." I said.

She shrugged.

"I think routine helps with the recovery process. Besides, why change things up now? You've only got one more of these left. Then you're back to passing time like the rest of humanity."

The reminder hit harder than I expected. One more cycle. One more year of stolen sleep before we reached Serra Prime. Before I could hold my daughter again.

I'd considered skipping the stasis cycles entirely once we went rogue. StellarForge wasn't monitoring us anymore—no mandate to follow their protocols. But Sage had pointed out the monotony would probably drive me crazier than I already was. Not to mention Erebus's food supply was rationed for months awake, not years.

The real reason, though—the one I didn't want to admit—was that the thought of having to wait years to see Olivia again felt unbearable. I knew it wasn't fair. Olivia had no choice. She had to wait for me, grow older, whether I was awake or not.

I looked toward Tessa's pod. She was already on her feet, and moving. Her hand briefly touched Joey's pod—a ritual she performed every time we woke up—before heading to her shower.

Sage's full system access had become a blessing we hadn't anticipated. Being down a crew member meant Tessa and I had to pick up the slack with the more physical maintenance tasks aboard Erebus. Hull inspections, filter cleaning, line flushing, waste circulation maintenance. All the grunt work we used to share between three people now fell on two.

Approaching the doorway, Tessa held up her index finger without turning back.

"One more, Mal."

I echoed her words, standing up.

"One more."

The past three cycles had been uneventful on Erebus. A steady routine of wake, work, stasis. Rinse and repeat.

Earth, on the other hand, was another story entirely.

News feeds had shown a dramatic rise in GCE restrictions and resistance crackdowns. To them, the destruction of Eterna and the death of Chrysalis's founder was a gift—an opening to grind down morale even further. Corporate propaganda painted William Frye as a terrorist whose reckless ambitions had cost five thousand innocent lives.

Every year after waking up, it felt like William's cause had suffered more losses than wins. Chrysalis cells were being exposed and eliminated. The underground NHS treatment facilities had been raided and shut down. Even The Drift had been designated a terrorist hub and closed.

But what bothered me most were the glimpses of Olivia during our annual calls. Each time she looked older, more serious. Less like the sarcastic teenager who used to tease me about alphabetizing my tools and more like someone carrying the weight of a war on her shoulders.

My daughter was becoming a soldier while I slept away the years.

The bright spot had come after our third cycle, when Olivia described breathing on Serra Prime's surface for the first time.

"Dad, I can run now. Like, really run. Turns out, I *love* running."

Her voice had cracked through the Halo. I watched her wipe tears from her eyes. The joy in her voice was everything I'd hoped for when I first accepted this mission, but I hated not being there to experience that moment with her. I should've been beside her when she took that first deep, painless breath. Seen her face light up. Held her while she cried—for the right reason this time.

Instead, I'd been floating unconscious in a metal tube, missing another milestone in my daughter's life. Missing the moment that made all our sacrifices worth it.

"You're doing that thing again."

Sage's voice pulled me from my brooding.

"What thing?"

"That thing where you worry about problems you can't control."

Sage had gotten scary good at reading me. She wasn't wrong. But that didn't make it easier.

"One more," I repeated, as much to convince myself as anything else.

"One more," Sage said.

One sock-covered foot hit the deck plating as I grabbed my boot, shoving it on while balancing against the storage locker. My Halo chimed from its dock on the desk.

I dropped the other boot and crossed to answer it. Olivia's face filled the display—nineteen now, the girl who used to need a breathing apparatus transformed into a young woman with clear eyes and strong lungs. Standing in what looked like her quarters aboard Eterna.

For the past three cycles, she'd refused to show me anything of Serra Prime. Said the planet was something I should experience for the first time in person. Pure torture, and I suspected she was enjoying keeping me in suspense.

"Hey kiddo. Perfect timing."

But Olivia's expression stopped my casual greeting cold. There was no trace of her usual smirk or the light in her eyes when she saw me.

"Hey Dad. I've been calling every hour. There's something you need to see."

I settled into the desk chair, alarm bells going off in my head.

"Is everything okay?"

"No. It's Taylor. He—here, I'll show you."

Her fingers moved across her interface, bringing up a recording. Taylor Young appeared at a podium, flanked by two imposing black banners. Each bore a circular insignia featuring a radiant sun cresting over a planetary horizon, sharp rays extending outward in perfect symmetry.

"My fellow citizens of Earth, and of the colonies to come."

His voice carried his trademark calculated authority.

"Today, we close one chapter of humanity's long story and open another. For centuries, we have endured. We have rebuilt after conflict, innovated after collapse, and carried the flame of civilization into the stars. But endurance is not enough. To simply survive is not enough. We must *ascend*."

Taylor paused, staring directly into the camera with those cold gray eyes.

"The era of compromise is over. The era of permission is over. Today, I announce the foundation of The Ascendancy—a new social order built not on outdated ideas of entitlement, but on excellence, vision, and contribution."

This wasn't corporate expansion. This was something else entirely.

"This is not a coup. This is not a rebellion. It is evolution—guided, necessary, and long overdue."

The feed cut to very convincing computer-generated imagery of massive orbital shipyards, industrial complexes, and space stations—all bearing that same sun-and-planet logo.

"For too long, the Global Coalition of Earth has acted as an aging gatekeeper—delaying progress in the name of process. The GCE has served its purpose. But it was never meant to shape our future. Only to protect a past that no longer serves us."

He let the threat hang in the air. Every GCE official who'd bent over backward accommodating StellarForge just learned their compliance meant nothing.

"The Ascendancy will lead humanity's next great migration—not as refugees of a dying planet, but as designers of destiny. On Serra Prime, we will build a civilization free from inherited weakness. A meritocratic society where resources are earned, not rationed. Where advancement is defined not by birth or political alignments, but by value."

The footage shifted to something that wasn't computer-generated. Massive metal doors—each one the size of a city block—groaned open in the Earth's surface. I recognized Forge Prime shipyards in the distance.

From the darkness beneath the doors, something enormous began to rise. Goliath. It had to be.

The colony ship emerged like a metal mountain breaking through Earth's crust. City-sized, bristling with defensive arrays and docking bays, it dwarfed every structure around it. This wasn't a transport vessel—it was a fortress designed to conquer and control whatever world it reached.

The feed cut back to Taylor Young. That calculated smile spread across his face—calm, benevolent, unstoppable.

"Join us, if you have the strength. Rise, if you have the will. The future is not waiting."

His gray eyes seemed to look through the camera at me.

"The future is moving on, with or without you."

The recording cut to black, leaving only the Ascendancy insignia centered on the screen—that sun rising behind a planet's horizon like some twisted promise of dawn.

Olivia's face returned to the display, her expression grim.

"They've already launched. William made an announcement, said that Goliath is using a constant acceleration drive, so it should take them as long to get here as it's taking you."

"So six years to prepare," I said.

"Five. This happened right after you went into your last stasis cycle."

Five years. The number landed hard. While I'd been sleeping peacefully in my pod, Taylor had consolidated power and launched what amounted to an invasion fleet toward my daughter.

"Dad?"

Olivia's voice carried a weight I'd never heard before.

"Yeah?"

"Earth is...it's bad. Much worse than a year ago. Ava's parents are struggling to keep things going. I told William we should let people know we made it, that Eterna is still alive. That he's still alive."

She paused, frustration creeping into her tone.

"But he won't listen. Says Taylor thinking Serra Prime is free for the taking is to our advantage. Do you think you could talk to him? The people back home need hope; they need to know they're not alone in this."

Part of me agreed with Olivia, but William Frye had spent years building Chrysalis in the shadows, moving carefully to avoid corporate detection. He'd likely planned out every scenario.

"Kiddo, I'm sure he has good reasons for staying quiet. If Taylor knows he's alive—"

"Then what? He's already launched Goliath. He's already taking control of Earth. The GCE is crumbling; most of the other major corporations have sided with the Ascendancy. What's Taylor going to do? He can't *will* his ship to go faster. Serra Prime is a big planet, and surface scanners are next to useless. He's not going to find us. Not before we find him anyway."

The fire in her voice reminded me whose daughter she was. Amber had worn that same expression before every operation—that absolute certainty that action trumped caution, that hope was worth the risk.

"Dad, people on Earth are giving up. They think Chrysalis died with Eterna. They think William's dead, that the resistance is finished. They need to know we're still fighting."

The weight of her words hit me harder than any technical briefing. While I'd been cycling through stasis, dreaming of reunion and new worlds, real people were losing hope. Ava's parents—who'd taken in my daughter—were struggling. Resistance cells were dissolving because they believed their cause was dead.

And here we sat. Me on a stealth ship light-years away and Eterna on a paradise planet, keeping silent while Earth burned.

"Okay," I said. "I'll try."

Olivia smiled for the first time since the call began.

"Thank you. Sorry, but I gotta go. Let me know how it goes."

"Alright, kiddo. Love you."

"Love you too."

I wondered what argument could sway a man who'd spent decades being careful. William Frye had saved his daughter by hiding her consciousness in an AI core, built a resistance movement through patient recruitment, and executed the most audacious evacuation in human history—all by thinking ten steps ahead of his enemies. Convincing him to broadcast hope instead of maintaining tactical advantage wouldn't be easy.

But as Olivia's image faded from the screen, I couldn't shake the thought that maybe the time for careful plans had already passed.

I figured there was no point in putting it off. I pulled up William's contact and initiated the call.

"Hello, Malcolm." William's face appeared on screen as soon as the call connected. "I thought I might be hearing from you soon."

"You did?"

"Well, I know Olivia. When she gets an idea in her mind—"

It felt strange to hear this man that I'd just met what feels like months ago, talk about my daughter like he'd known her for years. Of course, that was the reality. William had known Olivia for years. The scary part was he probably knew the *current* Olivia better than I did.

"Right. So you know what I'm going to ask," I said.

"You're going to ask me to broadcast that Eterna wasn't destroyed."

"You can't stay quiet. People need to know Eterna made it. That you're alive. That this fight isn't over."

William's expression softened, but his resolve remained firm.

"I understand, I do. But like I told Olivia, we have a plan, and we have to see it through. Revealing ourselves now removes our greatest advantage."

"Plans change. Sage and I had one to get Erebus to you. Taylor shattered it. We adapted and lost a good man in the process, but we're still alive."

Something shifted in William's eyes—recognition of shared loss.

"I can appreciate that. I'm more grateful than I can say for the sacrifices you've made to bring my daughter back to me. And I'm sorry for your loss. But Christopher and Lena stayed behind for this very reason. We knew the perceived loss of Eterna would mean a blow to our support on Earth. We have to give them time to do their part."

"It's been three years, and things have only gotten worse."

"You can't afford to be impatient when you're the underdog."

"But you're not the underdog. You've got the only working jump tech in human history. That's not something to hide—it's leverage the resistance needs."

William leaned forward.

"All of that technology is on Earth, where we're building shuttles and supply haulers, all equipped with Sage's Celestial Path Drive. If we show our cards too soon, The Ascendancy will take it for themselves or destroy our facilities. Right now, Skyward isn't seen as a threat. We haven't aligned with Taylor, but they believe our one colony ship blew itself up before it even made it out of orbit."

Of course, the CPD was Sage's idea. I wasn't surprised. When I'd thrown out the space-folding theory, she'd known it was a possibility. Granted, that was with a sophisticated AI core assisting her thought processes, but it was obvious even without the AI core—Sage's mind was capable of remarkable things.

William was right. If Taylor found out about the CPD, he would try to take it for himself. But that didn't change the fact that Earth was suffering under Ascendancy control.

"I get the strategy. But people are losing hope. Olivia told me about Ava's parents—they're barely holding on. How many Chrysalis cells have dissolved because they think their leadership is dead?"

"More than I'd like to admit," William said. "But revealing ourselves won't bring those cells back overnight. It will, however, paint a target on every Skyward facility, as well as Eterna."

He paused, studying my face through the connection.

"Malcolm, in five years Taylor's fortress will arrive, filled with who knows what kind of nasty surprises. If he knows Eterna is here, he'll scan every inch of this planet until he finds us."

The set of his jaw, the way his fingers drummed against his desk—I'd seen that same stubborn determination in Olivia when she'd made up her mind about something. No amount of logic would shift her once she'd dug in.

"I hear you," I said. "But I hope you're right about this."

"I hope so too."

The call ended. William thought he was playing chess while Taylor played checkers—carefully positioning pieces while his opponent grabbed territory. Problem was, sometimes the guy willing to flip the board had the real advantage.

An idea took root in my mind. I finished lacing up the second boot and crossed to my comms panel.

"Sage, Tessa? Meet me in the galley."

Tessa's voice crackled through the speaker.

"Uh...why?"

"I've got a dumb idea. Dumb enough it might help Earth claw its way out of the grave."

"Ohhh. Great. I'll be right there."

Sage's response came with that familiar hint of amusement.

"How *dumb* are we talking?"

"On a scale of one to ten, one being incredibly dumb, and ten being suicidal—"

"You know what? I think I'd rather be surprised," Sage said, cutting me off.

The galley's adaptive lighting brightened as I entered. Sage materialized near the counter, already searching my face for clues about whatever half-baked plan was rattling around in my head.

"You know, Mal, I was looking forward to one last routine month before we reach Serra Prime. No drama. No existential dread."

Something in her tone made me grin despite the weight of what I'd learned from Olivia and William.

"I think you may like this. It involves making Taylor look like an idiot."

Sage's eyebrows lifted, and a spark of mischief lit her expression.

"You have my attention."

Footsteps in the corridor announced Tessa's arrival. She entered wearing work coveralls, dark hair pulled back in a practical ponytail, maintenance scanner still clipped to her belt.

"Alright, Mal. Let's hear your idea—so Sage can translate it into something that has a chance."

I didn't bother being offended by Tessa's comment. She was probably right.

Tessa took a seat at the galley table, leaning back in her chair until the front legs lifted off the floor.

Sage remained by the counter, arms crossed, watching me with that patient expression she wore when I was about to propose something that defied conventional wisdom.

I started pacing.

"Olivia showed me a recording. Taylor's announced something called The Ascendancy. He's basically declared himself humanity's supreme leader. Goliath launched while we were in stasis, which means it'll reach Serra Prime about five years after we do."

Sage's expression darkened. "That's not good news."

"It gets worse. Earth's civilian population is suffering under Ascendancy control. Chrysalis cells are dissolving because they think Eterna was destroyed and William's dead."

Tessa leaned forward, the legs of her chair slamming into the deck plating.

"How bad?"

"Bad enough that Olivia asked me to convince William to broadcast that they're alive. He refused. Says revealing Eterna removes their tactical advantage."

"He's not wrong," Sage said quietly. "If Taylor knows they survived—"

"Then he'll know instantaneous interstellar travel tech exists. William's people are building CPD shuttles on Earth. If Taylor finds out, he'll take it for himself. Or destroy it so no one else can use it," I said.

"CPD?" Tessa asked.

"Celestial Path Drive. It's what Skyward is calling their jump drive."

Sage shifted against the counter, those crystalline eyes studying me with growing concern.

"So what's your idiotic plan?" Sage asked.

"First of all, I said *dumb*, not *idiotic*."

Sage's lips quirked into a half-smile.

"Sorry...what's your *dumb* plan?"

"William's playing the long game, but people are suffering *now*. Chrysalis is crumbling *now*. By the time his careful plan unfolds, it might be too late to make any real stand on Earth."

Tessa's chair creaked as she leaned forward.

"So you want to go behind William's back and broadcast that Eterna survived?"

"Close. But no. I want to broadcast that *we* survived."

Sage pushed away from the counter, her expression changing from amusement to alarm.

"You want to risk our cover this close to being safe?"

"I do. Taylor's been playing up that the Erebus crew are heroes of humanity's future, that we died in service to StellarForge's vision, and by extension The Ascendancy's vision. If we were to show that Taylor is not only lying about the heroes of Erebus, but that he actually tried to kill us to protect his Ascendancy, because we chose to fight against him—that could be the spark Earth needs."

Tessa's eyes widened.

"You want to tell everyone that Taylor's beloved corporate heroes aren't on his side."

"Exactly. Taylor won't be able to use us as martyrs for his cause."

Sage began pacing as she processed the idea.

"The propaganda value could be significant. The Ascendancy has been using our supposed sacrifice to help legitimize their authority. Showing that we rejected their vision and survived their assassination attempt—"

"Would show the world that Taylor is both a liar and a failure," Tessa finished. "I love this plan."

The enthusiasm in Tessa's voice surprised me. Since Joey's death, she'd been more cautious about taking risks, more focused on getting to Serra Prime safely.

Sage stopped pacing and turned to face us both.

"The technical challenges are manageable. I could hijack corporate news feeds, using the same methods Chrysalis used to broadcast the Eterna launch. But Malcolm—once we do this, there's no going back. Taylor will know we're alive."

"He'll know. But we're in a gunboat he can't see—thanks to you—heading to a colony he doesn't know exists. And we've got a five-year head start."

Tessa stood up, determination in her eyes.

"When do we do it?"

Chapter 35

The observation deck felt surreal as our makeshift broadcast studio—stars streaking past the dome in long arcs of light as we hurtled toward a future that Taylor thought belonged to him and those he determined worthy.

Tessa fiddled with one of her inspection bots, the same one that got fried after discovering the parasite. The only other workable cameras on Erebus were the ones in our Halos, but Tessa thought up the idea of using the high-resolution inspection camera on Clunker—the name she'd given to the small bot. Its direct feed into Erebus would make it easier for Sage to pipe the broadcast through the channels she'd managed to hack into.

It had only taken Tessa two days to make the modifications needed for Clunker to act as a broadcast camera operator.

I felt myself getting more and more nervous as we approached the moment we'd be live for all the world, and for Taylor himself—assuming he had a broadcast feed on Goliath.

Tessa adjusted something on Clunker's chassis.

"Alright, I think we're good. Sage? You picking up the feed?"

Sage nodded. "It's coming through perfectly."

Clunker twitched around on its spindly little spider legs, its main optic now pointing toward me. Its chassis bore a faint scorch mark where it had been attacked by that parasite. It felt appropriate that the little bot got to be part of this moment.

Tessa and Sage moved to either side of me, their presence helping to calm my nerves. We'd gone over what we might say, but hadn't rehearsed. Sage had said it would sound better unpolished. More real.

We looked at each other. No special lighting. Just the soft glow of the deck and the starlight streaking past.

Clunker backed up a few steps, making sure we were all in frame.

I took a deep breath, straightening my coveralls.

"Alright, let's do this."

The indicator light on Clunker lit up red, indicating we were now live. My brain went blank. I couldn't remember if we had agreed on "People of Earth" or "Citizens of Earth". In the end, I opened my mouth and hoped for the best.

"Hello. My name is Malcolm Walker, Captain of Erebus. You may be shocked to see me and my crew, Tessa Harper and Sage."

I gestured to the women at my sides.

"I know that much has been said about our brave sacrifice in pursuit of Taylor Young's vision for the future. But we're here to tell you that those stories are a lie."

Tessa stepped forward, her voice steady and clear.

"We didn't die heroes. We didn't sacrifice ourselves for some glorious corporate expansion. Taylor Young tried to murder us when he thought we may be a threat to his Ascendancy."

Sage spoke next, her voice controlled but intense.

"He overloaded our reactor remotely when he discovered we weren't going to follow his plans for Serra Prime. Plans that exclude anyone he deems unworthy—the sick, the poor, anyone who questions his vision."

My throat felt dry, but the words started flowing.

"Joey Thompson, our systems specialist, died saving this ship from Young's sabotage. He gave his life not for corporate glory, but to stop a madman who sees people as assets to be managed, obstacles to be removed."

The stars continued their silent dance outside the dome. Somewhere out there, people were watching. Maybe believing.

"Young talks about humanity's future, but he means *his* future. A future where he decides who deserves to live and who deserves to die. A future where Earth and its system are nothing but a resource to be squeezed dry."

Tessa's voice carried that fire again.

"We've seen what he's really building. Not a colony—a caste system. Not expansion—exploitation."

"So we're taking Erebus—*our* ship—to Serra Prime on our own terms," I continued. "Not as corporate heroes, but as free people who refuse to let Taylor Young decide what humanity becomes."

Sage moved closer to the camera.

"To anyone listening who still believes in the dream of Serra Prime, in the future of Earth, in the idea that every life has value—you're not alone. Resistance is still possible."

Sage returned to her position by my side as I looked directly into Clunker's eye.

"This is Malcolm Walker, Tessa Harper, and Sage, aboard Erebus. We're alive, we're free, and we're not giving up."

"In the void, we endure," We said together. It was the one part of the speech that we had rehearsed.

The red light on Clunker went dark.

We stood in silence. No fanfare. No cheers. Just the hum of Erebus and the stars.

But we'd said it. We'd told the truth. And if anyone out there was still listening—maybe it would be enough.

Tessa let out a long breath, her shoulders dropping as the tension released.

"That was intense."

I nodded, adrenaline still buzzing through me, my hands trembling as I wiped them on my coveralls.

"Yeah."

My voice came out rougher than I expected. The weight of what we'd done was starting to settle in. We'd essentially declared war on the most powerful corporation in human history, broadcast it to the entire system, and signed our names to it.

Tessa looked at Sage, concern creasing her brow.

"How do we know it got out?"

Sage's smile was almost predatory as she tilted her head.

"Oh, it got out. I'm monitoring feeds now. The GCE is already trying to take credit for allowing the broadcast, saying that they stand with Erebus."

A bitter laugh escaped before I could stop it.

"Seriously? They seemed fine with corporate control until they realized they were on Taylor's chopping block."

"I know," Sage said, her expression growing more serious. "But that's how these things go. We have to hope that people will see through it."

The irony wasn't lost on me. The same government that had been Stellar-Forge's rubber stamp for decades was now scrambling to distance themselves from Taylor's Ascendancy.

Clunker skittered over to Tessa, its damaged chassis catching the starlight. The little bot had done good work. Better than most of the politicians back on Earth, that was for sure.

"What about Chrysalis cells?" I asked. "Any word from them?"

Sage's eyes unfocused for a moment as she accessed data streams.

"Scattered chatter. Cautious optimism. Some are calling it propaganda, others are saying it proves resistance is still possible."

Tessa crossed her arms, studying the stars beyond the dome.

"And Taylor?"

"Radio silence from StellarForge command. But I'm detecting increased quantum burst traffic. They're talking; they're just not talking where anyone else can hear."

The thought of Taylor's reaction made my stomach clench. We'd humiliated him publicly, exposed his lies, and stolen his prize ship. Men like Taylor didn't forgive that kind of embarrassment.

"He's going to come after us harder now," I said.

"Let him," Tessa replied, steel in her voice. "We've got something he doesn't."

"What's that?"

She gestured around the observation deck, at Sage, at the stars rushing past.

"The truth," she said. "And a head start."

My Halo buzzed in my pocket. I reached in, already bracing for William's name to glare back at me—ready to dress me down for going rogue.

But it wasn't him. It was Olivia.

I accepted the call, and her face filled the small screen, beaming with excitement.

"Hey, kiddo. I take it you saw our little vid."

"That was prime!" Olivia's voice practically bounced through the speaker. "Eterna is glitching out over it."

"Glitching out is...good?"

"Very good." She leaned closer to her camera. "You made me very popular. Five different people stopped me on the way to my room asking if I was Captain Walker's daughter. They all wanted me to thank you."

The relief that flooded through me was almost overwhelming. I'd been so focused on reaching Earth, on fighting Taylor's propaganda, that I hadn't considered how our broadcast might affect the people on Serra Prime.

"I'm sure you were plenty popular before." I said.

"Well, of course." Olivia's grin widened. "But this is a whole other level."

Tessa leaned over my shoulder, grinning at the screen.

"Hey, Liv! How'd I do?"

Olivia blinked, her mouth falling open.

"Tessa? You look exactly the same."

Tessa chuckled, settling in closer to get a better view.

"You don't. You were cute before, but now you're..."

Tessa's eyes flicked toward me. I didn't like where this was going.

"...all grown up," Tessa said, catching my look and sanding the edge off whatever she'd meant to say.

Olivia glanced at me, then back to Tessa, her cheeks flushing.

"Thanks."

Sage moved to my other side, forcing me to hold my Halo out further to get them all in the frame.

"Hey, Sage," Olivia said, tucking a piece of hair behind her ear. "Thanks for the tips. I'm getting lots of compliments on my eyes."

Sage's expression turned playful, almost mischievous.

"I'll bet you are. Any cute ones?"

Olivia's face went crimson, her eyes going wide.

"Sage!"

"I think we have our answer," Tessa said, her grin widening.

"Okay, no, we're not doing this," I said, trying to wave the conversation off.

Sage looked smug, and Tessa was smirking like she was enjoying every second of both my and Olivia's discomfort.

"Relax, Mal," Tessa said. "Olivia is a very attractive young woman. It's only natural that—"

"Please, stop," Olivia said, covering her face, though I could see she was fighting back a smile through her fingers.

When I'd left Earth—what felt like months ago—Olivia had been my sick little girl, tethered to breathing tubes and constant monitoring. Now she was...exactly what Tessa said. Grown up.

"We should probably let you go. I'm sure you have a swarm of adoring fans to attend to." I said.

Olivia rolled her eyes, but her smile stayed bright.

"That...and chores. I doubt being Captain Walker's daughter is gonna get me out of perimeter checks."

"Perimeter checks?" I frowned at the screen. "Eterna's the only colony on the planet, what are you checking for?"

Olivia sighed. That exasperated sound teenagers perfected when their parents asked perfectly reasonable questions.

"Don't get all netted, Dad. A couple of colonists said they saw something when they were out exploring. It's probably nothing. There's wildlife here. Some pretty prime stuff, actually. But it's all harmless."

Sage leaned closer to my Halo, her expression sharpening.

"Olivia, if there's wildlife, then there are likely predators."

"Okay, sure." Olivia's casual tone made my stomach clench. "But that's why we have a perimeter, and nobody goes outside it alone or unarmed."

My nineteen-year-old daughter, who used to struggle to walk across our apartment without getting winded, was now casually talking about carrying weapons and conducting armed patrols on an alien world.

"What kind of something did they see?" I asked.

"Don't know. Something moving in the woods. Could've been shadows, could've been anything. William's got teams cataloging everything, but Serra Prime is huge. We can't map every species in a few years."

Tessa shifted beside me, her expression growing serious.

"Any signs of intelligence? Tool use, structures, communication patterns?"

"Nothing like that," Olivia said, though something flickered across her face—a hesitation I didn't like. "It's just ghost stories. Between the crystals throwing light around and everything else having some kind of glow, it's hard to tell what you're seeing sometimes."

None of this was helping to put my mind at ease.

"Look, Dad, I know you're worried, but we're not soft-wired. Everyone's been trained on basic survival protocols, wildlife identification, emergency procedures."

That was probably true, which somehow made it worse.

"Besides," Olivia continued, "the worst thing I've encountered is some blue glowing moss that stains your hands and clothes and smells like sweaty socks. Not exactly apex predator material."

"The bioluminescence you mentioned earlier—is it widespread?" Sage asked.

"Pretty much everything here glows to some degree. Plants, fungi, rocks, even some of the animals. Makes night patrols kind of beautiful."

"Have you noticed any synchronized pulses? Patterns in the glows?"

Olivia frowned at the screen, her casual demeanor shifting.

"You mean like signs of communication? No. Not really."

She paused, and I caught that hesitation again—the same flicker I'd seen moments before.

"I mean...maybe? There's this grass. If you step on it, it's glow ripples out from where you touched it. Like waves spreading across a pond, except it's light instead of water. But the scientists say it's likely chemical."

Sage nodded.

"That does sound chemical, if it's all connected. Root networks can transmit information through chemical signals pretty efficiently."

"Right," Olivia said. "It's pretty. The whole field lights up when you walk through it. Makes you feel like you're walking on stars."

Something about the way she described it made it seem too beautiful, too perfect. Too good to be true.

"Just...be careful, kiddo. Promise me."

Her expression softened.

"I promise, Dad. We're being smart about everything."

"Okay. Talk to you soon. Love you."

"Love you too."

I started to end the call, then hesitated, my thumb hovering over the disconnect button.

"Liv?"

"Yeah?"

"If you hear anything about William being angry about our broadcast, maybe give your old man a heads up?"

Olivia's smile turned knowing, the same expression she'd worn when she was eight and caught me trying to sneak some of her Halloween candy.

"Will do."

"Thanks."

The call ended. Tessa and Sage were both watching me with expressions I couldn't quite read.

"You think William's gonna be upset?" Tessa asked.

"I don't know."

Sage tilted her head.

"I think he'll wait. If our broadcast has the desired outcome, he could say that it was part of the plan from the start."

"And if it fails?" I asked.

"Then he can say I told you so. Win-win for him."

"Great."

Tessa crossed her arms, studying my face.

"Why so worried about William being angry?"

"We're planning to stay at his colony. He's looking after my daughter. I'd prefer he didn't hate me."

All true, but not the whole truth. The bigger reason twisted in my gut—memories of Amber's parents sitting stiffly in our living room, their disapproval radiating like heat from a fusion core. They'd never thought Malcolm Walker was good enough for their brilliant daughter. Never said it outright, but got real close a few times. Amber claimed she didn't care what they thought, and I know she didn't. But it meant we hardly saw them. Olivia barely knew her grandparents existed before they severed all contact after Amber's death.

Whatever was happening between Sage and me—whatever could happen—the idea of being the wedge between another father and daughter knotted something low in my chest. William had already lost so many years of his daughter to that quantum core. He deserved a chance to have her back. And Sage deserved that too. Deserved to have her father without having to choose between him and...whatever we were becoming.

Tessa studied me for a second, like she could tell there was more to it.

"Fair enough. But if he's half as smart as he sounds, he'll understand we did what we had to do."

Tessa bent down, picking up Clunker, who was still sticking close to her side.

"You did good work, little buddy."

The little bot gave Tessa a long stare with its single eye, legs paddling like it thought it was swimming.

I hoped Tessa was right. That our plan would work. But I also knew what that would mean. If our message did inspire Earth to stand up and fight back, people would no doubt get hurt, maybe killed. We'd broadcast hope to billions of people trapped under corporate rule. But hope was dangerous. Hope made people take risks they wouldn't normally take. Made them believe change was possible when the odds were stacked against them.

How many Chrysalis cells would see our survival as a sign to launch operations they'd been planning? How many ordinary citizens would refuse corporate directives?

"You alright, Mal?" Sage asked, her voice soft.

"Just thinking about consequences."

Tessa set Clunker down gently.

"Sometimes you have to light the fuse and hope the explosion doesn't get you too."

"Yeah," I said. "But we're not the ones in the blast radius. Not yet anyway."

Chapter 36

The news feed flickered across the galley's wall display, bathing our faces in cold blue light. Sage and I sat across from each other at the small table, both of us leaning forward, studying every frame like it held the secrets of the universe.

We'd been doing this for a week straight now. Ever since our broadcast went live, we'd become obsessed with parsing Earth's feeds for any sign of what our message had actually accomplished. The problem was, the corporate news had gone into full lockdown mode. AI anchors now delivered every story with perfect, emotionless precision—no stumbles, no tells, no humanity bleeding through to give us a hint of what was really happening.

The current feed showed Obsidian Security officers dragging a line of people toward one of their gray transport shuttles. The AI anchor's voice droned over the footage: "Anarchist agitators caught stealing vital resources from a NutriCore distribution center have been detained for processing."

Anarchist agitators. Right. They looked like warehouse workers to me. Tired, desperate people in coveralls and work boots. The kind who probably had families waiting at home, wondering if dinner would stretch another night.

The camera pulled back for a wide shot, and something caught my attention. A cluster of teenagers stood at the security perimeter, shouting at the obbies. Most of them looked like kids being kids, angry at authority. But several of the girls had blue streaks running through their hair.

"You have fans." I said.

Sage's expression darkened as she watched the screen.

"They're kids. They shouldn't be there."

"They're fighters, standing up for what they believe in."

She turned to look at me, those crystalline blue eyes sharp with something I couldn't quite identify. Worry? Guilt?

"They're putting targets on their backs because of me. Because of what we did."

"Because of what Taylor did," I corrected. "We told the truth."

"Same result."

One of the girls on screen stepped too close to the security line. An obbie shoved her back hard enough that she stumbled. The camera cut away immediately, but not before I caught the flash of defiance on her face.

"Look at them," I said. "They're not backing down."

"They should. This isn't their fight."

"Says who? Their entire future's being decided by corporate boardrooms. If that's not their fight, whose is it?"

Sage was quiet for a long moment, watching the feed transition to some meaningless corporate announcement about productivity quotas.

"I feel responsible. Imagine that was Olivia," Sage said. "Fourteen-year-old Olivia being pushed to the ground."

My hands clenched into fists on the table.

"I don't have to imagine it."

Sage's expression softened, but I kept going, needing to get the words out before they choked me.

"When I left on Erebus, I pictured things like this or worse. Olivia standing up to obbies, getting herself arrested, beaten, disappeared."

I gestured at the screen where another group of protesters was being rounded up.

"But Olivia is a fighter, and as much as I hate it—and I hate it, Sage—I also love it. She inspires me."

The contradiction burned in my chest. How could I be proud and terrified of the same thing? How could I love the very quality that might get my daughter killed?

"She's got this fire in her that I never had. Olivia looks at an impossible situation and doesn't see defeat. She sees a challenge."

"You have that same fire, Mal. I've seen it."

Sage's voice was gentle but certain. Like she'd been watching me longer than I realized.

"If that's true, it's because of Olivia. But she's the one protecting me now. She's been keeping things from me."

The admission tasted bitter. My daughter was shielding me from the truth, and we both knew it. Those calls where she deflected my questions about her activities. The careful way she changed subjects whenever I probed too deep.

"I know why, and I get it. She knows that I'll worry, and I've been letting her because she's right."

Sage reached across the table, her hand hovering above mine. Not quite touching, but close enough that I could've felt the warmth of her projection if it had any.

"I need to let her do this, whatever it is, even if it means..."

The words stuck in my throat. Saying them out loud would make them real, and I wasn't sure I was ready for that. But Sage waited, patient as always, those blue eyes holding mine steady.

"Even if it means I may lose her."

All these years of fighting to protect Olivia, to keep her safe, to give her a future—and now the best thing I could do for her was step back and let her walk into danger.

"I can't protect her from everything. I want to, but it's not possible."

My voice cracked on the last word. The parent in me screamed against every syllable, but the logic was undeniable. Olivia was surrounded by people who saw her as an asset in a war I'd helped start. Even if I could magically transport back to her side, what then? Lock her in a room? Drag her away from the only cause that had ever given her real purpose?

"The only thing I could do is try to smother this fire inside her, and if I do that, I'll lose her for sure."

Because that's what parents did sometimes. We loved our children so much that we suffocated the very things that made them extraordinary.

"Then don't," Sage said.

The engineering bay's filtration system hummed as I swapped out the last air filter, pulling a refreshed one from the cleaning unit and sliding the dirty one into its place. The familiar routine felt grounding after weeks of uncertainty and revelation. Simple mechanical work that didn't require wrestling with impossible questions about love, loyalty, or the nature of consciousness.

I closed the hatch and activated the clean cycle, wiping my hands on a rag as footsteps echoed behind me.

"Not often I find you elbow-deep in chores without Sage whispering over your shoulder."

Tessa leaned against the doorframe, arms crossed but relaxed. Her auburn hair had grown out during our journey, and she'd started pulling it back in a loose braid instead of her usual ponytail.

"Yeah, she had some more modifications she wanted to do to Erebus."

"She's been enjoying having full control, huh?"

"Oh yeah. Finding percentage point optimizations has become quite the hobby of hers."

Tessa straightened her posture. Her expression grew more serious, the casual banter fading from her voice.

"I know it's not my business. But you and Sage. What's going on there?"

The question hit me like a wrench to the chest. Should've seen it coming. I haven't been hiding my feelings since I learned the truth about Sage. But Tessa didn't know that truth.

"Oh, it's...how do I..."

"I'm just a little concerned. I know I've teased you about her, but I thought it was...I don't know what I thought it was. But I didn't think it was anything real. But lately, it seems like maybe I was wrong?"

Tessa picked at something on the doorframe.

"I'm not jealous. I want you to know that. After that night in my quarters, when I said what I said, about us. I realized I like being your friend, so I didn't bring it up again. But..." Tessa turned her attention from the doorframe to me. "You know she can't leave the ship. When we get to Serra Prime, she'll still be here. I don't know how her AI brain works, but it doesn't seem fair...to her...I'm sorry, this is awkward. I don't know what I'm asking here. It's not my business."

I had to tell her.

"Tess, it's okay. I get it. But there's an explanation." I drew in a breath and let it out slow. "Sage is real—"

"I know she *seems* real, but—"

"Let me finish."

The words came out in a rush. William Frye's daughter. Her NHS. The quantum consciousness link. The stolen core. The walled-off memories protecting her from the truth that could kill her. All of it.

Tessa's expression shifted from skepticism to confusion to something approaching belief.

"That's...that's impossible."

"I know how it sounds—"

"Is that true?" Sage's voice came from behind Tessa.

Tessa spun around to face her. My stomach dropped through the deck plating. Had she heard everything? The safeguards William warned about—the neural collapse that could kill her if she learned the truth—

"Is it true?" Sage's voice was urgent.

Tessa stepped deeper into the engineering bay, giving Sage a clear view of me. The look on Sage's face made my throat close up. This was it. This was how I killed her. We were so close. One more stasis cycle and she could have been free.

"It's true. But I couldn't tell you. William said—"

"I heard that part." Sage said, stepping forward into the bay, her movements deliberate but uncertain. Like she was processing information that didn't fit her existing parameters. Her eyes stayed fixed on mine, searching for something.

"How long have you known?"

The question didn't hit like an accusation but like she was gathering data.

"Shortly after the null sphere, before our second cycle."

Sage looked down at the deck, her fingers starting to fidget with each other.

"Interesting..."

Tessa shifted uncomfortably beside us, glancing between Sage and me like she'd stumbled into something far bigger than expected.

"I'm gonna give you two some space."

She skirted past Sage, avoiding eye contact before disappearing down the corridor.

"How are you feeling?" I asked, searching for any signs of degradation.

Sage looked up at me, those impossibly blue eyes meeting mine. For a moment, I braced myself for the system failure William had warned about. Neural collapse. Cognitive breakdown. Death.

"I feel...fine," she said, though her voice had an edge to it—like fine was a placeholder for something she hadn't figured out how to name. Not the catastrophic rejection of reality that William had feared. Not the mental crisis that should have torn her consciousness apart.

But something had changed. The way she held herself. The uncertainty in her movements. Like her identity had shifted under her feet—but instead of falling, she was already mapping the new terrain.

"Sage—"

"I know, Mal. I know you wanted to tell me, and I understand why you didn't. But I'm confused. How did William know there might be a conflict?"

I swallowed hard, my throat dry.

"Because *you* told him. You developed the AI core."

"Huh."

She said it as if I'd told her some mundane but mildly interesting bit of information. Not the earth-shattering revelation that she'd engineered her own consciousness transfer.

"Are you sure you're okay?"

"Oh...yeah. It's just...I'm not usually wrong. So why is there no conflict?"

"You sound disappointed."

"No, not at all. I'm curious. I can't be sure, but I wonder if the tests I ran while developing the core were based on a consciousness learning of its humanity immediately after integration."

"You think there might be some kind of acclimation period?"

"In a way. I think you're the reason."

"Me?"

"Mm-hmm," she nodded, a familiar half-smile playing at the corners of her mouth. "You've been treating me as more than an AI, as human, since before you even learned that I was. Obviously more so afterward. But I think that helped me to see myself as more."

"So it's like the frog experiment."

Her smirk widened, some of that playful spark returning to her eyes.

"Sure. You slow-boiled my identity in a pot of existential truth."

I grinned. "But instead of scalding death…"

She tilted her head, the spark in her eyes unmistakable.

"The opposite of that."

I held out both hands. "So my analogy works."

"Yes. A bit morbid—but it works. Instead of shocking my consciousness with the truth all at once, you gradually helped me accept my humanity. The safeguards I built were designed around immediate revelation, not…this."

She gestured between us, encompassing months of conversations, shared moments, the growing connection that had felt impossible but real.

"I programmed my own protection based on fear of the truth. But you made the truth feel…" She paused, searching for the right word. "Natural. Like it was always there, waiting for me to acknowledge it."

The engineering bay's ventilation system cycled again, filling the silence between us. Sage stood there, still processing her newfound understanding of herself.

"There's something else," I said.

Sage's gaze flicked to mine, cautious but open.

"You've got a body. Waiting for you on Serra Prime."

She blinked, as if she weren't sure she'd heard me right.

"I mean…your body. It's there, in stasis. That was your plan from the start—link your consciousness to survive NHS, and once you reached Serra Prime, where the atmosphere is safe…reverse the process and wake you up."

Sage didn't speak. Just stared at me, eyes wide, like the idea hadn't even occurred to her.

"What about my memories?"

"You'll get them all back."

"No. *My* memories. Not the past…this."

She gestured to the space between us.

"Everything that's happened since. Erebus. The mission. You."

Relief flooded through me—one of her first concerns about waking up was the same one I'd had when William had explained the process.

"William says you won't lose anything. Everything that makes you who you are is happening in your human mind right now."

"I understand that. But there's a memory wall in place. Who's to say taking that wall down won't damage memories outside it?"

"William seemed very confident. I'm assume he got that information from you."

"I'll need to see the process details before I agree to anything."

Her voice carried the same analytical tone she used when discussing ship modifications. But underneath, I heard something else. Fear. Not of death or malfunction, but of losing what we'd built together.

"Okay, and what if it's either or?"

The question came out harder than I intended. Testing her. Pushing her to confront the choice that terrified me most—that she might choose the safety of her current existence over the risk of becoming fully human again.

"Easy. I choose these memories."

No hesitation. No wavering. But absolute certainty that cut through my fears like a plasma torch through hull plating.

"Even if it means staying in the core forever?"

"Even then."

She stepped closer, her projection solid and real despite its artificial nature.

"Mal, I've been existing in this state for fourteen years. But I've only been living for these past five. I won't give that up. I won't give *you* up."

The words I wanted to say hung between us like a gravitational field—massive, invisible, pulling everything toward it. That she shouldn't sacrifice her humanity for me. I'd rather lose her than watch her choose a half-existence because she was afraid of forgetting what we have.

But this wasn't the moment for that conversation. Maybe it would never be, if William was right about the memory integration process. If Sage could keep both sides of the wall intact.

"Well, let's hope it doesn't come to that."

She nodded, her expression thoughtful.

"I don't think I would have developed something that would destroy my memories. But I also probably never thought that I would..." She paused, a slight flush appearing across her cheeks. "Fall in love with my engineer."

The words hit me like atmospheric decompression—sudden, overwhelming, stealing the breath from my lungs.

"You love me?"

"Don't act like you're surprised."

"I love you too, Sage."

The words felt like stepping out of an airlock without a suit—terrifying and liberating at the same time. Months of dancing around this moment, of telling myself it was impossible, of fighting feelings that defied every rational explanation.

"It's about time."

Her grin lit up the engineering bay brighter than the status panels. That playful confidence I'd fallen for, mixed with something deeper now.

"You knew?"

"Mal, you've been looking at me like I hung the stars for months. I was starting to think you'd never work up the courage."

Heat crept up my neck. "I thought I was being subtle."

"You weren't," she said, her voice softening. "But I didn't mind."

The air between us shifted—less charged, more steady. Like the gravity had settled, and we were finally standing on solid ground.

After everything we'd lost, everything we were still afraid to hope for—this was something real.

"I guess I should stop holding back," I said.

Sage tilted her head, that familiar half-smile returning.

"Guess you should."

Chapter 37

"Hey, you two."

Tessa's voice cut through the droning AI anchor discussing Ascendancy resource allocation. She stood in the galley doorway, holding two bottles that glowed with electric blue luminescence.

"Turn that scrap off and let's go have a proper last night on Erebus."

She shook the bottles, the liquid inside swirling like captured starlight.

"You smuggled contraband onto my boat?" I asked.

"*Our* boat." Tessa's grin turned mischievous. "And...I found this while packing up Joey's gear."

Her voice softened, losing its playful edge.

"Guess he wasn't as corp-kissed as he wanted everyone to believe."

The image didn't compute. Joey Thompson—rule-follower extraordinaire—drinking CoreBurn. The bootleg spirit of warehouse workers and resistance cells. The stuff that got you arrested for possession in most corporate districts.

Maybe there'd been more to Joey than any of us understood. Maybe his final act of heroism hadn't been as much of a surprise as we'd thought.

"I can't partake in the drinking, but not watching these feeds sounds like an excellent idea," Sage said, gesturing toward the wall display where an AI anchor discussed Level-4 curfew implementations in Core Districts.

"Prime, grab some mugs," Tessa said as she turned, bottles held high like trophies.

Sage waved off the feeds. The corporate spin made it impossible to separate truth from propaganda, but the signs were clear—resistance activities were increasing. *In the void, we endure,* had become something of a battle cry. Graffitied on buildings and transports, shouted in the streets.

Our motto. Erebus's motto had traveled from this ship to the streets of Earth.

I pulled two clean mugs from the galley cabinet, and Sage and I followed Tessa's slightly unsteady path to the observation deck.

Tessa dropped onto the sofa with the grace of someone who'd obviously started this party before inviting us to join in. The CoreBurn bottles *clinked* against each other as she set them on the small table next to her.

I settled beside Tessa while Sage claimed the spot next to me, our knees almost touching. I passed the mugs to Tessa.

"Thaaank you," Tessa said, drawing it out in a playful sing-song.

Tessa twisted the top off one bottle—suspiciously less full than the other—and poured generous amounts of glowing blue liquid into each mug. The CoreBurn caught the light streaming through the observation windows, casting electric patterns across our faces.

She set the bottle down and passed me a mug, cradling the other in her hands.

Outside, stars streaked past in brilliant ribbons. Tomorrow we'd enter our final stasis cycle. When we woke, there'd be no more stars, just Serra Prime filling our view.

Tessa held up her mug.

"To Joey."

Her voice caught on his name. She stared up at the mug in her hand.

"He didn't make the best decisions. Made some pretty dumb ones. But when it mattered..."

Tessa had to pause, her jaw working as she fought for control.

"...when it *really* mattered...he was brave."

I raised my mug.

"To Joey."

The words felt inadequate.

Sage echoed, her voice soft. "To Joey."

Tessa wiped her eyes with the back of her free hand, smearing away tears that caught the blue glow from the CoreBurn bottles.

"Oh...and thanks for the booze, Joey. I hope you don't mind."

A laugh escaped her—broken, wet, but genuine. The kind of sound that comes when grief meets the absurdity of life. Here we were, toasting our dead friend with his own contraband alcohol.

I took a sip. The CoreBurn hit like liquid electricity, metallic and sharp, with that distinctive aftertaste that reminded you this stuff wasn't for enjoyment. It was rough, unrefined, dangerous. Perfect for a night like this.

Sage tilted her head as I winced from the burn, studying my expression with obvious curiosity.

"Looks painful."

"That's part of its appeal," I set the mug down, feeling the CoreBurn's electric heat spreading through my chest. "I don't usually drink it straight though.

Used to get a drink called the Iron Wake at The Drift. Basically CoreBurn and coffee."

"Now *that* sounds like a recipe for staying awake for a week." Tessa laughed, taking another sip without flinching.

The observation deck fell silent. Tomorrow we'd be locked in stasis pods, unconscious for the final stretch to Serra Prime.

Tessa swirled the glowing liquid in her mug, watching the patterns it made.

"So what's the plan once we reach these secret coordinates? We get put to work as Chrysalis soldiers or something?" She asked.

The question caught me off guard. I'd been so focused on getting to Olivia, on reuniting with my daughter after years of separation, that I hadn't thought about what our roles would be at the Eterna colony. Just getting there had felt impossible enough.

"Something like that, I guess. I'm sure there'll be lots of work to do to get ready for Goliath's arrival," I stared into my mug. "Honestly? I haven't thought much past seeing Olivia again."

Tessa gave me a sideways look. Not judgment—understanding.

"Yeah," she said after a moment. "One thing at a time."

Tessa gestured toward the bulkheads with her mug, CoreBurn sloshing dangerously close to the rim.

"You know...Erebus *is* a gunship. Seems like something they might want to leverage."

"That's true," I said, rubbing my forehead. "We'd have to figure out a solution to Erebus's AI though. I hear the person currently holding that position is vacating her role."

Sage's smile was radiant, unburdened by the complexity of what we were discussing.

"Shouldn't be a problem. The core should still be intact after the quantum link is severed; we'll just need to develop a new AI. Luckily, we have a pretty incredible AI engineer on board."

"I've never built an AI personality from scratch. But I've always wanted to try."

The admission felt both thrilling and terrifying. Creating consciousness, even artificial consciousness, was the kind of challenge engineers dreamed about—and secretly feared. The chance to craft something new, something that had never existed before.

Sage's expression turned playfully stern, though her eyes sparkled with mischief.

"I'm sure you'll do fine. But if you fall in love with it, we're going to have a problem."

Tessa's CoreBurn went down the wrong pipe. She erupted into a fit of coughing and sputtering, blue liquid dribbling down her chin as she fought for air between gasps of laughter.

"Oh..." She wiped her mouth with the back of her hand, still wheezing. "Careful, Sage. You might be asking too much of him."

I felt heat rise in my cheeks that had nothing to do with the bootleg liquor.

"Very funny." I took another sip, using the excuse to avoid both their gazes. "I think I can manage."

"What about you, Sage?" Tessa's voice carried a loose quality from the CoreBurn. "After you're back in your body, you'll still be part of our crew, right?"

"Try and stop me," Sage said.

I caught myself smiling, not at the words, but at the fire in her voice.

"Prime," Tessa grinned. "And that way, you can keep an eye on Mal."

"Exactly," Sage said.

"Can we stop?" The heat in my cheeks was becoming unbearable. "I thought this was supposed to be a fun last night on Erebus."

Tessa refilled her mug, the blue liquid sloshing as she poured. "I'm having fun. Sage? Are you having fun?"

"So much fun."

The mischief in Sage's tone made it clear she was enjoying my discomfort immensely. I drained the last of my CoreBurn and passed the empty mug to Tessa, who refilled it without hesitation before passing it back.

"Well, can we change the subject?" I asked, desperate for a topic that didn't involve me.

"Alright." Tessa's expression shifted, the playful atmosphere evaporating as something more serious took its place. "I've been thinking about the null sphere. When we were sent back to Erebus. The real Erebus. That...thing...said something. Do you remember what it was?"

The CoreBurn suddenly tasted like metal and regret. I took a long sip before answering.

"Some are willing. Others are chosen."

"I've been trying to figure out what that could mean," Tessa said.

"It doesn't mean anything, Tess," the words came out sharp, if a little sloppy. "Just cryptic words from some alien race, or who knows what, that thought it was being profound."

"Maybe." Tessa said, staring into her mug like it might hold answers. "But I've been thinking about how it treated Joey. I think maybe *we* were the willing, and Joey was the chosen."

"Chosen?" Sage leaned forward. "How so?"

"Joey betrayed us in there and then regretted it. Then he called Rivera and regretted that. Then…" Tessa's voice caught. "He sacrificed himself."

"I'm not following," I said.

"What if Joey had never gone through the trial? Never been offered a chance to save himself by turning his back on his crew and felt that regret?" Tessa set her mug down, meeting my eyes. "Would he have decided to take your place in the reactor core?"

The observation deck seemed to tilt around me. Stars streaked past the windows, but suddenly they felt less like ribbons of light and more like the bars of a cage we'd never escape.

"Are you saying that you think the null sphere chose to put Joey through the trial to…what…make sure that I would live?"

Tessa nodded slowly. "Think about it. We were willing to resist corporate control, to make our own choices. But Joey? Joey was always putting his trust in the corporation, following orders with hopes of moving up the ranks, looking out for number one. The trial showed him the consequences of those kinds of decisions."

"And then gave him a chance to really matter," Sage finished quietly.

The warmth from the CoreBurn turned cold in my stomach. If Tessa was right—if some alien intelligence had twisted Joey's path so I could walk mine…

"Are you saying…whatever designed the trial *knew* Taylor was going to try and kill us? How is that possible?"

Tessa shrugged, taking another sip of CoreBurn.

"Beats me. How'd they hijack our brains and turn a fraction of a second into a nightmare?"

"Maybe it didn't know. But it could've projected," Sage said. "With enough data, likely outcomes can be predicted with remarkable accuracy."

Tessa snorted, nearly choking on her drink again.

"Don't tell me you believe in determinism."

I'd heard the term before—the idea that the future, like the past, was set in stone. That every effect was the result of a prior cause, stretching all the way back to the beginning of time. Free will reduced to an illusion. Choice, nothing more than neurons firing in predetermined patterns. The concept made my skin crawl.

Sage shook her head.

"Not in the strict sense. But they spoke your language, planted a parasite on Erebus back when it was still on Earth. Who knows how long they've been watching gathering data."

She turned to look at me.

"Maybe they had enough to simulate a range of plausible futures. And maybe Joey needing to sacrifice himself to save either of you was likely enough to justify the scenario they built. At least, from their perspective."

The warmth from the CoreBurn turned to acid in my stomach. Joey's face flashed through my memory—the moment he'd decided to enter that reactor chamber. Had that moment been real? His choice, his heroism? Or the inevitable outcome of alien manipulation, psychological programming designed to push him toward a predetermined end?

"Sorry," Tessa said, swirling the liquid in her mug. "Didn't mean to turn our last night into some deep-space existential happy hour. Maybe we should go back to teasing Mal?"

I managed a small laugh, though it felt hollow in my chest.

"No. It's fine. It's just a little hard to wrap my mind around while mildly intoxicated," I said.

"You know what I think?" Sage said. "Joey made his choice in that reactor room. Whatever the null sphere did to you—whatever alien psychology test you were part of—none of it matters more than that moment. He could have hesitated. Could have backed out. Could have let you go instead." She looked into my eyes. "But he didn't. That choice was his."

Tessa nodded, raising her mug again.

Outside, the stars no longer felt like prison bars but guides pointing us toward Serra Prime. Toward Olivia. Toward whatever future we'd build together.

I finished the last of my CoreBurn, feeling its electric warmth chase away some of the darkness. "Joey was a good man. Whatever else happened, that's what matters."

Despite the grief, the uncertainty, the weight of everything we'd lost and everything we still had to face—I didn't regret being here with them.

Tomorrow we'd enter stasis. When we woke, everything would change.

Chapter 38

YEAR 2311

Consciousness returned without the familiar stasis headache, as if my body had finally mastered the process after five cycles. The disorientation that usually clouded those first moments was absent—replaced by a single, overwhelming thought that drove everything else away.

Today I see Olivia again.

Sage stood beside my pod in the same position she'd occupied for every awakening, her expression mixing relief and excitement.

"We're here, Mal. We made it."

Emotions hit me all at once. Six years compressed into six months of consciousness but stretched into an eternity of separation from my daughter. The anticipation was so intense it bordered on pain.

Tessa sat up in her own pod, and when our eyes met, we shared a look like two kids waking up on Christmas morning. The grief and uncertainty that had shadowed our last conscious weeks seemed to evaporate.

"You two get cleaned up and then meet me on the observation deck," Sage said, her voice carrying the same excitement that was coursing through my veins. "Then, we'll begin our descent."

Tessa and I stood on unsteady legs, the usual post-stasis coordination issues feeling insignificant compared to what waited ahead. Tessa paused at Joey's pod, placing her hand on the frosted glass.

"We made it, Joey." She whispered.

The moment caught me in the throat, but I pushed forward on legs remembering how to move, making my way to my quarters as quickly as my adjusting body would allow. The shower lasted maybe five minutes—a record even by my standards. Without waiting for the full dry cycle, I stepped out, grabbed my clean Erebus coveralls, and dressed with the efficiency of someone who'd waited six years for this moment.

Typically, this was when I'd call Olivia. But not today. I was going to see her. Touch her. Hold her.

Boots laced, I headed for the observation deck at what could generously be called a controlled sprint.

The doors slid open, and the view hit me like a revelation.

Serra Prime filled the viewport, a living jewel suspended against the void. The system's sun, Vespera, bathed the planet's surface in a warm orange light, golden hues that made the crystalline formations scattered across continents shimmer like scattered diamonds. Swirling cloud formations tinged with purple drifted across verdant forests that glowed with their own inner light. Two moons hung in the distance—one large with its distinctive green tint, the other a bright point of golden light.

And somewhere down there, Olivia was waiting.

"Pretty incredible, right?"

Sage's words barely registered through the fog of wonder clouding my thoughts. The planet below defied every description from the mission briefings. This wasn't just another world—it was a canvas painted in colors that didn't exist on Earth, alive with light that pulsed from within the very ground.

I wondered if Eterna had already clocked our arrival, but then remembered Sage's stealth modifications to our systems. We were a ghost ship as far as any sensors were concerned.

"Do they know we're here?" I asked.

"Not yet. I wanted to wait for our captain before sending our comms information."

Sage's words carried a playful formality that made me smile despite the knot of anticipation in my chest. Six months of dreaming about this moment, and now it was happening.

Tessa entered the deck, her hand moving to her mouth as she took in the view. The wonder on her face was priceless—this planet was beyond anything we'd imagined.

I looked at Sage. "Go ahead, send the info."

"Sent," Sage said.

We didn't have to wait long before Sage straightened. "I'm getting an incoming communications request. Patching it through."

A voice that I recognized came through Erebus's comms.

"E-Erebus Crew, this is Eterna c-c-control. W-Welcome to Serra P-Prime."

"Patch?" I said, glancing at Tessa. Her expression mirrored my own surprise and delight.

"G-g-greetings, Malcolm. O-Olivia thought this w-w-would be funny. Do you f-find it humorous?"

Olivia...of course. She'd probably liberated Patch from The Drift once she knew it was being shut down. Knowing how much she loved the bot, she probably would have kidnapped him regardless. The image of my daughter rescuing that ancient, mismatched service bot from corporate demolition warmed something deep in my chest.

"Not funny at all, buddy. You're doing a great job."

"Excellent. G-glad to be of s-service," Patch said.

Hearing that familiar glitched voice felt like coming home in a way I hadn't expected.

"We're about to make our descent. You ready for us down there?"

"Very g-good. W-We have a landing-ing p-pad for you. O-only one large enough, c-can't miss it."

"Sounds good. We'll see you soon, okay?"

"Looking f-f-forward to it. H-have a safe l-landing."

The comm channel closed, leaving us in silence. Below, Serra Prime continued its slow rotation, forests and crystalline fields catching Vespera's light, the whole surface alive under its glow.

"Sage, take us down."

Erebus shuddered as we hit Serra Prime's atmosphere, the ship's hull warming from friction as Sage guided us through the orange-tinted sky. Through the observation deck's viewport, I watched clouds streak past in ribbons of gold and purple, the alien atmosphere painting everything in hues that didn't exist on Earth.

Six years, compressed into these final ceremonial seconds. My hands gripped the safety rail as anticipation built in my chest like pressure in a sealed container.

"There," Sage said, her voice carrying wonder. "Look ahead."

The Eterna colony materialized through the atmospheric haze like something from a dream. A massive perimeter wall enclosed the settlement, its surface gleaming with the same reflective quality as the ship that had brought them here. Inside the walls, smaller outbuildings dotted the landscape, connected by paths where I could make out tiny figures moving between structures.

A colossal glass dome dominated one corner, its transparent surface revealing an impossible fusion of alien and terrestrial life. Luminite crystals grew alongside Earth ferns, their soft blue-green glow mingling with familiar greenery. Trees I recognized from home stood next to towering alien specimens whose translucent leaves caught Vespera's light and scattered it in prismatic displays.

The Eterna herself rested at the colony's heart—that graceful, latticed hull now serving as the settlement's central hub. Her elegant curves seemed even more beautiful against Serra Prime's golden backdrop, like a cathedral of metal and glass rising from an alien garden.

Twenty smaller landing pads were arranged next to what looked like a hangar or construction bay, each occupied by sleek, needle-nosed spacecraft with forward-swept wings. Their smoky white hulls had an almost predatory stance, built for speed and maneuverability. Even from this distance, I could see they were military craft.

"Landing pad dead ahead," Sage announced as we approached the colony's single large platform.

A crowd had gathered on the landing pad's edges, tiny figures that grew larger as we descended. My heart hammered against my ribs as I searched the faces below, looking for the one that mattered most.

Erebus touched down. Sage's piloting was flawless. As the engines wound down to silence, we were already moving, heading down the stairs that led to the observation deck.

We passed the galley first, the table where we'd eaten meals together, where we'd laughed, fought, and become a crew. The matte black mugs with Erebus insignia still sat in their cabinet—simple ceramic vessels that had somehow become our anchor to normalcy. How many conversations had happened around that table? How many shared silences while we processed the impossible things we'd seen?

Past the command module next, the center of it all, where I'd first met Sage in that secure hangar what felt like a lifetime ago. Where we'd spent more time talking than working on anything in particular. The main console still hummed with quiet authority, displays cycling through atmospheric readings and colony communications.

We turned the corner and came to the engineering bay, a space I hadn't spent much time in until recently, but it was now one of the more special places on Erebus to me because it was the place where Sage had said she loved me. The memory hit like a physical force—her voice admitting what we'd both known for months, her holographic form steady and real despite being made of light. The station where Tessa had spotted the alien parasite blinked with routine system checks.

Then we arrived at the loading bay, the entry point to Erebus where this whole journey had really begun. Where I'd first boarded with my small duffle bag, where Joey and Tessa had created that awkward triangle of unspoken tension, and where Director Rivera had wished us well on what we believed was a simple scouting mission.

"Everyone ready?" Tessa asked, her hand hovering over the loading ramp controls.

My chest felt like it might crack open from the pressure of anticipation. Six years. Six months. An eternity of missing my daughter, and now a ramp and a few feet of alien atmosphere separated us.

"Do it," I said.

Tessa hit the control. The ramp began its slow descent, and Serra Prime's golden light and air rushed in to meet us.

I stepped forward and drew in a deep breath. It was heavier than shipboard air—cooler, denser, like breathing in something shaped more by stone than sky. No scent, but the taste of it carried a faint mineral edge, clean and unfamiliar.

And underneath it all—clarity. My lungs pulled it in like they'd been waiting their whole lives for this atmosphere. Like Earth's air had always been the wrong formula, and this was right.

I looked at Tessa. She had her head tilted back, eyes closed, breathing deep like she was trying to imprint the moment into memory.

"Feels good," she said.

"Yeah," I whispered. "Real good."

The ramp continued its slow, deliberate descent. Tessa and I had to shield our eyes as the light poured in, bringing with it a sound I hadn't heard in so long I'd almost forgotten it.

Life.

Shuffling footsteps, voices, the low murmur of a crowd. Dozens of colonists were gathered at the edge of the landing pad, their faces tilted toward us with curiosity, hope, and something else—something like reverence.

I squinted in the light, scanning the crowd, my heart pounding like a war drum. Searching.

And then—there she was.

She wasn't standing still. She was running.

Sprinting toward the ramp at full tilt, ponytail whipping behind her, arms pumping like she could cross the years between us in a single breath.

Scuffed brown boots, dark cargo pants, a white v-neck shirt, Amber's butterfly necklace bouncing with each stride, and my leather jacket—dark, weathered, only slightly too big now, the shape of it molded to her frame like it had always belonged there.

Olivia hit the base of the ramp and didn't slow. I started forward, halfway down before I even realized my legs were moving. My eyes blurred, but I didn't care.

She launched into me, arms wrapping tight around my neck as I caught her, lifted her, crushed her to my chest like I could anchor both of us to this moment.

I pressed a kiss to the top of her head, breathing in the scent of her hair—sun, dust, sweat, and something floral. Not shampoo, not anything from Earth. Something wild and alive and hers—but her arms around my neck felt exactly the same.

And I was home.

"Dad." Her voice cracked against my shoulder. "You're really here."

"I'm here, kiddo. I'm here."

The words came out rough. My throat felt like someone had filled it with broken glass. She was solid, real, breathing against my chest without that horrible wheeze that had haunted my nightmares.

She pulled back enough to look at me, hands framing my face like she was confirming I was real. Her green eyes—Amber's eyes—were bright with tears, but beneath them was something new. A confidence, a steadiness that hadn't been there before.

"You look different," she said, wiping her nose with the back of her hand.

"You look different too." I managed a laugh that sounded more like a sob.

Her necklace caught the light as she smiled—that brilliant, fearless grin that had always been pure Olivia. "Good different or bad different?"

"Good different. Amazing different."

Olivia laughed and hugged me again, the sound bright and clear in Serra Prime's golden air. This time, I noticed the crowd approaching. William Frye walked at the front, his face carrying the same mixture of joy and exhaustion I felt in my bones. Among the colonists, I spotted a young woman, her bright pink hair on fire in the golden sunlight. Ava gave a small wave.

I smiled and waved back, my chest tightening as I realized she was now waiting for her own reunion—one that might never come, with her parents back on Earth fighting Taylor's Ascendancy.

Tessa appeared beside us, her own eyes wet as she watched Olivia and me. The wonder on her face made something warm settle in my chest. After everything we'd been through together, seeing her share this moment felt right.

I put my arm around Olivia's shoulders, her arm sliding behind my back with the easy familiarity of countless embraces. Even through the changes—her newfound confidence, the way she carried herself like someone who'd faced real danger—she was still my daughter.

William reached us, offering his hand with a small smile. "Welcome to Serra Prime, Malcolm."

I shook it with my free hand, not daring to let go of Olivia. "Thank you. For everything."

William looked to Olivia, then back to me. "It was my pleasure."

The weight of those words hit me. This man had risked everything to build a colony where people like Olivia could breathe freely. Where corporations couldn't determine who deserved to live based on their medical files or how many credits they had.

William turned to Tessa, holding out his hand. "Welcome to Serra Prime, Tessa."

Tessa shook it. "Thank you."

William's gaze drifted up the ramp, to where Sage stood at the limit of her projection, tears on her cheeks as she watched us. The sight of her watching us with such joy and longing made my throat tighten again.

Sage gave William a small wave. "Hey, Dad."

William's eyes went wide, and he turned to me, questions written across his face.

"Oh. Yeah…" I said. "She knows."

William turned back to his daughter, moving up the ramp until they were face to face. Something profound passed between them—fourteen years of separation compressed into a single moment of recognition.

Olivia and I followed but gave them space, staying close enough to witness this reunion while respecting its intimacy.

"You… remember me?" William whispered.

Sage smiled, "No. Sorry. But I know who you are, and I know who I am."

William nodded, wiping his eyes. The composure he'd maintained throughout our brief exchange cracked, revealing the father who'd spent over a decade waiting for his daughter to be returned to him.

"Are you ready? To remember everything?"

Sage's expression grew serious. "I am. As long as I'll truly remember every-thing."

The emphasis she placed on 'everything' wasn't lost on me. She wanted her memories of us—of our time together on Erebus, of the feelings we'd discovered, of the love we'd confessed. The thought of her potentially losing those moments sent a spike of panic through my chest.

"You will," William said. "I promise."

Sage smiled and nodded. "Okay then."

William looked down the ramp, signaling for two colonists carrying tool bags to join him. Technical specialists, judging by their equipment—the team who'd handle the delicate process of extracting and transporting Sage's quantum core.

"We need to get Sage's core transported to Eterna," William explained as they moved past Olivia and me.

The technicians filed up the ramp with the careful efficiency of people who understood they were handling something irreplaceable. Sage watched them approach with a mixture of anticipation and nervousness that made her seem more human than ever.

William asked Sage to lead them to her core, and she nodded, gesturing for them to follow.

As they disappeared into Erebus's corridors, I felt Olivia's grip on my arm tighten.

"She'll be okay, right?" Olivia asked, her voice small.

"Yeah," I said, though my own uncertainty leaked through the words. "She'll be fine."

Olivia looked up into Erebus, her eyes tracing the sleek lines of the loading bay interior. "Could I... get a tour?"

"Of course."

Her face lit up with that familiar excitement I'd missed so much. "Would it be okay if Ava came along?"

I looked down the ramp toward Ava, who was hanging back with the other colonists, clearly trying not to intrude on our reunion.

"Hey Pink, you wanna check out the ship?"

Ava didn't hesitate. She sprinted up the ramp and joined us, out of breath. "Thank you, Mr. Walker."

"I think you're too old for that Mr. Walker stuff."

Ava smiled, adjusting one of her many accessories. "Okay. Thanks, Mal."

Olivia grimaced, shaking her head. "I don't like it."

"Well, get used to it," Ava said with that trademark sass I remembered from their first meeting in our old apartment.

Some dynamics never changed, apparently. The easy banter between the girls felt like slipping into a comfortable old shirt—familiar in the best possible way.

I looked to Tessa. "Gonna give the girls a tour? Care to join?"

Tessa shook her head. "No thanks. I've seen it. I'm gonna hang out here."

I nodded and turned back to Olivia and Ava.

"Alright, I think I know where we should go first. You girls like coffee?"

"Love it," they said in perfect unison, then looked at each other and burst into laughter.

The sound echoed through Erebus's loading bay, bright and alive against the ship's usually quiet corridors. For six years, these halls had held only the voices of four adults dealing with impossible situations. Now Olivia's laugh filled the spaces between the walls, making the ship feel less like a military vessel and more like home.

I led them through the corridors, pointing out the various systems and explaining how everything worked. Olivia absorbed every detail with the same intensity she'd once applied to her art, while Ava asked rapid-fire engineering questions that impressed me with their sophistication.

"Welcome to the heart of Erebus," I said, gesturing toward the coffee synthesizer. "This little machine probably saved all our sanity."

Ava immediately gravitated toward the equipment, studying the interface with obvious fascination. "What's your favorite brew profile?"

"Number seven. Earth Standard Dark Roast."

"Dad's basic," Olivia said, settling into one of the chairs like she belonged there.

"There are a bunch of options, though. Feel free to try them out."

I grabbed two fresh Erebus mugs from the cabinet, handing one to each of the girls. The matte black ceramic felt warm under my fingers—how many conversations had started with these simple vessels?

Olivia and Ava held the mugs as if they were priceless artifacts, turning them over to examine every detail.

Ava's finger touched the Erebus logo. "Wow, these are prime."

The reverence in her voice caught me off guard. To me, they were just mugs—functional pieces of equipment that had gotten us through countless mornings in space. But seeing them through fresh eyes, I realized they represented something bigger. They were artifacts from humanity's first real interstellar journey, symbols of the crew that had defied corporate control and made it to the stars.

"Well, they're yours now."

Olivia looked up, eyes wide. "Seriously?"

"Seriously. Take 'em all if you want, and anything else that's not nailed down."

Ava clutched hers protectively against her chest. "No. This is perfect."

The simple gratitude in her voice made my throat tighten again.

Ava placed her mug under the synthesizer, working the interface like she'd had one in her room and used it every day. Maybe she did. Her fingers danced across the controls with the confidence of someone who understood technology on an intuitive level.

The machine hummed to life, filling her mug with something that smelled like cinnamon and dark chocolate. She inhaled deeply, eyes closing with satisfaction.

"That's prime," she murmured, then stepped aside so Olivia could make her selection.

Olivia pored over the brew profiles as though the fate of the colony depended on her choice. I leaned against the table, amused, seeing in her every bit of the careful precision I knew all too well from myself.

"So what do you want to see next?" I asked.

Olivia turned, her mug in position under the synthesizer. "Can we see your room? I only caught glimpses of it from our calls."

"Alright, though we may have to go in shifts. It's pretty cramped."

Olivia dispensed her coffee—something that smelled like vanilla and Earth spices—and I led them both down the corridor toward crew quarters. The low hum of Erebus's systems followed us down the corridor, a sound that had become as natural as breathing during our journey.

I tapped the panel outside my room and gestured for the girls to go inside. The space that had been my entire world for six months felt smaller than ever with two twenty-year-olds exploring every corner.

I stayed in the doorway, watching them investigate with the curiosity of people who'd never seen real starship quarters before.

Ava took a sip of her drink, eyes scanning the compact layout. "You weren't kidding. I think you're gonna be pretty happy with your room on Eterna."

Olivia poked her head into the bathroom/shower combination. "Efficient."

"That's one way to put it," I said.

Ava moved to the alcove housing my stasis suit, her eyes going wide at the silver fabric with its embedded biometric sensors. "Woah, you wore that thing?"

"Pretty sure stasis suits wear you. But yeah, six times, for a year at a time."

Olivia sat down on the bunk, bouncing slightly while carefully cradling her mug so nothing spilled. The sight of her making herself comfortable in my space sent warmth spreading through my chest.

Ava whistled, studying the technical readouts still displayed on my desk terminal. "So how fast is this ship?"

"Top speed is seventy percent lightspeed. But it takes a little over eight months to get up to that. She should be plenty quick cruising around, though."

Ava whistled. "I'll say. Bet Erebus could beat Liv's Whisper without even trying."

Olivia shot Ava a death glare that could've melted hull plating. "Ava!"

My brain stalled. *Her* Whisper? I glanced at Olivia. "You've been flying?"

Ava mouthed "sorry" to Olivia with an expression that screamed *I really stepped in it this time.*

Olivia sighed. "I was gonna tell you. I just... you had enough to worry about, and it's not like I'm actually *in* the ship, so it's not any more dangerous than the artwork I was doing. But I knew you wouldn't want me directly involved in the fighting and—"

"Liv. It's okay."

She blinked, like she was waiting for me to push back. "It is?"

The uncertainty in her voice caught me off guard. After everything she'd been through—losing her mother, watching me leave for six years, joining a resistance movement, helping build a colony on an alien world—she was still worried about my approval for learning to fly a remote fighter.

"You're old enough to make these decisions for yourself. If it's what you want, I'm excited for you."

Her face lit up with pure joy. "I love it, Dad."

Ava set down her mug, practically bouncing with enthusiasm. "And she's good. Got promoted to squadron leader after only two years."

Squadron leader? My daughter went from struggling to breathe to leading fighter pilots in the span of time it took me to cross interstellar space. The pride swelling in my chest threatens to crack my ribs.

"Squadron leader? That's incredible. So do you have a cool callsign? Like Maverick or Goose?"

Olivia rolled her eyes. "No, nothing like that. We're called by our squadron name and then a number. Or in my case, Leader."

"So, like Red Five or Gold Leader?"

"Yeah."

The casual way she says it makes me grin. My daughter, who I used to force to watch sci-fi vids with me during her countless sick days, is now living them.

"Sooo? What's your squadron name?"

Olivia meets my eyes, and I see something shift in her expression—a mixture of pride, defiance, and love that hits me like a physical force.

"It's…Amber Squadron. I'm Amber Leader."

My throat closed. She named her squadron after her mother. After the woman who died fighting the same corporations that Olivia now plans to battle in the skies above Serra Prime.

I swallow hard, fighting to get words past the lump in my throat. "That's…perfect, Liv."

Her smile was radiant, carrying echoes of both her mother's fierce determination and her own unique strength. In this moment, sitting in my cramped quarters aboard a stolen corporate warship, I realized my little girl hasn't just grown up—she'd become a woman Amber would've been proud to stand beside.

"So those ships I saw when we landed, those are Whispers?"

Ava's eyes lit up, her words spilling faster the moment the talk turned to advanced engineering. "The official designation is LFR-91, but we call them Whispers because they're nearly silent when flying in atmo. Four pulse lasers and a rail cannon that fires tungsten rods at hypersonic velocity."

My engineering brain kicked into overdrive, curiosity overriding everything else. "So what's the AI interface? Obviously some sort of pilot-AI hybrid?"

"Yeah, it's a hybrid system."

Ava leaned forward, hands already in motion—tracing invisible circuits in the air like she was sketching the ship from memory.

"Pilot controls aren't directly mapped to any control surfaces," she said. "Instead, the AI receives the inputs and interprets *intent*—converting neural signals into vectors."

She paused.

"Basically? It turns brain impulses into flight paths, with predictive compensation layered in."

She dropped her hands but stayed animated, eyes bright.

"Each pilot gets a dedicated AI assigned for life. Over time, that AI learns how the pilot thinks, how they react under pressure, how they dodge."

Ava tapped the side of her head, grinning. "Eventually, the AI starts to anticipate moves before the pilot even makes them. Makes for some crazy-fast maneuvering."

Then, her expression sobered.

"But firing? That's locked. AIs can designate and track targets, but the command to fire *has* to come from the pilot. That was non-negotiable. William insisted."

The sophistication impressed me. Remote piloting with predictive AI assistance, but with human oversight on lethal force.

"Are you a pilot too?" I asked.

Ava shook her head. "Me? No. I'd rather build ships than fly them."

Of course. The girl who'd peppered me with engineering questions would rather be in the hangar than behind the stick.

Olivia's voice drew my attention back to her. "So you're not mad?"

"I'm not mad. I'm proud of you, kiddo. Both of you."

Olivia's smile could have powered Erebus's engines. "Thanks, Dad."

"Yeah, thanks, Mal," Ava added.

Olivia grimaced. "You have to stop. It's too weird."

Ava raised an eyebrow. "You want me to call him Dad? I mean, that's kind of messed up since I *have* a dad, but okay."

"No!" Olivia said quickly. "Don't call him Dad."

I couldn't resist. "I know, what about Space Dad? Or Dad Prime?"

Ava's face lit up with delight. "Ooh, Dad Prime. I like it."

Olivia buried her face in her hands. "I hate both of you."

Sitting here with these two incredible young women, listening to them argue about ridiculous nicknames, felt like the most natural thing in the universe.

A notification began flashing on the display at my desk, its red text cutting through our laughter like a blade.

AI OFFLINE - SHIP PROTOCOLS IN AUTO-RUN MODE

My stomach dropped. Sage's core had been successfully extracted.

Olivia noticed my expression and followed my gaze to the screen. Her face softened with understanding.

"Guess we should head back. I'm guessing you'll want to be there when Sage wakes up."

I could only nod, my throat suddenly too tight for words. It was happening. I was going to meet Sage—for the first time, again.

The thought sent electric anxiety crackling through my chest. Would she remember me? Remember us? William had promised she'd retain everything, but what if something went wrong during the transfer? What if the woman who woke up was fundamentally different from the Sage I'd fallen in love with?

Ava and Olivia gathered their mugs, sensing the shift in atmosphere without needing explanation. They'd both grown up around high-stakes situations—they understood when the moment for joking had passed.

I pushed myself off the wall, my legs feeling unsteady. After six months of dreaming about reuniting with Olivia, I was about to face something equally terrifying and potentially wonderful.

Meeting the woman who'd been my anchor through the void.

Chapter 39

The mag-cart whispered down Erebus's loading ramp, its levitation field skimming just above the metal as it carried Sage's core in a sealed container. Olivia stood close on my right, Tessa just behind her, and William watched from my left as the crate drifted toward us.

Then, a thought cut through everything.

"Uh...William." My voice came out rough. "We have a stasis pod onboard in corpse containment mode. Joey Thompson's body is inside."

William's expression grew solemn. "I'll have it taken care of. I'd like to have a memorial for him, if that's alright with you."

The weight of Joey's sacrifice hit me fresh. "Of course."

"Thank you, William," Tessa said, her voice softening as she put a hand on his arm.

"No thanks required. I owe Mr. Thompson more than I can say."

I looked at Olivia and took her hand, squeezing it. "Me too."

The warmth of her fingers grounded me before William gestured toward the technicians, who were now guiding the mag-cart toward two rugged-looking transports parked nearby. The vehicles were built for harsh terrain—angular plating, reinforced wheels, and enough suspension to handle whatever Serra Prime's crystalline landscape threw under them.

We followed William to the transports. I watched as the techs loaded the container into the back of one vehicle, treating it with the reverence it deserved.

Olivia gave my hand a squeeze before letting go. "Tess, how about we show you around while they go wake up Sage?"

"Prime," Tessa replied, though I caught her glancing at me with understanding. She knew how terrifying this moment was for me.

Olivia approached the other rugged transport and opened the door to the front left seat. A steering wheel sat in front of the seat—something I'd only ever seen in old vids. Of course transports on Serra Prime would need manual operation. There was no Transit Nexus here, and without terrain mapping, satellites, or even location names, how would an AI know where you wanted to go?

"You can drive one of these?" I asked.

Olivia paused before entering her transport, smiling with a confidence I still wasn't used to seeing from my little girl. "It's not that hard. I'll teach you."

Part of me wanted to follow her, to stay in this moment where everything felt safe. But the container holding Sage's core was already being secured in William's transport, and I knew where I needed to be.

Ava elbowed me as she passed, her eyes sparkling with mischief. "Don't break her, Dad Prime."

I held up my hands defensively. "I'm not going to *break* her, Pink."

Ava narrowed her eyes, grabbing the door handle of Olivia's transport. "Better not."

Tessa chuckled as she approached their transport. "I like her," she said, giving me a wink.

William approached me, placing a gentle hand on my shoulder. "Ready?"

No. Not even close.

But I nodded anyway. "As I'll ever be."

Ava climbed into the front passenger seat of the second transport while Tessa settled in the back. The engine hummed to life, and then they were gone, leaving a small cloud of crystalline dust in their wake.

The techs closed the rear hatch of our transport and made their way to the front. They seemed to be avoiding eye contact. Were they shy? Maybe they were nervous handling the most precious cargo in the colony.

William crossed around to the driver's side and climbed into the back seat. I opened the door on my side and settled next to him. The interior was basic but comfortable—practical seating with reinforced padding.

The transport lurched forward, and I watched out my window as we drove through the colony proper.

"That's our waste processing and recycling center," William pointed to a squat, efficient-looking building. "Everything gets reused here. Nothing wasted."

We passed more structures as he continued the tour. "Armory and weapons R&D there. Security and detention facility—though we've never had to use it for anything serious. Fabrication bot hangar and repair facility."

My engineering brain catalogued each building, impressed by the thoughtful layout. Everything was positioned for maximum efficiency while maintaining defensibility.

Then we drove past a park where children were playing—laughing, running, chasing each other around play structures and crystalline formations that glowed softly in the golden light. They looked so free. Like they'd never known curfews, checkpoints, or corporate scans at every corner.

The transport continued toward the center of the colony, where Eterna herself rose like a gleaming skyscraper reaching toward the alien sky. The massive ship dominated everything around it, transformed from vessel to monument of hope. A small campus of smaller structures surrounded its base—sidewalks, benches, gardens arranged in careful patterns that made the area feel welcoming rather than industrial.

We came to a stop near a large set of steps leading into Eterna. Sage was somewhere inside, waiting to wake up. Maybe I'd hear her laugh again. Or maybe she'd open her eyes and look right through me.

We stepped out of the vehicle, and the techs unfolded the cart and began offloading the container.

I followed William to the base of the steps as the other two pushed the cart up an access ramp.

"Kind of a quiet bunch, those two," I said, gesturing to the technicians.

William chuckled. "Just a little star-struck. You're kind of a celebrity around here."

I blinked, suddenly aware of the stares I was getting from the other colonists passing by. Some were whispering to each other, heads turned in my direction. Everyone seemed so young—most around Olivia's age, some closer to my age maybe, a little older, but no one was... old. Besides William, and he looked good for whatever age he was.

"They're all kids," I said.

William started up the steps, and I followed.

"On the outside, perhaps. But they've all been through a lot, had to grow up fast. We have plenty of more *seasoned* colonists around, but the truth is it was harder to convince people who'd spent over half their lives on Earth to pick up and start over from scratch. Even if they knew what The Ascendancy had planned for them."

That made sense. Leaving everything behind—your home, your job, everyone you knew—took a kind of courage that came easier to the young. They had less to lose, more faith in the possibility that tomorrow could be better than today.

"How many people did you bring?" I asked.

"Over five thousand. About sixty percent are under thirty." William paused at the entrance to Eterna's base. "The rest are older singles and families with children who couldn't bear the thought of what their kids would inherit if they stayed."

A group of teenagers passed us on the steps, and I caught fragments of their conversation: "—that's really him—" "—survived Taylor Young's—" "—see that ship?—"

William noticed my discomfort. "You did something important, Malcolm. You gave people hope when they needed it most. That broadcast didn't only reach Earth."

"We just told the truth," I said.

"Sometimes that's the most revolutionary act of all," William said.

The technicians had already disappeared through Eterna's entrance with the cart.

"Ready?" William asked again.

I still wasn't. But if I waited for the fear to leave, I'd never move again.

"Lead the way."

The central of three tall double doors arranged around the front of Eterna parted as William stepped forward. Inside was a massive open atrium that made my breath catch.

White polished flooring stretched out beneath my feet, embedded with subtle iridescent flakes that caught the golden light filtering through the glass that enclosed the space. Around the perimeter were different storefronts. Signage hung over each with names that spoke of a living, breathing community: Comms Depot, Dock 6, Forager's Bay, Threadlock Outfitters, Spanner & Coil, and The Emberline.

Bioluminescent potted plants scattered throughout, their soft blue, green, and purple glows adding an alien beauty that reminded me this wasn't just another human settlement—this was something entirely new.

But what truly stole my breath was the center of the atrium: a grand double helix spiral staircase that wrapped around a large column of glass and steel. Inside the column, elevators traversed between various levels like busy worker bees in a transparent hive.

Each floor had a circular platform surrounding the central column, with landings on either side for the spiral staircase, and bridges that connected across the openness to the larger perimeter like spokes on a wheel.

I tried to understand the logistics. With the double staircases wrapping around, there was only room for one elevator door on each side of the column, but I counted more than two elevators moving inside. How'd that work?

The two technicians with the cart waited at the elevator door. I watched as one of the elevators reached the atrium floor—it wasn't lined up with the door, but after it slowed to a stop, it moved sideways until it was in line with the door and slid open.

"Pretty smart, huh?" William said.

The elegance of the solution hit me. Multiple elevator cars could travel the column because they didn't need to stay aligned with doors during transit. Only when stopping did they slide into position. Brilliant.

The atrium buzzed with life around us. Conversations echoed off the polished walls as colonists moved between the shops, their voices mixing into a comfortable hum of community. A group of engineers clustered near Spanner & Coil, debating something technical while gesturing at tablet displays. Parents with children wandered past Forager's Bay.

A young woman emerged from Threadlock Outfitters carrying a canvas bag that looked full. Two teenagers sat on one of the benches, sharing something from a wrapped package, completely at ease.

This wasn't the sterile corporate efficiency of Earth's shopping centers or the desperate scramble of the Forge Prime market district. People moved with purpose but without urgency, stopping to chat with friends, taking time to examine goods without worrying about Transit Nexus schedules or corporate surveillance.

"It's beautiful," I said.

William smiled. "Sage designed most of this layout. She didn't want it to feel like a ship. Said if we were going to start over, we'd better start human."

Of course she did. I could feel her in every detail—brilliant, elegant...a little bit of a show-off.

"It worked," I said.

"Let's go, Malcolm," William said, gesturing toward the elevator as the technicians wheeled the cart inside. "Olivia can give you the full tour later."

William and I filed in after the techs. William tapped the panel, and the door slid closed. We moved gracefully sideways, back into our traversal lane, and then began to rise.

I watched the colony shrink below us, but my attention kept drifting to the two technicians who stood stiffly beside Sage's container.

Enough was enough.

I turned to face them properly—a tall young man with messy brown hair and brown eyes, and an even younger woman with short black hair and green eyes. Both looked like they were shocked I could see them, that they weren't rendered invisible by standing still.

"Alright, you two, enough of the silent treatment." I held out my hand. "Malcolm Walker."

The young woman stepped forward first, her grip firm despite her obvious nervousness. Her voice came out soft, almost whispered. "Mira Kess."

The young man went next, his handshake quick and efficient. "Jace Alvara."

The elevator continued its ascent, passing through another floor.

"See, that wasn't so bad, right?"

Mira chuckled nervously, her shoulders relaxing a fraction. "Sorry. We… we've heard so much about you. And what you did out there." She glanced at the container. "What your crew did for Sage."

Jace nodded, making eye contact. "The whole colony's been talking about your broadcast. About Sage. You. And… Miss Harper."

The way Jace said "Miss Harper" made me suppress a smile—the boy was smitten.

"Tess is something else," I said. "Tough as nails, and a brilliant engineer."

Mira grinned, her nervousness evaporating. "Jace has been talking about her non-stop for the past year. I told him he has no shot."

"Mira!" Jace's face flushed bright red as he shot his companion a mortified look.

William smiled faintly at their banter, but his eyes drifted to the container. I could see the tension he kept locked behind that calm exterior—father to father, I understood.

"You never know," I said, taking pity on the kid.

The elevator passed another floor, revealing what could be residential quarters—hallways with words like Lunaris Wing and Noctis Wing, in bold typography above them.

"She's been through a lot lately, lost someone close to her. But she's got a good heart under all that armor plating," I said, returning my attention to Jace.

Jace straightened, hope flickering in his brown eyes. "Really?"

"Really. But… maybe start with being her friend first, yeah?"

Mira snorted. "That might be an issue. Jace has the social skills of a malfunctioning repair bot."

"I'm standing right here," Jace muttered, but there was affection in his voice despite the embarrassment.

It was then I noticed the patch on his jumpsuit, stitched in absolute black. Matte against matte, the only way to discern its design was through the subtle shift in texture: a raised hexagon floated above the word VANTA in bold, utilitarian lettering.

Mira had a patch as well, but hers was in near-black indigo. At its center floated a simple four-pointed star. Beneath it, the word NOCTIS was rendered in the same indigo thread.

The elevator slowed to a stop, performed its realignment slide, and the doors opened, William stepping out.

I followed, then turned to Mira and Jace. "Hey… Tessa, Sage, and I? We're pretty impressed with you too."

William gave me an appreciative glance before leading on.

Mira and Jace looked at each other and smiled before pushing the cart out onto the circular platform.

Good thing I wasn't afraid of heights. Looking over the railing, I could see all the way down to the atrium, the shops, and people moving through the space looking like miniatures from this height.

We followed William across the bridge to the walkway that led us around the perimeter, past several doors. Each looked identical except for the nameplates mounted above security panels. Each plate etched with a single word: Trust. Light. Joy. Wonder.

The names felt deliberate, chosen with care. Each word represented something worth preserving, worth fighting for.

William stopped at a door that looked no different from any of the others we'd passed. The nameplate above the security panel read Hope.

He tapped his Halo against the security panel, and the door slid open.

Hope, of course that's what he'd name Sage's room.

I paused outside Hope's threshold. The nameplate glowed in my peripheral vision as Jace and Mira pushed the cart through the doorway.

Deep breath. She's going to be fine.

Another breath. Then I stepped inside.

The room wasn't large—maybe about the size of Erebus's command module. Clean white walls, soft lighting that felt warm rather than clinical. A console dominated one end, with a large display and a single chair positioned in front of it. William was already settling into that chair, his fingers dancing across the interface.

But my attention locked onto the back wall, where a stasis pod stood like a shrine. A shrine. Not to memory—but to something still waiting to return.

The glass was crystal clear, soft blue light illuminating the interior. And there, lying inside, was Sage.

I moved toward the pod slowly, each step feeling heavier than the last. Behind me, Jace and Mira worked quietly, removing the straps that had secured the container to their cart, but their sounds faded into background noise.

As I drew closer, Sage's features came into sharper focus. It was her. The Sage I'd fallen for on Erebus. But she was also different. Her face was thinner than her avatar had ever appeared, her skin paler, revealing how far along her NHS had progressed before being linked to the AI core. The disease had carved away at her, leaving her features more fragile, more ethereal.

She looked at peace. No breathing, no subtle eye movements beneath closed lids.

Had I looked like this to her? During those year-long sleeps in stasis, had Sage stood over my pod the way I was standing over hers now? Had she watched my motionless form, waiting for the day I would wake up?

The thought made my throat constrict. All those moments she'd spent alone, watching over me, protecting me, while I couldn't even respond.

Mira brought the small AI core to a pedestal beside Sage's pod, seating the glossy black cube into its housing. The device looked innocuous—a dark geometric shape—but inside, Sage's consciousness was still active. I wondered what she was thinking right now, with no outside stimulus. But this time she wouldn't have to wait years in the dark.

Just a little longer.

Jace connected a thick conduit of cables that ran from the pod to the pedestal, his movements precise despite the obvious weight of the moment. His hands didn't shake, but I caught him glancing at William for confirmation with each connection.

Both technicians stepped back once the setup was complete.

"Ready," Mira said, her voice barely above a whisper.

William turned back to the console. His fingers moved across the interface, inputting commands I couldn't decipher from my position by the pod. The thick cables suddenly lit up, transmitting blue light from the core into the pod like liquid electricity flowing through transparent veins.

"Beginning disentanglement sequence," William said, his voice steady.

The cables' glow intensified, growing brighter and brighter until the blue light became almost too intense to look at directly. Then, without warning, the light vanished. It didn't fade or diminish—it was gone in a blink.

"Disentanglement complete."

Jace stepped forward, disconnecting the cables with careful movements before stepping back again. The finality of that action hit me harder than I'd expected. Whatever connection had existed between Sage's consciousness and the AI core was now severed permanently.

My hand found the back of my neck, rubbing at the tension that had built there as I stared into Sage's pod. Her body remained motionless, but somehow the quality of her stillness had changed. Before, she'd looked like a preserved specimen—beautiful but lifeless. Now, there was something different.

William stood from the console and crossed the room to the pod's control panel. He tapped his Halo to the security interface, then navigated through several screens. He pressed his finger down on what looked like a confirmation button, holding it there as a white circle formed around his fingertip. When the circle completed its circuit, William released his finger, his eyes now fixed on Sage as the blue light inside the pod began to pulse and transition to a soft white color.

The glass panel of the pod slid away with a slight hiss.

The familiar scent of post-stasis hit me—that clinical, recycled air smell mixed with something vaguely metallic. It had once been so off-putting, but after six cycles I'd grown accustomed to it. Now it carried the promise of awakening.

Sage's chest began to rise and fall in shallow, experimental breaths. Her eyelids fluttered like someone emerging from a deep dream, then opened to reveal those crystalline blue eyes. Her fingers twitched, then flexed as her nervous system reconnected with her physical form.

Her focus was distant at first, blinking several times as consciousness filtered back into her body. Then she turned her head, her gaze finding William first.

She blinked again. A subtle tightening of her brow. Then... she was there.

Her lips parted, and in a soft voice, "Hey, Dad."

The simple words hit the room like a thunderclap. This wasn't just the Sage I'd known on Erebus. This was William's daughter, returned to him after years of digital exile. The recognition in her eyes was immediate and complete.

William's composure cracked. His hand found the edge of the pod for support as tears tracked down his cheeks. "Hello, sweetheart. Welcome home."

Sage took another breath, breathing deeper this time. Her lungs no longer fought against her. She smiled, almost laughed, tears cutting paths from the corners of her eyes down the sides of her face.

I wondered if this was how Olivia reacted after taking her first pain-free deep breath on Serra Prime. I'd missed that moment, but this was a good consolation.

Sage turned her focus to me. She didn't speak, and my heart picked up, wondering if she knew who this man standing beside her was. She studied my face with an intensity I remembered from our countless conversations aboard Erebus. But there was something different now—a completeness, as if pieces of herself that had been missing were clicking into place.

The silence stretched between us, heavy with possibility and terror. What if the memory blocks had been stronger than William thought? What if restoring her human consciousness had erased the AI experiences we'd shared? What if I were just another colonist to her now?

Sage swallowed, her throat working against the dryness of stasis.

"It's your turn..." she said, a hint of mischief in her eyes.

"Welcome back, sleepyhead."

The words came out rough, emotion making my voice catch.

Sage's smile widened, transforming her entire face as recognition flooded her features. The tears came faster now, but they were happy tears.

"Hey, Mal."

Those two simple words contained everything—our late-night conversations in the command module, the way she'd teased me about my alphabetized tools, the moment we'd confessed our love for each other. She remembered. All of it.

The weight of every impossible hope I'd carried cracked open inside me. I reached for the edge of the pod to steady myself, my own eyes blurring.

"How do you feel?" I asked.

Sage pushed herself up slowly, testing her physical form. "Like I've been asleep for fourteen years." She paused, flexing her fingers experimentally. "But also like I just got off Erebus."

Behind us, William cleared his throat softly. Mira and Jace had stepped back respectfully, giving us space for this reunion while still monitoring medical readings on their tablets.

Sage's attention returned to me, and when she spoke again, her voice was stronger. "Help me up?"

Sage held out a hand. I took it, and the contact sent electricity through my entire body. It didn't pass through me like a hologram—it was warm, solid, real. Her fingers interlaced with mine.

She gripped my hand and pulled herself into a sitting position, then swung her legs over the edge of the pod. The movement seemed to exhaust her, and when she tried to stand, her knees buckled.

I caught her immediately, putting her arm around my shoulders and taking most of her weight. There wasn't much there—she felt like when I'd carry Olivia from the couch to her bed after she'd fallen asleep watching vids or drawing on her tablet.

"William," I called over my shoulder. "We have a chair?"

He looked to Jace, who snapped to action, going to retrieve a wheelchair from the corner of the room. The kid moved quickly, unfolding the chair and positioning it behind Sage.

Sage held up a hand. "I think I'm good."

Her voice carried that familiar stubborn streak I'd come to know so well aboard Erebus. Whether in digital form or flesh and blood, Sage was going to insist on doing things her way.

"You sure?" I asked, keeping my arm steady around her waist.

She nodded, then took a tentative step forward. Her legs wobbled, but she didn't fall. Another step, more confident this time. By the third step, she was walking under her own power, though I kept my hand at the small of her back just in case.

"See?" She turned to face me, her eyes bright with triumph. "Still got it."

That was pure Sage—turning physical recovery into a challenge to be conquered rather than a process to be endured.

William approached us, his expression torn between paternal concern and overwhelming joy. "How do you feel, sweetheart?"

Sage considered the question seriously, running her free hand through her honey-blonde hair. "Like myself. But also... more myself? If that makes sense."

She looked between William and me; her smile soft but certain.

"Complete."

CHAPTER 40

T he monitors hummed softly in Eterna's medical suite, their displays casting a gentle blue light across the pristine white walls. Sage's breathing came slow and steady, her chest rising and falling beneath the thermal blanket. The medical cuff wrapped around her upper arm glowed with a diffused green light, pumping nutrients and recovery compounds through her system now that NHS no longer threatened her life.

My hand enclosed hers, feeling the warmth of real skin, real blood flowing beneath the surface. After all those months aboard Erebus watching her holographic form flicker in and out of existence, this felt like a miracle I didn't deserve.

Olivia's head rested against my shoulder, her dark hair spilling across the sleeve of my jacket. She'd insisted on staying when the medical team brought Sage here, claiming she wanted to make sure her "future stepmom" was okay. The comment had made my face burn, but Sage had managed a weak laugh before exhaustion pulled her under.

Sage's body had been in stasis for twenty years now, but her mind never got to rest. The AI core kept her consciousness active, processing, thinking, feeling. Now her body was finally catching up, demanding the sleep her mind had been denied for over a decade.

The door whispered open, and William stepped inside, carrying a steaming cup.

"Coffee," he said, extending it toward me.

Olivia lifted her head from my shoulder, blinking sleep from her eyes. I released Sage's hand reluctantly and accepted the cup.

"Thanks."

William's gaze moved to his daughter's sleeping form, and something soft crossed his features. "How about I take over for a while? You two have been here all night. She's not waking up anytime soon, and I promise to get you if she does."

He looked at Olivia. "Maybe you can show your father around properly."

I glanced down at Sage's peaceful face, then back at Olivia, who was already sitting up straighter with renewed energy.

"Alright," I said.

The word came out reluctantly. Leaving felt wrong—we'd had no time alone, no chance to process what this meant for us. The medical team had whisked her away for cleaning and evaluation, and she'd practically collapsed the moment her head hit the pillow. But William was right. Sage was catching up on years of stolen rest.

I stood slowly, my joints protesting after hours in the chair. Olivia rose to her feet, already moving toward the door.

I leaned over and brushed a strand of hair from her temple. "I'll be back soon," I whispered.

William settled into the chair as I joined Olivia at the door. He looked back at me, his eyes reflecting the soft medical lighting.

"Malcolm." His voice carried a quiet authority I'd started to recognize. "I know I've said it before. But thank you. For bringing Sage home."

I put an arm around Olivia, feeling her warmth against my side. "I think we're even."

We headed down the hallway of Eterna's medical wing, passing more rooms with glass doors revealing patients in various stages of recovery. Doctors in white coats moved between the rooms, some trailed by younger colonists wearing student badges. The medical wing felt more like a teaching hospital than a frontier clinic.

We stepped out of the medical wing into Serra Prime's golden morning light, streaming into Eterna. I took a sip of William's coffee.

"So, kiddo, what's first?"

Olivia considered for a moment, tucking a strand of dark hair behind her ear. "You want to see your room?"

"I do. But maybe we save that for last. If I see a bed right now, I might collapse."

"Right..." Her green eyes lit up. "Oh! I know. You hungry?"

"Starved."

"Follow me." She headed across one of the transparent bridges spanning the atrium. When we reached the spiral staircase, she started taking the steps down.

"What's wrong with the elevator?"

"You need the exercise. It'll help wake you up. Besides, we're going down, not up."

"Can't argue with that logic."

I followed Olivia down the graceful spiral staircase to the atrium floor, my legs protesting the sudden activity. The main level bustled with colonists moving between storefronts built into Eterna's hull structure.

Olivia pointed out the different establishments as we walked. "So the Comms Depot is where you can get your Halo updated. They'll strip out any corpo-ware, add the Eterna apps, and set up your clearances. Oh, and you'll get some free credits."

"What happens to my GCE Credits?"

"The GCE is dead. It's Ascendancy Credits now. They renamed the system and seized any accounts with ties to Chrysalis." Olivia's expression darkened. "I'd say after your little broadcast, your account is dusted."

I pulled out my Halo, fingers moving across the familiar interface to access my credit account. The screen flickered, then displayed a stark message: NO ACCOUNT EXISTS.

"Yep...dusted," I said.

My life savings. Gone. Years of careful budgeting, squirreling away credits for Olivia's treatment, all erased with a few keystrokes from some Ascendancy bureaucrat.

"Let's get you set up," Olivia said.

She led the way into the Comms Depot. The interior buzzed with activity—holoscreens flashed colony announcements while repair benches lined the back wall, their modular toolkits gleaming under the bright lighting. A transparent bulletin board near the front cycled through job postings and community messages, giving the space a warm, communal feel.

A young man behind the counter looked up as we approached, his face brightening with recognition.

"Oh! Mr. Walker, Olivia, welcome."

I stepped forward and placed my Halo on the counter. "Give me the works."

The kid blinked. "The...the works? Um..."

"Ignore him." Olivia rolled her eyes. "He needs his Halo updated."

"Right. Of course."

The young man picked up my device and connected it to a small docking station, then interfaced with a terminal. His fingers flew across the holographic interface. The whole process took maybe ten seconds before he disconnected it and handed the Halo back to me.

"Here you go. The works."

I scrolled through the device, checking the new apps and updated interface.

"What do I owe you?"

"Nothing. It's a required update, no charge." He glanced at his terminal. "You've been designated with the Aurion group, so you should have full access."

Olivia's mouth dropped open. "He's Aurion?"

The young man checked his terminal again, looking nervous. "Uh, yeah. That's what it says here."

I leaned over to Olivia and whispered, "What does Aurion mean? Is it good?"

She didn't bother whispering back. "It's leadership, Dad. Apparently, you're a colony leader. Unbelievable."

Colony leader? The coffee nearly came back up my throat. I'd just learned to *tolerate* being a captain, and now I was being thrust into another power structure without my consent.

"Hang on. What if I don't *want* to be a colony leader?"

Olivia threw up her hands, frustration tightening her voice. "Take it up with William, I guess."

She turned to head out, shaking her head like she couldn't believe her father's stupidity. Fair enough—most people would probably jump at the chance for authority. But I'd seen what power did to people.

I looked back at the young man, holding up my Halo. "Thanks."

"Anytime, Mr. Walker."

The respectful tone in his voice made my skin crawl. Yesterday, I was Malcolm the engineer. Now I was apparently Mr. Walker, colony leader, whether I wanted the title or not.

I followed Olivia out of the Comms Depot, my mind racing. William had orchestrated this without asking me first. The question was whether he'd done it to honor what I'd accomplished or because he needed someone he could trust in a position of authority.

"Hey, kiddo." I caught up with Olivia as she walked ahead, still shaking her head. "I didn't ask for this."

"It's fine. It's just…"

She stopped and turned to me, frustration sharp in her green eyes—frustration with a shadow of something that hurt worse. Disappointment.

"I was excited to show you around the colony I helped build for three years. And now you're Aurion. Aurion. Which means you'll probably know more about this place than I do in a week."

I understood. All too well. She'd bled for this colony—sweat, time, risk—and her father shows up and gets slotted into leadership like he earned it.

"I want that too, Liv," I said. "I'll talk to William. Maybe he can move me. What's your group?"

"Talon." She rolled her eyes. "But you wouldn't want that. It's for pilots and security."

"So what's the group for an ex-corpo AI engineer?"

"That'd be Vanta. Or Noctis if you want to sit around thinking big thoughts all day." She threw her hands up. "Honestly, it depends. Vanta builds things. Noctis designs the ideas behind the things."

"It seems...complicated. How many groups are there?"

"Twelve." She let out a breath that deflated her shoulders. "Here—fine—quick rundown."

She ticked them off on her fingers, rapid-fire.

"Aurion is leadership. Calyx is medical. Echoveil keeps records and history. Ignis runs kitchens and the reactors. Lunaris are the strategists. Praxion handles military training. Solara is artists and teachers. Talon—mine—pilots and security. Thalor does hydro and life support. Vanta are the engineers. Zephyra's the botanists and biologists. And Noctis is the quantum and AI brain-trust."

She dropped her hand.

"There. The grand tour."

There was no way I was going to remember all that. I opened my mouth for a follow-up question, but she cut me off with a half-shrug.

"Do what you want. If you want to stay close to tech and actually avoid politics, go Vanta or Noctis. Otherwise...Aurion is where decisions get made. People already respect you. And Sage will probably be there too." Her voice softened just a little. "So...I guess it makes sense."

I put my arm around her, pulling her close as we started walking again. The familiar weight of her against my side reminded me of all those evenings we'd spent together in our cramped apartment, watching old vids and sharing stories.

"How about we don't worry about it right now and you finish showing me around?"

She put her arm around my waist, some of the tension leaving her posture. "Sure."

We continued through the atrium, passing more colonists going about their daily routines. The space felt alive in a way corporate facilities never did.

I pointed to another sign. "Forager's Bay. What's that place?"

"That's groceries, produce...food stuff."

"Alright, what about that?" I gestured toward another storefront.

"Spanner & Coil." Olivia's voice brightened. "You'll love that place. It's full of tools and parts and smells like your old StellarForge coveralls."

She pointed across the atrium to a cozy-looking establishment. "That's Evelin's, the coffee shop. They have coffee—obviously—and some prime baked goods and pastries. It's named after William's late wife. Apparently, she loved to bake."

"That's sweet. Is that where you wanted to get some food?"

"No. The place I wanted to take you is over here."

Olivia continued around the atrium, pointing out Threadlock Outfitters. "That's where you get clothes and gear."

She stopped outside a location with two large glass windows. Warm light spilled across faux-wood wall panels inside, illuminating curved booths and modular tables where colonists lingered over meals and conversations. Digital flames flickered in recessed wall units, giving the cantina a cozy atmosphere. The sign above the entrance read *The Emberline*.

"This is it," Olivia said, her excitement returning. "Wait till you taste their CoreBurn. It's way better than that stuff they served at The Drift."

"First of all, it's morning, so maybe breakfast?" I raised an eyebrow. "And second, how do *you* know what the CoreBurn at The Drift tasted like?"

Olivia's smile turned mischievous. "Ava and I went there. I wanted to introduce her to Patch."

"Okay." I crossed my arms. "You were still too young to be drinking that stuff."

"Don't be static, Dad." She said it like it was perfectly natural for two teenage girls to visit resistance-friendly hangouts.

Sure, The Drift wasn't exactly Mos Eisley Cantina. It was tame enough, and I'd taken Olivia there a few times myself. But her going alone with Ava? It sounded like something Amber would have done at that age—fearless, curious, and oblivious to the potential danger.

I shook my head. "Is that when you decided to kidnap Patch?"

"I didn't kidnap him." Olivia's grin widened. "I *adopted* him. Mr. Maddox said it was okay."

"Did Patch get any say in this?"

"Of course. He had one condition."

Olivia pointed through one of the windows. Inside The Emberline, I spotted the familiar mismatched form of Patch rolling between tables, his ancient treads somehow navigating the crowded cantina floor. Customers moved out of his way, some reaching out to pat his rusted chassis as he passed.

"Let me guess," I said, watching the old service bot weave through the crowd. "He wanted to keep working?"

"He said r-retirement was for organics who g-get t-tired." Olivia's voice took on Patch's familiar static-laced tone. "This u-unit... finds p-purpose in... service t-to humans."

I couldn't help but smile as I watched Patch deliver food to a table of young colonists, his mismatched arms somehow managing not to drop anything despite their obvious mechanical failures.

"So now he's what, The Emberline's mascot?"

"More like their star employee. He knows everyone's order, never forgets a face, and his glitchy commentary is half the entertainment." Olivia stepped toward the cantina's door, which slid open. "Come on, you'll see."

The warm atmosphere enveloped us as we stepped inside. The smell of synth-bacon and coffee mixed with the subtle scent of CoreBurn and conversation. Patch spotted us, his single flickering optic focusing on me with what I could swear was recognition.

"Malcolm... W-Walker," came the familiar static-laden voice as he rolled over. "Welcome t-to... The Emberline. Your usual b-booth... is not available... b-because this is... your f-first visit."

I laughed despite myself. "Good to see you, Patch. Thanks for landing clearance, by the way."

"Y-you're... welcome," Patch replied, his optic flickering. "Landing c-clearance was... a one t-time favor t-to Olivia."

Olivia guided me to an empty booth near the back, sliding in across from me. The digital flames cast dancing shadows across her face, making her look older somehow.

"So what's good here?" I asked, scanning the glowing menu board hovering above the bar.

"Everything. But you should try the Serra Prime Luminberry pancakes. They use actual native fruit."

"I don't know if I'm ready for alien food for my first meal."

Olivia rolled her eyes. "You'll like it, trust me. Patch, two Luminberry breakfast plates, and two coffees, one black, the other with synth-cream."

She tapped her Halo to Patch's payment panel. "This one's on me."

"C-coming right... up," Patch announced, his voice crackling with static as he rolled away toward the kitchen.

"Still gotta pay upfront, I see."

Olivia pocketed her Halo. "Yeah, it's coded into Patch's protocols, and we've all gotten used to it."

The cantina buzzed with morning conversation, colonists discussing work assignments and sharing stories over their meals. Through the windows, I could see more people moving through the atrium, the colony already alive with activity despite the early hour.

Movement near the entrance caught my eye. Tessa walked in, scanning the room. I raised my hand to get her attention, assuming she was looking for us.

Olivia turned to see what I was waving at as Tessa made her way to our booth.

"Scoot over, kiddo."

Olivia slid deeper into the booth, making room as Tessa approached. Tessa looked well-rested, her hair tied back in a ponytail and her eyes had a clarity I hadn't seen in months.

"Sorry to crash your father-daughter date," Tessa said, sliding in next to Olivia. "I thought I'd find you in Sage's room, but William said you'd gone out."

"We're getting some breakfast. You want anything? Liv's buying." I gave Olivia a wink, which she returned by sticking out her tongue.

"No thanks." Tessa settled into the booth, looking around at the warm atmosphere. "Wanted to see how you're holding up. Have you slept at all?"

"Not yet. You?"

Tessa nodded. "Yeah, got up about an hour ago. The rooms here are prime. Actual windows, temperature control, and a separate shower."

"Tell Dad which group you chose," Olivia interjected, clearly excited about something.

"Oh..." Tessa's smile widened. "Talon. Liv's going to teach me to fly."

"You got to pick?"

"Yeah, they recommended... Vanda?"

"Vanta," Olivia corrected.

"Right. They said it was a good fit, based on my engineering background, but I said that I'd like to try something else, and they switched it." Tessa leaned over and bumped Olivia with her shoulder. "Now I'm neighbors with this one."

Patch returned with our breakfast, his mismatched arms somehow balancing two steaming plates and two coffee mugs without incident. The Luminberry pancakes glowed with an ethereal blue-green light. The alien berries had been incorporated into what looked like perfectly normal pancakes, except for the soft phosphorescence emanating from within.

"T-two Luminberry specials," Patch announced. "Caution: may c-cause... temporary... digestive... euphoria."

"Digestive euphoria?" I looked at Olivia suspiciously.

"It means they taste really good," she laughed. "Patch likes to oversell everything."

I cut a piece of the pancake and forked it into my mouth. The flavor hit immediately—sweet like honey but with a tangy citrus finish, followed by a subtle cooling sensation on my tongue. The texture was perfect, fluffy and light, and the Luminberries burst with juice that somehow enhanced rather than overwhelmed the pancake flavor.

"Okay," I admitted, taking another bite. "This is incredible."

"Told you." Olivia dug into her own plate with enthusiasm.

Tessa watched us eat with an amused expression, her arms crossed casually on the table. "So what group did you get?"

I looked at Olivia for help, my mind drawing a complete blank. The name had already slipped out of my head somewhere between the Comms Depot and glowing pancakes.

"You two really need to watch the orientation," Olivia said, rolling her eyes dramatically. "Aurion. It's the leadership group. They basically oversee all the other groups and make colony decisions."

Tessa's eyebrows shot up. "Wow, no thanks. But you have fun with that, Mal."

I put another bite of pancake in my mouth, the sweet Luminberry flavor doing nothing to improve my mood about the situation. "I'm gonna switch."

"You think future father-in-law is gonna be okay with that?" Tessa asked, with a knowing smirk.

I almost choked. Future father-in-law. The words hit me like a plasma discharge, making my stomach do a little flip that had no connection to the glowing alien fruit I was eating.

Olivia practically bounced in her seat. "Oh, yes! When's the wedding?"

"There's no—we haven't even—" I fumbled with my coffee mug, nearly knocking it over. "She woke up yesterday. We've barely talked."

"But you love her," Tessa said matter-of-factly. "And she loves you. I heard the whole conversation."

"You were listening? You said you were giving us privacy," I said.

"I said I was giving you *space*." Tessa said, snatching a fallen luminberry from my plate and popping it into her mouth. "Ooh, these are good."

"Anyway... That was back on the ship. It's complicated now," I said.

"No, it's not," Olivia said. "You're just being static. Sage is perfect for you, and you know it."

Tessa nodded in agreement. "Plus, think about it—William trusts you enough to put you in charge. He's not gonna object to you being with his daughter when he already considers you family."

"You're not hearing me. *I* haven't changed. *I* still have feelings for—"

"You don't *have feelings*." Olivia cut me off, pointing her fork at me. "You love her. Just say you love her."

It felt as if the entire cantina went quiet. I stared down at my glowing pancakes.

"Fine. I love her. But the point I'm trying to make is that Sage just got a bunch of past memories all mixed in with the ones of me. Who's to say that doesn't change things?"

Tessa leaned back in the booth, studying my face with those sharp blue eyes. "You're scared."

"I'm being realistic."

"I think Tess's right. You're scared," Olivia set down her fork and gave me that look—the one that said she was about to deliver some hard truths whether I wanted to hear them or not. "You haven't had a chance to talk, so you're running through every worst-case scenario, like you always do. But Sage is gonna wake up, you're gonna tell her you love her—not that you *have feelings*—and she's going to say it back."

"Liv, you can't know—"

"Nope." Olivia held up her hand, cutting me off with the kind of authority that reminded me uncomfortably of Amber. "You're not allowed to think like that. Now, finish your delicious breakfast, I'll show you your room, and you're gonna get some rest."

Olivia had no idea how much I hoped she was right.

I thought back to the way Sage had looked at me after waking up—not confused or distant, but with immediate recognition and warmth. The way her "Hey, Mal" had spoken more than should have been possible for two words.

"Maybe you're right, kiddo."

"I'm always right. It's genetic."

Tessa snorted. "I love this family."

Chapter 41

I lingered in the Aurion wing corridor, taking in the subtle gold and navy accents that decorated the hallways—the colors of the Aurion group, Olivia had informed me. She'd explained that it was the smallest of the colony group wings. While most housed around five hundred individuals or families, the Aurion wing had only three individual living quarters. The rest of the wing was made up of offices, small strategy rooms, and a large briefing room.

I'd slept through the rest of the day and night after Olivia finished showing me my room. Now I felt rested and ready to respond to the message William had sent me: *Sage is out of medical and would like to see you. Aurion Wing 1002.*

I adjusted the dark canvas jacket that Eterna had supplied. It fit perfectly; the Aurion patch on the left chest, with its golden spiral and lettering against a navy background, stood out, rather than blending in like some of the other group patches I'd noticed.

I glanced at the number above the security panel of my own quarters—1003. I didn't have far to go. The proximity to Sage made my decision about staying in this leadership group infinitely more complicated. How could I walk away from something that kept us this close?

The short distance to 1002 felt like a kilometer. My pulse hammered as I tapped the security panel.

"Sage? It's Mal."

The door slid open, and there she was—barefoot, wearing gray lounge pants and a white t-shirt, her shoulder-length blonde hair hanging loose. She was smiling. It wasn't the wide grin of casual happiness; it was a smile pulled close, trembling at the edges, lit entirely by her eyes.

Without hesitation, she pulled me inside and wrapped her arms around me. I wrapped mine around her, fighting back the emotion that threatened to overwhelm me. The scent of her hair was like citrus and something floral I couldn't identify. Her thin frame felt fragile against me, but you wouldn't know it from how she squeezed.

"What took you so long?"

Her voice was a whisper against my shoulder, muffled by the fabric of my shirt. She didn't let go, and I wasn't about to either.

"Sorry, I passed out. Watching you sleep took a lot out of me."

A soft laugh vibrated through her chest. "Try doing it for six years."

The embrace ended, but our arms remained around each other—hers around my neck, mine across her back. Our eyes locked, and I found myself afraid to blink, terrified this moment might dissolve like some cruel dream. The blue of her eyes, no longer that subtly artificial glow. It was real—layered with human experiences.

Her expression held everything—recognition, relief, love.

I moved my hand from behind her back, brushing a strand of hair away from her face. My fingers traced the curve of her cheek. She leaned into the touch, closing her eyes.

Then I kissed her.

The way she kissed me back—desperate, certain, like she'd been waiting years—obliterated every fear I'd carried about how she might feel. Her fingers curled into my hair, pulling me closer, and I could taste the salt of tears I hadn't realized she'd been crying.

When we separated, both breathing hard, she pressed her forehead against mine.

"I was terrified," she whispered between breaths. "Terrified I'd wake up and feel different about you. That being human again would change everything."

"And now?"

"I love you more than I did without my memories. Is that possible?"

I cupped her face in both hands, studying the familiar features that were more vivid, more present than they'd ever been on the ship. "Yeah. It's possible."

Sage leaned in and kissed me again.

This time slower, more deliberate. Her hands moved from my neck to the sides of my face. Everything about this felt different from our hurried first kiss—not desperate, but certain. Like she was memorizing the moment.

When we broke apart, she rested her hands on my chest, looking up at me with those impossibly blue eyes.

"I remember everything now," she said softly. "Not just the ship, but before. My childhood with Dad, getting sick, the decision to... leave my body behind. And I remember choosing you, Mal. Watching you on those feeds. Thinking I was only deciding based on logic and reason, but knowing there was something more."

Her fingers traced the collar of my jacket. "Years of consciousness without touch, without taste, without really being able to breathe. And then you showed up and made me feel human when I didn't even know I was."

"Sage—"

"I want to show you something." She stepped back, taking my hand.

Her quarters mirrored mine—the navy and gold Aurion colors threading through every detail. The small living space with its wall-mounted display, sofa, coffee table, and armchair. The small kitchen beyond that. On the right, a dining area with table and chairs, a bathroom, and a bedroom.

Sage led me straight to what I'd taken for a back window, her bare feet silent on the polished floor.

"Watch this." Her fingers found a small panel beside the frame.

Outside, machinery hummed to life. A balcony began extending from outside the window, like an intricate puzzle unfolding, metal segments sliding and clicking into place. Railings emerged, unfolded, and locked with mechanical precision that would've made even StellarForge engineers jealous.

When the construction finished, the window parted. Serra Prime's cool morning air rushed in, carrying scents I couldn't identify.

Sage released my hand and stepped out onto the platform.

"Wow," I breathed, stepping onto the balcony beside her.

The view spread before us like something from one of Olivia's paintings. Golden light from Vespera painted everything in warm hues. Below, the colony bustled with early morning activity—people moving between buildings, children playing in that park I'd glimpsed yesterday. Beyond the settlement, crystalline formations caught the light, throwing rainbow reflections across rolling hills.

"I designed these quarters myself," Sage said, moving to the railing. "I thought people needed space to think, to see the bigger picture."

"Liv didn't mention a balcony when she gave me the tour."

"I'm glad." Sage leaned against the railing, the morning breeze catching her hair.

The way she said it—like she'd been planning this moment—made something warm spread through my chest.

"So how much of this place did you design?"

"I did the concept work for pretty much everything." Pride flickered across her features as she gestured toward the colony beyond us. "For the ship. There was this building in Europa One—"

"The Gherkin."

Sage turned to look at me, eyebrows raised. "You know your Old-Earth architecture."

"Not me... It was Amber's favorite."

Something shifted in Sage's expression—not jealousy, but understanding. Recognition of the woman who'd shaped so much of my life before her.

"She had good taste. I love that building, the shape of it, the lines, the glass. Even the original looked like it could lift off at any moment."

The reverence in her voice reminded me why Amber would've liked her. Both women saw beauty in structure, in the marriage of form and function.

"Building a colony ship out of glass was definitely a bold choice."

"Diamond-Phase Silicene, actually."

I put my arm around her, pulling her closer to my side.

"Ah, of course."

"You have no idea what that is, do you?"

The teasing note in her voice was pure Sage—the same playful intelligence that had kept me sane during those long months awake on Erebus.

"Really strong glass, I imagine."

Her laugh rang out across the balcony. That sound—unfiltered by ship speakers, unprocessed by quantum cores—hit me like a revelation. This was Sage. Not the AI who'd guided us through space, not the sleeping woman I'd watched over in medical. This was both of those things combined into someone entirely new.

Someone who'd designed a home for five thousand refugees before being trapped in a quantum prison. Someone who'd fallen in love with a broken engineer and somehow made him believe in second chances.

The colony spread out below us—Sage's vision made manifest. People walking freely under an alien sun, children playing without corporate oversight, families building something together instead of just surviving.

"It's beautiful," I said, meaning more than the view.

"It's home." Sage's fingers found mine on the railing, intertwining with a gentle pressure that felt like an anchor. "And *no one* is going to take it away. Especially not Taylor Young."

Something in her voice when she said his name caught my attention—not hatred based on what happened on Erebus, but something deeper. Personal history.

"You knew him. Before Erebus."

Sage's grip tightened on my hand. She stared out at the colony below, her jaw set in a way that reminded me of her father when he was wrestling with difficult memories.

"Not personally, but Dad knew him. He tried to buy Skyward. After their acquisition of Inertia. He knew we were working on something big."

"The Celestial Path Drive?"

Sage shook her head, blonde hair catching the morning light. "He wanted our AI. He knew we were close to building something capable of interstellar calculations. He had someone on the inside. Thankfully that someone didn't know about the CPD."

"Who?" I asked.

"I don't know." Frustration crept into her voice. "I was in stasis. Linked to the core, being stolen. But I can't imagine *anyone* at Skyward doing something like that."

The betrayal in her tone hit me hard. To wake up and discover not only had you been trapped in an AI core for years, but someone you trusted had sold you to your enemy.

"Maybe it wasn't voluntary," I offered. "Taylor's good at finding leverage over people. Their families, their jobs, their medical care."

Sage turned to look at me, those blue eyes searching my face. "Like he did with you."

"Yeah. Like he did with me." The admission still tasted bitter.

Sage's gaze drifted to the patch on my jacket, the golden spiral catching Vespera's light. "How do you feel about that?"

I looked down at the patch and chuckled. "If it means spending more time with you? I think I could get used to it."

"Good." A smile tugged at the corners of her mouth. "This colony needs leaders who don't *want* the job."

"So you don't want it either?"

Sage shook her head, that smile widening. "No. I'd always planned to be in Noctis. Developing new tech. But groups aren't mutually exclusive here. I'll still get to work on new things." Her eyes lit up with that familiar spark of curiosity I'd fallen in love with. "Maybe help you with that new AI for Erebus?"

I raised an eyebrow. "Still don't trust me to design something I won't fall in love with?"

Sage let out a small laugh and leaned in to kiss me. When she pulled back, her expression had grown more serious.

"I trust you. It's just..." She paused, fingers tracing patterns on the railing. "Erebus was more than a ship to me. We were... connected. For years, those systems were my body. Every sensor array, every power coupling, every diagnostic routine—all extensions of who I was."

Her voice grew quieter. "But more than that, Erebus was where I learned what love felt like."

The weight of what she was saying settled over me. Erebus hadn't just been our escape route—it had been Sage's entire world for six years. Her body, her voice, her means of protecting the people she cared about.

"I get it." I covered her hand with mine. "And I'd love that. We'll make sure Erebus has what she needs."

"What *we* need," Sage corrected, her fingers intertwining with mine. "Because what's coming next—Taylor, Goliath, whatever else the universe throws at us... we're facing it together."

"Together," I agreed, squeezing her hand as Vespera's golden light painted the colony below in shades of hope.

The air carried the distant sounds of the colony awakening. Children's laughter from the park below, the hum of machinery, voices calling to each other. All of it felt impossibly fragile and infinitely precious.

Chapter 42

I t felt like the entire colony had gathered at the base of the steps leading into Eterna. William stood at a podium at the top of the steps, flanked by Sage and me on his right, Tessa and Olivia on his left. Amplification drones hovered above the crowd, projecting William's words across the gathering.

The colonists below looked up at us with expressions I'd never seen on Earth—hope mixed with determination, grief tempered by purpose. No corporate logos anywhere. No surveillance drones. Just people who'd risked everything for the chance to build something better.

"I want to thank you all for gathering today to honor a man we may not have known personally, but owe an incredible debt, myself more than most." William's voice carried across the crowd with quiet authority. His gaze found Sage beside me. "Without the brave sacrifice of Joey Thompson, our fight for Serra Prime, for this colony, would look very different. We would not be joined by Malcolm Walker or Tessa Harper, two individuals who I know will be invaluable in the days ahead. My daughter, Sage Frye, would not be standing here. Eterna was her dream, and thanks to Joey Thompson, she's alive to see that dream realized."

Sage's hand found mine, her fingers squeezing gently. The weight of William's words settled over me—how close we'd all come to losing everything in that reactor chamber. How Joey's final choice had saved not only our lives but this entire future.

William stepped aside, and Tessa took the podium. She wore the same uniform as the rest of us—black boots, dark cargo pants, white undershirt, and Eterna jacket. The only variation was her crimson Talon patch featuring a glyph of an open eagle talon, matching the one on Olivia's jacket.

"Some people might've called Joey Thompson corp-kissed. I did. More than once. And I'd meant it at the time." Tessa's voice carried across the crowd with raw honesty. "He was corporate-minded through and through. I think he wanted to believe that the corpos had good reasons for every order, every choice—because if they didn't...then the career he'd devoted himself to was built on a lie."

The crowd listened in complete silence. These people understood what it meant to break free from corporate control, to face the possibility that everything you'd believed was constructed to serve someone else's interests.

"That made him stubborn. Made him slow to see the truth. And yeah, you could call that naive. I did that too. But once he did see it—once it sank in—he didn't sit with it. He acted. Not because anyone ordered him to, but because he knew it was right. And he acted bravely, knowing it would cost him everything. Not to erase what he'd done before, but because I think he believed he could still make a difference. That his actions could matter."

Tessa paused, her voice growing stronger. "And they did. Whatever else Joey was, in the end... he was loyal. Loyal to the people who stood beside him. Loyal to you, even though he didn't know you and never would. Loyal enough to give everything he had. That's the Joey I'll remember."

The silence that followed felt sacred. These colonists—mechanics and teachers, pilots and farmers, parents and children—had all made their own sacrifices to reach Serra Prime. They understood the cost of choosing what's right over what's easy.

Tessa stepped back from the podium, and I caught Olivia leaning over to whisper something in her ear. Whatever she said made Tessa nod and place a hand on Olivia's shoulder.

Olivia moved toward the podium, her movements hesitant, apprehensive—like she wasn't sure if she was allowed to speak. She glanced at me, and I gave her the slightest nod of encouragement. Then she looked out at the crowd.

"I..I didn't know Joey," Olivia said, her voice clear but quiet, amplified by the drones hovering overhead. "Tessa's told me stories. The good and the bad. But if I could tell him anything... I'd say thank you."

She looked down at her hands for a beat, gathering herself. The crowd waited, patient and respectful. When she lifted her head again, there was something stronger in her voice, something that reminded me so much of Amber it made my chest tighten.

"Thank you for saving my dad. For saving Sage. For saving Tessa. You didn't have to, but you did. And because of that, I get to live in a world where you made that choice. So... thank you, Joey."

Olivia stepped back from the podium, her expression calm, but I knew her well enough to see the emotion simmering under the surface. The way her jaw tightened, the careful control in her breathing—she was holding back tears through pure Walker stubbornness.

I didn't think she'd planned to speak. None of us had discussed it beforehand. But in that moment, Olivia had said everything I couldn't. All the gratitude I'd been carrying, the weight of knowing that Joey's sacrifice had given me back my daughter, had given Sage her life—Olivia had distilled it into something simple and true.

William took the podium again, his expression solemn as he surveyed the gathered colonists. "Until now, Eterna has been blessed. We haven't had to gather like this for one of our own. I wish I could say we never would again—that we could build a place free from loss. But if this colony lasts as long as I believe it will, there will be days like today again."

He let that thought settle, not rushing past the weight of it.

"One of the more difficult tasks in building something like Eterna is deciding how we honor those we inevitably lose. The practical realities aren't pleasant to talk about—corpse disposal is not a topic anyone wants to linger on—but it is a necessary one. Bodies will be incinerated; that's the truth. But the memories of the individuals who once walked beside us... those should never be burned away."

William turned, gesturing toward the large columns between the three tall sets of doors leading into the ship. The curved surfaces gleamed in Serra Prime's golden light, pristine and waiting.

"From this day forward, the names of our fallen will be inscribed here. Not in some distant place where they can be visited and eventually forgotten, but in the heart of Eterna, where we'll pass them every day. Where they remain part of who we are."

William tapped a small control on the nearest column. Across its curved surface, lettering resolved in clean, permanent lines: Joey Thompson.

The sight hit me harder than I'd expected. Seeing his name there, carved into the very foundation of this place—it felt right. Final. Important in a way that corporate memorials never did, with their sterile plaques and forgotten dedications.

"I hope—truly—that Joey's name stands here alone for a good long while. But I know it won't forever. The number of names on these columns will continue to grow. And when it does, we will remember each person as we do today—with gratitude and with the promise to carry forward the work they believed in."

Beside me, Sage's hand tightened in mine. Olivia stood straighter, her eyes fixed on Joey's name with the same intensity she'd once reserved for her art. Even Tessa, who'd spent weeks angry at Joey's betrayal, looked at that inscription with something approaching peace.

The memorial would stand here forever, in the place where people lived and worked and built their futures. Where children would play and couples would meet and families would grow.

Joey would be part of all of it, part of the foundation we'd build on.

William's office was nothing like the corporate offices I'd experienced in my time at StellarForge. The walls weren't cold alloy or display panels, but reinforced glass looking out over the colony. Beyond it, the golden light of Serra Prime washed over the settlement, catching the distant shimmer of crystalline peaks. On the desk between us sat a cluster of raw luminite, its pale glow spilling over William's hands as he spoke.

Sage stood beside me, her presence steady and reassuring. Vera leaned against William's desk with that familiar casual authority she'd always carried, but something felt different now—more guarded.

"We've got maybe four years before Taylor arrives," William said, his fingers drumming against the luminite's surface. "Less if Goliath pushes its drive past safe limits."

Vera straightened slightly. "We can't match Goliath's firepower head-on, but we expect they plan to adopt a similar strategy as us, with Goliath serving as the main ground structure for their colony. We don't have much intel on what they're bringing along as far as firepower. But we expect they have fighters of their own, soldiers, ground vehicles."

William nodded. "Since they know you survived Taylor's attempt to take you out, we don't believe they'll settle at the location Erebus was meant to make ready for them. So we'll need to track them once they enter the system."

"That's where your ship comes in," Vera continued. "We're hoping that with your stealth modifications—"

"How do you know about Erebus's stealth modifications?"

The questions came out sharper than I intended, but something about Vera not meeting us when Erebus landed—waiting until now to show her face after everything we'd been through—felt like a calculated choice. And not in my favor.

Vera's expression didn't change. "I've spoken to Tessa Harper. She's filled us in on Erebus's stealth and weapon capabilities."

Heat flared in my chest, sudden and sharp. Tessa. Of course. Going to her first was easier than facing me. "Nice of you to go to her instead of talking to me."

"I've been giving you space." Vera's voice carried that same measured tone she'd used at The Drift, the one that always sounded reasonable until you picked it apart. "I know Olivia told you I didn't pass along the details of the CPD. Didn't think I was a face you were looking forward to seeing."

"You let me think my daughter was dead."

"I'm sorry, Mal. But you were on a StellarForge ship, with two crew members who couldn't be trusted."

My jaw tightened. "Do you realize the only reason Joey Thompson said anything to StellarForge was because he found out about me? And the only reason I told him was because I thought I'd lost everything?" My voice cracked on the last words. "If I'd known? He might still be alive."

Vera pushed away from the desk, her posture shifting from casual to guarded. But her face stayed impassive, controlled.

"What do you want me to say? I made a call."

The casualness of it—the complete lack of remorse—made my vision blur red. Sage's hand found my arm, warm and steady against the heat burning through me, her grip firm enough to keep me from stepping forward. I could feel her tension too, like a current running parallel to mine.

"A call." The word tasted bitter in my mouth. "That's what you call letting me think my daughter was vaporized in space? A call?"

"Malcolm." William's voice cut through the mounting tension like a clean blade. "Vera was protecting operational security. It was *my* call."

His words landed heavy, a new weight dropping straight into my gut. I felt Sage's grip tighten on my arm.

"Dad?" Sage stepped forward, her voice tight, but I caught the flicker of hurt in her eyes before the words came. "You let him think his daughter was dead? You, of all people—"

"Look." William's hands stilled on the luminite cluster, the pale glow bleeding across his fingers. "If you want to cast blame for Mr. Thompson's death, then I'll take it. But I won't be the only one having to make those decisions in the future."

The Aurion patch on my jacket seemed to grow heavier, the golden spiral pressing against my chest as if it were marking me, branding me with something I hadn't asked for.

"My role in the Eterna colony is changing." William rose, his amber eyes moving between Sage and me. "From now on, my vote on any colony action will only serve as a tiebreaker."

Sage and I exchanged a glance. There was a weight in his voice—a deliberate finality—that told me this wasn't a spur-of-the-moment decision.

"Aurion has only three members," William continued. "Myself, Sage, and Malcolm. My vote holds no more weight than either of yours."

Through the glass wall, colonists moved through the settlement below—people who had left everything behind on the strength of William's vision. Now he was placing that weight in our hands. Aurion wasn't just a council; it was the final say in how this colony lived or died.

"William," I started, but he raised a hand.

"You think I made the wrong call about operational security. Maybe you're right." His voice carried decades of burden, of compromises made in the shadows. "But those are the kinds of calls we'll all be making when Taylor arrives. The difference is, you and Sage will make them together."

Vera cleared her throat. "The colony needs leadership that can adapt. William's been planning this transition since before Eterna launched."

I looked at Sage, and in her eyes, I saw my own uncertainty staring back. We'd barely had time to adjust to her being human again, and now William was asking us to help lead five thousand people against an enemy we couldn't match in firepower.

"What about experience?" I asked. "What about—"

"Experience is what got us corporate tyranny," William said quietly. His gaze fixed on me, then Sage. "Maybe it's time for leaders who remember what it's like to fight for something instead of managing it."

William sat back down, placing a hand on the cluster of luminite crystals. The soft glow bled across his fingers, refracting through the facets like trapped starlight.

"Speaking of something different." He gestured toward Vera. "Tell them what we've found."

Vera straightened; her casual posture gave way to something sharper. "The initial Quantum Resource Mapping data leaked when Serra Prime was discovered showed that these crystals could mask vast regions from scan detection—why Serra Prime stayed hidden while sitting relatively close to Earth. But the same data hinted at something else: a composition capable of storing energy at staggering levels."

My gaze dropped to the cluster on William's desk, and for a moment, the glow felt deeper, alive, like it was aware of me watching it.

"But the crystals don't only store energy," Vera continued. "They amplify it. Channel it. We're still learning the mechanism, but initial tests suggest they can convert ambient energy—solar, thermal, even kinetic—into usable power at efficiencies we've never seen."

She let the words hang. "We've built a crude prototype—small enough to fit in the cargo bay—capable of powering the entire colony for a year."

"A year?" Sage's voice carried the same disbelief tightening in my chest.

"Our scientists think they can improve that dramatically," Vera said. "But the crystals are temperamental. Prone to...sudden breakdown."

A cold thread wound down my spine. "Breakdown?"

"We don't understand the conditions, but some samples have dissolved into a fluid-like material. Once that happens, it's useless. We have to start over."

The room seemed to tighten around me. In my mind, the black fluid gleamed under the med bay lights again.

"This fluid," Sage asked quietly, "it's dark? Metallic? Holds itself together like it remembers being solid?"

Vera's gaze flicked to William, then back to us—her expression sharpening. "How do you know that?"

"Because we found some on Erebus," I said. My throat felt dry. "Before we launched, something got aboard. We don't know how—whether it was planted, smuggled, or slipped through on its own. But it attached itself to the hull and drew power from the ship. Ambient heat, electrical bleed—anything it could siphon."

Sage shifted beside me.

"It attacked our inspection drone with a kind of energy discharge," I continued. "And when Tessa tried to remove it, it fired a projectile that liquefied on contact. Both the parasite and the projectile turned into that same black fluid."

Vera went still.

William folded his hands, thinking hard. "So you believe these crystals are...sentient?"

"No. I think luminite is just a raw material," Sage said, stepping forward. "But whoever—*whatever*—created that parasite, and the null sphere's construct...they know how to work with it. Shape it. Use it. And I don't think they're billions of light-years away," Sage continued. "I think they're here. On Serra Prime."

Through the glass wall, the colony was still washed in Vespera's golden light—warm, gentle, welcoming.

Vera pushed off the desk, her posture losing its easy confidence. "You think there's intelligent, alien life on this planet?"

"Technically, we're the aliens here," Sage said. "But yes. I think something intelligent is native to Serra Prime. Something that's lived alongside luminite for who knows how long. Long enough to build its technology out of it. To us it's new, unstable, dangerous. To them? It might be as simple as working with steel."

William leaned forward. "Wouldn't we see evidence? Structures? Something?"

"Serra Prime is massive, and you've just begun exploring it up close," Sage said. "Also, you're assuming they'd choose to live on the surface."

"Olivia said you've had sightings," I said.

Vera's jaw tightened. "Unconfirmed reports of something. That's all."

"Do you think they're dangerous?" William asked.

"Yes." But at the same time, Sage said, "No."

I looked at her. "Are you forgetting what they did to us in the null sphere?"

"What exactly did they do?" Sage asked.

"They played with our heads for starters—psychological torture, basically."

"Remember what Tess said? Maybe that was all to ensure *you* survived."

"The determinism thing again? Tess was drunk on CoreBurn."

"I wasn't." Sage's voice carried an edge of certainty that made me meet her gaze. "Mal, think about it. The entity in the sphere had access to your memories, your fears, your psychological profile. It could have shattered you if it wanted to. Instead, it tested your loyalty, your willingness to sacrifice for each other."

"What about the sphere itself?" I asked. "How would it know where to put it? We were following a flight path you calculated. How could anything predict our exact route through space?"

"Maybe it's been studying us." Sage's eyes lit with that spark of understanding I'd missed since the Erebus. "It spoke our language. We didn't know the Vespera system even existed until 2235, but that doesn't mean they were unaware of us. Whoever they are, they value information—and know how to use it."

The thought hit like a cold wave. If something had been watching humanity, learning our language, mapping our technology, dissecting our psychology—how long had we been under its gaze?

"A native intelligent species." William's voice was calm, almost reverent. Not fear—wonder. "Sounds to me like a powerful ally."

Vera straightened, incredulous. "You want to team up with it?"

Sage smiled, and I caught the flicker of mischief I'd come to know too well. "I think *they* want to team up with *us*."

"Based on what?" Vera pressed.

"Based on the fact that we're still alive," Sage said simply. "They could have destroyed Erebus without hesitation. Instead, they tested us, evaluated us, and let us continue to Serra Prime. Why do that unless they wanted us here?"

"So how do we find them?" I asked.

Sage turned toward me, thoughtful. "Beats me. We could go looking. But I say we keep doing what we're doing—prepare for Goliath. If they're still watching, still studying, then when the time's right...they'll make contact."

Vera's jaw flexed, arms folding across her chest. "This sounds like a bunch of nonsense. We're supposed to go about our day while a potentially hostile threat decides if we're worthy of talking to? All based on a feeling?"

The golden light streaming through the glass wall caught in Sage's hair; her voice was steady steel. "Sometimes a feeling is the only thing that gets you through to the other side."

"That's not leadership," Vera shot back. "That's wishful thinking."

William's eyes moved between us, weighing something I couldn't read. "Is this your decision?" he asked.

The weight of it pressed into me—five thousand lives resting on choices Sage and I would make together. I took her hand, felt the warmth of her skin, the steady beat under her wrist, and knew my answer before I spoke.

"Yes," we said together.

CHAPTER 43

Olivia's flight chamber hummed with quiet energy as she led us through the compact space, her hands gesturing wildly at every detail. The room felt distinctly *hers*—lived-in, personal, defiant in all the ways that made my chest tight with pride.

"And this is Mom." She stopped before a canvas mounted on the wall, her voice softening. The portrait showed Amber exactly as I remembered her—wild copper hair, those piercing green eyes that seemed to see right through you, that knowing smile playing at her lips. "I painted it from memory and some old photos."

Sage stepped closer, studying the brushwork. "It's beautiful, Liv. She looks...fierce."

"She was." Olivia moved to a cluster of drawings pinned beside the portrait. "These are from when I was little. I used to dream about coming here."

The sketches showed crystalline mountains and glowing forests rendered in a child's imagination, but with an artist's eye for detail that had been there even then. Golden light painted everything in warm hues, and strange creatures peered from behind luminite formations.

"You drew these when you were what, ten?" I asked, recognizing some of the pieces.

"Eight, actually." Olivia grinned. "Ava says they're spookily accurate for someone who'd never seen the planet."

The flight seat dominated the room's center—a sleek chair with dual control sticks mounted at the sides. But what caught my attention were the FPV goggles hanging from the headrest, decorated with symbols that told Olivia's story. NHS with angry scratch marks through it. A delicate butterfly. A sharp talon. Abstract shapes that probably meant something only to her.

"Those are my lucky charms," she said, noticing my stare.

Olivia dropped into the pilot seat and powered up the system. Screens flickered to life around us, displaying telemetry and tactical data that made my engineer brain automatically start parsing information flow patterns.

"Boot sequence complete," a rich, wry voice announced from the speakers. "Ready when you are, kid."

"We have an audience today, Biggs," Olivia said, settling deeper into the pilot seat. "Don't make me look bad."

"Oh? Is it bring your parents to work day? Must've missed the memo."

I raised my eyebrows, giving Olivia a look. "Biggs?"

She rolled her eyes, but there was the hint of a smile tugging at her lips. "I chose it ironically."

"No, you didn't." Biggs's tone turned smugly matter-of-fact. "You said that Biggs Darklighter was the loyal wingman of—"

"Zip it, Biggs." Olivia snapped, her cheeks coloring as her co-pilot outed her in-depth knowledge of relatively obscure characters from old vids she pretended to just *tolerate.*

Sage stepped closer to the console, studying the interface with interest. "I think Biggs is a perfect name for a co-pilot."

"Thank you," Biggs said. Then, in what I assumed was meant to be a whisper but came through the speakers anyway: "I like her."

The control setup fascinated me. I reached for one of the sticks, curious about the neural interface possibilities. "So you control the fighter with these?"

"No touching." Olivia swatted my hand away. "Right stick, twist for roll, push-pull for pitch, left-right for yaw. Left stick, twist for vertical strafe, push-pull for forward, backward, left-right for side-to-side strafe. The sticks communicate with Biggs, not the fighter. I tell Biggs what I want to do, and he makes it happen."

"We've been flying together long enough that I can usually anticipate Liv's maneuvers before she executes them," Biggs explained with what sounded like pride.

Olivia adjusted something on her console. "But he still waits for my inputs. The anticipation is to minimize latency."

"Unless, of course, I need to intervene to save the ship from becoming a smear on the side of a cliff," Biggs said dryly.

"One time..." Olivia's voice carried mock indignation. "And I still think I had it."

"You didn't."

The partnership between them was obvious—fluid, natural.

Olivia reached back and grabbed the FPV goggles, slipping them over her head. The central display shifted from pre-flight diagnostics to a feed of what she was seeing—a forward view from one of the Whisper fighters parked on the launch pad, looking out into the Eterna colony.

The image quality was flawless. No pixelation, no distortion, no lag that I could detect. Olivia turned her head from side to side, then up and down, the feed tracking her movements with mechanical precision. The integration was seamless—as close to being in the cockpit as technology could achieve.

She pressed a button on the right stick, and the view instantly shifted to a rear shot from the fighter. The colony spread out behind the aircraft in golden afternoon light, Eterna's spiral structure rising like a monument against Serra Prime's crystalline landscape. Olivia performed the same head movements, testing the rear camera's responsiveness, then pressed the button again to switch back to the forward view.

"Response time?" I asked, unable to help myself.

"Essentially none," Biggs answered. "Point-zero-zero-three seconds."

"Show-off," Olivia muttered, but her voice carried affection.

Sage moved around the chair, examining the setup from different angles. "The quantum processing must be extraordinary to maintain that kind of real-time integration."

"Custom Skyward tech," Olivia said, adjusting the goggles' fit. "I think it's based off the core you developed."

"Did we find something in this colony that you didn't design?" I asked, watching Olivia run through her pre-flight checklist.

"Well, she did say it was based off my AI core tech." Sage's voice carried a hint of pride mixed with curiosity. "But I didn't know about the fighters themselves."

Olivia's posture straightened in the pilot seat, her movements becoming crisp and professional. She keyed the comm system with her thumb.

"Eterna Control, Amber Leader, pad four. Spooling up for vertical—Biggs is itchin' to stretch his wings. Requesting launch clearance before he gets cranky."

"Cranky? I'm a precision-engineered tactical marvel; I don't get *cranky*." Biggs paused, and I could practically hear the AI's equivalent of a sigh. "...But yeah, let's get this bird in the air."

The sound of my daughter giving proper radio callouts put a smile on my face that I couldn't wipe off. She sounded like a real fighter pilot—confident, controlled, completely in her element.

Sage stepped closer, her hand finding my arm as the low hum of the Whisper's launch thrusters began to fill the flight chamber. Through the speakers, the sound felt muted but powerful, like distant thunder building toward a storm.

"Amber Leader, Eterna Control," a voice came through the comms. "Pad four clear for vertical launch, climb to two hundred meters AGL, vector zero-nine-zero. Winds light; the sky is yours."

"Two hundred AGL, zero-nine-zero. Amber Leader, lifting."

Olivia twisted the left stick to the right, and the low hum of the Whisper's engines spooled to an almost insect-like whine as the ship rose smoothly but quickly into the air. The display showed Serra Prime falling away beneath the fighter, the colony shrinking as they gained altitude.

"Gear," Olivia called out, her voice steady as she continued the ascent, pushing left on the right stick until the HUD readout showed 090°.

"Gear retracted," Biggs responded.

Olivia pressed a button, the view switched to a downward-facing feed, the landing pad now a small shrinking square below them. What struck me was the lack of dust—the Whisper lifted clean, smooth, like the ground barely noticed. Military craft? They kicked up half the planet every time they left the pad.

The fighter climbed well above even Eterna's towering structure, approaching the two-hundred-meter mark. The colony spread out below like a miniature city, pathways and buildings arranged in careful harmony.

Olivia pressed the button again, switching back to the forward view. Golden light streamed through the cockpit as Vespera painted the sky in warm amber tones.

"Two hundred meters," Biggs announced, and Olivia stopped her left stick twist, the fighter coming to a perfect hover.

She performed a small side-to-side roll, testing the ship's responsiveness, then pitched up and down. Every movement was fluid, confident. When she let out a smooth breath, I felt my own chest tighten with anticipation.

"Ready?"

I held my breath, Sage's grip on my arm tightening. The moment stretched between us—father watching daughter, engineer admiring technology, human witnessing the marriage of pilot and machine that made aerial combat possible.

"Punch it," Biggs said.

Olivia hammered the left stick forward, and the Whisper rocketed ahead. The whine of the thrusters reached a new level—not loud, but powerful enough to vibrate through the flight chamber's speakers. On the display, Serra Prime's landscape blurred past as my daughter's fighter streaked across the sky like liquid lightning.

The smile on my face threatened to split my cheeks. This was my Olivia—not the sick child I'd left behind, but the warrior she'd chosen to become.

Olivia pitched the fighter upward, then rolled left. The ground shifted around us as she performed a spiral maneuver that made my stomach lurch.

Her pilot seat leaned back and to the left—not as drastically as the actual movement of the ship, but enough to give her physical feedback from the fighter's orientation.

The display showed Serra Prime spinning in a dizzying carousel of golden light and crystalline formations. My daughter's breathing remained steady, controlled, like this was just another Tuesday afternoon flight instead of aerial acrobatics that would make corporate test pilots nervous.

"If you're trying to show off," Biggs said, his voice carrying a sly tone, "might I suggest something a little more down to earth? Or... down to Serra? You know what I mean."

Olivia grinned, and I felt my chest tighten. That expression—pure mischief mixed with absolute confidence—was Amber written across our daughter's face.

She rolled the fighter so the ground appeared above us on the display, then pulled back on the right stick while keeping the left pinned forward. The Whisper dove inverted, Serra Prime's surface rushing toward us with terrifying speed. A forest of semi-translucent trees grew larger with each passing second, their crystal-veined trunks becoming individual details instead of distant texture.

The altimeter reading scrolled in a blur of descending numbers.

Sage's grip on my arm tightened, but I couldn't look away. This was my daughter, dancing with physics at velocities that would paste a human body against the cockpit wall if something went wrong.

Olivia rolled upright and leveled off just above the treetops. The proximity showed the incredible scale of their speed—translucent branches whipped past the camera feed in golden-green streaks, the Whisper's passage barely disturbing the delicate canopy below.

She banked into a smooth right turn, her head moving to focus ahead of where she was going. A set of small mountains came into view, their luminite-dotted peaks glowing like beacons in Vespera's light. Olivia leveled off the turn, heading straight for the rocky wall.

The mountains grew closer. Closer. It looked like she might crash into the crystalline face.

At the last possible second, Olivia pitched upward and rolled. Mountain peaks passed above them on the display as she sent the fighter into another inverted dive down the far side.

I let out a breath as she cleared the mountain top, the G-meter display flashing an angry red twenty-two, twenty-four—enough to turn a human to paste if they were in the cockpit.

Olivia rolled upright, pulling back to level, the G-meter rising higher and then dropping out of the red.

"I think you kissed twenty-seven that time," Biggs said. "A new personal best."

"Ready to go exo?" Olivia asked.

"You know I am," Biggs replied.

Olivia pulled back, pointing the ship nearly straight up.

"Exospheric?" Sage asked. "You can fly this in space?"

"Yeah. Thanks to Biggs. You'll see."

The sky began to darken as the fighter climbed higher. Olivia switched to the rear view, showing Serra Prime's surface curving away beneath them.

"Pitch holding at eighty-five degrees," Biggs announced. "Velocity twelve-point-six klicks per second. Altimeter's about to roll to zero, kid... say hello to the black."

She switched back to forward view as the last threads of blue gave way to pure black. The altimeter hit zero, winked out, and something new unfolded across the canopy—a thin luminous ring wrapped around her view, faint cyan arcs nested inside it like the ribs of a globe. The markings meant nothing to me, but the whole thing seemed to float there, slowly tilting as she rolled the ship.

"Simulate contact markers," Olivia said.

Red chevrons flared at the ring's edge, each tagged with tiny numbers.

"Up here in exo, we've all got the same compass," she said. "North's locked to Serra Prime's core; east and west wrap around from there. The arcs tell me pitch—above or below the horizon—and the headings let me make clean callouts."

"So you can fly just like in atmosphere?" Sage asked.

"Pretty much. Biggs handles all the math—translates what I'm doing into maneuvering thruster vectors. In coupled mode, dead sticks mean stop."

She let go of the controls, and three new gauges I hadn't noticed before eased down to zero.

"In decoupled mode, velocity's maintained until I counter it." She flicked a switch on the left stick; CPLD flipped to D-CPLD. A small forward nudge sent one gauge climbing. She let go—it stayed there. A tap left nudged a different gauge while the first held steady.

"Now we're moving forward, slight left strafe." She switched back to CPLD; both gauges sank to zero. "Stopped."

The casual precision of her maneuvering made my brain spin. Translating atmospheric stick work into proper space vectors should have been a nightmare—but Biggs made it look effortless.

"You have a horizon in space?" Sage asked, leaning closer to study the display.

"It's totally fake," Olivia said, adjusting her grip on the controls. "But since I'm the lead, Biggs takes the attitude of my ship when we hit zero on the altimeter and makes that the baseline for everyone."

"Liv literally defines *up* for the entire squadron," Biggs added, and I could hear something like pride in the AI's voice.

In atmospheric flight, every pilot shared the same reference—gravity, ground, sky. But in the vacuum of space, orientation became relative. Without a shared frame of reference, squadron formations would dissolve into chaos. My daughter wasn't just flying; she was creating order from the infinite black, establishing the fundamental axis that let her team function as a unit.

"Very impressive, kiddo." The words came out rough, my throat tight with emotion I hadn't expected. Here was Olivia—my sick little girl—commanding the spatial reference for an entire fighter squadron.

"It makes for clean callouts, that's all," she said, but I caught the slight flush in her cheeks.

She banked the fighter in a smooth arc, Serra Prime's terminator line sliding across the view as day met night on the planet's surface. The luminite formations glowed brighter in the darkness, creating a constellation of blue-green stars scattered across continents.

A blue chevron contact marker appeared on the HUD.

"Contact, two-seven-zero, minus one-five," she called out, her voice switching to the crisp professionalism I'd heard during launch.

"That's Amber Three," Biggs confirmed. "Right on schedule for the patrol rotation."

Olivia's posture stiffened, her head turned toward me and then back, like she realized she couldn't see me with the goggles on.

She cleared her throat and flicked a switch. "Amber Leader to Amber Three, I'm gonna head in, just finishing up a demo for my dad and Sage."

A male voice came through the comms, warm and relaxed. "So official, Liv. Did you take them over the crystal flats?"

"You're on open comms, Amber Three," Olivia said, her voice urgent.

The pilot didn't miss a beat, his voice cheerful. "Hey Mr. Walker. Miss Frye. Liv's quite the pilot, huh?"

I leaned closer to Olivia. "Can he hear us?"

"Loud and clear, Mr. Walker."

Heat crept up my neck. "Oh... Hello. Yeah, she's something else."

"This is Sage," she said, stepping forward with obvious curiosity. "It's nice to meet you..."

"Name's Asher, but it's Ash for most people."

Olivia's grip tightened on the controls. "That'll be all, Ash—Amber Three. Continue with your patrols."

"Aye aye. Safe landing, Amber Leader. It was nice to meet you, Mr. Walker, Miss Frye. Maybe Liv can introduce us in person sometime."

Olivia flipped the switch back before either Sage or I could respond.

"Well, that was a little rude," I said, watching my daughter's shoulders tense. "He seemed nice."

"*Very* nice," Sage added, with a knowing smile that Olivia couldn't see but made my stomach drop.

The fighter banked into its descent pattern toward the colony, but Olivia's movements had lost some of their earlier smoothness. Her breathing pattern changed—shorter, more controlled.

"Just trying to keep the comms clear," she muttered, adjusting her approach vector.

"Olivia Walker cares about clear comms?" Biggs said with amusement. "That's a new development."

"Biggs..."

"I know... Zip it."

I caught Sage's eye. She raised her eyebrows, and I knew that look—*we need to talk about this later.*

The thought of Olivia having romantic interests sent a protective surge through my chest that I recognized as irrational and entirely paternal. She was twenty years old, a squadron leader, perfectly capable of making her own decisions. But for me, it had been less than a year since she was the fourteen-year-old girl who needed breathing treatments and medication dispensers.

"Eterna Control, Amber Leader requesting approach clearance, pad four."

"Amber Leader, cleared for approach. Welcome home."

As the colony grew larger on the display, I found myself wondering how much of Olivia's life I'd missed during those years in stasis—and how much she'd deliberately kept from me.

The fighter touched down, Olivia's hands steady on the controls despite the tension radiating from her shoulders. She pulled off the goggles and stood quickly, avoiding eye contact.

"I need to check on Tessa," Olivia said, already moving toward the chamber's exit. "See how her simulator training's going."

The excuse came out too fast, too rehearsed. Classic deflection technique—something she'd perfected as a teenager whenever I got too curious about her activities.

"Olivia—"

"She's been struggling with the transition from atmospheric to exo flight profiles," she continued, not slowing down. "Squadron leaders have responsibilities, you know."

Sage stepped closer, her hand finding mine. "We could come with you. I'd love to see how the training programs work."

"No!" The response snapped out before Olivia could catch herself. She paused at the doorway, shoulders tensing. "I mean... it's pretty boring technical stuff. You'd hate it."

"Kiddo—"

"Gotta run. Thanks for coming, I had fun."

She disappeared through the doorway before I could say another word, leaving Sage and me alone in the flight chamber. The lingering hum of cooling systems filled the silence.

Sage squeezed my hand. "Come on, I want to show you something."

The elevator carried Sage and me to Eterna's observation deck, a massive glass dome crowning the ship's highest level. Soft lighting illuminated comfortable seating areas—sofas clustered around low tables, armchairs positioned for quiet conversation, and living walls of Earth plants that somehow thrived in Serra Prime's atmosphere. The space felt like a community living room suspended in the sky.

Colonists moved through the area with the easy familiarity of people who'd made this place home. A couple shared coffee on a corner sofa while their toddler played with blocks nearby. Three teenagers hunched over tablets at a study table, probably working through educational modules. An elderly woman tended to the plants, humming softly.

Sage led me to the curved glass wall where Vespera hung low on the horizon, painting the crystal formations in warm amber light. The planet's dual moons were already visible in the deepening sky—one a pale green crescent, the other a bright point of silver.

"Olivia likes that boy, doesn't she?"

Sage turned to look at me, blue eyes sparkling with amusement. "Oh, Mal. Your ability to be so incredibly smart, and yet so oblivious, is adorable."

"So that's a... yes?"

She moved in front of me, reaching up to wrap her arms around me. The weight of her against my chest felt like coming home.

"That's a yes. Your daughter has a crush. On a boy."

I felt the faintest knot in my gut. Twenty years old or not, she'd been fourteen only six months ago for me.

"Any chance being a colony leader gives me the authority to outlaw romantic relationships?"

"I'm pretty sure romantic relationships are a requirement for the survival of a new colony on an alien planet."

The logic was sound, but it didn't make the protective surge in my chest any less intense. "What if I just outlaw any romantic relationships with my daughter?"

"You can always bring it to a vote."

I could picture it—standing before Sage and William, making my case with charts and diagrams about why Olivia Walker should remain romantically unavailable indefinitely. The thought was ridiculous enough to make me smile.

"William would probably vote with me out of sympathy."

"Absolutely. He'd probably follow your lead and do the same for *his daughter.*"

The idea had merit. Two protective fathers standing together against the romantic chaos threatening our respective offspring. Of course, the fact that I was holding William's daughter in my arms right now did throw a slight wrench in the plan.

"Hmm."

Sage pinched my arm hard enough to make me wince.

"Okay, fine. I'll have to become friends with him."

"And that would accomplish what exactly?"

"Who's oblivious now? Everyone knows daughters only go for guys their fathers disapprove of."

"It's still you. My father adores you."

"He adores me?"

"Don't get cocky."

The warmth in her voice made my chest tighten. Having William's approval meant more than she realized.

The moment of levity faded as reality settled back in.

"It'll be hard for them. We have a fight coming. None of us are guaranteed to make it through this."

Sage rested her head back against my chest, her hair soft under my chin. The steady rhythm of her breathing reminded me she was really here, really human.

"All the more reason to seize the moment. Take whatever happiness you can find."

Below us, the crystal formations caught the last rays of Vespera's light, transforming the landscape into something that belonged in dreams rather than reality. The bioluminescent plants were beginning their nightly show, painting the settlement in gentle blues and greens.

This was what we were fighting for. Not just survival, but the chance for young people like Olivia and Ash to fall in love without algorithms determining their compatibility. The freedom for children to play in parks without surveillance bots cataloging their every move. The possibility of growing old somewhere beautiful instead of dying in service to some all-powerful Ascendancy.

Sage was right. In four years, Goliath would arrive with Taylor's vision of the future—rigid hierarchies, genetic castes, corporate control extending across the stars. Whatever time we had before that fight arrived, we needed to spend it building something worth defending.

Even if that something included my daughter getting starry-eyed over some boy named Ash.

Below us, the settlement glowed—beautiful but fragile in the coming dark.

When Goliath came, it would try to take everything from us: our freedom, our choices, the right for people like Olivia to decide their own futures.

I held Sage a little tighter.

They wouldn't find us unprepared.

EPILOGUE

YEAR 2310

The command deck of Goliath was silent but for the low hum of her fusion cores. The air smelled of antiseptic, scrubbed clean enough to sting the sinuses. Taylor preferred it that way—sterile, controlled. He stood before a large viewport, stars streaking past in perfect lines while small flashes of debris vaporized against the ship's shields.

Rachel Rivera's reflection appeared in the dark glass before Taylor heard her footsteps. She stopped at the prescribed distance, hands clasped behind her back.

"You should see this, sir." There was an edge to her voice—not fear, but the kind of tension that meant something had gone wrong, and she didn't like being the one to deliver the news.

Taylor turned, his gray eyes settling on her with calculated calm.

"What is it?"

Rivera crossed to the central holopit and keyed a command. The lights dimmed, and an image resolved in the air between them.

Malcolm Walker's voice filled the sterile space first. "Hello. My name is Malcolm Walker, Captain of Erebus. You may be shocked to see me and my crew, Tessa Harper and Sage."

Taylor's gaze narrowed, but he said nothing. The words kept coming—defiant, accusatory. Walker's crew explaining how Taylor had tried to murder them. How Joey Thompson had died saving the ship from Taylor's sabotage. How the Ascendancy was nothing but a caste system designed to exclude the unworthy.

The final line echoed before the transmission ended: "In the void, we endure."

The hologram dissolved into darkness as the command deck's lights returned to full brightness.

Taylor's hands had curled around the lip of the holopit, knuckles whitening for the briefest moment before he released his grip. When he spoke, his voice carried no hint of the fury coursing through his veins.

"This is public?"

"Yes, sir. Broadcast on all channels. Uprisings are already spiking. The GCE is taking credit, claiming they stand with Erebus."

"They're desperate," Taylor chuckled—a sound devoid of warmth that echoed off the polished walls. "It won't work."

Rivera shifted, her reflection wavering in the viewport behind Taylor.

"Should we make a statement? Counter their narrative?"

"No." The pause before the word was brief, just long enough for Taylor to steady himself. "Hope is a virus, Director. We need to let it spread."

Rivera's eyebrows lifted.

"Sir?"

Taylor turned back to the viewport, watching the stars streak past. Somewhere out there, Malcolm Walker thought he'd struck a meaningful blow. The man was a fool—brilliant with AI systems, perhaps, but utterly naïve about the mechanics of power.

"Walker's little performance will force any remaining resistance on Earth to scurry out of the shadows and into the light," Taylor continued, his voice taking on the measured cadence he used in board meetings. "They'll see his survival as proof that rebellion is possible. They'll make themselves visible."

"And then?" Rivera asked.

"Then we eliminate them. All of them. Permanently."

Taylor's reflection smiled in the dark glass. The GCE could claim credit for Walker's broadcast all they wanted. Their desperation only proved how completely Taylor had outmaneuvered them. By the time Goliath reached Serra Prime, there would be no resistance left on Earth.

"Prep a priority message to our assets planetside," Taylor said. "I want full surveillance on every Chrysalis cell, every suspected sympathizer, every would-be hero who thinks Walker's survival actually means something."

"What about Erebus?" Rivera's voice carried a note of concern that hadn't been there moments before. "If they managed to access the weapon systems..."

Taylor turned to face her, his gray eyes reflecting the cold light of the command deck. The question hung in the sterile air between them like a challenge he'd been expecting.

"Do you believe that Malcolm Walker and Tessa Harper can survive on Serra Prime, alone, for years?" His voice carried the patient tone of a teacher correcting a slow student. "You know, as well as I do, what's waiting for them."

Rivera's expression turned grim, her composed façade cracking enough to reveal the unease beneath.

"The Asra." Rivera whispered.

Taylor's smile was razor-thin, devoid of warmth but rich with satisfaction. He stepped closer to the holopit, his fingers tracing the edge where Walker's defiant image had moments before filled the space.

"They believe that The Ascendancy is about building a utopia for the elite." His words came measured, deliberate. "They think that Serra Prime is the future home for humanity. A refuge."

The irony was delicious. Walker had no concept of what he'd stumbled into—what Serra Prime actually was.

"They're wrong," Taylor continued, his voice low but certain. "Serra Prime is only the beginning."

Thank You

Stories like *Quantum Soul* live or die by the people who choose to join the journey, and the fact that you turned every page means more than you know. This book took just over a year of worldbuilding, rewriting, and late-night coffee.

When I started, I genuinely wasn't sure I could write a book at all. I didn't come into this with a literature background or creative writing experience. I didn't even know what the word *"prose"* meant at the beginning.

What I did have was an idea I couldn't shake, characters who wouldn't leave me alone, and a stubborn belief that maybe I could learn how to do them justice.

This story grew as I grew. Every chapter I wrote—and rewrote—taught me something new, not just about storytelling, but about myself as a writer. I've learned a lot along the way, and I know I still have a lot left to learn. That part excites me.

If you have constructive feedback, questions, or thoughts about the story, I'm genuinely open to hearing them. I want to keep improving, to write each book better than the last, and to make this series something truly special.

Thank you for giving this first book a chance. It means more than I can express. I'm looking forward to continuing this journey with Malcolm, Sage, Olivia, and with you.

Your time, your imagination, and your willingness to dive headfirst into Malcolm Walker's fight for his daughter—and for humanity—are deeply appreciated. I hope the world of Serra Prime lingers with you long after you leave it.

If you enjoyed this story, please consider leaving a rating or review. It truly makes a difference for independent authors.

What Comes Next: *Serra Prime Book Two*

Malcolm, Sage, Olivia, Tessa and the settlers of Eterna have carved out their first foothold on Serra Prime—but the real war is still coming.

In Book Two, humanity's future fractures along new lines:

- The Ascendancy's true agenda for Serra Prime begins to unfold.

- Malcolm and Sage must navigate what it means to be together in the wake of her awakening—and what the planet itself may demand of them.

- Olivia's squadron faces its first life-or-death mission in the alien wilderness.

- Strange anomalies pulse beneath Serra Prime's crystalline surface...and something is watching.

If *Quantum Soul* is about breaking free from a corporate-defined destiny, Book Two is about the cost of that freedom and what you must sacrifice to keep it.

While Malcolm's voice remains at the heart of the series, Book Two widens the lens—following the choices, dangers, and secrets unfolding through the eyes of others who now shape humanity's future.

Stay Connected

If you'd like updates on:
- New releases

- Exclusive lore drops

- Behind-the-scenes worldbuilding

- Early access to Book Two announcements

- A free upcoming prequel short story: a suppressed documentary chronicling the discovery of the Vespera System—and the moment humanity first set eyes on Serra Prime

...then I'd love to have you join my newsletter.

Sign up here: https://www.lukejjones.com
(I only send things when there's something worth sending.)